The Bridegroom

X

JOAN JOHNSTON

The Bridegroom

Island
BOOKS

ISLAND BOOKS
Published by
Dell Publishing
a division of
Random House, Inc.
1540 Broadway
New York, New York 10036

ISBN: 0-7394-0254-4

Printed in the United States of America

Published simultaneously in Canada

This book is dedicated to my editor, Maggie Craw-ford, who besides her marvelous editorial and mar-keting talents, loves chocolate desserts, Broadway theater, and spending a sunny Sunday afternoon at a Dolphins football game as much as I do.

Chapter 1

"STAY AWAY FROM HIM, REGGIE. HE looks dangerous."

Lady Regina Wharton eyed her twin sister, Rebecca, Lady Penrith, from behind her fan, then shifted her glance back to the tall, dark-haired, dark-eyed lord who had recently arrived at Viscount Raleigh's ball. "I need something to relieve the boredom, Becky. Since no other gentleman here seems up to the task, I suppose I shall have to appeal to this newest addition to the *ton*. Whom do you know that might be willing to introduce us?"

"The Earl of Carlisle is not someone you should know," her sister admonished. " 'Tis said he was a pirate!"

Reggie laughed. "Yes, the Sea Dragon. I heard that ridiculous rumor. Though he does look rather like a fire-breathing dragon with those dark eyes of his burning holes in everyone he spies."

" 'Tis said he killed a man with his bare hands!'' Becky hissed.

Reggie raised a finely arched brow. "I find that difficult to credit.'' She eyed the broad shoulders that strained beneath an exquisitely cut jacket by Weston, then perused the narrow waist and muscular thighs revealed by skintight breeches. "Not that I doubt he has the strength to accomplish such a feat, but most gentlemen vanquish their foes with sword or shot.''

" 'Tis said he dresses in black to mourn the death of his wife in childbirth, though his year of mourning ended some little while ago,'' Becky said. "I doubt he is desirous of innocent female company.''

Reggie studied the hawkish features set off by snowy white linen and saw the ravages of grief reflected in the earl's stern mouth and brooding eyes. She knew from her father's grief over the past ten years for the babies her stepmother Kitt had miscarried how such a loss could hurt. She could not imagine the melancholy Carlisle must feel at having to bury his wife as well.

Suddenly, the dragon's fiery eyes were focused on her.

Reggie was shocked at the heat she felt, until she realized it was her own blush flooding her cheeks. She knew she had been staring, but now, so was he. She refused to be the first to look away. She lifted her chin and boldly met his gaze.

His lips lifted at the corners before he turned away in what, if she had been a less confident female, might have seemed like the cut direct.

"I am determined to meet him,'' Reggie said to her

sister. "If you will not name someone to introduce us, I will manage an encounter myself."

Reggie had already snapped her ivory fan closed and was threading her way through the crush at the edge of the ballroom in the earl's direction, when Becky caught up to her.

"I will introduce you," Becky said breathlessly.

Reggie eyed her sister. "Why did you not tell me you had met the earl? It is not like you to keep secrets, Becky."

"Penrith introduced me to him at Lady Harmley's musicale," Becky said. "You had the headache and did not attend, as I recall."

"Lady Harmley's musicale would have given me the headache," Reggie said dismissively. "Which is the same thing. And what was Penrith thinking to introduce his own wife to such a havey-cavey character?"

Becky paled, and Reggie was immediately sorry. William Hastings, Viscount Penrith, whom Becky had met and married during her first Season, did not treat his wife nearly so well as Reggie would have liked. His insults extended further than the simple discourtesy of introducing Becky to the wrong sorts of people. He criticized her housekeeping and the tables she set for company. He denied her funds of her own and rarely permitted her to travel abroad without his escort, making her a veritable prisoner in her own home.

Reggie had watched helplessly as Penrith slowly but surely crushed her sister's spirit. Becky rarely painted or made up wonderful stories or played the pianoforte anymore. The sad thing was, Reggie had been as easily fooled by Lord Penrith as had her sister. She had actually liked the handsome young man, until greater acquaintance had revealed his true nature.

If it had not been for the birth of Lily within a year of the marriage, her sister might have become a wraith. But the mischievous sprite never gave Becky the opportunity to become blue-deviled. The result was, while Penrith's behavior had Reggie surveying her suitors with a jaundiced eye and all but abjuring marriage, Lily's cherubic smile and open arms made her wish for a child of her own. How to have the child without the irksome husband was a quandary she had not yet resolved.

"At least this once Penrith has done me a favor," Reggie said, biting her tongue on further criticism of her sister's husband. "What else can you tell me about Lord Carlisle?"

"Only that he is a rogue and a scoundrel and not at all the sort of person whose acquaintance you should seek."

"Which means, of course, that he will be a fascinating man to know," Reggie replied with a teasing smile.

"Please don't make me do this," Becky pleaded. "Why not discourse with Mr. Tumlinson?"

"He writes bad poetry and insists on reciting it."

"Lord Larkin," Becky offered.

"He cannot admire anyone so much as himself."

"Viscount Scarborough?" she said desperately.

"Rotten teeth," Reggie whispered. "We have arrived, my dear. Make the introduction, please. I will survive the encounter, I promise you."

"Why, good evening, Lord Carlisle," Becky said, a

hesitant smile on her face. "What a surprise to see you here."

"Indeed," the earl said, his eyes moving from Becky to Reggie and back again. "I heard you had a twin, Lady Penrith. I see you are very much alike in looks, but not at all the same."

Reggie's nostrils flared with indignation as, with a brief, all-inclusive glance, Carlisle undressed her with his eyes—and apparently found her wanting.

She resisted the urge to whirl in a flurry of skirts and stalk away. The earl was *not* a nice man, and his behavior proved it. But she was no missish miss, no craven coward, to go running at the first sign of trouble.

Reggie nudged Becky with her fan, and her sister made the introduction. "Lady Regina Wharton, may I present Clay Bannister, Earl of Carlisle."

"Enchanté, mademoiselle," the earl said, bowing slightly.

He made no move to reach for her gloved hand, and Reggie barely stopped herself in time from offering it. How had he managed to be both charming and insulting in the same breath? She unclamped her teeth and smiled. Brilliantly. With all the seductiveness she had learned in four Seasons of enslaving prospective suitors.

The earl's lip curled. In scorn.

"Oh, the music is starting," Becky said. "Will you excuse us please, my lord? I am promised for this dance."

"I am not," Reggie said, focusing her gaze on Carlisle, daring him to ask.

It was well known that Lady Regina Wharton did not

dance. At least, not with anyone who might be considered a suitor. A gentleman might ask on his peril but was bound to be refused. She willed Carlisle to speak. *Ask me to dance, and see what answer you get.*

"It is a waltz," Carlisle noted. "Do you know how to waltz, Lady Regina?"

"Yes," Reggie said through tight, smiling lips. *But that is the only yes you will ever hear from me!*

"Very well then," he said. "We will dance."

"I—"

Reggie felt herself being swept onto the dance floor by a strong arm around her waist. She stumbled, and the earl's grasp tightened, pulling her even closer.

"You promised you could dance, my dear. Do try to keep up."

So many sensations assaulted her at once—the feel of her breasts crushed against the strength of his chest, the heat of his thigh pressing against her own—that Reggie could not catch her breath. There was simply no air with which to utter the scathing setdown on the tip of her tongue. They were whirling in the center of the ballroom by the time she could speak.

"What do you think you're doing?" she gasped.

"Dancing. Waltzing, to be more precise," Carlisle said as he twirled her in another circle.

"Stop that! You're making me dizzy."

He responded by whirling her faster, making the room spin. Reggie was no match for Lord Carlisle physically, but over the past four years she had learned the use of other weapons to bring a man to his knees.

"Is it true, my lord, that my father had you stripped of

your title? That he had you bound in chains and transported to Australia?''

His grip tightened painfully at her waist. ''Is that what he told you?''

She forced herself to meet Carlisle's gaze and flinched at the contempt she saw. ''Papa has never mentioned your name to me,'' she admitted, lifting her chin. ''But in the year since you returned to London, I have heard tales—''

He made a disdainful, dismissive sound deep in his throat. ''Banbury tales,'' he muttered.

''Then you were not a pirate?'' she asked.

He lifted a dark brow in mocking amusement. ''I was. But, as you can see, the *ton* has forgiven that indiscretion.''

''That seems a great deal to dismiss,'' she said bluntly.

He shrugged. '' 'Twas your own father made me respectable again.''

''How?''

''He advised the House of Lords he was mistaken in his accusations against me. Within the past year my title and estates have been restored. All is as it was before.''

Carlisle said the words, but it was clear from the turmoil in his fierce gaze, from the way his gloved hand crushed her own, that nothing was as it had been twelve years ago. How could it be? He had become a pirate. His wife and child were dead. And there was that other shocking rumor to be confronted.

''There is one thing more I would like to know,'' she said.

"You have asked enough," he replied curtly. "And been answered."

But Reggie would not be denied. "Did you kill a man with your bare hands?"

His eyes narrowed. The creases around his mouth deepened in displeasure.

An instant later Reggie found herself being waltzed through the open French doors and out onto the balcony. There was no time to gather her wits before she was being ushered down the steps and hurried along one of the moonlit pathways in Viscount Raleigh's rose garden.

Reggie tried digging in her heels, but they skidded on the gravel path. She wished she had not asked that last question. It seemed to have spurred the earl to some dire action. "Stop. Stop this instant, or I shall scream!"

The rogue dragged her inexorably into the dark.

Reggie realized Carlisle had deduced she could not very well scream without bringing ruin on herself. If she had been a true lady, that is to say, if she had been genuinely helpless and demure, there was no telling how Carlisle's kidnapping might have ended. But Reggie's docile outward manner was a thin facade, which Carlisle's boorish—and frightening—behavior tore asunder.

Kicking him would have been satisfying, but dancing slippers would not have caused much damage. She waited for him to stop and turn to her before she acted.

"Now, my lady, we will—"

She hit him in the stomach as hard as she could with her balled fist. An instant later, she grabbed her hand and bit back a yell, as agonizing pain shot all the way to her elbow. Hitting his belly was like hitting one of the gray stone walls at Blackthorne Abbey.

Carlisle shook his head, his lips tilted in what was undeniably a smile. "You're a feisty little thing."

It was humiliating to be reduced to an object of amusement. She struck back with words, since her fist had done little good. "You scoundrel! Libertine! Turk! You—"

"That is quite enough, Lady Regina," he said in a cutting voice. "I have taken your point."

She drew herself up, shoulders back, chin high. But her chin began to quiver, and tears welled in her eyes. She blinked hard, determined he should not see her routed. Lady Regina Wharton *never* cried!

"I do not know what it is you hope to gain by humbling me," she said. "I concede your superior strength. Where do we go from here? Will you ravish me? My father will kill you for it. Or would, if I were to tell him of your incivility."

"And you would not?"

She shook her head. "The battle is between us, my lord. I will win or lose on my own."

He nodded. "Very well, my dear. I accept your terms."

She tried to hold herself still as his thumb gently brushed away the damnable tear on her cheek, but her body quivered at his touch. She felt his dark eyes on her again, felt the heat again, but this time in her very marrow. She looked up and met his gaze. She had wanted relief from boredom, but she had discovered something a great deal more perilous than the mere entertainment she had sought.

"What do you want from me?" she whispered.

"Perhaps the same thing you want from me," he murmured in return.

Her eyes sought his. "A diversion?"

"A distraction from life's sorrows."

"My life is happy enough."

"Is it?" he said. "I would have sworn you looked disconsolate when I observed you with your sister."

"You were watching me?" she asked, intrigued by the thought he had noticed her.

"How could I not?" he said. "You were like a particularly succulent flower surrounded by buzzing bees. I wanted to be the one to sip your nectar."

It sounded too much like the flummery offered by the innumerable suitors she had rejected. "That is the first false coin you have offered me," she said, pursing her lips and shaking her head. "I expected better of you, my lord."

He laughed. "Do you think it impossible I should desire you?"

"Not at all," she said. "I am well aware of my superior attributes."

He laughed again. "No false modesty, I see. And I must agree. You are lovely beyond compare. Eyes that sparkle like—"

"Sapphires," she said, filling in the usual simile.

"A brook coursing over stones," he surprised her by saying. "Lips as dewy as—"

"Rosebuds," she interjected.

He smiled. "Grass in the early morning sun," he countered. "A complexion like—"

"Peaches and cream," she could not help interrupting.

"Cream," he countered, "without the peaches. Hair as dark and shiny as—"

She hesitated, then guessed, "A raven's wing?"

He shook his head. "Actually, the thing it most reminds me of is my horse, Balthazar. I imagine your hair must be as soft as his silky black nose."

Reggie laughed delightedly. "You are original, my lord, I will grant you that. I cannot quite believe it, but I am not even insulted. For if your Balthazar is as beautiful a black beast as my Beelzebub, then you have paid me a great compliment indeed."

"What is more," the earl continued, "There is substance to go with the beauty. You are every bit as fascinating as the tales I have heard of you."

"What tales?" she asked suspiciously.

"That you are an ice princess, beautiful but untouchable, desirable but unapproachable."

"How do you explain all those buzzing bees?" she asked archly.

"Have any sipped your nectar?"

She blushed hotly. "That is none of your concern."

"Then you are untouched?"

"I find this conversation tedious," she said, turning to march back toward the house.

He caught her arm and whirled her around to face him. "Stay."

"I see no purpose—"

"I want you for myself."

Her gaze shot to his face, and she found his intense dark eyes staring back at her. An odd sensation curled in her belly. Her heart began to pound. Whatever he had done in the past, her own father had made him respectable again. And yet, he still had not answered that last question. Had the earl killed a man with his bare hands? "What makes you think I would consider marriage to a rakeshame like you?"

"I do not remember offering marriage."

It took her a moment to take his meaning. "You are offering me *carte blanche*?"

"Why not?"

"I am a lady, an innocent—"

"Your innocence is a bit of a problem." He brushed a knuckle across her cheek. "But that can be remedied."

Reggie jerked away, unable to speak, she was so incredulous.

He laughed. Again. "You are much too naive, my dear. And predictable. I am afraid we would never suit."

"What if I said I accept? What would you say then?" she demanded, incensed at his dismissal of her as unworthy of his regard.

His eyes narrowed. "I wish I were as true a blackguard as you have painted me. But even such miscreants as I have scruples."

"Are you refusing me?" she asked in disbelief.

"I will take a kiss," he said. "As the price of your foolishness in playing such games."

"I will never—"

His lips were firm and damp on hers, eliciting a moan

of pleasure before she could squelch it. His tongue traced the seam of her mouth, but she kept her teeth tightly clenched, determined not to give more than he had already taken.

He let her go and stepped back, his eyes gleaming in the moonlit darkness. "You are a tempting morsel, my sweet. But it is time we returned to the ballroom. Our absence will no doubt have been noticed."

Reggie's eyes went wide. It was odd enough that she had danced with Carlisle. Their exit onto the balcony most certainly would have been remarked upon. Her continued absence with such a notorious figure would already have been the cause of speculation. "Was scandal your purpose all along?"

"You elicited the invitation to dance, my dear."

Reggie knew he spoke nothing but the truth. Her behavior over the years had crossed the line beyond propriety on occasion, but being a great heiress—and the Duke of Blackthorne's daughter—had given her a great deal of latitude and smoothed a great many important ruffled feathers. This time she might have gone too far.

"Reggie? Are you out there?"

"Is that you, Becky?" Reggie replied in response to the whispery voice.

"Where are you?"

Reggie walked along the gravel path, trailed by Carlisle, until she met her sister coming from the opposite direction. "What are you doing out here?" Reggie asked.

"Looking for you," Becky said in exasperation. "I

followed you out onto the balcony almost as soon as you left, hoping to prevent gossip.''

''That was cleverly done, Lady Penrith,'' Carlisle said. He turned to Reggie and said, ''Thanks to your sister's quick thinking, you may escape with your reputation. All we three need do is return to the ballroom together.''

''I would not accompany you—'' Reggie began.

''For my sake,'' Becky said. ''Please do as Lord Carlisle asks.''

Reggie remained silent and did as she was told. Her sister would bear the brunt of the blame if she were found to have been compromised. There was no telling what penalty Penrith would exact from his wife if he heard of Reggie's unchaperoned escapade. ''Very well,'' she conceded. ''We will return to the ballroom together.''

''Smile,'' Becky hissed as they moved from the dark balcony into the candlelit ballroom, where the waltz was just ending.

To Reggie's surprise, Carlisle was the soul of propriety, bowing over her hand and thanking her and her sister, in words loud enough to be heard by those assembled, for the pleasure of their company during the dance. ''I will look forward to calling on both of you tomorrow,'' he said.

Reggie was appalled by Carlisle's obvious intention of furthering the acquaintance, considering how outrageously he had behaved during their *tête-à-tête*, but with so many gossips about, there was no way she could voice her objections.

"We will look forward to your visit, my lord," Becky replied with a smile.

She and Becky were left standing arm in arm as Carlisle made his way back across the ballroom. Reggie snapped open her fan and used it to cool her face. "I want to go home."

"I am afraid that is not possible just yet," Becky said.

"Why not?"

"You must play the game a little longer."

At Reggie's inquiring look, her sister explained, "To prove nothing untoward happened during your absence from the ballroom."

Reggie's chin jutted. "I don't give a fig what anyone thinks."

"A scandal will do none of us any good," Becky said.

Reggie saw the plea in her sister's eyes and relented. "Very well. I shall be a flower and let the bees buzz around me for another half hour at least. Will that suit you?"

"Yes, it will. Afterwards, I shall be glad to escape along with you."

Over the next half hour, Reggie laughed and smiled until her jaws ached. She was aware, the entire time, of Carlisle's heavy-lidded gaze watching her from the other side of the ballroom. He spoke to no one. He danced with no one. Until at last the moment came when she looked for him, and he was gone.

"Please, Becky, may we leave now?" she said.

Becky squeezed her hand. "I think we have done as much as we can tonight. I will send a footman to find

Penrith in the card room and tell him we are ready to retire.''

On the ride home in the carriage, the thoroughly foxed viscount raged incessantly at his wife. ''I feel certain my luck was turning when you sent for me,'' he ranted, the words slurring together. ''As it is, I left at least a monkey on the table.''

''You could have stayed, my lord,'' Becky said meekly. ''We would have been happy to return home without you.''

''What? And have it said I let ladies under my protection go about unescorted?'' Penrith snorted. ''I know where my duty lies. Even if it costs me dearly at times.''

There was no winning the argument, as Becky well knew, yet Reggie watched her sister attempt to soothe her cupshot husband.

''Regina met an acquaintance of yours this evening,'' Becky said.

''What? Who's that?''

''Lord Carlisle,'' Becky said.

''Good man to know,'' Penrith mumbled.

''Why is that?'' Reggie inquired.

''Rich as Croesus. Been advising me which funds are best in the 'Change.''

Reggie frowned in confusion. ''Did I understand correctly? You are taking *investment* advice from Lord Carlisle?''

''Why not? Man has a fortune. Must know what he's about, don't you think?''

''I think he made his fortune as a pirate,'' Reggie said dryly.

Penrith shook his head. "Shows what you know, missy. He earned a bit from shipping, but he doubled that in the funds."

"Why is he so willing to share his knowledge with you?" she asked.

"Likes me," Penrith said. "Said so himself."

"One scoundrel recognizes another," Reggie muttered under her breath.

"What's that?" Penrith asked.

"Lord Carlisle is coming to call on Regina tomorrow," Becky said, stepping into the breach.

Penrith's eyes focused slyly on Reggie. "There's a match I would pay to see. Such a man would soon put you in your place, young lady."

"Oh?" Reggie said, arching a disdainful brow.

Becky shot her a beseeching look, but Reggie was still stinging from her encounter with Carlisle and was in no mood to back down. "What place is that?" she demanded.

"Lying beneath him," Penrith said, his eyes glittering.

Becky gasped. "How dare you—"

Penrith's hand lashed out and caught Becky on the mouth. The slap was loud in the carriage, and the sound of it echoed—along with Reggie's cry of alarm—in the silence that followed.

Reggie was already half out of her seat when her sister cried, "No, Reggie!" It took every ounce of restraint Reggie possessed to sit back down.

She watched, tight-lipped, as Penrith reached out with a trembling hand to touch the edge of Becky's lip, where blood had begun to seep. "I did not mean—I would never—" he stuttered. "It was an accident."

Becky fumbled to open the drawstring on her reticule, and Reggie reached across and opened it for her, drawing out a lace handkerchief and thrusting it into her sister's shaking hand. Head bowed, Becky pressed the cloth against her wounded lip.

Reggie was still in shock. She had known Penrith was not the best of husbands, but during the entire four years Reggie had been living with Becky in London, she had never—not once—witnessed any physical mistreatment of her sister. But there was no denying what she had just seen. Reggie felt sick to her stomach, wondering what Becky might have been enduring behind closed doors.

What Reggie found most difficult to credit was Penrith's evident remorse. She watched in disbelief as he brushed a trembling hand across Becky's hair, smoothing a stray curl from her brow, and pressed a gentle kiss to her temple. "Forgive me," he whispered. "Please."

Becky glanced across at her, then looked down at her hands and whispered, "I forgive you, William."

Reggie's nose curled in distaste. It could have been the offal she smelled on the cobblestones as they drove by. But it was not. Her teeth were gritted, and her fingers were so tightly threaded she could feel the bite of her fingernails, even through her gloves. Penrith's behavior could not be allowed to continue. She would inform Papa of the situation in the next mail, and he would—

Reggie realized that was exactly what she could *not* do, for the same reason she could never tell Papa how Lord Carlisle had treated her this evening. Papa would demand to meet William on a field of honor. Reggie was not willing to take the chance that William's aim with a dueling pistol might be true. Even worse, if Papa killed William in a duel, three-year-old Lily would be left without a father.

But there was someone who might be able to help.

"I have been thinking of inviting Michael O'Malley to come for a visit," Reggie said. "What do you think, Becky?"

"I think Papa needs Mr. O'Malley to help oversee his estate in Scotland, especially now, with Kitt due to deliver at any time."

"I shall write to ask Papa if Mr. O'Malley can bring the news of whether we have a new brother or sister in person," Reggie said. "Surely Papa will let him come."

In the flickering light from the gas lanterns on the street corners, Reggie could see that Becky's face looked stricken. And well it should. Ever since their father had brought Michael O'Malley home with him as a gangly boy of fourteen, he had been like an older brother. Mick would be incensed when Reggie told him how badly Penrith was treating Becky.

Reggie was sure that together, she and Mick could come up with a way to make certain that William never laid another violent hand on his wife . . . even if it meant finding a way to end the marriage.

"If I am not mistaken, Rebecca, you enjoy Mr. O'Malley's visits," Penrith said. "I will add my letter to Regina's."

It was clear to Reggie that Penrith's offer was intended as an olive branch. She watched to see whether Becky would accept it.

"Very well," Becky said at last. "I will prepare a room for his arrival."

As they left the carriage and entered the Penrith town house on Berkeley Square, Reggie reached out and squeezed her sister's hand. "Shall I say I am ill and ask for your company tonight?" she whispered.

"Please don't," Becky whispered back. "All will be well. Go to bed."

Reggie watched as William solicitously escorted Becky up the stairs, as though the blow had never happened. She would not sleep tonight until she had written to her father and to Mick. It would not be fair to Becky to tell Mick precisely what had happened tonight, but she could hint at some trouble Becky was having that required Mick's assistance and encourage her father to send him to London.

But even after she had written her letters, Reggie tossed and turned in bed, plagued by a pair of dark dragon's eyes that would not give her peace.

Chapter 2

"REVENGE IS A DIRTY BUSINESS. I thought you had decided to leave the second chit out of it."

Clay Bannister eyed his solicitor, and former classmate at Oxford, Roger Kenworthy. "My plans changed," he replied, returning his attention to the precise mathematical he was creating with his neck cloth.

Roger settled back more comfortably in the wing chair in the far corner of Clay's dressing room. "When did this change of heart occur?"

Clay smiled at his friend in the looking glass above his dressing table as he struggled with the resistant neck cloth. "The instant I laid eyes on her. Or rather, the moment she laid eyes on me."

"You were not so enchanted when you met her twin. What makes this one so different from the other?" Roger asked.

"Everything."

Roger chuckled. "Well. That clarifies the situation."

"You would have to see them together to understand. They are identical, and yet as unlike as a rose and a peony, as a terrier and a spaniel, as a Thoroughbred—"

"You are determined to have her?"

Clay's eyes narrowed. "She will make a formidable weapon in my hands against her father. I will make Blackthorne rue the day he had me transported to Australia for a crime I did not commit."

"You are not the same man I knew at Oxford," Roger said quietly.

Clay's eyes took on the look of obsidian, cold and hard. "That blameless boy died twelve years ago. In his stead was born the Sea Dragon, merciless pirate, plunderer, plague of the Seven Seas."

"Are you sure you did not conjure this marauder from a lady's novel?" Roger asked, his lips curling with amusement.

"He is real enough. And ruthless enough to take the vengeance that is his due."

"In the year since you reappeared, the duke has made an honest effort to undo the harm he did. He has had your name cleared by the House of Lords and your title restored."

"Too little, too late," Clay said bitterly. "Blackthorne must pay."

"To what purpose?" Roger questioned. "Revenge will not bring back what you have lost. Why not forget the past and go on from here?"

"I cannot. I want Blackthorne to know the depths of despair, the loss of all hope. I want him to know how it feels to lose what he loves most in the world. I want his life ruined, as he destroyed mine!''

Clay realized his hands were shaking and grasped the neck cloth more firmly to hide his agitation from his friend.

Roger rose and crossed to stand at Clay's side. The two men eyed each other in the looking glass. One was the epitome of British manhood, blue-eyed with fair hair cut in a stylish Brutus. The other was dark, his skin bronzed by the sun and weathered by the sea wind, his unruly hair the color of soot, his eyes as black as his soul.

''Bringing about the financial ruin of Blackthorne and his family is one thing,'' Roger said. ''Despoiling an innocent is another thing entirely.''

''You knew what I planned when you agreed to act as my solicitor.''

Roger shook his head. ''I did not realize the extent of your hatred for the man.''

''Are you quitting me, Roger?''

''I would like nothing better. However, I think I may have more chance of convincing you of your folly if I stay involved in your affairs. If the chit is everything you say, perhaps she will not be as vulnerable to your wiles as you believe.''

Clay gave a wolfish grin. ''She will be a challenge. Of that I have no doubt.''

Roger reached for the bouquet of wild red roses that sat on the dresser to take a sniff, yelped when he got pricked, and dropped it. He brought his forefinger to his lips to suck on the wound. "Be careful," he warned. "Roses always come with thorns."

"You forget, my friend. Before I became the Sea Dragon, I spent five years under the lash on one of His Majesty's frigates. I'm not likely to be brought down by anything less than a wound to the heart."

"That is precisely what I'm afraid of," Roger muttered as he took his leave.

"Never fear. I know what I'm about," Clay replied as the door closed behind his friend. "Pegg," he said in a quiet voice. "I'm ready to be poured into that jacket."

A huge man stepped through the door that led from Clay's bedroom into the dressing room. He wore a small gold hoop in his left ear, a patch over his left eye, and his left leg ended at the knee and had been replaced by a wooden peg. The burly Scotsman had been transported to Australia on the same convict ship as Clay, and they had been together ever since.

"Ye did a fair job with the neck grabber," the giant conceded as he held up an exquisitely tailored jacket.

Clay eyed the mathematical critically in the looking glass as he allowed Pegg to drag the tight-fitting garment up his arms and onto his shoulders. "Symmetrical, at least," he conceded.

"Chokes ye just the same, whether it be tied foul or fair," the big man mumbled.

"Agreed," Clay said. "But my purpose is to appeal to one of the fairer sex, who have definite ideas about what is proper fashion for a gentleman of the *ton*. So, Pegg, will I do?"

Pegg studied him, then snorted in disgust. "Seems a

lot of bother for one small girl. Ye should just steal the
lass and run. What could her father do?''

''Kidnap her?'' Clay said in surprise.

''Why not? The *Sea Witch* is tied up at the London
docks. We could set sail with the mornin' tide. The
duke'd never find us.''

Clay considered the possibility. It might come to that,
if he could not convince the girl to wed him. But his
revenge would be all the sweeter if he could flaunt the
chit's misery—and he would make her miserable—right
under her father's nose. He could take her to his estate in
Scotland, which bordered Blackthorne's property to the
north. When the duke's daughter had given him a son to
replace the one he had lost, he would take the child and
abandon her.

''No kidnapping,'' he said at last. ''We will try this
course first.''

''Foul weather ahead,'' Pegg muttered.

''Yes, Pegg,'' Clay said grimly. ''Foul indeed.''

Clay was too engrossed in his own thoughts to acknowledge the smiles and nods of those he passed in his
curricle during the journey from his town house on
Grosvenor Square to the Penrith town house on Berkeley
Square. The instant he lifted the knocker, his heart began
to thump harder.

His revenge had begun a year past, when he had returned to England after an absence of eleven years. He
had begun by making certain Blackthorne found no
ready market for his wheat during the harvest. He had
arranged to meet Lord Penrith and gained his trust. And
he had begun a search for the missing Mr. Ambleside,

Blackthorne's former steward in Scotland, the villain who had embroiled him in the affair that had led to his arrest, and who must certainly share in Blackthorne's fate.

Clay regretted nothing he had done so far in the name of vengeance. The more harm he caused, the better. Lady Regina was a chick ripe for the plucking. What she had gleaned from gossip did not tell the whole story, and it was plain she had no inkling of how much hatred he harbored toward her father. And he had no intention of enlightening her.

Clay had been careful not to show any overt animosity toward the duke since his return to England, though he had consistently refused to see Blackthorne on those occasions over the past year when the duke had presented his card and sought an audience. He did not want to hear the duke's explanations or his apologies. He did not want to hear Blackthorne's plea for absolution. There was no forgiveness in his heart.

It had been easy to justify his financial manipulation of Blackthorne's son-in-law. Lord Penrith knew the whole story, had even been a part of the House of Lords all those years ago, insisting that if Carlisle had done what Blackthorne accused him of doing, he should be stripped of his title and transported. Clay had befriended the man, pretending that the past was the past, advising Penrith to invest in ventures risky enough to cost him a fortune. It would not be long before the duke's elder daughter was married to a financially ruined man.

But Roger was correct in his conjecture that ruining a woman's reputation was another matter entirely. And

Clay did plan to ruin her—to wed her and bed her and then abandon her.

Nevertheless, he felt no regret for what he was about to do.

In his mind's eye, Clay pictured the graves of his wife, and the son he had never seen, overgrown with eleven years' worth of weeds and thistles. He felt the coarse texture of the gravestones beneath his fingertips, the utter cold of the ground in which they had been buried while he was chained hand and foot on a ship bound for Australia.

And felt all the anguish of his loss anew.

He had loved Lady Marjorie Wren more than life but had despaired of ever having her, especially when he learned that his elder brother Charles had gambled away the entire Carlisle fortune before he'd died. Virtually everything was gone except a crumbling castle in Scotland and the Carlisle town house on Grosvenor Square, both of which were entailed. Once the exact nature of Clay's affairs was known, Lady Marjorie's family had forbidden the match.

Clay would have lost her, in truth, believed he *had* lost her, except their dalliance at a weekend house party had resulted in the expectation of a happy event. Her parents had relented and allowed them to marry, holding a quiet ceremony outside London, despite the allegations hanging over his head.

They had been happy for those few months before his trial. He had watched his wife's belly grow, had laid his cheek against her flesh and spoken to the child inside her, promising he would be a better father than his own had been.

He had been so naively certain he could prove his innocence—because he *was* innocent. But Blackthorne had brought all his considerable power to bear, and the true villain, Mr. Cedric Ambleside, had disappeared, leaving Clay to suffer the full measure of the duke's ire.

Clay's lips thinned with resolve as the front door to Penrith's town house opened. Blackthorne deserved to be robbed of any joy he might find in his family, or which his family might find in their fortunes . . . or reputations.

"My lord," the butler said, bowing low. "You are expected in the drawing room."

Clay followed the butler upstairs, where he was startled to find only one of the twins. She was dressed in a bright yellow day dress that did not do her beauty justice. Her blue eyes were anxious, and she unknotted her fingers as she rose to make her bow to him.

He waited for the butler to leave before he spoke. "Good afternoon, Lady Penrith."

"How did you know it was me?" she asked as she sank back onto the brocade sofa. "We are identical, you know."

And nothing alike, Clay thought. "Lady Regina has a tiny scar at the edge of her mouth," he said, as though that were the only difference he had noted.

"You are very observant, my lord. Will you join me for tea?"

"Where is Lady Regina?"

"She will not be joining us," Lady Penrith announced as she poured a cup of tea. She held it out to him, the china rattling slightly, and Clay found himself taking the few steps necessary to retrieve the delicate cup and saucer. He handed her the bouquet of roses in return. "I brought these for Lady Regina."

"I will make certain she gets them." She carefully set the roses on the table beside her without smelling them.

Clay settled on the cushioned chair across from Lady Penrith, who remained perched on the edge of the sofa as though she were a canary and he a cat about to pounce.

"I hope Lady Regina is not indisposed," he said.

"My sister is otherwise occupied this afternoon," Lady Penrith said.

"Does she always disappear when company is expected?" he asked, unable to keep the irritation from his voice.

"She had a prior engagement which she had forgotten."

"I see."

"Do you?" Lady Penrith said, her eyes searching his face. "My sister will not be bullied, my lord."

Clay lifted a brow. "That is frank speaking."

"I believe the truth will serve best."

"And what is the truth, my lady?" Clay asked.

"You know that better than I. Why did you come, my lord? You cannot be looking for a wife."

Clay considered what to say and finally replied, "I came for tea and conversation."

"Very well," she said. "It is fine weather we are having, is it not?"

Clay found himself unexpectedly admiring Lady Penrith's poise under what were difficult circumstances. It was too bad she had such a blackguard for a father. "A beautiful day, indeed," he said. "I am only sorry your sister is not here to drive out with me."

"Perhaps another time, my lord," she said.

He was disappointed that Lady Regina had avoided the skirmish he had planned, but this was only the first sortie. When the butler arrived to announce another guest, Clay rose and excused himself. "Please tell Lady Regina I was sorry to have missed her."

"I will give her your message," Lady Penrith promised with what could only be described as a relieved smile.

As Clay stepped up into his curricle and took the ribbons in hand, he saw a slight female dressed in a ragged gray dress, a black woolen shawl draped over her head, scurrying around the side of the town house. At first he thought she was a servant, but when the figure cast a single furtive look over her shoulder, she gave away the game. He would have recognized those delicate features anywhere. It was Lady Regina.

Why, the chit was in the house all along! He had suspected as much but had been willing to give her the benefit of the doubt. For a moment he considered letting her escape. A second look revealed no maid had joined her. Where was Lady Regina going unchaperoned, in such a disguise—and in such a hurry?

He followed her at a distance, keeping his cattle in check. He tried to imagine where she might be going. The only thing in this direction was a neighborhood that catered to ladies of another sort entirely. She walked several blocks before stopping on a corner, where she stood looking anxiously about her, leading him to believe she was waiting for a carriage to carry her to an assignation.

Clay's stomach knotted. Who was it? What man had she agreed to take as her lover? He tried to remember whom she had graced with her smile the previous evening. Lord Malroux. Davison. Willowby. Even Viscount Sheppard. He could name a dozen others. The chit had smiled at all of them with innocent allure. He had even succumbed, momentarily, to that smile himself.

Clay remembered too vividly the kiss he had taken from her, how soft her lips had been, how she had trembled in his arms. He had not believed his heart could be touched, and yet he had found himself in turmoil when their lips parted. Wanting more. Needing more. Determined to have more.

His cattle were restless by the time the chit finally turned the corner, after one last furtive look around for the lover who had not arrived. Her step continued toward the part of town where gentlemen kept houses for their ladybirds. Surely she did not mean to walk there! It would be dangerous for any woman alone in such sordid surroundings, but especially so for a gently bred young lady.

Clay could think of only one reason why a lady might travel disguised into such a neighborhood, on foot and without her maid. The Ice Princess had obviously melted for some gentleman or another, fooling him—and a great many others.

Clay realized he was disappointed. And furious at having been duped the previous evening. He should have allowed Lady Regina to accept his offer of *carte blanche*. He might even now be enjoying her favors.

He could see no reason to avoid confronting her with what he knew. Perhaps he could tempt her away from her current lover with the offer of some bauble. He would not need to marry her to ruin her. He need only expose her current behavior to the light of day.

At any rate, he meant to have her, if for no other reason than to throw his conquest of her in her father's face. He gave his cattle a taste of the whip and pulled alongside her. "Good day, Lady Regina. Fine weather we are having."

She stopped in her tracks and stared at him. The shocked O formed by her lips was almost comical. It was followed by a shuttered look of guilt—for having been found out, no doubt—and then a flush of what appeared to be embarrassment, though he suspected that was counterfeit. He would wager this was not the first time she had snuck out alone, though perhaps it was her first time to be caught out at it.

"May I offer you an escort to your destination, my lady?"

"What are you doing here?" she said breathlessly.

For a moment he was speechless, entranced by the sheer beauty of her face in the sunlight. He cursed himself for being transfixed by a pair of wide eyes that only *looked* innocent and said in a voice that insinuated everything he believed, "*I* am enjoying the spring air. What are *you* doing here?"

Her cheeks heated under his stare. "That is none of your concern." She turned abruptly and began walking again, more briskly than before.

He gave his perfectly matched bays enough rein to keep pace with her.

She turned to eye him suspiciously. "Why are you following me?"

"It appears you have been abandoned by your escort, my lady. I only sought to offer you my protection." He barely managed to avoid giving the words a different, and altogether more suggestive, meaning.

She sighed, looked desperately around her, then chewed on her lower lip in a way that made his insides draw up tight. "It is a very long walk," she said. "I suppose it would not be so very scandalous if I were to accept your offer. After all, we have been formally introduced."

"I have even been to Penrith House to visit you, though you were not there to greet me."

Her face flushed, but her eyes flashed defiance. "There could be no purpose in meeting you, since I have no intention of furthering the acquaintance."

"I see."

"What is it you see, my lord?"

"That it will take a bit more persuasion to convince you to accept my suit. Unless you would prefer the *carte blanche*?"

She wrinkled her nose in disdain and marched away in high dudgeon. "I have changed my mind about the ride. Good day, my lord."

Clay found himself smiling. He was glad she was not

making it easy. His spirited bays fought the bit as he kept them to a pace equal to hers. "Perhaps I should submit to your father for permission to wed you," Clay said, thinking how much he would relish such a meeting with Blackthorne.

"My father would never—"

"Are you sure you would not prefer to sit up here with me? At least then we could keep this conversation between ourselves."

He watched as she noticed they were attracting an audience of street peddlers, beggars, and other less savory characters. She shivered, wrapped her shawl more closely around her, then continued on her way. "I am not afraid, my lord."

Apparently not. But he was becoming alarmed on her behalf. The way had narrowed, and little sunlight made it past the close-set buildings. The shadowy streets were filled with refuse so foul that even these poor souls could find no use for it.

Clay glowered at a sly-looking beau-nasty who was following her too closely. "You there, step back and give the lady room."

For his efforts, he got a leer that exposed blackened teeth. Clay regretted not bringing a carriage that required a tiger who could attend his team while he walked beside her, since the neighborhood was becoming more and more threatening.

"If you are afraid to ride with me, of course I will understand," he said.

She whirled to face him. "Stop your curricle, my lord."

Clay barely managed to avoid grinning. Plainly, the best way to manage her was to challenge her. "Can you reach the step by yourself?"

She had clambered into the high seat beside him before he finished speaking. She looked straight ahead, her black-gloved hands hidden in the folds of the faded gray dress. "Continue to the corner and turn right, please."

Clay turned right at the corner and recognized the street as one where he had rented a house for his first mistress. He had been a boy of one-and-twenty, a younger son dependent on his elder brother, then Earl of Carlisle, for his subsistence. In those days, he had spent—overspent—his quarterly allowance on gambling, women, and wine. No wonder Blackthorne had believed the worst of him.

"Why did you follow me?" Lady Regina asked, interrupting his thoughts.

Clay stared down into a pair of blue eyes that stared right back. There was nothing coy or practiced about her, he realized. "What makes you think I followed you?"

She rolled her eyes. "It must have been obvious I did not wish to see you today. Why did you insist upon forcing an encounter?"

"Do you always abandon your suitors to your sister?"

"I had forgotten a previous appointment," she said, sticking to the story her sister had given him.

He snorted in disbelief. "An assignation, you mean."

"What?"

"I recognize the neighborhood, Lady Regina. Who is he?"

"What?"

35

"The name of the gentleman you are meeting. Come, come. Let us be honest. I will match his price, whatever it is."

Her lips pursed in annoyance, and for a moment he thought she was going to deny his accusation. She shook her head, opened her mouth, closed it again, and finally said, "If you must know, there are two gentlemen."

"Two!"

"Mr. Edwards and Mr. Connelly . . . Simon and Harry. I try to see them at least thrice each week."

"You don't find that a bit . . . fatiguing?" Clay asked through tight jaws.

"Why, of course I do," she admitted with amazing candor. "But when I see the smiles on their faces after I have hugged them and kissed them and made them as comfortable as I can, I feel the effort has been worthwhile. I would see them every day if I could manage it, but social engagements interfere far too often."

The chit wasn't even blushing! "It cannot be easy for you to engage in such activities unnoticed by your sister."

"She is indulgent, my lord, as you can see."

"Does she know you entertain two gentlemen at once?" he asked, unable to keep the edge from his voice.

"Of course."

Clay could not believe he was having such a conversation, neither the fact of it nor the matter of it. He would not need to indulge in debauchery to ruin the chit. She was already beyond redemption. All he need do was inform her father of her activities and . . . and be laughed out of the duke's house. Who would believe it of her? He could scarcely believe it himself. He needed proof. "I will *double* whatever they have offered," he said.

Her chin slipped up a notch. "Simon and Harry need my attentions far more than you ever could, my lord," she said. "Turn right at the corner, please."

Clay concentrated on keeping the ribbons loose, though his hands had tightened into fists.

"Furthermore, I am convinced there is no way you could match what they give me in return for my affection. Stop here." She was stumbling onto the uneven cobblestones before he had brought the high-wheeled curricle to a complete stop.

"Wait!" he exclaimed. "You will hurt yourself—"

She had already disappeared into a dark, narrow alley between two houses. "What the devil are you—?"

Damn the chit! He tied up the ribbons and leapt to the ground in one graceful move. His hand clamped onto the filthy shirt of the first street urchin he saw. "Watch my cattle. There will be something for you, if they are safe when I return."

"Aye, milord," the boy said, his chest puffing out in importance as he looked around to see who might have noticed his improved station in life.

Clay eyed the boy askance, not at all sure his favorite bays would be there when he returned, but leaving them was a necessary risk. An infamous procurer kept a houseful of *filles de joie* not a block away. If Lady Regina was not careful, she might very well find herself forced into a life even he could not condone.

He glimpsed the hem of her skirt disappearing beyond a pair of iron gates, which clanged shut behind her. Had she gone inside willingly? Or had she been taken prisoner?

Clay hurried forward, only to find the gates had been locked behind her. "Open the gates!" he ordered the woman who was rapidly retreating along with Lady Regina.

The middle-aged woman dressed severely in black bombazine turned, her face filled with surprise and concern, increasing Clay's fear that Lady Regina had fallen into the worst sort of company. Some of the most notorious Covent Garden abbesses looked like simple governesses.

"Let me in," Clay said. "I have business with the lady."

"Ye'll have to take yer turn, sir," the woman said with a chortle. "The lady is much in demand."

Clay ground his teeth with impatience as she unlocked the gate with a skeleton key attached to a chain at her waist. Then he shoved his way inside, grabbed the woman by her shoulders, and demanded, "Where is she?"

"Why, inside with the youngest of the gents. Where else would she be?"

Clay let the woman go so abruptly she nearly fell and hurried toward the double doors that led into a kind of hell he was afraid to imagine. He could hear shrieking even through the heavy wooden doors beyond the inner courtyard. He reached for the latch, half expecting the door to be locked, but it opened with a screech of unoiled hinges. As he stepped into the gloom, his jaw dropped.

Lady Regina stood haloed in a shaft of light, holding a gurgling baby in her arms. A "younger gent"—a mere three years, at a guess—held tightly to her skirt with one hand, while the thumb of the other was stuck firmly in his mouth.

Clay crossed to her without speaking and stood staring at her in fascination.

"This is Simon," she said, brushing at the blond curls on the baby's head. She looked fondly at the child at her knee and added, "This young man is Harry." She turned to glance at the myriad other children crying and shrieking as they played around her. "It will take me a while to introduce the rest. I believe there were forty-eight at last count."

"This is an orphanage," Clay said, a relieved bubble of laughter building in his chest.

She shot him a mischievous grin. "Yes, my lord, it is. What else could possibly lure me into such a disagreeable neighborhood?"

Chapter 3

REGGIE KNEW IT HAD BEEN OUTRAGEOUS of her to confound the earl, once she realized he had so totally misunderstood the situation, but she had been unable to resist teasing him. It was not at all ladylike behavior, but no one could ever accuse her of acting as she ought. It was a flaw in herself she could not seem to mend.

"You had me in a fine coil, Lady Regina," the earl said.

"You deserved every moment of discomfort I could give you for thinking so badly of me," she said, returning his chagrined smile with a look that begged forgiveness.

"I suppose I deserved to be roasted," he admitted with a laugh. "I could think of no other explanation for why you would come here."

"Do you always think the worst of people?" she asked.

His features abruptly sobered. "I try to see people as they are, not as I would like them to be."

"What is it you believe I am?"

"An enigma," he murmured.

Reggie felt her blood begin to thrum at the earl's steady regard and realized her ready wit had deserted her. Fortunately, her uncle Marcus, once a major in the Prince of Wales's own Tenth Royal Hussars, had taught her that retreat was occasionally the better part of valor.

"I thank you for your escort, my lord," she said to the earl. "Now that I am safely arrived, please feel free to go about your business."

She shifted the baby so he lay over her shoulder, then took the toddler by the hand and headed for one of the two long trestle tables set for luncheon. The tables were situated near an immense brick fireplace where a coal fire burned, taking the chill from the room, but leaving everything in a layer of soot. To her dismay, the earl followed right behind her.

"I had reserved the afternoon to spend with you," he said, stopping beside her at the table closest to the fire.

"Oh. I am—"

She was distracted by three-year-old Harry's grunts as the child tried to hitch himself up onto the wooden bench at the table. She waited to see whether Lord Carlisle would offer to help. When he did not, she thrust the baby into his arms in order to help Harry herself. "Will you please hold Simon for me?"

"See here, my lady," the earl protested. "You cannot be shoving babies at a fellow—"

Simon, looking not at all happy about the switch, began to howl.

Before Reggie could reach Harry, he fell, scraping his elbow on the rough stone floor, and began shrieking like a banshee.

"Try feeding Simon some bread from the table, soaked in milk," Reggie instructed the earl over the two wailing children, "while I tend to Harry's hurt."

"Don't leave me—"

Reggie had already forgotten the earl, so absorbed was she in soothing Harry and finding a clean cloth and water in the kitchen to wash the dirt from his wound. It was Harry's, "I'm starvin', Reggie," that reminded her she had left the earl at the luncheon table with a howling baby. Except, she realized suddenly, it was now deathly quiet.

Reggie hurried back to the dining room where, to her amazement, she saw forty-seven children seated at the two tables, all quiet as mice. The reason for their silence was plainly the predatory creature sitting in their midst.

Her attention was drawn to the grimy hand of a small girl, up on her knees beside the earl, tugging on his no-longer-immaculate white linen neck cloth.

"What is it, Charity?" the earl asked.

"May we eat now?"

"When Lady Regina returns."

"She says to call her Reggie," a gap-toothed girl across the table said.

" 'Cause she's our friend," the towheaded boy beside her added.

"And friends can call each other by their given

names," the girl in tight brown braids sitting beside him chimed in.

"I see," the earl said. "And what is your name?"

"Melinda, sir. Melinda Smythe."

"It's Smythe 'cause she ain't got no name of her own," a boy at the foot of the table said. "Seein' as how her mum's a—"

"I'm pleased to make your acquaintance, Melinda," the earl said, adroitly cutting off the boy's explanation.

The girl was old enough, Reggie saw, to blush at the earl's formal greeting.

"What shall we call you?" the gap-toothed girl asked the earl.

Reggie was very much a part of the expectant hush, waiting to hear how Lord Carlisle would reply.

"You may call me—"

The baby in his lap let out an impatient shriek and reached with both hands toward the table.

"Your manners are execrable, young man," the earl said, restraining the child. Nevertheless, as Reggie watched, Carlisle picked up a loaf of bread from the center of the table, broke off a piece, and dipped it into a cup of milk in front of him. He handed the portion to the baby in his arms, who leaned back against him and sucked noisily on the offering.

"What's yer name?" an impatient child at the other table demanded.

"My name is Clay," the earl said.

"Pleased to make yer acquaintance, Clay," the tow-headed boy said with a grin.

"Likewise, I'm sure," the earl replied with a smile. "And who are you?"

"I'm Freddy Jenkins," the towheaded boy replied.

The room erupted with names being offered to the earl, until someone spied Reggie at the door.

"It's Reggie! Hurry up, Reggie, and sit down," Freddy urged.

"Clay says we have to wait for you," Charity piped up.

Fists pounded on the table. Shouts erupted. A fight broke out.

"Silence!" the earl roared.

The mice froze in place.

"You're frightening them, my lord," Reggie said in a soft voice. "Is such a fierce look really necessary?"

The earl's features eased as he said, "I always look like this when I'm famished. Dig in, mates."

Every eye shifted to Reggie, who nodded.

A clatter of plates and a clash of silverware followed, as the children grabbed for bread and hunks of cheese.

"I can take Simon now," Reggie said as she settled Harry in an empty space and then took the last bit of bench left—beside the earl—for herself. "He is not the neatest of children."

The earl surveyed the bread crumbs soaked in milk which Simon had deposited on Clay's black breeches. "I have a passing acquaintance with dirt, my lady," the earl said. "And the damage is already done. Simon will be fine here," he said, brushing a hand gently across the child's blond curls.

Her jaw was still hanging in amazement when he said,

"I would love to know what brought you here in the first place, Lady Regina."

"Won't you please call me Reggie?" she said. "At least while we are here."

He shot her a grin that took years from his face. "Only if you agree to call me Clay."

"But—Oh, very well."

"Very well, Clay," he intoned.

"Very well, Clay."

"Will you answer my question?" he asked.

"I have forgotten it," she said with a laugh.

"What are you doing here, Reggie? It is not often one finds a lady, indeed, a duke's daughter, playing nursemaid to a bunch of orphans."

"It is quite simple, really," Reggie replied. "When I was ten, my father brought home a fourteen-year-old orphan named Michael O'Malley to live with us at Blackthorne Abbey, my father's estate in Kent. Mick became a beloved brother. He works for my father now managing his estate in Scotland, Blackthorne Hall, but he will be coming to London within the month to bring news of whether I have a new brother or sister. I am sure you will find him as fine a man as I do."

"This O'Malley is the source of your interest in orphans?"

Reggie nodded. "It took some time, but my sister and I finally pried the truth from Mick about how awful life was for him and his two younger brothers and two younger sisters in a Dublin orphanage. After a beating one day, he finally ran away, but not before promising to return for Corey and Egan and Glenna and Blinne when he had made his fortune. Unfortunately, his sister Blinne was sold away before Mick could get back to them.''

When she finished, Reggie's throat was tight with emotion. Mick was still searching for his lost sister.

Reggie met the earl's gaze and said, ''When I heard Mick's story, I vowed that someday, when I was old enough, I would do what I could to help such unfortunate souls.''

''You really think coming here makes a difference?'' the earl asked.

''Yes, I do. My pin money contributes enough to provide milk and cheese to go with the bread which was all the children had before I began coming here two years ago.''

''How did you find this place? It is nowhere near any of the parks where I would expect a young lady to spend her time walking. In fact, the neighborhood—''

''Is not a very nice place,'' she finished for him. ''If you must know, Freddy slipped out and made his way to St. James's Park, where I was walking with my sister, snatched my reticule, and ran. I doubt he expected me to run after him, but I did—and caught him! Once I found out he was only hungry, I offered to help and . . .'' She shrugged. ''Here I am.''

''What about the dangers of frequenting such a neighborhood?'' Carlisle asked.

''Oh, 'tis perfectly safe,'' Reggie said. ''A hackney is usually waiting for me at the corner, and I always leave before dark. Something must have delayed Bascombe today.''

The earl shook his head. ''You are naive to think no

harm could befall you in such a place. A young woman alone—''

"You will not sway me from my purpose. Besides, you need not fear for me, my lord, I—''

"Clay.''

Reggie had encouraged the familiarity, so she could hardly object to it now. "Clay,'' she said, feeling her stomach turn over as his hand covered hers. She eased her hand free and set it in her lap. "I am careful to bring nothing of value with me when I come, and I dress as meanly as the least servant, so that no one will suspect my true station in life. Indeed, when Bascombe did not arrive with the carriage today, I considered returning to the house. I would have done so, if it were not for Freddy's birthday.''

She watched as the earl sought out the rail-thin boy with lank blond hair and large brown eyes who had identified himself as Freddy Jenkins.

"Freddy is twelve today,'' Reggie continued. "So this is his last day here at Miss Henwick's Home for Unfortunate Children.''

Clay turned to meet her gaze. "Where is he going?''

"Out into the world.'' Reggie paused and took a calming breath. "You see, the lady who left this house to be used as an orphanage stated it was to be employed for the aid of children only until their twelfth year.''

The earl frowned ominously. "And what are Freddy's plans, if I may ask?''

"I . . . he . . . If I had my own establishment, I would hire him myself,'' Reggie said. "But Penrith says he has all the servants he can use, and I—''

"Freddy," the earl said, addressing the child. "How would you like to work for me?"

"What?"

"I need a groom. Would that suit you?"

The boy leapt to his feet. "Workin' with prime bits o' horseflesh?"

"The very best," the earl assured him.

"How much does it pay?" the boy asked.

Reggie groaned. "Freddy, really, you should be grateful—"

"A bed, all you can eat, and a bit to spend on Sunday to start. We can negotiate again when you're sure you like the work," the earl said.

"Blimey!" Freddy exclaimed. "When do I start?"

"You can start by checking to see if my curricle is still out front where I left it." Carlisle flipped the boy a coin and said, "Pay the lad who's waiting there. I'll join you shortly."

Freddy caught the coin in the air and with a shout of pure joy, raced from the room.

Reggie could barely swallow past the sudden lump in her throat. She turned away from the earl, but he reached out and caught her chin and angled it toward him. She could feel the tears welling in her eyes and knew she must not blink or one would fall. "That was a lovely gift," she said softly.

"The world is a frightening place when you have nothing. I can spare him that discovery for a little while, at least."

"How can I ever thank you?"

"Come to the theater with me on Thursday. I have a box at Covent Garden."

"Pardon me?" Reggie said, startled by the shift in their conversation.

"I would like to see you again," he said, his voice low and coaxing. "Please come with me."

"I see no purpose to be served by continuing our acquaintance."

"I hope to persuade you I am different from the men who have left you so disappointed in the past. Will you give me a chance to do so?"

Reggie could not conceive of any man of her acquaintance who would have made such an unselfish offer to a child he barely knew as the one Carlisle had made to Freddy. Surely for that reason alone, the earl deserved a second opportunity to make a good impression. "Very well. I will attend the theater with you on Thursday."

His eyes narrowed distrustfully at her easy capitulation. "You won't abandon me to your sister?"

"I promise I will be there when you call for me." Reggie fully intended to keep that promise. In fact, she and Becky would both be waiting when the earl arrived.

"Lord Carlisle has invited me to attend the theater with him on Thursday," Reggie announced at supper that evening. "I was wondering, dear brother, if you could spare my sister to play chaperone."

The startled look on Penrith's face told Reggie she might have raised her brother-in-law's suspicions by speaking to him in such a friendly manner. But it had occurred to her, as she was dressing hurriedly for supper after having stayed until long after dark at the orphanage, that she had the perfect opportunity to separate her sister from Penrith's company.

She would simply spend all her time with Carlisle, and insist on Becky as her chaperone, until Mick arrived from Scotland to help rescue her sister.

"Well, well," Penrith said, a lurid glint in his eye. "Now there is a match made in heaven. The man is rich as Croesus, a member of the Four-in-Hand Club, handy with his fives at Gentleman Jackson's Saloon. When all is said and done, he would make a handsome brother-in-law." Penrith's eyes narrowed assessingly. "Tell me, Regina, where did you meet the fellow?"

Reggie suddenly realized how truly castaway Penrith had been the previous evening. He seemed to have no recollection of their discussion in the carriage. "Why, I met him at Viscount Raleigh's ball last night," she said. "Do you not recall introducing us?"

Reggie ignored her sister's anxious hand signals and her disapproving faces as she baited Penrith. "You were effusive in your praise of the gentleman. I felt certain you would approve of our further association, which is why I agreed to attend the entertainment with him.

"Now that I think of it, you may even have put the idea in my head that my sister should chaperone. I believe you said Carlisle was a man you could trust, indeed, that you had trusted him to advise you on financial matters."

"Yes, well . . ." Penrith blustered. "I do have some other business requiring my attention these days. And

Lord Carlisle is a figure of some note. I suppose under the circumstances I can spare my wife to chaperone her sister.''

"Thank you," Reggie said, surreptitiously shooting Becky a grin of triumph.

After supper, Reggie and Becky left Penrith alone with his port and headed upstairs. It was dark in the upper hallway because, although Penrith insisted on expensive beeswax candles, he could not bear to burn them, so only a few of the wall sconces were lit.

"You are impossible. Incorrigible. Hopeless," Becky muttered as she marched down the hall toward the nursery.

"Why?" Reggie demanded. "Because I have contrived to have my sister come with me to the theater. You know you will enjoy it. You have not often had the opportunity to attend, since Penrith does not care for it. You should be thanking me."

To Reggie's surprise, Becky rounded on her. "This is not a game, Reggie. This is my life. I know you cannot like Penrith, but he is my husband. Please do not humiliate me again as you did at table tonight."

"What harm was there in confirming Penrith's overindulgence in spirits last night?" Reggie retorted. "You already know the worst. Indeed, you have suffered disgracefully for it. When Mick arrives we will contrive a way to free you from this marriage."

"Are you mad? Penrith will never let me go!"

"Why not?"

"He wants an heir," Becky said bitterly. "And I have not yet given him one."

Joan Johnston

"I should have considered that, of course," Reggie said, her lips pursed thoughtfully. "I had hoped a separation would be sufficient, but I see it will have to be something more permanent. An annulment, perhaps, so Penrith can remarry and have his heir."

Reggie glanced at Becky and saw that her sister's eyes were huge with disbelief. "What is wrong? Don't you want to be freed from this marriage?"

"I would like it above all things," Becky hissed, the words obviously wrenched from deep inside her. "But it is impossible!"

"If you desire it, I will manage it somehow," Reggie assured her. "Mick is certain to have some idea of how it can be done."

Becky groaned. "You know how your plans have a way of going awry, and that is putting things in their best light. Please don't do anything. And *please* don't involve Mick."

"But I know we could contrive—"

"You are forgetting one very important thing," Becky interrupted, her eyes bleak. "You may force Penrith to relinquish his right to his wife, but you will never convince him to give up Lily."

"Why would he care about Lily?" Reggie asked, confused. "She is a mere girl—not the heir he desires."

"You do not understand," Becky said, her voice filled with despair.

"Explain it to me," Reggie urged.

"You have seen how he does not ask to hold her, that he rarely even acknowledges her existence. But Lily is *his*. She belongs to him, as I belong to him, as the chairs

52

and sofas and silverware belong to him—something he can show off if an occasion arises, but which otherwise should stay in its proper place." Becky shook her head. "It is hopeless."

Reggie slipped her arm around Becky's waist in comfort and continued walking with her toward the nursery. "Nothing is ever hopeless."

"I don't wish to discuss the matter further."

"Will you still come with me to the theater?" Reggie asked.

Becky stopped outside the nursery door. "I don't understand your attraction to Lord Carlisle," she said with a sigh. "He is a totally inappropriate escort."

"But I told you how he gave Freddy a job. I think there is more to the man than meets the eye," Reggie said. "And what harm could befall me with you there to watch over me?"

Becky made a sound in her throat that suggested a great many things might go amiss in such an outing, but conceded, "I am no good judge of men, as this discussion has proved. Only promise me you will guard your heart."

In her sister's pained voice, Reggie heard more unhappiness than she could bear. She pressed a kiss to Becky's cheek and whispered, "I am in no danger there. With you as my chaperone, Carlisle will never get a chance to do more than speak flowery words, and you know I am immune to vows of eternal love spoken by callow young men."

"Carlisle is no callow young man," Becky warned.

"No, indeed," Reggie agreed. "I think he must be at least . . . three and thirty."

Becky laughed. "You are incorrigible."

"I know," Reggie said with an unrepentant grin. "And impossible and hopeless. Come, let us kiss our darling Lily good night and go to bed ourselves. You will need to be in fine fettle from now on to protect me from the earl."

Becky laughed. "I have never imagined myself as a knight in shining armor, but I stand ready to defend you. Forward into the fray!" she said as they stepped into Lily's bedroom.

Reggie was glad Becky did not realize that she was not entirely joking. She found Carlisle every bit as threatening as Becky had suggested. He had already destroyed her peace of mind.

Carlisle's past made him intriguing. The tragedy he had suffered made him a figure for whom she could feel compassion, especially considering her father's part in the catastrophe that had caused him to lose everything. The earl was attractive to her in a way she could not understand or define . . . or resist.

Oh, yes, he was dangerous.

But Reggie had no intention of making the same mistake as her sister. She would know her man before she married him. She would doubt him, dispute him, defy him. She would put Carlisle in every situation she could conjure that might reveal his true nature. When he had proved himself worthy of her love, then, and only then, would she consider giving him her hand . . . or her heart.

Chapter 4

HEADS TURNED. BROWS LIFTED. FANS snapped closed as the Ice Princess arrived at Covent Garden in company with the pirate. Although Reggie was certain Carlisle could not know it, he was already being measured against her list of Seven Deadly Sins in a Suitor. It had taken her an entire evening to compose it, and she had actually wound up with more than a dozen sins by the time she was through.

Will he ignore present company in favor of some prettier face or larger bosom? she wondered.

His eyes never left her, and they were filled with admiration. "That is a charming gown, Reggie," he whispered in her ear as he seated her in his box.

Reggie supposed she must allow the earl a passing mark on one point, at least: he did not appear to have a roving eye. *But will he show my sister equal courtesy?*

"May I take your wrap, Lady Penrith," the earl said solicitously.

"Thank you, my lord," Becky said.

Carlisle settled the Norwich shawl across the back of Becky's chair, which was in the row behind Reggie. "Is there anything else I can arrange for your comfort, Lady Penrith?" the earl asked.

Reggie conceded Carlisle's manners were impeccable. He was both considerate and kind. But she had known that already, from his behavior toward Freddy and the children.

She caught her lower lip between her teeth. The problem was how to test all those other sins. It might be possible to determine whether he was willing to spread vicious gossip, or whether he would bore her to death with his conversation, simply by attending the *ton* events to which she was regularly invited.

But how could she measure whether Carlisle drank to excess or gambled beyond his means? She had never been to a tavern, and Becky was not likely to agree to attend a gaming hell with her. That meant finding ways to spend time in Carlisle's company without Becky along to chaperone.

While the thought of being alone with Carlisle did not precisely frighten her, it did cause her a certain amount of trepidation. Nevertheless, she was determined to discover even those flaws it might be dangerous to encounter. *Was Carlisle the sort of man who might strike a woman?* Reggie was certain it would take some great provocation to know for certain, but that meant she must devise some means of protecting herself if the earl became violent.

There were also matters of a more personal nature to

be determined, matters about which ladies and gentlemen did not ordinarily discourse. *Did the earl believe it was his right to keep a mistress after he was married?* Reggie had made up her mind long ago that she could not bear to share her husband with another woman, even one he craved only for her body, which was the excuse Penrith had given Becky for why he kept a mistress.

And there were matters of character to be uncovered. *Would Carlisle take advantage of an innocent?* She could only know for sure by giving him an opportunity to seduce her in surroundings where they would not be fortuitously interrupted by her sister.

"You do not seem to be enjoying the play," the earl said.

Reggie started at the feel of his warm breath in her ear. "But of course I am," she protested.

"You are not laughing," Carlisle pointed out.

Reggie looked around and saw that the audience in the pit had broken into raucous laughter. She could hear Becky giggling like a schoolgirl behind her. "I was not . . . I mean . . ."

"Perhaps if you share your troubles, I may be of some help," Carlisle said.

Did one dare ask the fox to guard the hen coop? "No, my lord. I do not believe that would fadge."

"If the play bores you, perhaps you would prefer to engage in conversation," he whispered. "But not here."

He turned to her sister and said, "Reggie has a bit of the headache. We will walk in the hall for a while, where it is less noisy, and hope that helps."

When her sister started to gather her shawl, Carlisle

laid a hand on her shoulder and said, "I see you are enjoying the play, Lady Penrith. Pray continue to do so. You may trust me with your sister."

To Reggie's astonishment, Becky sat back in her chair and said, "Very well, my lord. I shall."

She and Carlisle made as unobtrusive an exit as they could through the rear of the box into the hallway beyond, which was indeed more quiet. Carlisle surprised her by stopping while they were still within sight, and easy calling distance, of her sister.

She turned and smiled at him. "Thank you."

"For rescuing you from your thoughts? I doubt I have done much but delay your distress. Will you not share the problem with me?"

Reggie took a deep breath and braced herself, as though she were preparing to dive into the icy pond at Blackthorne Abbey. "If you must know the truth, I was wondering how I might manage to attend a gaming hell."

He laughed. "Surely you jest."

"No, my lord—"

"Clay."

"No, Clay, I am not jesting," she said. "It is a matter of . . . of curiosity, you see."

"Curiosity killed the cat," Carlisle replied.

Well, Reggie thought wryly, the earl certainly had not pounced on the opportunity to draw her into flaunting convention. To be caught out in such a place could mean the ruin of her, but how else was she to discover what she needed to know. She had not heard any gossip about the earl's gaming habits, and she did not know anyone who knew him well enough to ask about them.

Reggie was not about to give up. Perhaps a little coaxing would do the job. She smiled prettily up at him, though she forbore batting her lashes. That was a coquette's trick. She only wanted to convince him, not seduce him. "Surely it could be arranged if I were in disguise," she suggested.

Before the earl could answer, a drunken fop laid a hand on her shoulder.

One minute the hand was there, the next it was gone, along with the castaway young man. He had been lifted bodily by his neck cloth and removed some distance down the hall by the earl, who said in a voice sharp enough to pierce even a drunken sensibility, "Kindly watch your step."

At the same time, Carlisle managed to bow and smile at Lady Hornby, the *ton*'s most notorious gossip, as she passed by.

Lady Hornby paused and lifted the lorgnette that hung from a ribbon around her neck to stare pointedly at the pair of them. "What are you doing out here with that chit, Carlisle? The play is inside."

"I might ask the same of you," Carlisle said, arching a black brow. "Are you in need of any assistance, Lady Hornby?"

Reggie watched in awe, as Carlisle not only deflected Lady Hornby's question, but left her flustered at the attention he paid her. It was difficult to tell, beneath all the powder and rouge, but Reggie would have sworn the old bat blushed!

"Enjoy your evening, Carlisle," Lady Hornby said. The ostrich feathers sprouting from her turban bobbed with each step she took, so she looked like that massive bird as she strolled regally down the hall toward the theater.

Reggie suddenly found the earl's eyes turned back to her, and she knew exactly how Lady Hornby had felt. There was nothing she could do to stop the rush of blood to her cheeks. If he was a rogue, he was certainly a charming and protective one.

"The answer is yes," he said.

Reggie barely managed to avoid blurting, "What is the question?" She merely smiled. Brilliantly. "When shall we go? How shall we manage it?"

"Leave everything to me. How does tomorrow sound?"

Reggie gulped. "So soon?"

"Do you have some other engagement tomorrow evening?"

"My sister and her husband are promised for dinner with the Covingtons, but I made my excuses." The last time she had dined with the Covington's, their nineteen-year-old son Harvey had cornered her in a dark hallway, sworn his undying love for her, and tried to prove it by forcing himself on her.

"I will pick you up at nine tomorrow night," Carlisle said.

"What costume shall I wear?" Reggie asked, both elated and terrified at the prospect of stealing away with the earl.

"The Smuggler's Den supplies masks at the door for

the disguise of their patrons," Carlisle said. "Be ready when I call. I will manage everything."

Reggie laid a hand on Carlisle's sleeve. "Thank you, Clay. I know I can trust you to take the best care of me."

He lifted her gloved hand, turned it over, and pressed a kiss to her palm. "You are precious to me in more ways than you can possibly imagine, my dear."

"Oh." She felt the heat of his breath again, this time on her flesh beneath the glove. She stood frozen, unable to move, unable to retrieve her hand or to offer him her lips as she had the undeniable urge to do. She could not ask for a more perfect suitor.

But he could not possibly be perfect. No man was perfect. She noticed a flaw in his perfection—and reached out to brush back the stray lock of dark hair that had fallen onto his forehead.

Reggie suddenly realized what she was doing and jerked her hand away. "Please forgive me," she said. "I don't know why I did that."

He stared at her, his dark eyes burning with some strong, frightening emotion she could not name. "There is nothing to forgive," he said at last. "Shall we return to the box?"

Reggie did not want the interlude to end, but she knew it was perilous to stay where she was. It was too private, and there was a tension between them now that had not been there before. "Of course," she agreed.

She tried to enjoy the rest of Sheridan's comedy, but her thoughts kept straying to her engagement with the earl on the morrow. The evening's entertainment at a gaming hell would offer her the opportunity to evaluate

Carlisle on more than one count, but it was also risky because she did not have a plan yet for how to save herself if the earl's behavior was not all it should be.

Reggie glanced at Carlisle and saw a man whose tailoring was impeccable, whose demeanor was entirely proper, but who reminded her of nothing so much as a caged jungle cat. "I am an idiot," she muttered under her breath. "Completely out of my mind. A fool on a fool's errand."

But it wasn't foolish, not really. She wanted a home and a husband and children. Until she had met Clay Bannister, she had not believed she would ever find a man she could respect and admire who also respected and admired her. That brief episode in the hall had been more than a little revealing.

Carlisle had dealt courteously with the importuning fop, but the fellow could not have mistaken his message. More impressive was the way he had dealt with Lady Hornby. And then there was that kiss on her hand. And the look in his eyes. For the first time in a very long time, Reggie had a hope that she might find . . . love.

Reggie had never allowed herself to dwell on the subject of love. At the same time, it had never been far from her mind since she had become old enough for her father to agree to a match. To be honest, she feared the emotion. Love exerted some magical power, created some powerful inner turmoil that allowed men and women to overlook the worst of faults in each other. Becky had allowed love to propel her into a match with Penrith, and look how badly that had turned out.

Reggie was quite certain she had never experienced

love, at least, not the sort that would allow her to overlook a fatal flaw in a man's character. She glanced at Carlisle from the corner of her eye, looking for the defect she was certain she would find. In his face and form she could find none. But physical assets—however pleasing to the eye they might be—were not what really mattered in a man, as she well knew. It was what was inside that counted. And that did not show at first glance.

She was determined to know the truth of Carlisle's character because she saw in him the sort of perfection a lover sees in her beloved. And Reggie knew how illusory that sort of perfection could be.

On the ride home in Carlisle's carriage, Reggie was so engrossed in her thoughts, and thus so quiet, that Becky asked, "Are you all right, Reggie? Has your headache passed?"

"What? Oh, yes, I am very well."

Becky turned to Carlisle and said, "It was kind of you to allow me to see the rest of the play while you walked with my sister."

"The pleasure was entirely mine, Lady Penrith," Carlisle replied. "Ah. We have arrived at Penrith House."

He stepped down from the carriage and helped Becky out first, then reached for Reggie's hand. Carlisle was everything that was proper. He waited at the door until Hardy, the butler, had let them in before he turned and headed back toward his carriage.

Reggie stood in the doorway, unable to take her eyes off of Carlisle. She had the strangest desire to run after him, to beg him to take her with him.

"Come inside, Reggie, and close the door," Becky

said, taking her by the arm and tugging her inside. "You are staring at Lord Carlisle as though he were a hot cross bun and you a starving child."

Reggie made a face. "Don't be silly. It was nothing of the sort. Although I do confess I like the man."

"*Like* is too weak a word for what I saw on your face. Be careful, Reggie."

"I thought the earl very well behaved tonight," Reggie said as she followed Becky upstairs.

"Oh yes, very well behaved. But I believe the earl to be capable of dissembling," Becky said.

Reggie hurried up two stairs to get in front of Becky and stop her. "Do you think he was? Dissembling, I mean?"

"His manners were not so nice at Viscount Raleigh's ball. Could he have changed so much in such a short time?"

Reggie sat down in the middle of the staircase and grabbed Becky's hand to tug her down onto the step beside her. "A man may have manners and yet not employ them," Reggie mused.

"I suppose so," Becky said. "But you must ask yourself what caused such a striking change."

"I suppose he wanted to impress me," Reggie said.

"Why?"

"What do you mean?"

"Why would a man as rich, as powerful, as determinedly unattached as Lord Carlisle, want to impress you?" Becky asked.

Reggie flushed. "He said he wishes to court me."

Becky frowned. "He wishes to court the daughter of the man who had him transported?"

"You are forgetting Papa has made amends."

"The earl is rich enough to attract a diamond of the first water from the current Season's crop of young misses. Why would he choose you, a female practically on the shelf?"

Reggie laughed. "Only you could insult me so thoroughly in the name of concern for my person. Perhaps he enjoys my company."

"I only pray that you will not make the same mistake I did," Becky said quietly.

Reggie put her arms around her twin and hugged her tight. "Oh, I will not. I promise I will not." She opened her mouth to explain her plan to expose any character flaws which Carlisle might possess but closed it again without speaking. If she included Becky in her plot, she might cause more trouble between Penrith and her sister.

"I understand there was a letter from Papa today," she said, subtly changing the subject.

Becky disentangled herself from Reggie's embrace and rose to continue up the stairs. "Papa promises he will send Mick to bring us the news when the child is born."

"I can hardly wait until Mick arrives," Reggie said, following after her.

"I wish he were not coming!" Becky said vehemently. "I don't know how I will bear it!"

Reggie caught her sister's elbow and urged her down the hall. "Come with me."

"Where—"

"Not another word," Reggie said firmly. Once they were inside Reggie's bedroom, she closed the door and turned to confront her sister. "Has Mick said anything, done anything to hurt you? I will pummel him into mincemeat. I will tear him limb from limb. I will—"

Becky giggled. "Oh, Reggie, you ridiculous creature. Mick has done nothing."

"Nothing?" Reggie asked suspiciously, crossing to the foot of the canopied bed where Becky stood and looking closely into her sister's eyes. "Then why don't you want him here?"

Becky sighed and levered herself up onto the foot of the bed. "You will think I am silly."

"I often think that," Reggie teased.

"He will know," Becky said.

"Know what?"

"That my marriage is . . . not entirely happy."

Reggie did not argue with her sister. Mick had always been good at reading faces, something he had learned in the orphanage in Dublin, where divining what someone was thinking might help him avoid a blow or manage an extra portion of gruel. And Reggie had to admit, Becky's face spoke volumes about the state of her marriage.

The slight puffiness in her lip had not lasted beyond the morning after Penrith had struck her, but the wounded look had not left her eyes. Mick could not fail to see it.

Reggie reached for her sister's hand and twined their fingers together. "I will not say a word about . . . about what I saw. I promise."

She felt Becky squeeze her hand. "Thank you, Reggie. I could not bear it if Mick were to learn the truth."

"He would not blame you for it," Reggie said.

"I know that. But he will pity me. And that is much worse."

"Won't you please let us help you escape this marriage?" Reggie asked.

When Becky shook her head, Reggie felt a hot tear spill onto her hand. She took one look at Becky, then gritted her teeth to keep her own chin from quivering.

She might not be able to save her sister, but she could save herself. If Carlisle failed even one test, she would dismiss him. Spending the rest of her life as a spinster or a maiden aunt, even being stuck on the proverbial shelf, was preferable to a life filled with disappointment, with disillusion, and with utter disdain for one's spouse.

Reggie's nose pinched as she entered the Smuggler's Den and was assailed by the smells of spilled wine, male sweat, and cheap perfume. A servant at the door handed them each half-masks, and Carlisle helped her to don hers before putting on his own.

The cacophony inside was punctuated by shouts of joy and groans of despair as patrons won or lost at the tables. Now she knew why such places were called gaming hells. How could any decent gentleman bring a lady to such a place? It seemed Carlisle had flunked a test she had not even meant to give.

Before Reggie could ask to be taken home, she felt the earl's arm around her waist ushering her through the jostling crowd. A moment later they passed through a door at the back of the room, and the noise was shut out behind them. She found herself in a quiet, elegantly decorated room where masked patrons like themselves stood or sat around tables where various games of chance were being played.

"What is your pleasure, Reggie?" the earl asked. "Hazard? Faro? Whist? *Rouge et noir?* Piquet?"

Reggie realized too late that there was a flaw in her plan to determine whether Carlisle was a high-flyer. The only sharps or flats she had ever come in contact with were on the pianoforte. And though she had heard of gambling vowels, she wasn't certain precisely how one obtained an I.O.U.

"How about whist?" she ventured.

"Very well. Come this way."

Carlisle led her to a square table where a lady and gentleman were sitting, but which had two empty seats. "May we join you?" he asked.

"Of course, Carlisle."

Reggie turned to the earl, her mouth rounded in surprise. "He knows who you are!"

The earl grinned. "May I introduce my friend and solicitor, Mr. Roger Kenworthy."

"But I thought—"

"So nice to meet you, my lady," Roger said, rising and bowing to her. He turned to the lady who had risen along with him and said, "May I introduce Miss Millicent Waters."

"So very nice to meet you, my lady," Millicent said with a bobbing curtsey.

Reggie leaned over to whisper to Carlisle. "I thought the purpose of coming here in masks was to remain anonymous."

"To everyone else here, you are anonymous," Carlisle assured her in a quiet voice. "Mr. Kenworthy and I were roommates at Oxford. I told him I would be bringing you here tonight and asked him if he would come and bring a partner in case you wished to play at cards. I thought you might be more comfortable playing with friends, rather than with strangers."

Reggie could not fault him on that. She had been afraid she might say something during play that would give away her identity. "Thank you. I would."

As Carlisle seated her in one of the two empty chairs, she examined the man he had named as his friend. It was good to know the earl was capable of making friends— and of keeping them—since Roger's friendship was apparently of long standing. Of course, that could also mean the earl had not made any friends recently. She had so much to learn about him!

It was difficult to tell much about Roger Kenworthy's face behind the half-mask he wore, although he had a nice smile, with one front tooth that slightly overlapped the other. His hair was chestnut brown and so curly it must be a trial to his barber. He was a portly man, and to judge from his lime green waistcoat, enjoyed bright colors. The woman with him was rather thin, her dress bare of ornamentation, though it still must be considered fashionable. Despite Miss Waters's austere attire, she wore a smile as warm as the one on Mr. Kenworthy's face.

Reggie was able to say with the greatest sincerity, "It is so nice to meet you, Mr. Kenworthy. And you, too, Miss Waters."

"The pleasure is entirely mine," Roger replied.

"Thank goodness we may play whist," Reggie said with a laugh. "It is the only card game I know. I enjoy playing it with my sister." She looked longingly at the hazard table, where she could hear the sound of dice against the baize. "Although I must confess, I had imagined playing something a bit riskier."

"Fortunes are won and lost playing whist," Roger said.

"Oh. Really?" Reggie said, her interest piqued. She glanced across the table at the earl, with whom she was partnered. "Shall we risk all, my lord?"

"Everything, my lady."

So, he could be tempted to gamble. And not just a little. Perhaps this was the Fatal Flaw in Carlisle's character. The next few hours would tell the tale.

Though the earl had allowed a servant to fill a crystal goblet with wine for him at the beginning of play, he did not drink from it more than twice during the next three hours.

So much for drinking to excess, at least while he is playing at cards, Reggie thought.

If she had hoped to see how much Carlisle was willing to lose gambling at cards, she should have picked another game. Because all he did was win. And win. And win. And that despite her ghastly play.

"Oh, that was the wrong card. Again," Reggie said. She had not purposely begun playing badly to test

Carlisle's patience and composure, but she had learned a few lessons there, as well. He never criticized her when she played the wrong card, but merely encouraged her when she was playing well.

He was infinitely patient.

He had no temper.

He was a paragon.

In fact, he was simply too good to be true. Except, she could not imagine what purpose the earl could have for pretending to be other than what he was. Unless Becky was right, and he had some unknown, nefarious motive for courting her other than the hope of winning her hand. Then, of course, he might be dissembling. If he was playing a deep game, she would uncover his deception. But she wanted to believe he was what he seemed to be.

This time her poor play caused them to lose. Reggie lifted her eyes to the earl's face, looking for signs of blame. But all she found in his dark eyes was esteem. And regard. And respect.

She felt buoyed. And elated. And delighted to be in his company.

Which made her all the more suspicious. Carlisle was not going to break down her wall of caution with a single night's good behavior. Oh, no. Anyone might manage to have a good day. She was certain this perfect, polite facade could not last. Perhaps she had not made the challenge sufficient to the task. Perhaps he needed greater provocation to reveal his true nature.

"I think I would like to try a game of hazard," she said.

The earl lifted a brow, but all he said was, "Very well."

"I think Miss Waters and I must take our leave," Roger said. "Until tomorrow, Carlisle," he said, making his adieus.

Once Roger and Millicent were gone, Reggie rose and began walking with Carlisle toward the hazard table. "I like your friend Mr. Kenworthy."

Clay smiled. "We got into a great deal of trouble together at Oxford."

Reggie stopped and turned to him. "What were you like then? I mean, before you became the Sea Dragon?"

"Foolish. Profligate. Licentious," he said curtly.

Reggie's jaw dropped. There were the flaws she had been seeking, named aloud by the earl himself! "I cannot believe you would describe yourself in such terms."

"Lying would serve no purpose. You need only ask any gossip to know what was said of me then."

"And now?"

"No longer foolish. Or profligate. Or licentious," he said with a wry smile. "Rather the opposite."

"Because of what my father . . . I mean . . . Because of what happened?" Being transported would have been a life-altering experience for anyone.

A fleeting look passed across his face—anguish or anger, it was hard to tell which, or perhaps it was both—before he focused his gaze once more on her. "My life was changed forever. But that is in the past. Suffice it to say, I am a different man now."

A better man, she would say, based on what he had said. It was a great relief to know her father's interference in Carlisle's life had not had disastrous consequences.

He slipped his arm through hers and began walking toward the hazard table. "Shall I explain the game of hazard, or would you prefer to watch for a while before you try it?"

"I have changed my mind entirely," she said. "I would rather hear more about your adventures—past and present," she added with a cajoling grin.

"Then perhaps it is time I called for the carriage."

Reggie wasn't sure whether that meant the earl wanted privacy to talk, or whether she had asked one too many questions, and he wished to put an end to the evening as quickly as possible.

She managed to hold her tongue until they were both settled in his carriage—which was tastefully opulent, if there was such a thing—before asking, "What was it like to be a pirate?"

He was sitting next to her, which meant she could only see his face in profile. She could feel the heat of him, feel the rigid tension in his body. She wished he would look at her. There was no light in the carriage, but the flicker of the gas lamps they passed on the street defined his strong cheekbones and the hollows beneath them.

"That is not a story fit for your ears," he said with a smile to ease the sting of his refusal to answer.

Carlisle's unwillingness to share the details of his past life was not a flaw, precisely, but it did leave her wondering what he might be hiding. "Did you ever have to fight for your life?"

He eyed her sideways and smiled. "You're a blood-thirsty thing."

But that was all he said.

She had nothing to lose by asking the question she had already asked once, but which he had never answered. "Have you ever had occasion to kill anyone?"

"Not lately," he shot back.

She caught a glimpse of eyes so full of malice, so livid with violence, that she would have screamed with terror, except her breath was caught in her chest.

As suddenly as the violence had flared, it disappeared, hidden behind shuttered eyes. As though he willed it to go, the tension left his shoulders and thighs. His lips curved in what could only be a smile, but which bore no joy. "I have not yet come to terms with what happened in the past. Sometimes it feels a part of my present. I apologize if I frightened you."

"Apology accepted," Reggie said. But she felt an overwhelming sense of despair.

She had found a reason to reject him.

Beneath Carlisle's perfect facade was a boiling river of rage. She had seen it. It had been almost real enough to touch. And yet . . . He had lifted no hand against her. He had done her no harm. He had remained in control.

Excuses. She was making excuses. Why?

Because behind the rancor I saw pain. And I would rather try to heal his pain than give him up.

She seemed to have even worse judgment about men than did her sister. Becky had chosen Penrith without knowing the dangers to be found in loving him. How could Reggie commit herself to a man she knew beforehand was fighting demons?

Then she realized the awful truth. She believed she could make the demons go away. She believed she could redeem his tortured soul. She believed if she loved Carlisle enough, they would end up living happily ever after.

Oh, dear. Time to take a step back. Otherwise, the Ice Princess would end up a muddy puddle at the pirate's feet.

Chapter 5

THE EARL OF CARLISLE WAS COMING TO propose marriage this afternoon, and Reggie had not yet decided what her answer would be.

After that first lapse, when she had seen evidence of a tortured soul, Carlisle had never again dropped his guard. In four weeks of outings, he had comported himself so well that she had abandoned her list of Seven Deadly Sins in a Suitor. She had stopped looking for flaws and begun to search for the assets she might desire in a husband—companionship and common interests and comfortable conversation.

Reggie had been delighted to learn that the earl planned to eschew the debauchery of London when he married and retired to his estate in Scotland. She had discovered that they both loved to ride neck-or-nothing, that they both played the pianoforte with gusto rather than precision, and that they both enjoyed reading. Which had led to a great many stimulating conversations, because they rarely agreed on the substance of what they read.

And yet, something about the earl troubled her. It was as though he wore a mask, and there was a part of him she could not see. He had never again spoken about the past, and when she raised the subject, he had pretended it was of no consequence. Reggie feared the secrets Carlisle's past might hold, feared that, like Becky, she might marry the man of her dreams and wake up in a nightmare.

"What has you so Friday-faced?"

Reggie turned to look at Becky, who had entered the drawing room with Lily wrapped around her like a limpet. "Come here, you scamp," she said to her niece, sitting forward in the wing chair and holding out her arms.

Becky set the little girl down, and Lily ran on teetering three-year-old legs, her arms swinging akimbo, into Reggie's embrace.

Reggie swept the child up into her lap and gave her a quick hug, then kissed Lily's neck below her ear, where she knew the child was ticklish.

The little girl squealed and writhed with delight. "Aunt Reggie, stop!"

Reggie merely switched her attack to Lily's rounded belly, drawing her dress up and blowing on her stomach to make loud, rude noises.

Lily giggled with glee.

"Stop that, both of you!" Becky said, sending a furtive look over her shoulder through the open door to the hallway. "Someone may hear you."

Reggie looked up, her enjoyment arrested by Becky's admonition. "It is your home, Becky. Who should say you nay?"

"Not me!" a male voice said from the doorway.

Becky spun, her hand to her heart. "Mick! Oh, my God, I thought—"

Despite the fact Becky was closer to the door, it was Reggie who reached Mick first, Lily clutched tightly in her arms. "Mick! How wonderful to see you! Your hair needs a trim," she said as she tugged on the wavy black hair that had grown over his collar. "But you look fit."

"I'm glad to hear I don't appear the total scapegrace," he said with a grin.

Reggie leaned back and examined his face, as though looking for evidence of his good character. A spray of crow's-feet framed his sky blue eyes, a result of his tendency toward frequent laughter, and two vertical lines marked the edges of a surprisingly sensual mouth. He was undeniably a handsome man. "You're a devilish rascal, if ever I saw one," she announced.

As he enfolded both her and Lily in his arms, Reggie could not help thinking how glad she was he had come. Perhaps Mick could help her figure out what it was about Carlisle that troubled her, and of course, there was Becky's problem with Penrith to be resolved.

Reggie stepped back and asked, "All right. What is it? A boy or a girl?"

"You have a sister, Lady Margaret Moira Wharton," Mick announced. "Better known as Meg. Mother and child are both doing well."

"Thank the good lord for that," Reggie said.

Mick chucked Lily under the chin and said, "You're a sight for sore eyes, little one."

Lily shyly ducked her head into the niche between Reggie's neck and shoulder.

"I guess she doesn't remember her uncle Mick," Mick said. "I cannot believe it has been two years since last I saw her." He turned to Becky. "Am I going to get a welcome hug from you?"

Becky stood rooted to the spot where she had been standing when Mick entered the drawing room, her hand still pressed against her heart, her eyes focused on him, her face ashen.

Reggie was sickened to think that Becky was so frightened at the thought of Penrith catching them in a moment of unreserved gaiety that she was near fainting. She opened her mouth to chide her twin for being such a peagoose, but at the last instant saw something in Becky's eyes that took her breath away.

Dear God. She is in love. With Mick.

Reggie's gaze shot to Mick's face where, to her shock and dismay, she saw the same desperate, longing look in his eyes. Love . . . and something more. Overwhelming despair.

Reggie felt the muscles deep in her belly squeeze up tight, as though she had just seen a raw, bleeding wound. She felt certain neither of them had intended for her to devine their feelings, and indeed, she wished she had not. Her heart ached for both of them.

As Reggie watched their stilted greeting, a hug that was brief and from which each immediately stepped back, she noticed that both were careful to conceal their forbidden feelings from the other. Reggie tried to recall whether their last greeting had been so awkward and reserved, but it had occurred nearly two years past, and she could conjure no recollection of it.

For one completely mad moment, Reggie considered how wonderful it would be if Mick and Becky were to marry. Mick would never mistreat her sister. Reggie knew he would make a perfect brother-in-law, because he had been a perfect "brother." Thanks to their father, Mick had even been educated at Eton. Standing before her in his tailored plum jacket, buckskins, and shiny black Hessians, he looked every bit the Corinthian.

But Mick was no gentleman. He was the bastard son of an Irish whore. There was no way Michael O'Malley could ever hope to marry a duke's daughter. Presuming Becky were free to marry. Which she was not.

It is impossible. Even if Becky could be separated from Penrith, Papa would never allow it.

On the other hand, why not? They could live in Scotland, far away from Society and its strictures.

Lily snuggled closer, her cold nose pressing against Reggie's neck.

Reggie looked down at the child in her arms and realized she was holding both the source of—and the primary obstacle to—her sister's happiness. Even her father's vast influence could not silence the scandal that would ensue if Becky married a whore's bastard son. Lily's chances of making a good marriage would be ruined. She would be refused admittance to the best houses. Whispers would follow wherever she went.

Becky would never trade Lily's happiness for her

own. And even if Becky were willing to take the risk, Reggie knew Mick would never sacrifice Becky's and Lily's happiness for his own satisfaction. It was a tragedy with no possible happy ending.

"It is good to see you again, Becky," Mick said. "You are looking . . ." A crease formed between his brows, and he turned to confront Reggie. "Have you been running your sister ragged, keeping her out all hours of the night at routs and balls? If you have, Reggie, I swear I will—"

"I am not the one to blame for her deuced appearance!" Reggie said, surprising herself with the strong language that popped out of her mouth.

"Then who is?" Mick demanded.

"Penrith," Reggie blurted.

Mick's frown deepened. He reached out slowly and laid his hand along Becky's cheek, caressing the shadow beneath her eye with his thumb. "Is there anything I can do to help?"

Reggie could see the struggle Becky waged between moving closer to Mick and stepping away from the comfort he offered. At last Becky said, "It is something William and I must work out between ourselves. But thank you for the offer."

Mick's hand dropped away, but their eyes caught and held.

Reggie felt her throat clog with feeling.

"The Earl of Carlisle," Hardy announced.

Mick and Becky sprang apart.

Reggie barely stifled a groan. It was Carlisle, come courting. She wondered if he would discern the feelings

Mick and Becky were being so careful to hide from each other, but which seemed so blatantly obvious, now that Reggie had become aware of them.

She sought Carlisle's eyes as he entered the drawing room for a clue to what he was thinking. She was flustered by the sudden flash of hunger she found in his gaze and stunned by the matching flare of desire that rose within her.

Carlisle was dressed, as usual, entirely in black with snowy white linen. She let her gaze follow the breadth of his shoulders to his narrow waist and hips, then down the length of strong legs outlined by tight-fitting breeches, to tasseled Hessians. Her perusal could not have taken more than a few seconds, but when her gaze returned to the earl's face, she found his eyes heavy-lidded with desire.

Reggie had never been so aware of a man in her life, but she felt helpless to extricate herself from what was fast becoming, in light of their audience, an unseemly encounter.

"Welcome, my lord," Becky said with considerable aplomb, as she made her curtsey. "You find us *en famille*." She crossed to take Lily from Reggie, leaving Reggie feeling even more nakedly open to the earl's regard.

"May I introduce my father's steward, Mr. O'Malley," Becky said. "Mr. O'Malley, the Earl of Carlisle."

Carlisle seemed to realize of a sudden that they were not alone. His eyes narrowed as they settled on Mick. "We have met before," he said in a voice Reggie hardly recognized, it was so cold and hard. "And parted less than amicably."

"I recall the moment vividly, my lord," Mick said in an equally unpleasant voice.

"Perhaps you would like to share your recollection," Reggie said to Mick.

Mick's lips curled down in distaste. "It is Carlisle's moment and therefore his to share."

Reggie was perplexed. She had never seen Mick take anyone in such instant dislike. Except, it was not *instant* dislike, she realized. The two men had obviously met in the past, and not on good terms. She was convinced by Carlisle's black looks that a request for elaboration would not be welcome. But if he were ever to become her husband, he would be seeing a great deal of Michael O'Malley. Better to know the worst now than to face calamity later.

"I think I must hear this story, my lord," Reggie said.

"I do not choose to tell it," Carlisle replied.

"If you do not, I shall," Mick retorted. "Especially in light of recent events."

"What recent events?" Reggie asked.

"The day before I left Scotland, the traces snapped on the carriage your stepmother uses when she travels to Mishnish. When the horses broke free, the carriage overturned and nearly slid over a cliff into the sea."

Reggie gasped. "You said Kitt and the baby were well!"

"She is well, only a little bruised. Meg was home safe with her nurse. But it was a near thing. It seems the leather had been cut nearly through with a knife." Mick focused his blue eyes on Carlisle as though expecting a response.

Reggie looked from Mick to the earl, whose face had become a wall of stone. "What does Lord Carlisle have to do with an accident in Scotland?" she asked.

"I had nothing to do with it," Carlisle said flatly.

"So you say!" Mick shot back.

"Why would you suspect the earl of such perfidy?" Reggie demanded, incensed on Carlisle's behalf.

"It is obvious Lord Carlisle has not told you quite all there is to know about himself," Mick said.

Reggie glanced at Carlisle and saw the flush—was it rage or shame?—rise on his cheeks. She had suspected he was keeping something from her, but obviously it was something of even greater import than she had imagined. But she could not imagine the earl being responsible for such a heinous act. "Lord Carlisle has been in company with me these past weeks," she said. "How could he be the one who cut the traces on Kitt's carriage?"

"He is rich enough to hire someone else to do his dirty work," Mick accused.

Reggie turned to Carlisle, whose dark, dangerous eyes were focused on Mick.

"If you were a *gentleman*," Carlisle said to Mick with a sneer, "I would challenge you for that."

Reggie's head snapped around to see how Mick had taken Carlisle's insult. He looked ready to launch himself bodily at the earl.

Becky grabbed Mick's arm and begged, "Mick, please, do not provoke the earl. My lord, I am sorry—"

"Don't apologize to him!" Mick snarled at her.

Becky looked stunned at Mick's attack.

Lily let out a howl of protest at all the shouting. Her eyes scrunched up and her fists clutched at Becky's hair, grabbing handfuls and holding on tight.

"Ow!" Becky cried.

Mick's attention was torn from Carlisle by the need to rescue Becky from Lily's painful hold.

Reggie took advantage of the commotion to announce, "I am afraid we will have to postpone our meeting, my lord." She took Carlisle's arm—it was hard as stone—and ushered him toward the door to the drawing room. She could not hear his addresses now, not before Mick's accusations had been explained away. And she wanted time to compose herself before she heard Carlisle's confession, whatever it turned out to be.

"I have had a message from Miss Henwick's Home beseeching my immediate presence," Reggie improvised. "I am sorry I was unable to advise you sooner and spare you an unnecessary visit."

"Reggie, I—"

"Please, my lord," she said, making it clear he was no longer welcome. "I cannot speak with you now."

He bowed to her and said, "I will see you soon, Lady Regina."

It sounded more like a warning than a promise. It was not until Carlisle was gone that Reggie realized he had not observed the courtesy of taking his leave of either her sister or Mick. When she turned to search them out, she saw why.

Mick was holding both her tearful sister and the whimpering child in his arms—in what could only be termed an embrace. Reggie took a deep breath and let it out. This would never do. She crossed the room and put her own arm around Becky, forcing Mick to relinquish his hold. But his eyes never left Becky's.

Reggie was annoyed by Mick's behavior. She had invited him to London hoping he would be a source of succor. But all he had done so far was create more problems with his amorous attentions toward her sister and his mysteriously violent attack on Carlisle. "Why do you think Carlisle is to blame for what happened to Kitt?" She demanded. "Papa made every effort to ensure Carlisle's lands and title were restored. Surely the earl must be grateful to Papa, not angry with him."

Mick made a face and shook his head, but said nothing.

"You will have to tell us something," Becky said in a voice intended to ameliorate Reggie's aggravated tone.

"I promised your father I would not accuse Carlisle without proof," Mick said disgustedly. "He says he has wronged the earl enough, and that he will not compound prior insult with further injury."

"So you are only speculating that the earl is to blame?" Reggie said, her face revealing her disappointment in Mick.

"It cannot be anyone else," Mick argued.

"Why not?" Reggie said.

"Carlisle is the most logical culprit."

"But he was here in England courting me."

"Why would a rake like him bother courting a woman known as the Ice Princess, a disagreeable female who has rejected every eligible suitor for the past four Seasons. Think, Reggie!''

Reggie stared at Mick. She felt nauseated. ''Are you suggesting the earl is courting me for some reason other than the pleasure of my company?''

Mick's face looked troubled. ''I'm sorry if you have let yourself like the man, Reggie, but I cannot believe it is simply coincidence that Carlisle sought you out.''

''I sought him out,'' Reggie countered, her face heating. ''Despite what you say, I believe the earl has developed a genuine fondness for me.''

''You are only fooling yourself,'' Mick said. ''I think—''

''Are you suggesting I'm incapable of knowing when a man is dissembling? Why do you think I have waited so long to marry?'' Reggie said angrily. ''I have never met a man I could like as much as I like the earl. I have tested him in every way I can conceive, and he has never failed to impress me with his goodness, his kindness, his—''

''Perhaps we should sit down and discuss this calmly,'' Becky suggested.

Reggie felt a knot in the pit of her stomach. She was afraid to examine Mick's accusations too closely. Afraid of what she would discover. ''I cannot stay. As you must have heard me tell Lord Carlisle, I have an appointment at Miss Henwick's Home this afternoon.''

Reggie felt like sobbing. And would have, if she were the sort of female who allowed herself to become a watering pot. She had an awful premonition that once Mick told her everything he knew about Carlisle, she might never want to see the earl again. Carlisle could not have kept the truth so well hidden from her. He must have a care for her; she would have discovered a lie. She was not like her sister. She had been so very, very careful to look before she leaped.

"I will return in time to join you for supper," Reggie said as she fled the room.

She would deal with everything at supper. She would listen to what Mick had to say about Carlisle. And she would distract Penrith, so he perceived no evidence of the obvious attraction between Michael O'Malley and his wife.

"Pike and Jarvey understand they're not to strike her?" Clay said to Pegg as they stopped near Miss Henwick's Home in a closed carriage that was purposely absent the Carlisle crest.

"They've been with ye since the Sea Dragon first set sail," Pegg said. "They'll do their best."

Which meant, Clay thought, they might be provoked to violence. He shoved aside any second thoughts. Reggie had given him no choice. "I should have kidnapped her a month ago and saved myself the trouble of a courtship," he muttered as he stared out into the black, starless night. A misty rain made the cobblestones glisten in the light from a flickering gas lamp on the corner.

" 'Twas not time wasted," Pegg said. "The lass trusts ye now. When ye rescue her from a fate worse than death, she'll be glad to marry ye."

Clay was upset with himself for not broaching the

subject of a leg shackle sooner with Reggie. He should have known his luck would run out. But he did not intend to see his plans foiled by the sudden appearance of Blackthorne's steward, Michael O'Malley, even if it meant arranging things so the duke's daughter would be forced to marry him.

He had not believed Reggie's story that she had an appointment at Miss Henwick's Home, so it had been a relief to see her leaving Penrith's town house within minutes of his own departure earlier in the afternoon. The foolish female had not even bothered to disguise herself in old clothes and had hailed a public hackney to reach her destination. She had stayed long past an hour when it was safe to be in such a disreputable neighborhood.

Clay was waiting now in the shadows for the drama he had set in motion to unfold. "I warned the chit she should not linger here after dark. She is fortunate no one else has done what I am about to do."

"When do we sail?" Pegg asked.

"Tomorrow morning with the tide." Clay patted the pocket of his jacket. "I have procured a special license that will allow us to be married at any time of day, and without the banns being read in church, in anticipation of precisely the situation which has presented itself. Have you arranged to bring someone aboard tomorrow morning long enough to perform the ceremony?"

"All is in hand," Pegg said. "Are ye sure ye want to go through with this, lad?"

Clay stared out the window to avoid answering. And

caught sight of Reggie being accosted on the lamplit street by two rough-looking villains.

The play had begun.

Clay watched as a grimy hand covered Reggie's mouth to cut off her scream. He pursed his lips in admiration when Reggie gave Pike a vicious jab in the belly with her elbow, causing him to lose his hold on her. Clay winced as she clawed red furrows down Jarvey's cheek, then laughed aloud when she took off running. Damned if the chit wasn't about to escape!

His amusement vanished when Pike caught her by the tail end of her skirt, reined her in like some desperate animal on a tether, then clouted her hard on the chin with his fisted hand.

Clay growled in fury and lurched toward the carriage door.

Pegg manacled his arm to hold him in place. "Ye must have known she would fight, lad."

"I warned them not to hit her!" he said in a savage voice.

Pegg pointed to the lifeless body being hoisted over Jarvey's broad back. " 'Tis better this way. By the time the lass wakes, 'twill all be over."

Clay settled back into the velvet seat, but his shoulders were knotted with tension. His insides turned when he imagined how Reggie's face would look, blackened and bruised by Pike's blow.

Clay turned away from Pegg, fearing the other man would see his anguish, hating himself for feeling sympathy for the daughter of his enemy. He reminded himself why he had begun courting the chit in the first place.

Made himself remember the bitter bite of the lash on his back, the agony of the saltwater that had been used to salve his wounds, the unending ache in his chest where his heart should be.

He had lost a wife and a son. In return, he would take Blackthorne's daughter from him and get on her a child to replace the one he had lost.

Clay watched, forcing himself to remain impassive, as the two men carted their burden down a darkened alley toward the brothel he had selected as the site of Lady Regina's ruin. He had arranged for her to be sold to the worst of the Covent Garden abbesses, a woman who catered to the worst lechers, the most depraved gentlemen. It would not be long now before Reggie's innocence was lost.

Once she was ruined, she would be glad to marry him.

Clay felt the bile rise in the back of his throat and swallowed it down.

He felt dread. And summoned hate.

He felt regret. And summoned rage.

He had been a victim. It was only fair that Blackthorne's daughter should suffer as he had.

But the mere thought of Reggie submitting to some wretched goat with sweaty hands and the money to buy her virginity made Clay want to do violence. Lady Regina Wharton was no longer merely his enemy's daughter. Sometime over the past four weeks, and despite his best efforts to avoid caring, Reggie had become a person to him, someone with wishes and hopes and dreams.

He knew she wanted children, several of them. He knew she wanted to be more than an object of beauty to her husband, that she wanted to share her thoughts with him and to have an equal say in decisions about their future. And he knew she was romantic enough to believe that passion should be a part of marriage.

He regretted never kissing her again, though she had given him opportunities enough to do so. They had even walked alone together along one of the darkened pathways in Vauxhall Gardens, stopping to admire the fireworks that had exploded overhead. Her eyes had glowed with excitement, and she had turned her face up to his, inviting his kiss, inviting his touch.

He had known it was a test. He had leaned close, his mouth a breath from hers and said, "You are tempting, my sweet. I would love a taste of your lips. But I can wait."

He had resisted the urge to drag her into his arms, to align them body to body, to feel her softness against the places where he was hard. He had felt a grim satisfaction in her small moue of disappointment and exulted in the knowledge that when she was his at last, his seduction of her would be all the more satisfying.

A sudden pounding on the carriage door startled Clay from his reverie. He opened the door and stepped out.

"The girl has been delivered—"

He hit Pike without thinking, flattening the man and making his nose spurt blood.

"Why'd ye do that, Captain?" Pike said angrily, as he shoved himself to his feet.

"That was for disobeying an order." The instant Pike was on his feet, Clay hit him again. "And that was for bruising the girl."

Jarvey kept his distance. "She's been sold to the School of Venus, Captain, like you said." Jarvey held out a wad of paper notes. "They was glad to get her, her bein' a virgin and all."

When Clay made an animal sound in his throat, Jarvey grabbed Pike by the arm to haul him to his feet, shoved the money into Clay's hand and said, "Pike and me'll just be headin' back to the ship."

Clay shook his hand to ease the sting in his torn knuckles. He turned to the coachman and said, "Take me to the School of Venus," then stepped back inside the coach where Pegg waited for him.

"I thought ye planned to leave her overnight," Pegg said.

"My plans have changed."

Clay stared at the wad of dirty paper that represented the value of Reggie's virginity. He set the money on the plush scarlet velvet beside him and did not look at it again. He still had not decided what course of action he should follow, when his carriage rolled to a stop before the School of Venus, the house of ill repute where Reggie was now held prisoner. "Wait here for me," he said to Pegg.

"What would ye be doin', if I might ask?"

"Rescuing the fair damsel," Clay said in disgust.

"But there hasna been time—"

"Stubble it, Pegg."

The door knocker at the School of Venus was made of iron and clanked in a minor key when Clay used it. The knock was answered by a sticklike woman, dressed very much like the caretaker at Miss Henwick's Home, who invited him inside.

The walls of the drawing room were covered with Chinese hand-painted wallpaper that featured pheasants and flowers, and Clay's boots sank in the plush weave of a Brussels carpet. A harp sat in one corner, while a gilded chaise longue with carved arms had been angled in front of a white marble fireplace. In the opposite corner, two Hepplewhite chairs braced a small parquet gaming table. The exquisite furnishings made it plain that the School of Venus catered to the Quality.

Clay knew there were gentlemen with an appetite for virgins, the younger the better, and the money to pay for such a treasure, but he had never let himself dwell on the matter. Now he could not force the thought from his mind.

"What can I do for you, milord?" the abbess asked.

"I have a fear of diseases," Clay improvised. "Have you any girls who are untouched?"

The abbess smiled, revealing a missing eyetooth. "You are in luck, milord. A girl came here only today from the country saying she was pure as snow and wanted a real gentleman to pluck the bud from her—"

"Are you sure she is untouched?" Clay demanded, his voice sharp with fear that he was already too late.

"I do not promise what I cannot deliver," the madam

said. "She is pure. I checked her myself. But the price—"

"How much?"

"A hundred pounds?" the abbess ventured.

"What does she look like?" Clay asked. It would be his luck to pay for a "virgin" who was not Reggie.

"Small and shapely, milord, with black curls above and below, eyes the color of the deepest blue sea, skin that will taste of peaches and cream, excellent teeth, sweet breath—"

"Done," Clay said, his mouth dry with unexpected desire.

Realizing that he would have paid much more, the woman said, "Of course, clean sheets are extra. And if you choose to spend the night—"

"I will take the room until tomorrow morning," he said. "How much?"

She named the amount she wanted, which he paid, along with the hundred pounds for Reggie's virginity. It was four times the amount for which she had been sold. Acid surged into his throat. He did not know why he had said he would spend the night. Surely he did not intend to do so. To take her against her will? To make her his own in a place such as this?

"Do you have a pen and paper?" he asked.

"On the desk against the wall, milord," the abbess said.

Clay scribbled a note and sealed it with wax from one of the three tapers burning in what appeared to be a silver candelabra on the desk, imprinting it with the Carlisle seal etched in the gold ring he had inherited from his brother along with the title.

"Deliver this to the man with a peg leg you will find waiting in the carriage outside," he said.

She eyed him askance but said, "It shall be done, milord."

"Now," he said. "Show me where she is."

He followed the abbess upstairs and then along a narrow, carpeted hallway, disconcerted by the serenity he felt in such a place. One would never have suspected the debauchery he knew must be occurring behind closed doors.

When they reached the end of the hall, the woman unlocked the door and shoved it open. Clay half expected Reggie to throw herself into his arms, but there was no sound, no movement, and very little light.

"Where is she?" he asked, taking a step into the gloom.

"There, on the bed."

Clay followed the woman's gnarled finger and felt his body tighten viscerally as he spied Reggie lying stark naked on the bed. Her hair tumbled across the pillow in abandon, and her legs were spread wide in readiness, but her hands were folded peacefully across her breasts. Clay swallowed hard.

"What is wrong with her?" he demanded. "Why is she so still?"

"Oh, well, I gave her a bit of laudanum. For the pain. And to make her compliant for whatever you wish, milord."

His mouth flattened in repugnance at the leer on her

face. "That will be all," he bit out. "Leave the key with me."

He closed the door, shutting out the world of demireps and doxies, then put the key in the bolt and turned it, locking himself inside with Lady Regina Wharton.

Chapter 6

Michael O'Malley believed devoutly in two things: hard work and Irish luck.

It was Irish luck that he had encountered the Duke of Blackthorne at a time when Alastair Wharton had amnesia and did not know he was His Grace and not the sort to be socializing with the likes of Mick O'Malley. It was hard work that had resulted in Mick's appointment as the Duke of Blackthorne's steward in Scotland.

On the other hand, it was damned bad luck that he had fallen in love with Lady Rebecca Wharton the first time he had laid eyes on her. Becky had been sitting on the lawn at Blackthorne Abbey, her lap full of daffodils, when he crossed her path, scythe in hand. She had looked up and smiled at him, a perfect stranger dressed in a coat with too-short sleeves, pants with too-short legs, and boots that were two sizes too large.

Mick had known even then, as a gangly boy of fourteen, that a duke's daughter was never going to marry an

Irish bastard. He had owed Blackthorne too much to lust after his daughter, when all it could lead to was heartache for both of them. Besides educating Mick and giving him a job, the duke had provided homes and positions for his half brothers Corey and Egan and his half sister Glenna.

To repay the duke's generosity, Mick had kept his hands and his thoughts to himself, watching Becky all of his life with his love well hidden behind a friendly smile.

Until today.

He did not quite understand what had happened. Perhaps Reggie's exuberant greeting had broken his reserve. Or perhaps it was the way Becky had stood so still, staring at him, her heart in her eyes. *Love* in her eyes. It was a dream come true, to have her look at him with such longing. He had been so stunned he had . . .

Oh, God, what had he done? Mick shoved a hand through his hair. He should never have let her see what he was feeling. How was he supposed to face her across the supper table tonight and pretend nothing had changed? Everything had changed.

No, that was not precisely true. She was still a married woman. That had not changed.

And he was still a whore's bastard son.

Mick groaned. He had no business even looking at Becky, let alone dreaming of what it would be like to kiss her, to hold her in his arms. It was blasphemy even to think of trying to steal her from her husband.

Mick realized that if he did not find something to keep his mind off of Becky for the rest of the afternoon, he would go mad. Or do something he would regret for the rest of his life.

A paper crackled in his coat pocket, and he pulled it out. It was a letter from a London solicitor urging Mick to see him "at your earliest convenience" on "a matter of great importance to·your future." Mick supposed some lord or another had heard of the modern farming methods he had employed at Blackthorne Hall and wanted Mick to come work for him.

Mick considered the prospect of leaving Blackthorne's employ. Perhaps that was the best solution. That would take him out of Becky's orbit. That would remove temptation from his path. Because, if he were honest, now that he knew Becky might return his feelings, he doubted he would be able to keep himself from reaching for what he wanted.

Making her an adulteress. Making yourself an ungrateful wretch.

Mick sighed and shoved himself off the four-poster bed in the room he knew Becky had prepared especially for him, because it contained a vase of his favorite flowers . . . daffodils. He imagined how Becky would look with a daffodil on each breast and a cluster of them decorating her mound of Venus. His body tightened viscerally, and he shook his head in disgust at the foolishness of indulging in such fantasies.

Perhaps he ought to take whatever offer was made by that London solicitor. It was an honorable way out of the coil in which he found himself. At least the visit would remove him from the house during the long hours that stretched before him until supper.

In clean linen, with his coat brushed free of dust from the road, his Hessians polished, and his unruly black hair combed, Mick presented himself at the address on Chancery Lane named in the correspondence he had received.

A rotund, bald-pated gentleman looked down his nose through a pair of wire-rimmed spectacles and asked, "May I help you, sir?"

Mick handed over the letter. "I received this from someone in your office."

The gentleman took one look at the missive, then leapt to his feet, bobbed his head, and said, "Oh, my goodness. So sorry, my lord. Come with me."

Mick stared at the man, who had become quite agitated. Before Mick could protest that he was plain Michael O'Malley, not lord of anything, the wizened fellow had cracked his knuckles on a door across the room, opened it without waiting for an answer, and announced, "He's here! Tenby's grandson is here!"

Another gentleman, even rounder than the first and with spectacles perched on a much larger nose, appeared in the doorway. "Oh, my. The resemblance is amazing."

"Yes, Mr. Ellis. Amazing," the wizened man agreed, tilting his head back and staring down his nose through his spectacles at Mick.

"Would you please come into my office, my lord?" Mr. Ellis said. "We have a great deal to discuss."

"I think there's been some mistake," Mick said.

"No mistake, my lord," Mr. Ellis assured him. "Please, come inside where I can explain everything."

Mick was intrigued. It sounded like a case of mistaken identity, with him being mistaken for some lord's grandson. But what if there was no mistake? What if he really was who they thought he was?

Mick's chest felt like some heavy piece of farm equipment had fallen on it. He couldn't seem to catch his breath. He and Corey and Egan and Glenna had often speculated on who their fathers might be. Of course, they had no way of knowing, since their mother had spent so many nights with so many different gents. But they had often imagined it was some lord or another and that someday he would come looking for his missing child, because he had no heir for his absolutely huge fortune.

The three boys had all agreed that if any one of them was claimed by Lord Moneybags he would help the others. Glenna had lifted her chin in imitation of some grand lady, patted Blinne's back to make her burp up a bubble of milk, and said, "If I turn out to be Lady Lots-of-Loot, I shall allow you to work in my stable." Which had seemed a grand idea to the boys, because there was nothing they craved so much as the thought of sitting astride some fine blooded animal.

Of course, no lord had ever shown up claiming any of them. Until now.

Mick's feet felt like two anvils; moving in any direction was impossible. He was afraid to hope his dreams had come true, equally afraid to discover they had not. But in this one shining moment, anything was possible.

Becky already has a husband. All the money in the world cannot buy her freedom. It is too late.

"My lord? Will you join me?" Mr. Ellis said, gesturing him into the chamber.

"Would you mind telling me what this is all about?" Mick asked in a desperate attempt to control the absurd fantasies of wealth and power that had his heart pounding in his chest.

"Certainly," Mr. Ellis said. "Please come in and make yourself comfortable."

Mick stepped inside the solicitor's office. Every surface was littered with stacks of paper and immense, leather-spined books filled cases that lined the walls. He sat in one of the chairs across from the desk, but getting comfortable was out of the question. He felt like he was sitting on pins and needles.

"May I offer you a glass of sherry?" Mr. Ellis asked as he seated himself across from Mick.

"Brandy would be better," Mick said, feeling the need for something stronger.

"Of course," the solicitor said. "Jensen, brandy please, and then you may leave us."

Moments later, brandy in hand, Mick found himself facing Mr. Ellis, who leaned back in his chair contemplatively, pudgy fingers steepled atop his rotund belly.

"I have a few questions," Mr. Ellis began. "First, what was your mother's Christian name?"

The personal nature of the question surprised Mick. "Why do you need to know?"

"Please humor me, my lord."

"I am not—"

"Your mother's name?" the solicitor interrupted.

Mick was halfway out of his seat when the solicitor said, "Please. If you will only be patient, all will be made clear to you. Your mother's Christian name?"

"Elizabeth," Mick said at last. It was such a common name he could not understand what help it could be to know it.

"Did your mother have any distinguishing marks, anything that would identify her to a stranger?"

Mick thought a moment, and a memory came rushing back.

He had woken up to find a strange man shoving his mother up against the wall, his hand fisted in her hair, his mouth pressed against her throat—apparently biting her, because she was moaning with pain.

He had attacked the man, trying to beat him off. The instant the man lifted his head, Mick had seen the red mark and thought his mother was wounded. It had enraged him enough to pummel the man with all his might.

It was much later, when his mother was pressing a cold cloth to Mick's blackened eye and swollen lip, that she lifted her hair to show him that the man had not hurt her and to explain that the small red mark had been there since birth.

"She had a strawberry mark on her throat, beneath her left ear," Mick said.

"Anything else?" Mr. Ellis asked.

"No. Nothing else."

The solicitor templed his fingertips before him and pursed his lips. Clearly he was expecting something else. Mick racked his mind to think what it might be.

"The tip of her right index finger was missing," he said at last, "but she always wore gloves, so no one would notice that."

"Very good," Mr. Ellis said, rubbing his hands together.

"She also had brown hair, blue eyes, and good teeth," Mick added brusquely. "Is there anything else you would like to know?"

"Hmm. Yes. I see. Well." The solicitor looked down at a paper on the desk in front of him and adjusted his spectacles.

Mick still did not understand the point of the solicitor's questions, especially when the only proof that the answers he had given were true was buried with his mother in a pauper's grave.

"When is your birthday, my lord?"

"I will be five-and-twenty tomorrow," Mick replied impatiently.

"May 14. Oh, yes. Happy birthday."

Mick rose. "If you are finished, I will be going."

Mr. Ellis levered himself to his feet and held out his hands, entreating Mick to stay. He spoke quickly, before Mick could get out the door. "I represent Harold Delaford, the Marquess of Tenby. The marquess has been searching the past twenty-three years for his late son's wife, Elizabeth, Lady Delaford, who stole his two-year-old grandson Michael Delaford, Earl of Stalbridge, and disappeared. We believe, my lord, that you are Michael Delaford, Earl of Stalbridge and heir apparent to the Marquess of Tenby's title, estates, and fortune."

Mick dropped back into the chair, stunned. And then burst out laughing. "Oh, this is marvelous. This is wonderful. The very best birthday present I have ever had." He had actually believed for a moment that he was heir to a fortune. He pulled a cotton handkerchief from his pocket and wiped the tears of laughter from his eyes. "Who paid you? Was it Corey and Egan? Or Glenna? It must have been all three of them," he concluded.

"You know," Mick said with a chuckle, "you actually had me believing you. Where are they?" he asked, rising and looking back toward the door through which he had entered. "I want to knock their silly heads together for spending money on such foolishness. I am sure your services did not come cheap."

"This is no joke, my lord. I am entirely serious. You *are* Michael Delaford, Earl of Stalbridge, Viscount Newbold, Baron Tredington, *et cetera* and so forth."

Mick sank back into the wing chair. "This sort of thing just doesn't happen," he said, rubbing a hand across the tension in his forehead.

"Not often," the solicitor agreed, resuming his seat.

"How do you know I am who you think I am? I mean, a first name and a missing forefinger and a strawberry mark . . . that doesn't seem much to go on."

"And a birthday. You are forgetting that."

Mick shook his head. "How in heaven's name did you put those puzzle pieces together and come up with me? And why did it take so long?"

"Actually, we found you purely by accident," Mr. Ellis said. "An American gentleman came to me recently seeking help in locating a female bondservant who had run away from his plantation in Virginia. Seems he was in love with her! Said he had bought her from a man who claimed she was purchased from an orphanage in Dublin. He thought she might have come back to England searching for her family."

"Blinne!"

"Yes, my lord, it appears so."

Mick leapt to his feet and grabbed Mr. Ellis by his neck cloth, yanking him out of his chair. "Did you find her? Where is she? How is she?"

Mr. Ellis made one vain attempt to free himself before he explained, "The American gentleman gave me a great deal of information, including the fact that the girl's mother was named Elizabeth and was missing the tip of her right index finger. I engaged the Bow Street Runners, who investigated thoroughly and—"

"Found me," Mick said. "But where is Blinne, sir?"

Mr. Ellis shook his head. "I am sorry, my lord. We were unable to locate her. She must still be hiding somewhere in the colonies."

"At least now I know where to look," Mick said, releasing the solicitor and heading for the door.

Mr. Ellis hurried after him. "Wait, my lord. There is more."

Mick stopped in the doorway and stared back at him, feeling dazed, wondering if he could stand any more good news. "What more could there be?"

"Your grandfather wants to meet you. He wants to get to know you. He wants you to come live with him at Delaford House here in London."

Mick could not help grinning. It was all simply too ridiculous to be real. "My grandfather is still alive?"

"But of course. Otherwise, my lord, *you* would be the Marquess of Tenby."

"I am not certain I want to meet him," Mick said, feeling a sudden constriction in his throat.

"Your mother's estate includes a trust for you of five thousand a year. If you think you could live on that—"

"Five thousand a year?" Mick said incredulously. "That isn't possible. If my mother had so much, she would never have let us go hungry. She would never have—" *Sold herself,* Mick finished in his head. "Why?" he asked, his voice breaking. "Why did she run away when she had everything!"

"Not quite everything, my lord," Mr. Ellis said. "She would not have had you."

"I don't understand."

"When your father died, your grandfather not only took control of all your mother's income, he became your legal guardian. He believed your mother was too indulgent, and he forbade her any contact with you."

"How could a mother be too indulgent?" Mick retorted. "What kind of ogre is he?"

"A determined one," Mr. Ellis said. "He foiled all your mother's plans to steal you away. Until the last one. She lost the tip of her index finger when your grandfather slammed a carriage door closed on it as she was fleeing Delaford Park."

"Why are you telling me all this, when you're my grandfather's solicitor?" Mick asked suspiciously.

"Because I also represented your father, Thomas Delaford, before his death," Mr. Ellis said, removing his spectacles and wiping them with the trailing end of his neck cloth. He replaced them carefully, looked Mick in the eye, and said, "I know he would never have wanted your mother to suffer as I have learned she did."

The blood leached from Mick's face. *Ellis knew his mother had been a whore.*

"I only know of one occasion after she ran away that your mother asked Tenby for money. That one time, he refused her."

Mick felt the bile rise in the back of his throat. "And now he wants me to have his bloody money? I don't want it or his damned title! I don't want any of it. Not after what he did to my mother."

"The choice, of course, is yours, my lord."

"My name is Michael O'Malley, sir. And our business is concluded."

Mr. Ellis bowed to him. "I think your father would have been proud of you, Mr. O'Malley. I also think he would have wanted you to have his title and his fortune. Please consider that before you make a final decision. When you are ready, come back and see me."

Mick's nose burned and tears blurred his vision. He hurried from the room before he lost his composure entirely.

Why, oh why did I let down my guard? Becky lamented. *I have been so careful for so long. How could I have let Mick see what I was feeling?*

If only he had not stayed away for so long! She had missed Mick so very much over the past two years. Letters had simply not been enough. When she had seen him, her first instinct had been to throw herself into his arms and cover his face with kisses. Thank God Reggie had reached him first!

But she had not been able to keep from devouring him with her eyes. And he had seen her need and revealed his own.

Now every interlude between them would be as awkward as their meeting today in the drawing room. There would be no more long, lazy walks in the park discussing Mick's work for Papa. No more cozy nights curled up before the fire in the drawing room making up wonderful stories to tell one another. Such meetings would be fraught with danger now.

One moment of weakness, and I've ruined everything.

Becky kept her head down and walked quickly through St. James's Park, ignoring the maid that trailed in her wake, hoping to find some peace of mind before she had to confront Mick at supper. But there was no peace to be had.

She moaned aloud, and her maid said, "Are you all right, my lady?"

"A pebble in my shoe," Becky replied.

"Shall we stop—"

"It has fallen out again," she interrupted. "I am fine, really, Brenda."

That was a falsehood. An absolute clanker. She had a stomachache, her dread of meeting Mick at supper was so great. "Why don't you rest here on this bench awhile," she said to her maid. "I will return to you in half an hour."

"But his lordship said—"

"You may tell Lord Penrith I never left your sight," Becky said patiently.

"Very well, my lady," Brenda said, settling onto a wrought-iron bench near the water. "I will be counting the minutes."

Becky gritted her teeth to keep from screaming in frustration. She hated being caged in the house, but going out meant acknowledging the bars that surrounded her. So far she had managed to keep the wretched state of her marriage a secret from Mick. What if, now that the wall between them had come tumbling down, he saw how bad things really were?

She had kept an even more perfidious secret from Mick.

What if he asked her when she had fallen in love with him? Did she dare tell him the truth?

I have loved you for years and years, but I never said anything because . . . I was afraid of what people would say.

If Reggie had been in love with Mick, Becky knew her twin would have married him, no matter what obstacles lay in her path. Reggie would have spit in the eye of anyone who criticized her. Becky had actually seen her do it once!

But although they were twins, they were not at all alike. Becky had married a man who appeared to be the perfect mate, rather than the man she loved, because she feared the certain condemnation of her friends and family when she told them she wished to marry a commoner—and not just any common man, but the bastard son of a whore.

"I did not expect to find you here. Where is your maid? Are you alone?"

Becky looked up to find Mick standing right in front of her, as though her thoughts had conjured him. There was so much she wanted to confess. So much she was loath to say. She only managed, "I left Brenda behind. For half an hour."

"Good," Mick said. "That will give us a chance to talk privately. I have so much to tell you!"

Becky was caught unawares when he reached for her forearm to wrap it around his own. She cried out as his fingers pressed against a bruise that was hidden beneath her sleeve.

"What's wrong?" Mick asked. "Did I hurt you?"

"No. I . . . That is . . . It is nothing," she said, tugging down the sleeve of her walking dress.

Mick took her hand in his and pushed her glove down and her sleeve up. She knew what he would find: the imprint of Penrith's thumb and four fingers, which had gripped her wrist when he had forced his attentions on her two nights past.

"Who did this?"

Becky hung her head. "It was my fault," she whispered. "I should not have refused William. I am his wife. It is my duty—"

"Oh, God. No, Becky." A moment later Mick's strong arms bound her tight against his chest. "He doesn't have the right to hurt you," he murmured in her ear.

She leaned her cheek against his shoulder. "It is the first time he has—"

He leaned back and tipped her chin up, forcing her to look at him. "Don't lie to me. Not to me."

She felt a knot grow in her throat. "Mick, please. Let me go. Someone will see us."

His hands dropped to his sides, and he took a step back. He offered his arm without touching her and said, "Shall we walk?"

"All right." She laid her gloved hand on his arm and walked with him toward a copse of birch and willow growing along the lake, where they were less likely to be discovered. "What was it you wanted to tell me?"

"I am . . ." He hesitated, then said, "I have had some news about Blinne. It seems she was sold as bond-servant to a gentleman in Virginia."

"Can you buy her freedom, do you think?"

"Perhaps. If I can find her. She ran away from him."

"Oh, no. The situation must have been very bad for her to take such a drastic step."

"I am afraid so." Mick stopped. "Especially when I see what you are willing to endure and still stay with your husband."

"I have Lily to consider," Becky said, leaving the impression that, if not for Lily, she would willingly leave Penrith. Would she? Given a second chance, would she have the courage to flaunt Society and marry her father's steward?

"Would you like to sit down?" Mick asked.

Becky realized they were hidden from sight beneath a willow. "The grass will stain my skirt," she said. Penrith noticed everything and was certain to ask questions she would rather not have to answer.

Mick tugged off his jacket and spread it on the ground. "Will that solve the problem?"

She settled onto his coat and waited as he sat down beside her.

"How are things at Blackthorne Hall?" she asked.

"I would rather talk about the bruises on your arm."

Becky shook her head. "There is nothing to be done, Mick."

"If your father knew—"

Becky put a hand on his arm. "Please don't tell him. It is my problem to solve."

"Reggie hinted in her last letter to me that there was something wrong. I never suspected this. I want to help, Becky. Tell me what I can do."

Becky averted her eyes, unable to bear the look of sympathy in his. "Nothing. There is nothing anyone can do."

The silence between them grew uncomfortable. Becky could feel Mick's eyes on her, and a slow curl of desire began to unfurl inside her. His hand reached for hers, and he threaded their fingers together.

Mick had held her hand a thousand times before, but it had never felt like this. Like they were connected. Like they belonged together.

"I cannot bear to think of him hurting you," Mick said. "When all I have ever wanted is to cherish you . . . and love you."

Becky raised her eyes to his. "Oh, Mick." She reached out to touch his face, as she might safely have done only a day before. But he reached up to cover her hand and his mouth closed over hers and she was lost.

114

There was nothing tentative about Mick's kiss—or her response. It felt as though they had been lovers for a very long time.

Mick's tongue traced the seam of her lips, and Becky opened to him. She made a grating sound in her throat and heard his answering moan. His hand cupped her breast, feeling the shape of it through her cambric gown. His thumb brushed at the nipple, which had already tightened into a hard nub.

Becky slid her hand into the hair at his nape to feel its silky texture, something she had often dreamed of doing. She nibbled on the lobe of his ear and kissed his cheek, rough with nearly a day's growth of dark beard. She let her lips learn the feel of his mouth as she tasted him, trying to memorize it all. Because this was forbidden. Because she must not let this happen again.

A dog barked, and they sprang apart.

They stared at each other for a long moment, realizing what they had found. And what might be lost to them forever.

Mick stood and reached down to help her up, brushing away the few blades of grass that had clung to her skirt. "You will need to fix your hair," he said.

She reached up and realized for the first time that he had removed nearly all the pins. She laughed. "What were you thinking?"

"That I wanted to feel your hair in my hands."

His honest answer sobered her. It was what she had craved herself. "This can never happen again," she said as she repinned her hair.

He said nothing.

"You agree, don't you, Mick. We mustn't be alone like this, ever again."

"Many wives have affairs—"

"Not before a man has his heir," she said brusquely. "And in my case, not at all. This was wrong, Mick. I'm not sorry it happened," she admitted. "But I will never meet you like this again."

Mick picked up his jacket and yanked it on. "I wish you had not married him," he said, as they began the short walk back to where she had left her maid.

"Then I would not have Lily."

"Do you think Penrith would be willing to divorce you?"

Becky shuddered. "If he did, he would most certainly take Lily from me. I could not bear that."

"A child belongs with its mother," Mick agreed.

"Unfortunately, the laws are all in the father's favor," Becky pointed out.

"That does not make them right," Mick said. "At least I arrived in time to save Reggie from an unfortunate alliance with the Earl of Carlisle."

"Why unfortunate?" Becky asked.

"The earl hates your father."

Becky stopped and stared. "That cannot be true. I must admit I questioned Lord Carlisle's motives myself at first. But in all his dealings with Reggie, he has never suggested the least animosity toward Papa."

"Which is all the more reason to distrust him," Mick said. "I was there on the docks with your father when Carlisle was transported. He stood there in chains and vowed he would come back someday and ruin your father's life."

"Dear God," Becky whispered.

"The story does not end there," Mick said. "Your father eventually determined that Carlisle was the innocent dupe of his steward, Cedric Ambleside. But by then, the convict ship was lost at sea, and Carlisle was presumed dead. What happened between then and a year ago, when Carlisle returned to England, is known only to him and to God. But you have surely heard the rumors."

"That he was a pirate? That he killed a man with his bare hands? Yes, I have heard them, but I gave them little credit."

"I believe every word of it. The earl is no gentleman. He is a savage bent on revenge against your father. I believe he hired someone to cause the accident that almost cost your stepmother her life."

Becky gripped Mick's arm. "Why would the earl so patiently woo Reggie, if he hates Papa and tried to kill Kitt?"

"I cannot believe he means to marry her," Mick said. "Perhaps he hopes she will allow herself to be seduced. It is possible he may even force himself on her."

"But if his intention is merely to ruin her reputation, why offer marriage? Reggie believed Lord Carlisle meant to offer for her this afternoon."

Mick shook his head, acknowledging that he was stymied. "Perhaps Reggie can tell us more about the earl's intentions at supper tonight."

"She will be heartbroken if he abandons her," Becky murmured.

"He is a scoundrel, a liar, and a cheat. And if rumor can be believed, a murdering pirate," Mick retorted.

"Even if everything you've said is true, none of it will matter to Reggie."

"Why not?" Mick asked.

"She is in love with him."

Chapter 7

REGGIE COULD SEE A MENACING MALE FIG-
ure outlined in the doorway but could
not move to cover her nakedness. Nor
could she manage the effort it would have taken to
scream or scratch or kick. It was as though her body
were an otherworldly thing over which she had no control. She knew what must be the result of this encounter.
She would be brutally raped. Her innocence would be
despoiled. She would lose whatever chance she might
have had for a happy life with Carlisle.

"Reggie?"

How strange. The man who had come to ravish her
spoke with Carlisle's voice. She searched in the shadows
for the awful face that went with the looming figure and
saw that it, too, had taken on Carlisle's familiar features.

"Clay," she whispered. "Oh, Clay."

She closed her eyes to shut out the truth of what was
about to happen to her. It was not Carlisle. It could not
be him. She flinched as callused fingertips traced her

119

collarbone. The touch was surprisingly gentle, almost reverent. She felt a curious languor, a desire to know what those warm, gentle fingertips might feel like on her breasts and belly. There were more delicious sensations, the gentlest brush of flesh against her ribcage before the caress moved downward, but she could not seem to stay awake to enjoy them.

Her last memory was the feel of cotton sheets being folded over her, of strong arms wrapping themselves around her body, and weightlessness as she was lifted into the air and floated away on soft, whispery wings that carried her into the darkness.

Clay had left Reggie in his cabin on the *Sea Witch* to sleep off the effects of the laudanum and then come here to the church graveyard where his wife and son were buried. He carried a lantern to light his way as he moved carefully through the tombstones, looking for the stone angels that marked the two graves he sought. When he found them, he set the lantern down so it illuminated the script on the two headstones. He dropped to one knee, but his head rose to the dark night, rather than bending in supplication. And it was no prayer to God that he spoke.

"I have your daughter now, you blackguard," he said. "I intend to make her pay for every humiliation of mind and body and spirit I suffered, every godforsaken moment of hunger and thirst, every strike of the lash that peeled the flesh from my back.

"Most of all, she will pay for the deaths of those I

loved, my wife and my son. I will get a child on her to replace the one you stole from me, and then rid myself of her, as I would discard a filthy rag. So much will I do to avenge my wife and my son and myself.

"May your soul rot in hell, Blackthorne, for all the harm you have done."

Clay felt an icy wind cross the back of his neck like a ghostly spirit. His heart was hammering, and a knot squeezed his throat. He glanced around, but the grave-yard was empty save for him. He reached out and traced his wife's name on her tombstone, then did the same for his son.

"You will both be avenged," he whispered. "I promise it."

Reggie's mouth felt stuffed with cotton, and her tongue was dry and swollen. Her body ached, though she was aware of lying on a bed of utter softness. It felt as though she were being rocked in a cradle. She could see a faint light beyond her eyelids, but she had no desire to leave the dark warm cocoon in which she lay.

"Here. Sit up and drink this. It will help rinse away the last effects of the laudanum."

Reggie recognized the voice at the same time she felt a muscular arm reach beneath her bare shoulder—oh, God, she was naked!—and lift her into an upright position. She experienced a moment of sheer panic, though it did not translate itself into action. Her limbs felt as though they were made of pudding.

It could not be Carlisle, not if she was in bed! She

must still be under the influence of whatever drug the villains had forced down her throat. Her eyelids were simply too heavy to lift. She felt the edge of a china cup against her lips and inhaled the strong smell of coffee.

Her captor must have sensed that she was afraid to drink for fear of being drugged again, because he said, "You're safe, Reggie. Drink now, like a good girl."

It sounded like Carlisle. It must be Carlisle. But what was he doing in her bedroom? Where was Becky? Shouldn't her twin be here with her? Things were too muddled in her mind to make sense.

Reggie swallowed a gulp of coffee that burned going down but took with it the ball of cotton that had made her mouth feel so dry. She drank again, lifting her hands—she could lift her hands!—to hold the china cup as she imbibed its contents.

She made a sound of satisfaction in her throat as the coffee warmed the cold places inside of her. She wanted to look into Carlisle's eyes and thank him for saving her. If only she could get her eyelids to cooperate.

"That's enough for now," he said as he eased the cup out of her hands and laid her back down. "Lie back now and rest. The Reverend Mr. Thompson won't be here to marry us for another hour."

Reggie's eyes flew open, and she sat bolt upright as though she were a toy springing out of a box. It took her a moment to realize the sheet had slid to her waist. She grabbed at it and dragged it up to cover her nakedness.

"Marry us?"

"After what happened tonight, we have little choice in the matter," Carlisle said.

Tonight? What had happened tonight? She remembered being accosted and carried away and then being forced to drink a cup of something awful-tasting. And then . . .

Reggie realized she had no idea what had happened afterward. Her glance darted from the man who sat on the narrow bed beside her toward the door—and spied the portholes in the walls through which she saw the blackness of night. Her stomach did a somersault and landed awry. "What time is it? Where am I? What is this place?"

"It is past midnight. You're in my cabin, on my ship, the *Sea Witch,*" he said. "There is no reason to be frightened."

"I'm not frightened," Reggie said, curling her legs tight against her body and gathering as much of the bed coverings—and her composure—around her as she could. "I am a bit . . . befuddled, if you please, as to how I got here. The last thing I remember was . . ."

What she remembered was the exquisite pleasure of a man's hand caressing her rib cage. And her belly? Or had she imagined that? At the time Reggie had been certain it could not have been Carlisle. But here she was. And here he was.

"It was you. The man in the room with me. It was you."

He nodded.

She was assailed by several feelings at once. Gratefulness that it had been Carlisle, and not some stranger, was paramount. And then embarrassment that he had seen her as bare as a newborn babe. She was both curious—

and suspicious—about how he had happened, so conveniently, to be there. And worried about what he had done to her afterward.

"How did you know I had been kidnapped? How did you find me?" she asked.

"By chance, really. I witnessed your abduction." He lightly traced the faint purple bruise on her chin, removing his hand when she winced. "I'm sorry I was not able to catch up to you sooner. By the time I arrived at the brothel where you had been taken, you had already been drugged," he said. "I am afraid there was no way I could take you out of there without stepping into that room and seeing you."

Reggie felt a flush on her throat that quickly crept up onto her cheeks.

"And seeing you," he continued inexorably, "how could I not touch you? And having touched you . . ."

Reggie looked into Carlisle's face, trying to determine whether he had actually done to her what he seemed to be implying that he had done. His dark eyes were inscrutable, revealing nothing.

It was impossible to believe she could have lost her virtue. She did not feel any different. Could Carlisle possibly have ravished her without her having any memory of the encounter? "Did you . . . ? Did we . . . ?"

"No," he said.

She heaved a sigh of relief. "Oh, then I can go home—"

He shook his head. "We will be married tonight."

"What if I don't want to marry you!" Reggie retorted.

"Neither of us has much choice in the matter," he snapped back. "Not after what happened tonight."

Reggie felt a sudden painful knot in her throat. "Surely there is another way out of this coil."

"Your absence has already been noticed. Your father's steward, Mr. O'Malley, has been to my town house demanding information concerning your whereabouts. We have no choice, Reggie."

It was, of course, possible to refuse the earl, but the consequences of such a refusal were daunting. In the world in which Reggie lived, a fallen woman was doomed to spend her life as a spinster. She would be ogled and ostracized. She would become a useless appendage in a social body that would rather cut her off than find a use for her.

But what about Mick's accusations against Carlisle earlier that evening? She still did not know the truth about the man who sat beside her.

But you do know the truth, another voice argued. *Would a villain have rescued you? Would a villain be offering marriage?*

Reggie had to admit that gambling on marriage with Carlisle was a better alternative than losing all hope of ever having a family of her own. But she rebelled at the thought of being forced into wedlock. "Perhaps we can keep what happened this evening a secret. No one else need ever know—"

"I will know. And you will know." Carlisle hesitated and added the words that sealed her fate. "And after Mr. O'Malley's inquiry regarding your whereabouts, my servants know."

Of course he could order them not to speak of Mick's visit. But all it would take was one slip. Even if he sacked the miscreant whose tongue got away from him, it would be too late. Once servants knew a thing, all of London soon knew it.

Reggie sighed. "I believe my father will still provide a dowry, even if I marry in such a havey-cavey fashion."

"I don't want your father's money," Carlisle said flatly.

Reggie frowned. "But—"

"Is it yes or no?"

"Did you do what Mr. O'Malley accused you of doing?" she asked quietly.

He did not pretend to misunderstand. "I am guilty of many things," he said. "Murder, even attempted murder, is not one of them."

Reggie knew that if she chose not to marry Carlisle she could survive. She would have the funds to support herself as an unmarried woman. She could live with her sister until she was five-and-twenty, at which time she would begin receiving an allowance from a trust fund her father had set up for her. She could bear to be a social pariah.

But she would never have the children she so desperately wanted.

"Even if I said yes, how is it possible for us to marry at night and without the banns—"

"I have a special license," he said, his gaze intent on hers. "I obtained it a short while past, when I began to have a hope you might accept my offer."

She stared at him in wonder. "Then you do love me."

Reggie could tell nothing from Carlisle's dark eyes, which remained unfathomable. But he lowered his head and his lips touched hers with a tenderness that made her chest ache.

"Will you marry me, Reggie? Will you be my wife and bear my children?"

"Yes, Clay," she whispered against his lips.

He deepened the kiss, his mouth capturing hers, until she felt breathless, her heart pounding, her head dizzy. She clutched his shoulders as he released her, and stared into his heavy-lidded eyes. "I love you, Clay. I love you."

He rose abruptly, grasping her wrists to free himself, and took a step back. "I have had a wedding gown made for you. I had intended it as a wedding present. It's hanging in the wardrobe. Everything else you need is in the trunk at the foot of the bed. When you're dressed, come up on deck. I'll be waiting for you there."

He lifted her hand, turned it over, and pressed a chaste kiss on her palm. When he looked up, she saw his eyes were filled with desire, and his lips had a certain rigidity she was learning to recognize. "I will leave you to dress," he said. "Otherwise, we are likely to anticipate the honeymoon."

A moment later he was gone.

Reggie felt frightened. Everything was happening too fast. It was only after Carlisle had gone that she realized she had not asked about having Becky and Mick present at the ceremony. On second thought, she realized it would be easier to marry now and explain everything to them later. Once they heard the story of her kidnapping—and knew how much in love she was with Carlisle—they would understand why she had agreed to marry him in such haste.

Reggie scooted to the edge of the bed and set her bare feet on the cold wooden deck. She tucked the sheet around her as she rose and moved to the trunk at the foot of the bed to retrieve the underclothes Carlisle had promised would be there. She supposed he must have made arrangements to obtain them, and to have the wedding gown moved onto his ship, while she was under the effects of the laudanum.

Reggie gasped as she lifted two handfuls of frail silk underthings from the trunk. Why, she could see her hand right through them! She searched through the trunk for something more substantial, but to her dismay, found nothing.

Reggie made good use of the pitcher of warm water and washcloth that had also apparently been left for her, patting gently around the bruise on her chin, before she put on the delicately stitched silk chemise and lace-trimmed pantalets. She caught a glimpse of herself in the looking glass and blushed. She was appalled to think that Carlisle would know how little she had on beneath her wedding gown.

Reggie opened the wardrobe and found herself staring at the most beautiful gown she had ever seen. She quickly forgave Carlisle for the flimsy undergarments. She reached out to touch the delicate bodice of the ivory silk gown. The skirt was decorated in lace and pearls in a design that intertwined Scottish thistles and English roses. A note pinned to the dress informed her that she would find a pair of ivory slippers at the base of the wardrobe and that the contents of the blue velvet box on the dressing table was a wedding gift to her.

As she drew the long-sleeved wedding gown up over her shoulders, adjusted it around her bodice, then struggled to button it, Reggie realized with a sinking feeling that the gown did not fit. Whatever modiste Carlisle had hired to create the marvelous gown had made a terrible mistake. Her breasts fit into the bodice, but a great deal of flesh—everything down to the edge of her nipples—could be seen above the square-cut neck. The gown was simply cut too low for decency.

Reggie groaned in disappointment. She did not want to take off the gown, but she did not see how she could wear it. She crossed to the trunk to see if there might be something else more appropriate. To her surprise, she actually found several more silk dresses. But when she held them up to her frame, she saw that—although each had a different neckline—every single one was cut as low as the one she had on. Reggie wondered, for the first time, whether the gown had actually been made for her. Perhaps it had been made for another woman. Perhaps it had been worn by Carlisle's first wife.

Or perhaps the London modiste he had hired had merely gotten the wrong measurements from her own modiste. Reggie stared at herself in the mirror. It was such a lovely gown. Except for the neckline. She looked for something to cover up the exposed flesh, but could not even find a scarf to serve as a substitute fichu.

Then she spied the net wedding veil hanging from the corner of the wardrobe. Reggie grabbed the veil and carefully separated the net from the rose-trimmed band. She then wrapped the net around her shoulders, criss-crossed it over her bosom and tucked it snugly into the bodice. She hurried to the looking glass to judge her efforts and gazed at herself in delight.

Barring the faint bruise on her chin, she looked lovely. Or would, as soon as she repaired her hairdo, which looked as though it had been through a storm at sea. Reggie used what pins she found in the tangles to gather her long black hair up onto her crown. A few curls dangled at her brow and temples and at her nape, but that could not be helped.

When Reggie finally opened the blue velvet box, she found a string of matched pearls and a pair of pendant pearl earrings. She put one of the earrings on but was startled into dropping the other by a knock on the door and Carlisle's, "Reggie? The reverend has arrived. Are you ready?"

"Come in, Clay," she called as she stooped to pick up the second earring and attached it to her ear.

When the earl stepped inside, her jaw dropped in surprise. Carlisle had changed his clothes for the wedding. He was dressed in a black tailcoat, tight-fitting black breeches with white stockings, and black patent leather shoes. He had made an attempt to tame his unruly hair, but a lock of it fell stubbornly onto his forehead.

Reggie had never seen a more strikingly handsome man, and she wished that she was being married in a church with all of her friends present, so that they might see him. She held out the pearl necklace, and he crossed and took it from her. She turned to observe the pair of

THE BRIDEGROOM

them in the looking glass as he clasped it around her neck.

"I'm afraid my hair is still a wild tangle—"

He brushed aside a dark curl at her nape and pressed his lips against her flesh. "It's beautiful and untamed, like you." He met her gaze in the looking glass and said, "You look beautiful to me, Reggie. And very desirable."

"I am barely a match for you, my lord," she said, letting him see her admiration.

He turned her in his arms and ran a finger along the edge of the bodice, where the net had been tucked in as a substitute fichu. "What is this?"

"The gown did not . . . I mean . . . It is lovely, but—"

"No matter," he said, giving her a quick kiss.

But their lips clung, and Reggie found herself leaning into Carlisle's body as his arms closed around her, pressing their hips together, revealing the hard evidence of his arousal. Reggie's heart was thundering in her breast with fear and excitement. She moaned deep in her throat as Carlisle tugged on her lower lip with his teeth and sucked it gently into his mouth.

"Clay," a gruff voice called through the door. "The reverend is waiting."

Carlisle reached up and eased her hands from around his neck—how had they gotten there?—and held them in his own. "Come, my dear. It is time to become husband and wife."

She allowed him to lead her from the cabin, but

131

stopped abruptly in the companionway when she saw the giant waiting there.

"This is my friend, Pegg," Carlisle said. "He's first mate on the *Sea Witch.*"

Pegg nodded his head. "Pleased to meet ye, lass."

Reggie made herself smile at the intimidatingly large man, whose black eye-patch and peg leg and golden earring made him seem quite foreign. "Hello, Pegg. I hope you will be my friend, too."

Pegg eyed the earl askance before he said, "Maybe. Could be. We'll see."

She had no time to puzzle out the meaning of his words because Carlisle was urging her up the steps to the upper deck.

"Come, my dear. The reverend is waiting."

When Reggie saw the reverend waiting all alone on the quarterdeck, she was more aware than ever of the lack of any friendly faces to support her. "I wish Mick and Becky were here," she murmured.

"I have had a message delivered to Penrith's town house informing your sister that we have been married by special license, and that we will be honeymooning at Castle Carlisle, my estate in Scotland."

"Maybe we could tell them ourselves tomorrow," Reggie suggested.

Carlisle shook his head. "The *Sea Witch* sails on the morning tide."

She looked around forlornly. The only witnesses to their marriage would be the giant with the peg leg, a few sailors who lingered on deck, and the reverend who married them.

Carlisle lifted her chin. "It will be better this way, my dear. It will give everyone time to accustom themselves to the fact that you are my wife."

The voice of reason inside Reggie's head was shouting, "Stop! Wait!" But sometime in the past half hour she had laid her heart in Carlisle's hands. If she fled now, she would be leaving without it.

"Very well, my lord," she said, turning to face the reverend. "Let us be wed."

Reggie had never before realized how short the actual ceremony of marriage was without the other public rituals that went along with it. It had taken an hour to seat all the guests for Becky's wedding at St. Paul's, and stirring musical themes by Bach and Beethoven had been played on the organ to entertain them during the wait.

Becky's walk down the aisle on Papa's arm had taken only a matter of minutes, but she had been preceded by the Duke of Braddock's two youngest daughters, Constance and Penelope. The three- and four-year-olds had the duty of scattering flower petals before the bride, a tradition apparently established at Uncle Marcus's wedding. It had taken far longer than a few minutes and brought indulgent and delighted smiles to the faces of all in the congregation.

Instead of beautiful music and the scent of flower petals, she had only the eerie creak of the ship and the smell of rotting refuse near the docks.

"Do you, Clayton Giles Bannister, take this woman, Regina Allison Wharton, to be your lawful wedded wife, forsaking all others, for as long as you both shall live?'' the reverend intoned.

"I do.''

"Do you, Regina Allison Wharton, take Clayton Giles Bannister to be your lawful wedded husband, forsaking all others, for as long as you both shall live.''

"I do.''

"Have you any rings?'' the reverend asked.

Reggie shook her head, realizing it would be one more thing that was missing at her wedding besides her family and her friends and scattered flowers.

"I have them,'' Carlisle said.

To Reggie's surprise, he handed the reverend two rings. One was a plain gold band. The other was inset with a large stone.

"Is that a diamond?'' Reggie whispered.

"The stone has been in my family for generations,'' Carlisle murmured. "The ring is worn by all Carlisle brides.''

Which meant it had been worn by the wife who had died, Reggie realized. She wondered what memories it conjured of his previous marriage. Judging by his grim expression, none of them was pleasant.

The reverend handed Carlisle the ring with the stone and instructed him to put it on the fourth finger of her left hand. Carlisle's eyes looked fierce and frightening as he repeated the words spoken by the reverend.

"With this ring I thee wed. With my body I thee worship. And with all my worldly goods I thee endow. In the name of the Father, Son, and Holy Ghost. Amen.''

"Amen,'' Reggie croaked. Sometime during the

words, her throat had swollen closed. But she was given no respite. The reverend handed her the plain band and instructed her to put it on Carlisle's finger. She had no recollection whatsoever of what she said, only of Carlisle's fierce dark eyes and his mouth as he said "Amen."

"Inasmuch as this man and this woman have pledged themselves to each other with the giving and receiving of rings, before God and these witnesses—" The reverend paused and said, "My lord, there is only one witness."

"There are sailors on deck," Carlisle said.

"Yes, my lord, but ordinarily—"

"Continue," Carlisle ordered.

"Very well, my lord. Where was I?"

"Before God and these witnesses," Carlisle provided.

"Before God and these witnesses," the reverend repeated, "I hereby declare you to be man and wife. In the name of the Father, Son, and Holy Ghost. Amen."

"Amen," Reggie and Carlisle said together.

Carlisle was leaning down to kiss her when the reverend added, "What God has joined together, let no man put asunder."

She felt Carlisle's hands tighten briefly on her shoulders before she felt his lips on her own. When he lifted his head, she searched his face, wondering if he had been as moved by the simple ceremony as she had been.

What she saw on his face alarmed her. Not joy. Not peace or pleasure. Only grim satisfaction.

"It is done," he said. "You are mine."

Reggie shivered as a chill ran down her spine. That

stark statement of possession should have made her feel
loved. Instead, she felt like a piece of chattel. She
touched the cold metal ring that bound them together for
life.

Dear God. What had she done?

Reggie lifted her chin and stared into her husband's
eyes. "Yes, my lord, it is done. But there is no longer a
yours or *mine,* there is only what is *ours.* Now and forever, we are one."

Carlisle looked shocked at her outburst. But Pegg
threw back his head and roared with laughter.

Chapter 8

THE BRIDEGROOM INTENDED TO STAY ON deck with his bride no longer than it took to be congratulated by the reverend. "Give every man a ration of rum," Clay said to Pegg. "And make sure we're not disturbed."

He laid his fingertips on Reggie's back to urge her toward the steps that led belowdecks. She looked up at him with a smile that made his breath catch in his chest.

"I would have liked to dance with you," she said wistfully.

"Ye can have your wish, lassie," Pegg said. "If ye dinna mind me playin' the tune."

Clay shot Pegg an aggrieved look, but the older man retrieved a hand organ from one of the other sailors, took a seat on an upturned barrel, and began to play a waltz.

Reggie laughed delightedly and turned to face Clay. "I had no idea a shipboard wedding could be so romantic. We have the stars and the moon above us and music as beautiful as anything I have ever heard in church."

Romancing his wife had not been Clay's intention, but he saw no reason to rob Reggie of whatever joy she might take in these few moments before he broached her. There would be little enough joy in her life from now on, if he had his way.

"Oh, my goodness!" Reggie exclaimed. "Is that Freddy?"

The boy swaggered up to her, grinning from ear to ear, and made a creditable bow. "It's me right enough, Reggie."

"Whatever are you doing here?" she asked.

"The earl says I'm to watch over his prime bits o' blood in Scotland," the boy said proudly. "I'm to have a home of my own someday near the castle and I—"

Clay caught Freddy's eye and made it clear the boy should take his leave.

"I'll be goin' to my berth now—to get my ration of rum," Freddy said.

"But, Freddy—" Reggie protested.

"Don't say I'm too young to be drinkin' rum," Freddy said as he backed away. "I'm a man now, Reggie, with a man's duties and—" He stumbled over a coil of rope, picked himself up with an embarrassed grin, and disappeared belowdecks.

Once the boy was gone, Reggie looked up at Clay, her eyes soft and full of pride—in him. "My lord, you have managed to surprise me again with your thoughtfulness. I have always believed you were a kind man, but this is the best wedding present you could have given me."

Clay felt his insides squeeze tight in response to the adoration in her eyes. He did not want her admiration, her adoration, or anything else resembling approval. His bride would soon learn that where she was concerned, he intended to be neither thoughtful nor kind. He had brought Freddy along only because he had seen the light in the boy's eyes when it became known he planned to take ship for Scotland.

"I will need help with my cattle in Scotland," he told Reggie, shrugging dismissively. "And the boy was willing to come."

She placed her palm on his heart. "Yes, my lord. I can see how such a young, inexperienced boy would be the perfect choice when you are setting up a new stable." She laughed. "You cannot convince me that what you did was not a noble gesture, or keep me from loving you for making Freddy so happy."

His throat clogged with feeling, making it impossible to explain that he had brought the boy for his own comfort. Neither her feelings, nor the boy's, had been any part of his decision.

He noticed her frowning at one of his men and turned to see who had caught her eye this time. Bloody hell! It was Pike. He stepped into her range of vision, circled her waist with his arm, and drew her close.

"That sailor looks exactly like—"

His mouth covered hers to distract her, while he used his free hand to wave Pike away, behind her back. He found himself caught up in the kiss, unwilling to let her go. His tongue slipped inside to claim her, as he had wanted to do since he had first laid eyes on her in the decadent wedding gown he had provided. She was pliant and sweet. "Come below with me," he murmured against her lips. "There is enough left of the night for me to make a wife of you."

Her eyes looked unfocused, and she seemed a little dazed. He had already taken another step toward the stairway with her before she remembered the forgotten waltz.

"The dance, my lord," she reminded him.

It would cause only a small delay in his plans. And he would still be holding her in his arms—indecently close, if he had his way. He took her palm in his, tightened his hold on her waist, and swept her into the dance. Pegg slowed the tune as it became necessary to waltz Reggie around the mast, under the boom, and across the hatches. He used his artful maneuvering around the ship as an excuse to pull her snugly against him, so that her soft, full breasts were crushed against his chest. He could feel her breathy laughter against his cheek as he danced her toward the companionway steps, intending to slip away even before the dance was done.

Pegg thwarted him by ending the tune abruptly. Clay turned to find out why he had stopped playing.

"I've forgotten the rest," he said with a grin. He rose and headed belowdecks. "I'll leave the night to the two of ye," he said with a wink at Clay.

Clay looked around and realized they were alone. He had his hand on Reggie's back, urging her toward the stairs, when she edged out of his grasp and headed for the ship's rail. She leaned so far over the rail, she was in danger of falling off the ship—and out of her dress. His body responded with violence to the brief glance he got of her nipples before she leaned back a little, and they were hidden from sight again beneath the square neckline of her gown and the makeshift fichu.

He joined her at the rail, standing beside her without touching. He searched for whatever had caught her eye and saw the lights of London on the opposite bank of the Thames.

"The city looks so beautiful at night," she said, her eyes shining in the moonlight.

"The dark does a great deal to conceal the poverty and filth," he said dryly.

"Your ship is certainly beautiful," she said, undaunted by his sarcasm. She turned to face the mainmast and laid her arms along the ship's rail. "Where did you get it?"

"I won it."

"I thought you did not wager for great stakes," she said, eyeing him askance.

"I never said that."

"What did you risk in return for such a great prize?" she asked.

"My life. Or, rather, my services for life."

"You wagered your freedom?" she said, aghast.

"At the time, it was all I had. I wanted—I needed—this ship, and a life spent sailing the Seven Seas did not seem such an awful fate if I lost."

"I am glad you won," she said fiercely, letting go of the rail and turning to face him. "And came back home to find me."

Clay looked down at the small, delicate hand covering his own, then back up at her intense gaze. She was pleased for him. Proud of him. *In love* with him. He felt his breath hitch in his chest. Time to get her below. Time to finish what he had started. He slid his arm around her waist. "Shall we go below?"

"Not yet," she said, resisting him with a coy glance. "Tell me about our new home. Is it very beautiful?"

He hesitated, wondering whether to force her to go with him. He could see from the way she peeked at him from beneath lowered lashes and then looked away, that she was nervous, anxious perhaps in the way a maiden would be on her wedding night. One more brief delay would not make any difference.

"Castle Carlisle is perched on a cliff above the sea," he said in answer to her question. "You can hear the waves crashing on the rocks far below if you try hard enough. I always imagined I could, anyway. As a boy, I used to stand on that cliff and look out to sea and wonder what was beyond the horizon."

"So you came by your love of the sea honestly," she said with a shy smile.

"I would never have chosen to see it the way I did," he said brusquely. He needed to remind her—and himself—of the passage he had made in chains. And finish what he had set out to do. "Come, my love, it is time—"

"Not yet. Please," she said, sliding farther down along the rail. "Tell me about your family."

"They are all dead."

She turned to stare at him, her eyes filled with sorrow, and he felt desire rise like a dragon inside him, talons ripping at his insides. He fought the fierce need, struggled to subdue it. He had only one use for her. He could not afford to indulge the dragon.

She stepped back when he reached for her and babbled, "I lost my mother when I was only six. A tragic fall down the stairs at Blackthorne Abbey."

"Gossip says she was drunk," he said ruthlessly. "And that your father pushed her."

"What a wretched thing to say! Especially when it isn't true!" She glared at him in indignation.

He stared at her, not backing down.

"Perhaps Mama was drunk," she conceded at last. "But Papa could never have done such a thing. He is too kind, too—"

"How did you get this scar?" he interrupted. He traced the tiny scar that sliced through her upper lip.

"Papa said—" She hesitated, then looked up at him. "I will not lie to you, my lord. Papa told me it was an accident, but one of the maids let the truth slip. Papa was sitting in a rocking chair, holding me over his shoulder, when Mama threw a crystal goblet against the stone wall near his head. The glass shattered and one of the fragments ricocheted and cut my lip."

He resisted the urge to kiss her, to take away the wounded look in her eyes. Instead, he said what he knew would cause her pain. "Rumor says the duke and his first duchess fought often and loudly."

"I don't believe—"

"And that your uncle is really your father."

Her face paled, and she looked at him with haunted eyes. "How dare you repeat such vicious, vicious blasphemy! Uncle Marcus would never— Papa is—" She stared at him, speechless with outraged hurt.

"Hearsay can often be mistaken for truth when you do not look hard enough to find the truth," he said.

He watched as understanding dawned in her eyes. "As my father did not look closely enough to see the truth about you," she said slowly. "And thus failed to discover your innocence."

He said nothing. He simply scooped her up in his arms and headed briskly toward the steps that led below. He tried to see her features in the dark companionway, but it was not until he had reached his cabin and shut the door behind them that he saw the hurt and confusion on her face.

He set her down and took a step back.

"My lord, can we not delay—"

"No."

"A gentleman would wait until his bride—"

"Take off that dress," he ordered.

"I will not."

Her anger only made him want her more. He reached behind her and gave a yank, and pearl buttons went flying. The gown fell away from her shoulders, leaving only the net fichu and the sheer chemise to cover her.

"Let's get rid of this," he said, pulling the net free of her shoulders and tossing it aside. He had purposely had the gown cut in a style more fit for a courtesan than a wife. After all, that was the role he had planned for her—a woman to be used and discarded when he was done with her. He had admired her ingenuity in creating a fichu from the veil, but her attempt at propriety had only made the dress more enticing. "Now, let me see what I have."

He surveyed her as he would a horse at Tattersall's, murmuring sounds of approval as his eyes lingered on the various assets he discovered. He intended to humiliate her. He intended to make her cringe from him. He intended to hurt her as he had been hurt by her father.

She stood before him proudly, daring him to touch her. Daring him to take her. She had no idea the harm he could cause if he chose. But he did not choose to wound her further tonight. And then he remembered. There was one more unavoidable wound to be inflicted—when he broached her.

"Perfect," he announced at last. "And every inch of that perfection mine to enjoy."

She stood like a beautiful marble statue as he began to kiss her, to touch her, to skillfully seduce her. The cold stone began to melt like ice in the heat of the sun. Her helpless, mewling sounds of excitement spurred him to touch more, to take more. He saw the surprised look in her eyes, the need she could not bear to feel, the pleasure she could not deny, and felt a surge of triumph.

By the time she decided to fight, it was too late. The battle was already won. Her hands clutched frantically at his hair while her body molded itself to his. It took little more effort on his part to urge her complete surrender.

"What do you want from me?" she whispered.

It was a plea for mercy. But there was no mercy in him.

Clay had nothing to lose. He decided to ask for what he wanted, pleasures a husband did not normally seek from his wife, but found only with his mistress. "Undress me," he said.

She looked at him in shock, but then reached with trembling hands for his neck cloth, pulling the ends and releasing the elegant *trône d'amour*. She slid the strip of linen from beneath his shirt and let it fall to the floor, then began unbuttoning his waistcoat.

He reached for the straps of the chemise and drew them down off her shoulders.

She quickly crossed her arms over her breasts to keep herself covered. "I would not have worn such a garment if there had been any choice. It was all I could find."

"I know," he said. "I chose it on purpose. I wanted to see you this way." *As a mistress. As a person intended for my pleasure. Not as a wife.* "Don't hide yourself. You are quite lovely." He unwound her arms, and the chemise slid to her waist. "And you are mine now."

She reached out in turn to unbutton his shirt, shoved it aside, and put her hands flat on his chest. "And you are mine."

She met his gaze defiantly, and he felt a sudden flare of desire. And unwelcome shame. And then anger, because she was only an instrument of vengeance. There would be no belonging of one to another, only his possession of her. She must submit to him; she was his wife.

He grasped her breasts roughly in his hands, intending to shock her, but her eyes slid closed, and she moaned deep in her throat. He kissed her hard, his teeth biting at her lips, his breathing harsh as his blood began to pound and his body hardened. He took her nipple in his mouth, biting and sucking as though she were an experienced courtesan.

She gave a guttural cry, and her hands tore at his hair.

He lifted his head, expecting her to punish him, but she wanted only her mouth on his. She returned the bites he had given her as her body arched against his own.

He clutched her hips, afraid she would lurch away with virginal fright when she felt his hardness between her thighs. But her body tipped into his own, and she rubbed herself against him, eyes closed, her head thrown back in total exultation, making an animal sound that provoked a lust he had never imagined he could feel.

He did not think, could not think, overwhelmed by a rapacious need that demanded satisfaction. He stripped her bare as she tore his clothes from him. Her hands found places he had not known could crave a woman's touch, and she moaned and writhed beneath the onslaught of his hands and his mouth.

They fell onto the bed together, their arms and legs tangled, their bodies already slick with sweat, their breathing labored.

"I feel so much," she said breathlessly. "More than I ever dreamed I would. And you are so beautiful, so strong and—"

"I am only a man like any other," he said, cutting her off. But he was entranced by her desire, enthralled by her need, and more aroused than he could ever remember being in his life. In his wildest dreams he could never have fantasized such an encounter. He could wait no longer to put himself inside her.

Then he felt her fingertips on his back, tracing the ugly ridged scars that crisscrossed his flesh. He sat up abruptly and would have left the bed, except she laid a hand on his shoulder and whispered, "Stay."

He quivered beneath her touch.

"Let me see," she murmured.

"My back is not a fit sight for your eyes."

But she had already resettled herself so she could see the damage done by a cat-o'-nine-tails laid on with a will. For a long time she said nothing. Then he felt her lips caress his skin, tracing the worst of the welted scars. His chin fell to his chest as he surrendered to her gentle ministrations. Her arms slid around his waist, and she laid her cheek against his scarred flesh.

He could feel her warm, moist breath as she said, "There will be no more pain, my lord. No more hurt that I cannot soothe if you will let me."

He felt his throat tighten with emotion and realized how easily she had slipped past his guard. Her father was responsible for the very stripes she was soothing. And Blackthorne could not be so easily forgiven.

He unclasped Reggie's hands from around his waist and turned to shove her flat against the feather mattress. He pinned her wrists to the pillow on either side of her head and quickly mantled her body with his own. With one quick thrust, one ragged cry of pain, he was inside her.

"You are only a weapon, my dear. A way to hurt your father. Nothing more. You will never be more than that."

He saw the shocked disbelief in her eyes before she made an agonized sound in her throat.

"I will never love you. I can never love you," he said in a harsh voice.

Her eyes caught his, holding him equally captive. "Don't do this, Clay. You do love me. I know you must.

148

I cannot have been so badly mistaken." Her body arched against him, enticing him, inflaming him, demanding a response.

It would have taken a stronger man than Clay was to resist her. The words she spoke meant nothing, he told himself as he reached between their bodies to touch her, to inflame her in return.

She made a whimpering sound, and he asked roughly, "Have I hurt you?"

"No, my lord," she gasped.

It was a foolish question to have asked, when he had professed his intention to hurt her, to hurt her father, to hurt everyone her father loved. He did not care. He could not care.

She hid her face against his neck as he began to move inside her. Her fingernails dug into his shoulders, and she choked back a cry of torment or delight or perhaps both.

He thrust hard and deep, ignoring the sounds she made, taking his pleasure without consideration for her feelings. She was only a means of vengeance against her father.

"My stepmother said we would find joy in this," she cried in a choked voice. "Please, Clay. Love me."

He shut out her plea for mercy. For love. He thrust deep and hard, urging her to feel the joy if she could, but not caring whether she did. He watched her struggle against the loss of control, felt her resist her body as it sought satisfaction. "Let the waves crest and ride down with them, as though you were adrift on the wide blue sea." It was all the help he was willing to give her.

He watched as her eyes slid closed. Her head arched back, and her neck muscles stretched tight as her jaws clamped down on a grating sound of satisfaction.

The feel of her body spasming around him brought his own climax. Too late, Clay realized the enormity of what he had wrought. He gave a cry of anguish and exultation as he spilled his seed in the womb of his enemy's daughter.

Chapter 9

"YOU SHOULD BE HOME WAITING FOR news of Reggie, not sitting here in a carriage wringing your hands," Mick admonished.

Becky shivered. "I had to come. I would have gone mad sitting home alone." The sun had disappeared almost as soon as it rose, and a fog had rolled in, bringing a damp chill. "Where is she, Mick? What could have happened to her?"

But Becky knew Reggie's likely fate without having to be told. It was the fate of any woman unfortunate enough to find herself alone and unprotected in such a neighborhood. "I warned her," she moaned. "I told her it was dangerous to come here. What if we cannot find her?"

"We will find her," Mick said. "Someone will have seen what happened to her."

A short, middle-aged workingman pushing a cabbage-laden cart tapped on the carriage window.

"Please tell him we don't want any cabbages," Becky said.

"He's not a peddler," Mick replied. "That is the private detective I hired to search for Reggie."

"Oh." At two o'clock that morning, when Reggie had still not returned home and discreet inquiries among her acquaintances had yielded no information about her whereabouts, Becky had wanted to call in the Bow Street Runners to search for her sister. "I believe that is what Penrith would do," she had said.

"Penrith is not here," Mick had pointed out.

Becky had been grateful for William's absence at supper, believing that Reggie's empty seat at the table was the result of some escapade that would shortly resolve itself. But when neither her sister nor her husband had returned by two in the morning, Becky had truly begun to despair.

Despite the fact William had never been a solace to her, she had wished for his company. However angry he might have been with her for failing to chaperone her sister properly, he would surely have used his influence as a member of the nobility to ensure that Reggie was found by the Bow Street Runners.

Becky could tell from the pity in Mick's eyes that he had guessed where her husband most likely had spent the night. She did not know why she felt so embarrassed that he had discovered that William preferred another woman's company—*body,* she corrected herself—to her own. It was simply one more in a multitude of small humiliations she had endured over the course of her marriage.

Only this time, Mick's look of sympathy made her wish she had confronted William and demanded he give up his mistress. She suddenly felt ashamed that she had accepted her husband's behavior, even if it was common among other men of his class.

At least she could do something to help Reggie. "Is there any reason why you and I cannot contact the Runners?" she had asked Mick.

"Unfortunately, it would announce to the world that Reggie is missing," Mick had replied. "I think I know someone who can look for her just as effectively, but much more discreetly. Will you trust me?"

"Do whatever you think is best," she had said, feeling grateful beyond words that he was there to help.

But that was six hours ago. It was eight o'clock in the morning, and there had been no word in all that time. Soon, she would have to return home and explain to Penrith, who usually reappeared at mid-morning on those evenings he spent away from home, why she had not immediately called in the Runners.

She eyed the cabbage peddler dubiously. "That is your detective?"

Mick grinned. "Believe me, Tim could find a three-toed rat on a sinking ship." He lowered the window and asked, "What news do you have?"

"Found her, Mick. Or rather, where she was taken. The abbess says a gentleman paid to have her, then stole her away in the middle of the night."

Becky had been sitting in the shadows, so her presence would not be noted by passersby, but she lurched forward into the light to confront Mick's detective. "What man? Where has he taken her?"

Tim seemed reluctant to speak in front of her.

"Please tell me!" she cried.

"Tell her, Tim," Mick said.

"From the description, it seems the lady was paid for by the Earl of Carlisle," Tim said. "He took her with him in his carriage. That's the last anyone saw of her."

Becky exchanged a shocked look with Mick. "No. It cannot be. He would not dare to keep her overnight!"

Mick's features contorted in anger. "That scoundrel would dare anything! I went to his town house last night, hoping he might know Reggie's whereabouts, but his butler claimed he was not at home. This time I won't be so polite!" He pounded on the roof of the carriage and ordered, "The Carlisle town house on Grosvenor Square. Make it quick, man!"

Becky could hardly sit still in the carriage while Mick knocked on the door to Carlisle's town house. To her surprise and dismay, he was not allowed inside. His face was so black as he walked back toward her, that she was afraid to ask what he had discovered.

"Penrith House," he instructed the coachman before he entered the carriage.

"Is it very bad news?" she ventured.

"His lordship and his wife are not at home," Mick said through clenched teeth. "They sailed this morning for Scotland."

"His wife?" Becky asked, her brow furrowed in confusion. "The earl is not married."

"He is now," Mick replied. "He and Reggie were

wed by special license last night. Carlisle's butler said the earl left a message to be delivered to Penrith House this morning, detailing the events that led to their nuptials."

"Why would Reggie agree to such a marriage, without any family in attendance?"

"I make no doubt he forced her," Mick said quietly.

Becky felt sick. "All Reggie ever wanted was to marry a man she could love. She cannot love such a man as that, can she, Mick?"

"One thing you may be sure of," Mick said. "If Reggie was forced into wedlock with Carlisle, your father's wrath will know no bounds. The earl will find himself in chains again before he can enjoy the fruit he has stolen. At least we know where to find him."

"There is one thing I don't understand," Becky said. "If Carlisle coerced Reggie, why would he tell us his direction? And why go to Scotland? It is the one place he is certain to encounter Papa."

"Because he wants to compel a confrontation with the duke," Mick said.

Becky's brow furrowed. "Why?"

"If you had seen the violence in Carlisle's eyes when he vowed to ruin your father, you would not be asking that question," Mick said. "I believe the dastard planned all along to maneuver Reggie into marriage. When I showed up, and he knew he had been found out, he grabbed Reggie and ran."

"But Lord Carlisle acted toward Reggie in all ways, and at all times, as a gentleman," Becky countered.

"Believe me, it was an act," Mick said. "From all

accounts, the Sea Dragon is a vicious marauder who takes what he wants and destroys anything that gets in his way."

Becky had been concerned when she believed Reggie might have spent the night in company with Carlisle, but not frightened. Now she knew enough to be truly terrified. "I hope and pray you are wrong, Mick."

It took a great deal of control for Becky not to race up the walk to Penrith House. The instant she was inside, she called for Hardy and asked, "Did any messages come for me while I was gone?"

"Yes, my lady. There is a letter in the dish."

Becky felt her heart leap to her throat as she accepted the parchment bearing Carlisle's seal in wax. She carried it with her into the drawing room to read it in private with Mick. "See that we are not disturbed, Hardy."

She tore open the letter and quickly scanned it. Her legs threatened to buckle, and she sank onto the sofa to keep from falling. "Oh, dear God. The situation is every bit as bad as you feared! Here. Read it."

Mick took the note and read aloud.

"My dear sister-in-law,

By the time this reaches you, your sister—whom I married by special license last night—and I will be on our way to my estate in Scotland. We are sailing with the morning tide on the *Sea Witch*. She is a fast ship. Do not waste your time trying to catch us. You are already too late.

You may inform your father that I have now

replaced the wife who died while I lay in chains, falsely accused by him of crimes I did not commit. I will shortly make certain he knows the agony of losing a child, since henceforth he will be allowed no discourse with my wife.

What harm I may cause to him and his, I will cause. We are enemies, his family and mine.

Yours, etc.
Carlisle"

Becky stared at Mick in shock. "I cannot believe Reggie married him knowing what he intended." She rose, knowing she must act, but uncertain what to do next. "I must go . . . I shall contact my father, and he will . . ." It was too late to save Reggie. Her twin had already fallen into the maw of the Sea Dragon.

When Mick opened his arms, Becky walked straight into them and clung to him as her ululating wail of despair echoed through the drawing room.

"Don't cry, Becky. Please, I cannot bear it," Mick said. "We will find a way to rescue her."

"I should have seen what he was and warned her away," she said. "She will surely bind herself to him before she learns the truth."

Once the marriage was consummated, it would be impossible to free her sister without an act of Parliament.

The door burst open, and Becky snapped her head around to confront whoever had dared to enter. "I said I should not be disturbed!"

"Excuse me, my dear, but this is my house. I will enter any room I please."

Becky jerked herself from Mick's embrace and turned to make what obeisance she could to her husband. She lowered her eyes and let her chin sink to her chest. "I am sorry, William. I did not realize you were home."

"Obviously," the viscount said, eyeing Mick suspiciously.

Becky felt a surge of indignation at even the suggestion that she would indulge in anything improper with Michael O'Malley. Until she remembered that they had, in fact, kissed in the park the previous afternoon. Nevertheless, she lifted her chin and raised her eyes to meet Penrith's accusing stare.

This incident, at least, had been innocent. He was the one in the wrong. Because he had not come home the previous evening, she had been forced to deal with the entire catastrophe of Reggie's disappearance without his assistance.

"If you had come home last night," she said in a voice she kept even only with the greatest difficulty, "you would know that Reggie went missing. Mr. O'Malley and I have discovered this morning that she married the Earl of Carlisle by special license, and that they have sailed on the morning tide to Scotland.

"Now, if you are through slandering my good name and that of a good man, I will excuse myself. I am feeling ill."

Becky marched from the room with her head high, but the moment she was out of sight of the two men, she picked up her skirts and ran. She had been robbed of her sister's comfort, which had helped to make her own unhappy marriage bearable, and she did not even have the comfort of knowing Reggie would be happy with Carlisle. Far from it. It was obvious the earl intended no good.

Becky had not yet reached her bedroom door when another thought struck her. Carlisle might have the worst of intentions, but he was sadly mistaken if he thought Reggie would give in to his strictures without a fight. A smile tugged at the corners of her mouth as she closed her bedroom door behind her.

Beware, my lord of vengeance. You may finally have met your match!

"What has her up in the boughs?" Penrith demanded, staring after his wife. "Carlisle would seem to be an excellent match for her sister."

"The earl has declared himself Blackthorne's enemy," Mick said, handing Carlisle's missive to Becky's husband. "See for yourself."

"Dear lord," Penrith said, sinking into the wing chair nearest the fire as he perused the note. "This explains a great deal." He leaned his elbow on the arm of the chair and dropped his head into his hand. "I wish I had come home sooner. Though I doubt I could have made much difference to the outcome. It appears Carlisle had his plans well in hand."

Mick bit his tongue on a sharp retort. It was galling to think Penrith had the right to lie next to the woman Mick loved but had chosen to spend the night with a mistress instead. "Your wife needed you," he said, which was as close to an accusation of infidelity as he dared to come.

"I am afraid in future she will be seeing even less of me," Penrith muttered.

"My lord, you cannot—"

Penrith waved a hand to cut him off. "Sit down, Mr. O'Malley. You need not rush to my wife's defense. I would not willingly leave her unprotected. But I am likely to find myself mewed up in prison before the year is out."

"Prison, my lord?" Mick asked as he sank into the other chair that faced the fire. "Why?"

"I am pockets to let. Under the hatches. At *point non plus*. Haven't a feather to fly with. In short," he said after the lengthy recital, "I am completely rolled up."

"That hardly seems possible, my lord. You could lose a fortune at the tables every night and not make a dent in your fortune," Mick said.

"True, true," Penrith agreed. "Nevertheless, everything that is not entailed, including my wife's dowry and every farthing of her trust fund, is gone."

"How is that possible?"

Penrith slumped back into the wing chair. "I lost it in the 'Change. On 'solid' investments recommended to me by . . . You will never guess who has advised me these past months," Penrith said with a bitter smile.

"It cannot be—"

"Carlisle," Penrith confirmed.

"But why would you have listened to him?"

"Why not?" Penrith asked. "The man obviously knows how to make money. He has enough of it himself.

Why should I have expected him to bear me any enmity? I am no more responsible for his fate than any other member of the House of Lords. And you do not see him ruining any of them.''

Penrith shoved a hand through his hair, leaving it askew. ''I would sooner blow a hole in my head than be known to the *ton* as a dupe and a fool. It is a better choice than debtor's prison, I make no doubt.''

''Perhaps all is not lost,'' Mick said.

Penrith lifted his head. ''Do you think Carlisle—''

''Forget Carlisle.''

''I cannot ask Blackthorne to redeem my I.O.U.s,'' Penrith said. ''I have no way to repay him, and I will not be in his debt.''

''Forget Blackthorne, too. This concerns you and me,'' Mick said. ''And your wife.''

''What has my wife to do with anything?''

''What if I could offer you a fortune in exchange for the annulment of your marriage and the release of your daughter to your wife's care?''

Penrith stared at Mick assessingly. ''My marriage annulled and my daughter forfeited in exchange for the return of my fortune,'' he mused. ''Are you in league with Carlisle by any chance, Mr. O'Malley?''

''I despise the man.''

''Then you must want my wife,'' Penrith said.

Mick could not stop the revealing flush.

''Ah. So that embrace I witnessed was not entirely innocent.''

''I merely offered your wife comfort,'' Mick said.

''I will not argue the matter,'' Penrith said with a

wave of his hand. "To be frank, Mr. O'Malley, your offer is intriguing. It is certainly a preferable alternative to sticking my spoon in the wall."

Mick let out a breath he had not known he was holding.

"Now that we have that settled," Penrith continued, "let us move on to a more pertinent matter. I see before me a duke's steward, a man who earns his living with his hands. What do you earn in a year? A hundred pounds? Where would you come by a fortune, Mr. O'Malley?"

"That is my concern, not yours," Mick said. "Assuming I could make you a rich man again, would you be interested?"

Penrith snorted. "Of course." He rose slowly and crossed to warm himself at the fire. He looked back over his shoulder at Mick. "I cannot imagine where you have found such a fortune, but I must suppose you are making this sacrifice out of love for my wife."

Mick said nothing.

"Do you really believe Rebecca will marry you, if she is free of me? She will never have you without the fortune, sir. You cannot win, Mr. O'Malley. Why play the game?"

Mick rose to confront the other man. "If I am willing to take the gamble, what does it matter to you?"

Penrith tilted his head in contemplation, then turned and extended his hand. "Very well. My hand on it. When the papers reach me confirming I am once again a wealthy man, I will arrange for the annulment."

Mick could not believe it had been so easy. He could

not believe that all it had taken was money to free Becky from Penrith's clutches.

"One thing more," Mick said. "You will send Lady Penrith to stay with her parents in Scotland—along with Lily—until the annulment is final."

Penrith turned back to the fire. "She is like a fish in bed. And the child is of no use to me. Take them and be welcome."

Mick grabbed Penrith by his neck cloth and planted him a facer. "The woman is your wife!" he snarled as Penrith reeled. "She deserves your respect!"

Penrith gingerly touched his nose and stared at the blood that came away on his fingers. "A body would think she was *your* wife, you defend her so ferociously."

"She will be!"

Penrith sneered. "You fool! She will never agree to marry so far beneath her. She is too much of a mouse to face the tabbies."

Mick put up his fives, and Penrith placed his palms face out in surrender.

"I will trade her to you for this mythical fortune you claim to have, much good it will do you," he taunted. "If she has her freedom, she will only find another like me to take my place. Now, if you will excuse me, I must see if my valet can stop this infernal nosebleed. It is ruining my favorite waistcoat."

Mick was left standing alone in Penrith's drawing room.

He felt devastated by Penrith's declaration. What if Becky would not have him without his fortune? If he gave away his inheritance, he would need to continue working as the duke's steward. Would he be able to convince Becky to take him as she found him?

Mick felt as though he had drunk too much. He could not find his center of gravity, and the room seemed to be tilting around him. His head was pounding, and his stomach felt queasy, as though at any moment he might cast up his accounts.

The only woman he had ever loved was suddenly within his grasp, but he was terrified to reach for her as plain Mick O'Malley. Because when he did, he would learn once and for all whether a duke's daughter could love a common man like him enough to forfeit all for love.

Chapter 10

REGGIE AWOKE ABRUPTLY AND SAT BOLT upright in bed. She was alone, her body sweat-soaked and trembling with agitation. She had been having a nightmare. In the dream, she had married Clay on board his ship, and on their wedding night, he had confessed that his entire courtship had been a sham. Reggie rubbed her eyes and shuddered. Unfortunately, the nightmare was real. For the past four days, she had been married to a man who had said he could never love her.

The morning after her wedding, Reggie had gone up on deck and seen the two men who had abducted her—working as sailors! She had run to Clay for help, crying, "They're here! On board ship! The men who kidnapped me!"

She had stopped short when he turned to face her. His hands were fisted on narrow hips, and his legs, clad in skin-tight black trousers that ended in knee-high black boots, were spread wide to counter the rolling of the ship at sea. He wore a blousy white cotton shirt, open halfway down his chest, revealing an embarrassing amount of dark curly hair—embarrassing because she found it arousing.

Her eyes had desperately sought his, only to discover those deep black wells as unfathomable as ever. His cheeks and chin were covered with a night's growth of rough whiskers, and if he had ever combed his hair, the wind had whipped it into a frenzy again. He looked altogether like . . . a dangerous pirate.

"Pike and Jarvey were acting on my orders," he said.

"*You* had me kidnapped and taken to that awful place?" she had asked incredulously. "You had me drugged and . . . and *touched* me!"

He nodded sharply. Forbiddingly. Reggie had felt a chill to her marrow and realized she was standing in the brisk wind with her bosom exposed—in one of the few dresses he had provided for her. She watched as his eyes lowered to stare at her nipples, which had peaked beneath the blue merino gown.

And it dawned on her that he must have known all along how low the bodices of all those dresses were cut, that he must have ordered that indignity as he had ordered the scandalous kidnapping. Her first instinct was to attack him, to strike back for the hurt he had done her.

But he had stood like a wall of stone, tall and impregnable, and she had known she would be the one battered in any physical confrontation. She had turned on her heel, head held high, and marched back down to the cabin, fighting her skirt as the wind whipped it up to expose her ankles, aware of the dozens of lecherous eyes that followed her, watching her ignominious retreat.

Reggie clutched the tangled sheets surrounding her and followed the stream of sunlight on the worn deck back to the portholes in the wall. After that first, ominous encounter with her husband on deck, she had reached a momentous decision. She was determined to fight for her marriage, fight for Clay's love, with all the feminine ammunition at her disposal. And somehow, some way, she would make peace between her husband and her father.

Reggie shoved the covers off and padded barefoot on the cold deck to the wardrobe where she had left her clothes the previous evening, the same borrowed men's attire she had been wearing the past three days. She had refused to wear another of those wretched dresses Clay had provided, clothes more fit for a mistress than a wife.

She pulled on a pair of tight-fitting trousers Pegg had acquired for her from a young man named Daniel and buttoned them in front, then slipped a blousy white shirt that belonged to Clay over her head, tucking it in and cinching it at the waist with a rope belt that Pegg had made for her. Finally, she pulled on stockings and a pair of half boots—which fit perfectly—that she had also found in the trunk.

She grabbed a bite of the toast that had been left for her on the captain's desk, swiped Clay's silver-handled brush through her tangled curls, then tied her long black hair at the nape with a ribbon she had pulled from one of the dresses, letting it fall free down her back. Then she hurried topside to begin her day of tempting Clay.

The first person she saw when she arrived on deck was Pegg. The giant had turned out to be a gentle man and had become her only friend on board besides Freddy, who was kept busy with shipboard chores. She searched out Clay and found him standing at the wheel, his face turned to the wind, looking as devilishly handsome as ever—and just as dangerous.

She crossed to the rail near where Pegg was sitting on a keg, braiding rope. She leaned across the smoothly varnished English oak, staring out at the horizon, making certain her buttocks in the skin-tight trousers were aimed in Clay's direction.

It was a blatant invitation to be mounted.

Clay had warned her, the first time he caught her bent over the ship's rail with her bottom in the air, that it was unseemly. She had laughed at him and replied, "Would you rather I wore a dress and allowed your sailors to ogle my bosom?"

A muscle had jerked in his cheek, but he had conceded the battle and stalked away.

Reggie leaned recklessly far over the rail to watch an albatross skip across the waves.

"Ye're a born sailor, lass," Pegg remarked. "But better ye should stay on board. The sea is cold and deep."

Reggie flashed the older man a grin, then turned her nose into the wind. She loved the salty smell of the sea, the rhythmic splash of the waves against the hull, the flap of the sails in the sea breeze, even the sea chanteys the deck hands sang as they went about their work.

"My father's first ship, the *Twin Ladies,* sank in a storm off the coast of Scotland years ago," she said.

THE BRIDEGROOM

"But he had another built, the *Scottish Lady*. He often took my sister and me sailing with him. Becky never found her sea legs, but I learned to love it."

"Best not let his lordship see ye again in them breeches," Pegg warned. "He'll have yer tail and mine, too. He near stripped my hide for askin' Danny for the loan of them."

Reggie flashed a glance in Clay's direction, but he was pointedly ignoring her. "My husband knows better than to complain, since he is the reason I have naught else to wear."

Reggie gripped the ship's rail tightly. Since that first night, Clay had not come near her. She knew he must sleep beside her, because the pillow bore an indentation. But he came to bed after she was asleep and left before she awoke. She also knew he must desire her; she felt the sparks whenever their eyes met. But she did not understand why he was not taking what he wanted.

She was clever enough to have figured out that the physical closeness between a man and a woman was a powerful means of binding them together. She needed Clay to give in to temptation. She needed him to want her.

Reggie turned to look at Pegg. The Scotsman knew Clay better than any other man. She felt awkward approaching him, but there was no one else to ask. She let go of the rail and crossed to where Pegg sat his peg leg braced on the deck, his left hands still braiding twine into rope. "May I ask you a question about the earl, Pegg?"

Pegg's fingers never missed a move, though his one

good eye left his work and focused intently on her. "What is it, lass?"

"Do you think perhaps Carlisle does not want . . . ? You see, he has not . . . Is it possible he did not . . . ?"

"Spit it out, lass."

Reggie swallowed hard. "I believe there must be some flaw in me that my husband cannot excuse. Perhaps he was offended by what he saw when he came to rescue me. Or perhaps I am not the sort of woman he desires. You see . . ." Reggie leaned close and whispered the rest in Pegg's ear.

The Scotsman stared at her in disbelief, then slapped his knee and guffawed. "I dinna believe it, lass! Are ye saying he hasna touched ye since that first night? Not once?"

"Shh!" Reggie cautioned, pressing her fingertips across his lips and glancing around her in search of the nearest sailor. "Someone might hear you."

Pegg made a *tsk*ing sound and shook his head. "Stubborn, he is. And honorable to a fault. It comes of having been accused of wrongdoing when he was innocent, ye see. 'Twas yer father did the blaming, and Clay canna forgive him for it. And he canna forget. Nay, I canna either, if the truth be known."

"Were you falsely accused, too?" Reggie asked.

Pegg chuckled. "Not me, lass. I was a thief, right enough."

"A highwayman?" Reggie asked, her eyes wide with wonder.

"Nothin' so fancy. A simple card sharp. I cheated the

wrong man and got caught." Pegg shrugged. "I had cheated more than him what caught me, so I suppose I deserved what I got. But it turned out more terrible than any of us ever guessed."

"What happened?" Reggie asked. "I have never heard the whole story."

"I shouldna be tellin' ye this," Pegg said.

Reggie shot him an imploring look and said, "Oh, please, Pegg. Please."

"Them bright blue eyes of yers turn my spine to mush," Pegg grumbled. "Here's the long and the short of it, then. We got caught in a storm, and the ship foundered. One of the guards took pity and began unlocking the chains, but it was too late for most. I was free . . . but Clay was not."

"Then how did he escape drowning?"

"Well, that's where I come in. Ye might have noticed, I'm a wee bit of a brawny fellow."

"A giant of a man," Reggie agreed with a grin. "Did you save him, Pegg?"

"I did," Pegg said, bowing his head modestly.

Reggie leaned over impulsively and kissed his grizzled cheek. "Thank you, Pegg. I'm glad you did."

Pegg's eyes focused on his hands again. "I pulled the rotten board that held his chains right out of the ship, I did, and hauled him with me up on deck. That was not the end of it, though."

"Because you were marooned at sea on a piece of flotsam," Reggie guessed, imagining in her mind's eye what it would be like to be caught in such a storm, to be certain one would drown, and then to be miraculously saved. "With no food or water and the hot sun beating down on you—"

"Who's tellin' this story?" Pegg asked.

"You are," Reggie said sheepishly. "Go on."

"When we saw sails on the horizon, we slapped each other on the back and grinned, though our lips cracked, they were so dry. It was one of His Majesty's frigates.

"The captain saw the metal cuffs on our legs and knew we were convicts, so he gave us a choice. We could go back to England and be transported again to serve out our sentences. Or we could serve with him for five years. So Clay and I joined the British navy."

"That doesn't sound so bad," Reggie said. "It must certainly have been a better fate than becoming a bond-servant in Australia."

"Aye, lass, so ye would think. But Captain Taylor was fond of the lash, and yer Clay was not a man to suffer fools gladly."

Reggie's eyes widened in horror. "Are you saying the English captain whipped him?"

"Aye, lass. We served with Taylor for five long years, but at the end of it, the captain said we'd misunderstood, that we must serve the full seven we'd have owed if we'd been transported. Not long after that, Clay and I slipped over the side at one of those Caribbean islands where the captain stopped to take on water."

"And that's where Clay won his ship and became the Sea Dragon?"

"Ye have the right of it. And a menacing creature he was, especially whenever he spied a vessel escorted by a ship in His Majesty's navy. To tell the truth, I think he was lookin' for Captain Taylor. Someone else got to the captain first, though the story told is that he fell overboard in a storm.''

"None of this explains why my husband is avoiding me,'' Reggie said.

"Dinna ye see, lass? Clay likes ye more than he wants to. But he canna let himself love ye, not when he hates yer father. He canna give up his vengeance. Not even for you.''

"Then why did he marry me?'' Reggie asked.

"Ye must see it, lass. Do ye need me to draw a picture?''

"Just tell me, Pegg. Why?''

"To punish yer father, lass. To make him wonder and worry if Clay is mistreatin' ye. To take from yer father what he thinks yer father stole from him—a beloved child.''

Reggie stared at Pegg in horror. "You cannot mean it.'' How had she fallen into Clay's web? How could he have dissembled so thoroughly?

" 'Tis sorry I am, lass. Ye asked, and I told ye. With all the demons the lad's fightin', ye should be grateful he's left ye alone.''

"I will give him more than demons to fight,'' Reggie muttered.

"Now, hold on there. What are ye plannin', lass?''

"Nothing that should worry you, Pegg,'' she said. She focused her eyes on the earl. "But Carlisle had better batten down the hatches!''

•　　•　　•

Clay saw Reggie coming and called a sailor to take the ship's wheel. He crossed to the rail and waited for her to reach him.

The wind had whipped her hair into curls around her face, and the blue ribbon that held her long black hair had come half undone. The sun had brought out freckles across her nose, and her cheeks were burned pink.

She was wearing one of his old shirts, open at the throat, the sleeves rolled up to reveal her bare forearms, the cotton so thin he could see a faint outline of her nipples beneath the flimsy chemise she wore under the shirt.

But the shirt was not the worst offense. She was wearing a pair of breeches that lovingly hugged her figure, making it easy for him to imagine slipping his hand between her legs to palm the heat and the heart of her.

He arched a disdainful brow. "Breeches again, my lady?"

"Would you rather I wore one of those dresses fit for a doxy?" she replied with a brow arched as high as his own.

"I have made my preference clear," he said.

"As I have made mine," she replied.

He took a step back and crossed his arms over his chest—to make certain he would not be tempted to reach for her. "Then what has you so bedeviled, my dear?"

"I have been a bride for three days," she said, closing the distance between them. "But I do not feel like a wife."

He perused her body in a way that suggested she most certainly was.

She looked up at him, temptation in her body, surrender in her eyes. He knew there must be a good reason why he should not enjoy her, but right now he could not think of it.

"Pegg said you only married me to punish my father, to make him know how it felt to lose a child."

"Bloody hell!" What the devil had Pegg been thinking, to speak so frankly? Of course, he had told her nearly as much himself on their wedding night.

Reggie reached out and laid a hand on his arm. Goose bumps rose the entire length of it.

"I'm your wife, Clay. If we are to have any hope of happiness—"

Clay snorted and pulled away, denying the need that made him quiver like a beast in rut. "My chance for happiness ended when your father watched me board that convict ship in chains. I lost everything I had, everything that was dear to me. Well, I have taken something dear away from him."

"I suppose I am dear to my father," Reggie said. "How were you planning to separate us? Are you going to make me walk the plank?"

"Don't be ridiculous."

Reggie raised a brow. "I promise you, nothing less than death could keep us separated for very long. I will seek him out when we arrive in Scotland. I love my father. I do not intend to give him up."

Carlisle did not argue with her, though the subject demanded discussion. He turned his face toward the horizon—and saw the faint outline of the rocky Scottish coast. "I intend to travel directly to Castle Carlisle once we reach port."

"You cannot keep me from seeing my father," she said. "You cannot guard me every minute of every day and—"

He turned to look down at her, feeling the blackness roil inside him. "I do not have to guard you," he said. "I will merely make it plain to the duke that if he ever speaks to you, if he ever so much as lays eyes on you, you will suffer for it. He will make certain he is never at home when you come to call."

Clay saw from the stunned look on Reggie's face that he was right. It was a diabolical plan, but it would work.

Her eyes brimmed with tears, but none fell. "Am I correct in assuming you would have no objection if I see my stepmother or my brother Gareth or my new sister?"

He shrugged. "My fight is not with them."

"How long must my father and I be parted?" she asked.

"I only ask that he suffer what I suffered," the earl said. "A child taken away for a child taken away."

Reggie's face blanched, and she wavered on her feet as a rogue wave rolled under the ship. Clay reached out to steady her, but she jerked herself free and said, "You are blaming my father for something over which he had no control. Your son died in childbirth."

"And do you know why my son died being born?" he asked in a ragged voice.

"It must have been God's will," Reggie said.

"God had nothing to do with it! My wife could not bear the shame of being married to a convict, a man who had been stripped of his title, a man who was nothing and nobody. She wanted to be free of me, and she most definitely did not want my son!''

Reggie put her hands over her ears. ''Do not say any more. I don't want to hear—''

He grabbed her wrists and shoved them behind her back, forcing her against his rigid body, forcing her to listen.

''She murdered my son. She tried to rid herself of the child growing inside her and died herself in the killing of him.''

Reggie stared at Carlisle in horror. ''No woman could do such a thing!''

''But she did,'' he said coldly. ''And who shall I blame for such a tragedy? An abandoned woman too weak to deal with the vagaries of life? Or your father, who helped sentence an innocent man to transportation and left that woman to fend for herself?''

''I'm sorry—''

He released her abruptly and stepped back, his features contorted with rage. ''A nice, neat apology will not bring back my wife or my son or my life before your father ruined it.''

''I should never have married you,'' Reggie said.

''But you did,'' Carlisle said. ''Till death us do part.''

Chapter 11

REGGIE STARED AT THE MAN SITTING ON the opposite side of the carriage. She could hardly imagine the horrors Clay Bannister had suffered in his lifetime, but every time she thought she had heard the worst, there was worse to be told. She still could not believe his wife had killed herself and their unborn child. No wonder he was such a bitter man. No wonder his heart was filled with so much hatred.

She chose not to converse during the ride from the docks near Mishnish to Castle Carlisle. She felt Carlisle's eyes on her as they drove past the turn that led to Blackthorne Hall, but she was not willing to give him the satisfaction of revealing how much she yearned to feel her father's arms around her in a comforting hug.

Several estates bordered the vast acres surrounding Blackthorne Hall, but Reggie had been too young when she was last in Scotland to know which of the neighboring estates belonged to Carlisle.

"There it is," Carlisle said. "Castle Carlisle. Your new home."

Reggie gasped. "But that's Sleeping Beauty's castle!"

At least, that was the name she and Becky had given the crumbling stone castle when they had stumbled across it on one of their afternoon forays. The Carlisle ancestral home truly looked as though it had been lifted from the pages of a storybook.

The turrets and crenels were even more overgrown with thorny vines than Reggie remembered. And there were no vestiges of the expansive lawn, only a dense growth of intimidating thistles. The path to the front door had disappeared entirely beneath a garden of weeds.

She turned to Carlisle and said, "You cannot mean to live here! It is not habitable. Except by rodents, a great many of which, I can assure you, must have taken up residence."

"Nevertheless, it will be our home."

"The front door is off its hinges," Reggie said, pointing to the off-kilter portal that had left the abandoned property so accessible to curious neighborhood children.

"A new one can be made."

"The windowpanes are all cracked and broken," she protested.

"How can you tell?" Carlisle asked. "I do not see any that are not overgrown with vines."

Reggie turned on him angrily. "Is this part of my father's punishment? To keep his daughter in a pigsty?"

Reggie saw the flash of pain in Clay's eyes and felt a

flicker of uncertainty. After all, this was his home, or what was left of it after years of neglect. Perhaps he had not realized the extent of the decay. She returned her gaze to the castle and tried to see it as it must have been when he was a boy growing up there.

She imagined the windowpanes sparkling in the sun, the severity of the gray stone walls relieved by a manicured layer of ivy. The path to the massive wooden doors, with their heavy iron hinges, might have been edged with a profusion of purple heather. And the lawn had surely been an elegant vista of rolling green that swept one's eye all the way to the sea.

"It is a hovel," Carlisle said, brusquely interrupting her daydream. "It will be your duty to make it a home."

Reggie surveyed the dilapidated castle. "I am sure I can do wonders with time and enough money."

"I have no desire to spend my hard-won fortune refurbishing Castle Carlisle. The only memories I have of the time I spent as master here are unpleasant ones. You will have to make do with what you find."

Reggie stared aghast at the ruins before her. "But you cannot wish your own comfort to suffer," she protested.

For the first time since they had argued on board ship, he smiled. "You need not worry, my dear. I have made arrangements to ensure my comfort."

Reggie noticed he had not said anything about *her* comfort.

She could not remember the last time she had been inside the castle, but it must have been nine or ten years past. Even then the furnishings had been in ruins. She wondered how much everything had deteriorated since then from the damp weather and the salty winds off the sea.

As a child, she had entered the castle through an opening at the base of the off-kilter door. But she had no intention of entering her new home by crawling in on her hands and knees. She waited impatiently for Carlisle to join her.

"Would you please pry open the door for me? I want to see inside."

It took Carlisle and Pegg working together to move the heavy portal aside. Carlisle gestured her inside before he and Pegg followed on her heels.

Reggie had opened her mouth to decry the condition of the house when she happened to glance in Carlisle's direction. She did not think, she simply reacted to the anguish she saw on his face. She linked her arm through his and pressed her body close, offering comfort for the spoiled ruins they had found.

"We can make it what it was, Clay," she said.

When he turned to her, his eyes were shuttered. "I am afraid the burden of repairing Castle Carlisle will fall on your shoulders, my dear. A more important matter will be occupying my time."

Reggie took a step back and stared at him in dismay and disbelief. "What could be more important than making this hovel a home?"

"Finding the miscreant who gave false information against me twelve years ago, the man who convinced your father I was guilty of forgery, theft, and attempted murder."

"How did my father come to suspect you in the first place?" Reggie asked.

"I had signed a contract to buy back a vast tract of land surrounding the castle, which my brother had sold to your father," Carlisle said. "I had no idea that the papers authorizing the transaction—on credit—had been forged without your father's knowledge or consent. Or that someone had tried to kill your father to make certain the deal was consummated."

Reggie frowned. "If you are not guilty, then who is?"

"Your father's former steward, Cedric Ambleside."

"Mr. Ambleside tried to murder Papa?" she said, aghast.

"Several times."

"Then why would Papa blame you?"

"Because Mr. Ambleside told him I was guilty."

"Where is he now?" Reggie asked.

Carlisle stopped pacing and turned to face her. "Ambleside disappeared twelve years ago."

"Disappeared? No one just disappears."

Carlisle shook his head disgustedly. "Cedric Ambleside did. I have had detectives searching the width and breadth of Scotland for the past year looking for the man and all they have been able to find out for sure is that he has done business recently in this neighborhood. I intend to find him. When I do, I will make him pay."

Reggie felt a shiver of alarm roll up her spine. "Pay how?"

"With his life," Clay said flatly.

Reggie stared at her husband with stricken eyes. Clay was planning cold-blooded murder. If he killed Mr. Ambleside, he would likely be hanged for it. She imagined Clay with a stiff hemp rope around his neck, imagined him choking, strangling. Suddenly, she could not catch her breath.

Her range of vision narrowed, and she felt as though she were moving down a long, dark tunnel. There was a light at the end, but she could not quite reach it. Finally, it seemed too much effort to try.

Clay caught his wife as she fainted.

"You were too hard on the lass," Pegg said, glaring at Clay, with his one good eye. "And she did nothin' to deserve it. Did ye hear her? 'We can make it what it was, Clay,'" Pegg said in a falsetto imitation of Reggie's voice. "By God, that's a woman, lad! Why are ye in such a hurry to give her up?"

"Shut your blabber, Pegg, and help me find a place to lay her down."

"Ye're not goin' to leave her to face this ruin alone, while ye go traipsin' around in search of Mr. Ambleside, are ye?" Pegg said, stumping back and forth angrily in front of Clay. "Not after she was so gallant. I'm tellin' ye here and now, I'll not force her to stay in this hellhole once you're gone. How can ye expect one of the Quality to manage amid such filth?"

Pegg's agitated stumping frightened an enormous rat out of hiding, and it scurried across the floor. "There, see. The lass was right. This is no fit place for humans."

Clay scowled. He had listened to Pegg rant on more than one occasion without giving in to the older man's persuasion. But it was hard to ignore Pegg's arguments while he held Reggie in his arms. She felt entirely too soft and warm and desirable.

And looked entirely too vulnerable.

Though he had planned to make her live in surroundings unfit for a lady, he had not been to the castle since he had left it twelve years past. He had known it would need repairs. But he was shocked to find it in such a state of ruin. He stared down into Reggie's face, noting how fragile her lashes were, how delicate the freckles on her nose. She had always seemed so strong to him. But she was only human. She had limits he was only beginning to learn. And there were some burdens too great even for someone with her great heart to bear.

He fully intended to bed her—if there was still a bed somewhere upstairs. He wanted an heir off of her before he abandoned her once and for all. But he was determined not to care for her. Or to worry about her. Pegg could do the worrying. In any case, he had always intended for Pegg to stand guard on her while he was away searching for Ambleside.

"I suppose I've let ye stand there feelin' the weight of yer folly long enough," Pegg said. "Take her upstairs, lad. There's a bed up there where ye can lay her down."

"How can you know that?" Clay asked peevishly.

"Because I had it put there," Pegg retorted. "Ye dinna think I'd bring a wee bit of a lass to a place like this without makin' sure she could manage, do ye? I had that Roger Kenworthy fellow look in here when ye said we'd be comin' back to Scotland. The man couldna believe what he found. It didna take much convincin' to have him fix up one decent place to sleep.''

Clay grinned. ''Bless you, Pegg. You're a good man.'' He clutched Reggie more tightly to him as he turned and headed quickly up the familiar winding staircase.

''I hope this means ye plan to make a go of it with the lass,'' Pegg called up after him.

Clay gently laid Reggie on top of the neatly made four-poster bed in what had been his father's bedroom. ''Long enough to get my heir, Pegg,'' he murmured. ''That long. But no longer.'' He crossed the room and closed the door, then returned to the bed, where Reggie was beginning to rouse. He looked around for a pitcher of water and was surprise to find one on the dressing table. Pegg had apparently had someone come in from the village to prepare the room for their arrival while they were unloading the cargo he had brought with him from London.

Clay poured some water into a bowl, dampened a cloth, and brought it back to the bed. As he laid the cool cloth on Reggie's forehead, her eyelids blinked open, closed as though to clear her vision, then opened again. ''We're upstairs,'' he said in answer to the confusion he saw in her eyes.

He watched as her darting glance took in the cleanliness of the wooden floor and the freshly painted walls. The windowpanes, two of which were cracked, were bare of drapes but were curtained on the outside by ivy. Aside from the neatly made bed, an end table bearing a candlestick, the dressing table with pitcher and bowl, a wardrobe, and an overstuffed wing chair by the fireplace, the room was devoid of decoration.

"How long have I been—"

"Not long enough for this room to be cleaned and furnished," Clay assured her with a wry smile. "Pegg had this done."

"Oh, bless him," Reggie said with a sigh. "At least I will have a vermin-free place to sleep."

"*We* have a place to sleep," he corrected her. He stared at her until she flushed, and he was certain she had taken his intent. There was no reason to keep his distance. She was his for the moment. And he must make love to her to get his heir.

Reggie stared at him without speaking, then dragged the cloth from her forehead and struggled to sit up.

"Lie down," he said, pressing firmly but gently on her shoulder. "You need—"

She knocked his arm aside, sat up so that her legs hung over the edge of the bed, then angled her face to look him in the eye. "Are you intending to sleep in this bed with me?"

"I believe it is the only bed in the house," Clay said.

She had changed into one of the low-cut dresses for the journey from the ship to the castle, but had used one of his linen handkerchiefs as a fichu. He reached out and removed the cloth, revealing the swell of her breasts almost to her nipples. He saw her eyes dart anxiously toward the door and back to him.

"You cannot escape, my dear. And besides, we are husband and wife."

She reached for his neck cloth and pulled it free. "I

did not wish to escape," she said, her bosom heaving practically beneath his nose. "I only wondered whether the door was locked. I would not wish to be disturbed."

Clay rose, crossed to the door, and turned the lock. Then he turned back to her, his body taut with expectation. "Very well, my dear. Our privacy is assured."

He began removing his clothing, quickly stripping off his jacket, waistcoat, and shirt. He sat down on a chair near the dressing table to pull off his boots and stockings. Then he stood barefooted, wearing only his trousers and smalls, and crossed to sit beside her.

She sat unmoving, her eyes wide, her lips half-parted. He brushed a hand across one of her breasts and watched as the nipple beaded obviously beneath the cloth. He leaned over and kissed the gentle swell of flesh revealed by the low-cut dress.

"My lord," she said, tugging on his hair. "Wait. We must talk."

He watched her eyes dilate and her breathing grow raspy as his hands played over her body. "Talk."

"I will need servants, help to—"

"You may have as many servants as you need to make such repairs as are necessary to live here without assault from the elements."

"Thank you, Clay," she said.

He could see her mind working, planning a great deal more renovation than he intended. He did not want the castle repaired. He wanted Blackthorne to imagine his daughter living in the hovel his home had become. But he could not help but wonder what they might make of the place together.

"I give nothing for nothing," he said in a hard voice, desperate to cut off such thoughts.

"What is it you want?" she asked.

"I want a son."

The silence was deafening.

He met Reggie's gaze and said, "You must have known I want an heir."

It was devilishly unfair to add children to the precarious scale on which their marriage was currently balanced. But life was rarely fair. Clay had learned to use whatever means were at hand—fair or foul—to get what he wanted. And he wanted a son.

"If only the future were not so uncertain," she murmured.

"Are you refusing me?"

"No. I only hope we do not end up faced with choices neither of us wants to make."

He wondered if she suspected that he intended eventually to abandon her—and to take the child with him. "Let us take first things first," he said.

"Where would you like to begin?" she asked.

He answered by kissing a spot at the base of her throat. He kissed his way up to the tender pulse beneath her ear, then turned her back to him and began undoing the buttons on her dress.

"I am itching to pull all those weeds from the front walk," she said as he pulled the dress away.

He turned her toward him again and began to work on the ties holding her chemise in place. "I would rather see you rescue my mother's rose garden," he replied in a raspy voice, as he saw her bare at last.

She moaned as he filled his hands with her breasts. "I do not remember seeing anything that looked like a rose garden," she grated out.

"It is completely overgrown with weeds," he said as he pushed her flat, then stripped her dress and pantalets down and off so that she was naked beneath him. He found her mouth and let his tongue intrude, mimicking the sex act. His body pulsed and hardened. "My father loved to look out at it from the library window," he managed to rasp.

"We will need a dozen gardeners just to trim all the ivy off these windows," she said as her mouth pressed kisses to his bare shoulders. "And two dozen carpenters to repair the shutters and the windowsills and the floors."

Clay said nothing to dampen her enthusiasm, but he had no intention of making any repairs that were not absolutely necessary. He spread her legs with his knee and settled himself in the cradle of her thighs. "There are some rotten boards on the stairs," he said. "They should come out first."

Her hips arched upward, and her hands clasped him tightly about the shoulders. "You will have to make a tour of the house with me to see if there is any furniture or carpeting or drapery that can be salvaged."

It would be easier to shovel everything out and start over, Clay thought, as he sucked on the flesh at her throat. If they were starting over. Which, he reminded himself, they were not. "Save what you wish. There is nothing here I care about."

"There might be some article that holds a special

memory for you,'' she said as she reached for the buttons on his trousers.

''I doubt it.''

He helped her shove the trousers and smalls down off his hips far enough to free his shaft. One thrust, and he was inside her.

Their eyes met.

''Life here can be good.'' She reached out with her forefinger to trace his lips, but he opened his mouth and sucked it inside. Her eyes closed, and her body arched upward as he began to move inside her.

There was no more time for talking, no more time for thinking, only the immense pleasure to be found inside her before he spilled his seed.

He must have slept, because he awoke to find her playing with the dark curls on his chest.

''Hello,'' she said, removing her hand. She lowered her gaze as a blush pinkened her cheeks. ''I didn't mean to wake you.''

''I didn't mean to sleep,'' he said brusquely.

''Wait,'' she said as he started to rise. ''One more question.''

''One more,'' he conceded.

''Were there ever happy days here for you?''

''I had a wonderful childhood here with my brother Charles and my parents. My mother always placed an enormous silver epergne, filled with the most fragrant pink roses, in the center of the table,'' he said, seeing it in his mind's eye. ''I think she did it to counteract the smell of tobacco in the room, because my father always insisted on blowing a cloud after supper.''

Reggie smiled. "They sound well matched."

"They were. I might have lived here quite happily, if your father—"

"And it will be a happy place again," Reggie interrupted, placing her fingertips against his lips to silence him. "In no time at all Castle Carlisle with be filled with the smell of roses on the dining room table, and . . . What would you most like to find here in the years to come, my lord?"

Clay met her gaze, kissed her fingertips, and said, "The laughter of children."

Becky had begun her overland journey to Blackthorne Hall from London without informing her father and stepmother that she was on her way. She simply could not find the words to express the disaster that had befallen her . . . or how much a blessing in disguise it actually was.

Her marriage was being annulled.

A mere week ago—could it be so little time had passed?—Penrith had sat across from her at the supper table and announced, "I have had a change of fortune, my dear, which will require me to travel abroad for some time to come. And since I cannot subject a wife and child to the rigors of such a lengthy journey, I am leaving you."

"You mean, you wish Lily and me to wait here in England for you?" she had asked.

"No. I mean I am having our marriage annulled."

Becky's heart skipped a beat. *Lily! Who is to get Lily?*

But she did not dare to ask. Any interruption of her husband before he had finished speaking had always been dealt with severely. Her pulse was so loud in her ears that she had to force herself to concentrate on what Penrith was saying in order to hear him.

"My solicitor has come up with a legal defect that will suffice to allow an annulment—the existence of a prior marriage contract between myself and another lady, I believe. In light of the fact I may be gone for as long as ten years or more—"

Becky could not restrain a gasp. He was not even pretending his case for annulment was valid. It was made up out of whole cloth! She bit her lip when Penrith's eyes narrowed and lowered her gaze submissively. "Please continue, William."

"It seemed better, in light of such an extended absence, that I should set you free to seek connubial bliss with someone else."

Becky's head jerked up, but she was still enough in control of herself to choke back the startled cry of surprise—and rage at his utter callousness—that sought voice.

Penrith sipped a spoonful of turtle soup, savored it, and swallowed it. "I assume you will not want to stay here in London. Indeed, I am closing Penrith House for the period I am gone. I have made arrangements to send you and Lily to stay with your father and stepmother in Scotland."

"Lily is to stay with me?" she croaked past the painful knot of emotion in her throat.

He waved his napkin in dismissal. "You may take the brat with my good will."

"Will I—"

"I do not care to discuss the matter further," he said. "My solicitor will call on you tomorrow to discuss any questions you may have."

Becky understood the cruelty—the total lack of any human kindness—in the man she had married when she realized William had not waited until the end of the meal to offer his news. He had done it during the first course. In order to escape, she would have to excuse herself before the meal was finished.

She would not do it. She would stay and choke down the rest of her meal if it killed her.

"Is the soup not to your taste, my dear?" he asked.

Becky swallowed a spoonful past the lump in her throat, so that she could say, "It is too salty."

"Then I will have Cheevers take it away and bring the next remove."

The only thing Becky wanted to remove from the dinner table was herself, but she merely nodded. When Cheevers returned, she accepted a slice of lamb with boiled cauliflower but refused the stewed eels.

The next course consisted of fried sole, potted pigeon, and a sweet, milky custard. She gagged on the custard.

"Are you unwell, my dear?"

She was in shock, her body so cold she was physically shivering. She could see that William relished her discomfort. It was a cat-and-mouse game they had played all the years of their marriage. This time he had cut her to the bone—in fact, given her a mortal wound—but she refused to give him the satisfaction of acknowledging the hit.

She managed a smile, a last courageous act in a marriage filled with far too much cowardice, and said, "I am merely fatigued."

He lifted his wine glass to her. "Then I will excuse you, my dear. You have a great deal to accomplish in the next few days. I am closing the house in a week."

She had stood and turned her back on him and walked away. But she had only made it to the bottom of the stairs before her knees gave out and she collapsed.

To her utter horror and humiliation, Hardy had called William to come and carry her upstairs to her bedroom.

Becky did not remember much about the five days that followed. She had expected to be able to rely on Mick to help her, but she received a letter from him explaining that he had been called away on business that could not wait. He hoped to see her the next time she visited her family in Scotland. She had set out for her father's estate in Scotland with all possible speed, encouraged by Penrith's threat to close the town house within the week. And the prospect of seeing Mick again.

Becky leaned back against the comfortable velvet seat of the carriage, hugged her sleeping child closer to her breast, and listened to the jingle of harness and the clop of the horses' hooves on the dirt road. They had left the last of the macadam roads just past Edinburgh. It would not be long now before she was home. She had done little on the journey but cry and sleep . . . and think.

She would never have betrayed her wedding vows by making love to Mick. But things were different now. She was once again an unattached female. Marriage to Mick was out of the question, considering the differences in their stations. But she was willing to consider a discreet liaison with him. They could be lovers.

Mick managed several properties for her father in Scotland, and he lived in a house on one of them, not far from Blackthorne Hall. It should be possible to meet there without being discovered, if they were cautious. They would be able to hold each other and to love each other.

Becky had a startling—and troubling—thought. What if Mick already had a lover? It was possible. There must be widows in the countryside who were willing to share their favors with a man as young and handsome as Mick.

Becky felt an ache deep inside at the thought of Mick with another woman in his arms and realized she wanted him all to herself.

Why not marry him?

It was impossible. She had been taught from birth the importance of her heritage, the need to marry well, to marry within her class. Mick was a whore's bastard son. The social stigma of marriage to such as he would be unbearable. She would become an outcast, and her daughter along with her. And, to be honest, Becky was not sure she could live without the comforts she had been raised to expect with an inexhaustible income.

Penrith had taken control of her trust upon her marriage to him and dissipated it entirely, so she had no wealth of her own. She could probably ask Papa for pin money, but she doubted Mick's pride would allow it. And she was not entirely sure Papa would not cut her off without a farthing, if she married without his approval. And as much as Papa admired Michael O'Malley, she could not believe he would approve of Mick as the proper husband for a duke's daughter.

So. It must be a liaison, or nothing. She did not even consider marriage to another man, not after her experience with Penrith. But the thought of spending life as an unattached female did not seem so frightening when she imagined herself being held snug in Mick's arms.

There was only one problem with her solution. What if Mick did not want to be her lover? What if he was offended by the fact that she did not consider him a man worthy of her hand in marriage. What if their friendship was blighted as a result? Or, worst of all, what if she really was as unsatisfying in bed as William had always said and she could not please Mick?

Becky had already chewed all her fingernails to the quick. She was forced to content herself with staring out the window at the rapidly passing countryside.

At least she would have someone to share all her troubles. Reggie was in Scotland. Surely, between them, they could figure out a way to make life turn out happily ever after.

Chapter 12

REGGIE SWIPED AT A DROP OF SWEAT streaming from her temple, then returned her attention to the fernlike weed she was pulling from the base of a rosebush. Her knees and shoulders ached from the unnatural position in which she sat, and her hands beneath a pair of leather work gloves were swollen with blisters. But she could see the beginnings of a rose garden. Somehow the roses had survived, despite a choking mantle of bracken and thistles.

Lightning streaked across the dark, distant sky and down into the sea. She waited for the clap of thunder that was sure to follow. *One, two, three, four, five* . . . The rumble in the distance was not so far away now. A zephyr swirled around her, bringing the sting of cool, salty air. The storm would be here soon, and she would have to stop.

She leaned back on her heels and glanced upward, searching for Carlisle's figure atop the peaked slate roof of the castle. Pegg had arranged for a bed and fresh bedding, but he had not repaired the hole in the roof above the bedroom. Fixing it had taken precedence over everything, even the journey to visit with her family that Carlisle had conceded she could make. That is, the visit with everyone except her father. He had insisted on accompanying her to make certain the duke kept his distance.

She had been tempted to stay inside today and avoid the possibility of an encounter with Carlisle. After her wanton behavior yesterday—making love with him in broad daylight—she still was not able to look her husband in the eye without blushing.

But a single glance through the ivy-choked bedroom window had revealed the weed-choked rose garden. She had not been able to resist the chance to begin the restoration of Castle Carlisle to its former beauty. Since there were no servants for whom she must keep up the pretense of being a countess, she had changed into the pair of Daniel's breeches she had confiscated on board ship and gone to work.

Reggie knew it would have been wiser to begin her repairs to the castle from the inside out. If she was going to be a prisoner in her own home, it behooved her to make her captivity as pleasant as possible.

But ever since Carlisle had mentioned his mother's rose garden, it had become a symbol to her of all he had lost. Perhaps if she could make the garden what it once had been, he might see the possibilities for what they could do with the rest of the castle—and their lives.

She was also determined to mend the breach between

her father and her husband, but she had no idea how to accomplish such a feat. Becky had always been the one to come up with the best solution for a problem; Reggie had been the one who carried it out. She would simply have to write to Becky and see what her sister suggested.

Reggie sighed as she perused the rosebushes, noting the absence of weeds and the fecund smell of the earth. She had never in her life done so much physical labor, been so sore, or so exhausted. Or so satisfied. Which was quite different from contented or happy. She was neither of those. She was drawing lines, of course, but what else could one do, when one was married to a man who fought the devil every day—and sometimes lost.

Reggie watched as the rising wind whipped at Carlisle's shirt, which was open at the throat and clung to his chest in sweaty patches. She had stolen glances at him throughout the afternoon as he stood with one hip cocked to maintain his shaky balance on the steep roof. Several times she had feared he would fall, but somehow, despite several near misses, he had not.

She knew he must be as aware of the coming storm as she was. Why did he not come down? It was dangerous to be so high above the ground in the midst of so much lightning. She had no desire to be a widow before she had really been a wife.

She had opened her mouth to shout at him to come down when a gust of wind stripped a lock of hair from the knot of curls at her crown. She tore off her gloves and reached up to try to keep her hair from falling down entirely. Her efforts came to naught as the wind tore at her curls, loosing pins that she could not find in the newly turned earth.

She gave up and pulled out the few remaining pins, shaking her head, running her hands through her hair, and rubbing her fingertips against her scalp to ease the pain where the pins had held her hair tight against her head. The stone in her wedding ring caught in a tangle, and she eased it free, then held her hand out before her to gaze at the ring.

The diamond was brilliant in the sunlight, a bright, beautiful symbol of their union. Except Carlisle had never intended their marriage to be a joining of two souls. She had been so unbelievably foolish for someone who had tried to be so careful. The encircling band of gold reminded her of a prisoner's manacle, and she suddenly wanted it off. But her fingers had swollen in the heat, and hard as Reggie tugged, she could not free herself.

When she looked up, she found Carlisle watching her, his dark hair riffled by the gusty wind that made his stance on the pitched roof so perilous. She felt herself go still inside.

Reggie thought it was fear for Carlisle's safety that made her skin prickle, made her heart begin to pound so hard it threatened to burst from her chest. But it was not. It was something else entirely. Something much more sinister.

Desire.

It was appalling to feel so much need for a man who had sworn to destroy her father, a man who had deceived her, disgraced her, and then coerced her into marriage.

And this was not even love, it was lust. Reggie felt ashamed. And then angry because Carlisle had no right to put himself in such mortal danger that she was compelled to worry about him, as she would worry about *anyone* in such dire straits.

"Come down," she mouthed distinctly, knowing her voice would be whipped away by the wind long before it reached him.

He shook his head and mouthed back, "Not yet."

She glanced worriedly at a flash of lightning over her shoulder and counted, *one, two, three* . . . before she heard the thunder. Dangerously close. The storm was nearly upon them. She stood up, her eyes never leaving Carlisle. He was down on one knee hammering again. She was so absorbed, she never heard Pegg coming until he touched her shoulder.

"Make him come down," she said, her voice sharp.

Pegg didn't even look up. "He'll come down when he's done, lass, and not before."

"But the storm—" she protested.

"Canna ye see he loves it? He dares the wind to blow him away, dares the lightning to strike him."

Reggie looked up and discovered Carlisle standing with his eyes closed, his face lifted to the storm. "Why isn't he afraid?" she whispered.

"I dinna believe he fears death. Sometimes I think he might even welcome it."

Reggie had no experience with wounds so painful that death would be a blessing. How could she hope to heal her husband if he nursed his hurt so carefully that it was still alive this long after it had been suffered?

Lightning crackled so close that the hairs on her arms stood on end. A boom of thunder followed almost immediately. She bolted for the tall wooden ladder that lay against the back wall of the castle, determined to bring Carlisle down. She could hear Pegg yelling at her to stop, but that only made her run faster.

She scurried up the ladder, anxious to get to the top before lightning struck again. The blisters on her hands protested as she clutched the rough wood, and she bit her lip to hold back a sob of pain. She was so intent on putting one hand above the other that she was startled when she found herself staring into Carlisle's dark, angry eyes.

He was down on one knee holding the ladder steady and greeted her with, "What in bloody hell do you think you're doing?"

A gust of wind shoved her backward so suddenly the scream of terror was caught in her throat. She felt Carlisle grab handfuls of the man's shirt she wore and yank her forward onto the roof. A moment later, she lay prone next to him, her head aimed toward the peak of the slate roof, her body tucked in the cradle of his strong arms. Icy rain splattered against her cheek before he pressed it hard against his chest.

"You willful little fool," he muttered in her ear. "You could have been killed."

She could no longer feel the cold rain, no longer smell the salty air. She could only feel the heat of his body along the length of her own and smell the sharp, acrid odor of male sweat which, surprisingly, she did not find unappealing. His hand palmed her head and held her tight against him as the storm raged over their heads.

"Did you finish?" she asked loud enough to be heard over the rain clattering against the slate.

"What?" He released her enough so that she could see his face.

She brushed a raindrop from his eyebrow. "Repairing the roof. Did you finish?"

"Just. At least we will sleep dry tonight."

Reggie shivered as lightning struck again, too close for comfort. "Assuming we are still alive. Why didn't you come down?"

Carlisle lifted his face to the threatening sky. "All the times I begged God to strike me dead, He never did. I doubt He would bother with me now."

"You've forgotten one thing," Reggie said.

"What's that?"

"He may decide He wants me and get you by mistake."

Carlisle grinned. "Then I had better take advantage of the opportunity to do something I've been wanting to do all day."

His lips were cold from the rain as he caressed the tiny, almost invisible scar near her upper lip, but his tongue was warm as he slid it into her mouth and tasted her thoroughly. She felt her body heating from the inside out, and the thunder overhead was eclipsed by the roar of her own blood rushing in her ears. Her hands crept around his waist, pulling him closer, while his hand settled on her hip, pressing their bodies together as she arched toward him.

Their precarious perch on the roof, the lash of the wind and the rain, and the urgency of Carlisle's kisses all combined to leave her breathless, aching for him, needing him desperately.

And then his kisses stopped.

Reggie opened her eyes and looked up at him, confused. "What's wrong?"

"The worst of the storm has passed," he said. "We can go down now."

She looked up at the sky and realized there were patches of blue among the clouds. She had been lost in some other world, and she was not yet ready to leave it.

Reggie felt bereft as Carlisle eased himself off of her and found purchase on the slippery roof, and then guilty, because she had succumbed to the desire—the lust—she felt for him, despite his avowed intentions toward her father.

"Be careful," he warned.

"I don't understand your concern for my well-being," she said. "I would have thought it would please you to leave my father with one less daughter."

"He will suffer more if you are alive, yet lost to him," Carlisle replied. "Besides," he added, "I don't yet have my heir."

Reggie could hardly believe this was the same courteous gentleman who had courted her so successfully in London. The man she had married had no heart, no shred of decency, no mercy for her or her father. When Carlisle reached out to her, she jerked her shoulder free. "Don't touch me."

She lost her balance and would have fallen, if he had

not grabbed a handful of her shirt. She glanced down and saw Pegg waiting far, far below, at the bottom of the ladder. Her heart was thumping crazily in her chest as she realized how close she had come to death.

She looked at Carlisle and realized she owed him thanks. But the words stuck in her throat. He had saved her because her death did not fit into his plans of revenge. In order to punish her father—and get his heir—he needed her alive. Well, he would have to wait to get his heir. She had no intention of giving him what he wanted before she had what she wanted.

"You will get your heir when you make peace with my father," she said. "And not before."

His brows lowered. "Are you refusing to lie with me?"

"I will fight you tooth and claw," she assured him. "Now, let me go, my lord. I can make my own way down." When he released her, she felt much less safe, but she was determined not to rely on him any more than absolutely necessary.

"I will go down first," he said, stepping in front of her. "To catch you if you fall."

"I have no intention of giving you the satisfaction of telling my father I am dead," she retorted. But he had already gone before her. She stepped onto the top rung of the ladder the instant his hand had left it. When she was ten feet above the ground, her foot slipped on a still-wet wooden rung, and she fell.

"Clay!" she cried. To her mortification, she landed in his outstretched arms. "Put me down!" she said, struggling to be set on her feet.

"You're shivering with cold," he said. "I've asked Pegg to draw a bath for you. I suggest you stay in it until you are warmed."

It would be idiocy to say she would not bathe. She barely managed to refrain from uttering just such a refusal. The dirt that had collected on her clothes in the garden had turned to mud in the rain. Her hair straggled around her face in wet clumps, and her body ached—and stank—from the hard afternoon's work. "Put me down," she insisted.

He slid her along his body, and in the sensual riot that resulted, she made the mistake of laying her blistered hands on his shoulders.

"Aaah!"

"What's wrong?"

"Nothing," she said, curving her injured hands close to her chest and turning away.

He reached out a hand to curb her, and she cried out in anguish. He grasped her wrists and turned her hands over, revealing the raw flesh and bleeding blisters. "Dear God. What have you done?"

His eyes were filled with concern as he met her gaze, and the defiant response she had intended caught in her throat. "I . . ."

He turned his gaze to the rose garden. Reggie looked along with him, feeling a great deal of satisfaction at all she had accomplished. A circular pattern of rosebushes could be seen, the dirt around them freed of weeds, the bushes themselves pruned so they might begin to grow again.

She waited for Carlisle to acknowledge her effort,

hoping he would be pleased. Instead she heard, "You should have left this work to someone better suited to it."

"I wanted to do it," she said. *For you. For us.* But those thoughts remained unspoken.

His gaze focused on her again, but what she saw in his eyes was not gratitude, but annoyance. "If you will not set limits for your own welfare, I will set them for you."

"No one tells me what I can and cannot do!"

He lifted an arrogant black eyebrow. "If necessary, I will keep you locked in your room."

Reggie's heart was thumping hard, and her body felt hot. Her throat ached from the wound to her pride he had so carelessly inflicted. "My father could not manage it when I was six, and I have learned a great deal since then, my lord."

He glanced at the roses again, then lifted her injured hands gently in his own, turning them to survey the damage. "Will you at least take better care of yourself?"

"It is only a few blisters," she protested, awkwardly pulling her hands free. "They will be gone in a matter of days."

"Come," he said, placing a firm hand at the small of her back and urging her toward the front door to the castle. "Pegg will know what to use on those blisters to ease your hurt."

Pegg met them as they entered the castle, and when Carlisle asked whether he had a salve that might help, the big man insisted that she bathe first. "Ye've got to get those hands clean, lass, or there'll be trouble later.

I'll give Clay somethin' to put on them when ye've finished yer bath.''

"But—"

"I have found it is a waste of breath arguing with
him," Carlisle said. "You might as well do as he says."

Reggie looked from one imposing male to the other,
then turned and headed up the stairs.

"That's a braw lass ye've married, lad," Pegg said as
he poured a cup of hot tea and set it on the kitchen table.
"Not many a wife would have worked so long nor so
hard for ye."

"I know," Clay conceded as he sat down and added a
lump of sugar to the hot tea Pegg had poured for him.

"Maybe ye ought to reconsider and—"

"Forgive Blackthorne?" Clay interrupted brusquely.
"Never."

"She's yer wife," Pegg argued.

"She's a pawn. A means to an end."

"I can see ye care for her."

"I need her healthy if she's to bear me an heir," Clay
said.

"Ye don't deserve her," Pegg retorted.

Clay stood abruptly, shoving the rickety wooden chair
back so hard it fell over with a clatter on the stone floor.
"Nevertheless, she's mine to do with as I like. I—"

Clay was cut off by the resounding clang of metal
striking metal at the front door of the castle. While Clay
had worked on the roof and his wife had worked in the

garden, Pegg had repaired the front door, adding a fantastical brass sea dragon as a knocker.

Clay turned to Pegg. "Are you expecting anyone? Servants? Gardeners? Grooms?"

Pegg shook his head.

It was nearly dusk, and Clay could not imagine who would be visiting them at this hour of the day, unless . . . "Come with me," he ordered, as he headed for the door.

Clay waited for Pegg to stump his way over to the front door before he opened it to find Reggie's father, the Duke of Blackthorne himself, standing on his doorstep. Though the duke was a man of five and forty years, he appeared quite capable of tearing Clay limb from limb. He looked almost sinister in a black, many-layered greatcoat.

Except for the gray that lightened his dark blond hair at the temples and the webbed lines at the edges of his eyes, he looked exactly as Clay last remembered seeing him, the day Clay had been transported to Australia. He remembered the vow he had made that day on the London dock, chained hand and foot like a common felon. *"You've convicted an innocent man. One day I'll come back to England. And when I do, I'll ruin your life, as you've ruined mine."*

Adrenaline raced through Clay's body, heightening every sensation. He could recall everything as though it had happened yesterday.

He remembered standing before the House of Lords in disgrace as Blackthorne accused him of forging documents that would allow him to buy Blackthorne Hall, along with the Carlisle land his elder brother Charles had previously sold to Blackthorne, *in the event of Blackthorne's death,* and then attempting to murder the duke in order to exercise his rights under the forged documents to claim the land.

He relived the frustration of trying to defend himself when the one man who knew the truth, and who was, in fact, the guilty party—Mr. Cedric Ambleside—had disappeared. And experienced the same impotent fury he had felt while Blackthorne watched him leaving England in chains, relishing the misery he had inflicted.

Clay had not forgotten any of it, nor the agony of the years that had followed.

His muscles tensed for action as his heart pumped blood to every extremity, preparing his body for this long overdue confrontation with his enemy. His hands curled into fists as he fought to bring himself under control.

"May I come in?" the duke said.

"You are not welcome here," Clay replied in a hard voice. He deliberately omitted the duke's title, to ensure that *His Grace* recognized the insult. He started to slam the door closed in Blackthorne's face, but the duke caught it with his open palm and shoved his way inside before the door banged shut behind him.

Blackthorne grabbed fisted handfuls of Clay's shirt and pulled him close so they were eye to eye. "I want to see my daughter."

"She's no longer your daughter," Clay shot back. "She's my wife."

"Bring her out where I can see her," the duke demanded.

Clay felt Pegg take a step closer to his side and said, "Keep out of this, Pegg."

Blackthorne's eyes never left Clay's. "I came because of your letter," the duke said. "I want an explanation."

"I thought it was clear enough," Clay replied, his lips curling derisively. "I have your daughter. She is mine. You are not to see her again. Ever."

The duke's piercing gray eyes searched the large entryway and the parlor beyond, and Clay could not help feeling shame at what he knew Blackthorne saw. The rotting gilt furniture with its worn cushions, the tattered velvet drapes, the stains left by rodents on a once-exquisite Turkish carpet brought home by a Carlisle knight who had fought in the Crusades.

He let hate rise up—it was easy after so many years of conjuring it—to take the place of shame. "Get out."

The duke's glance shifted to the shadows at the top of the winding staircase before it rested once again on Clay. "Is she upstairs? I want to speak to her." He used his hold on Clay to throw him aside and started up the stairs.

Clay did not attempt to stop him. "If you seek her out, I will make her pay for it," he warned.

Blackthorne halted on the third step and turned, his face a picture of fury and frustration. "If you harm one hair on her head, I will—"

"I am not the callow, untried boy you destroyed a decade past," Clay said. "Swords? Pistols at dawn? I welcome either challenge. I have had practice enough at both as the Sea Dragon. I will be glad to see you dead and your family left unprotected.''

The duke looked taken aback at the threat.

''But I would rather you lived, so you may suffer as I have suffered,'' Clay snarled.

Blackthorne clutched the wooden stair rail. ''I am sorry—''

''Apologies will not bring back my wife or my son or the years of my life you stole from me,'' Clay said in a cold, deadly voice. ''I meant what I said in my letter. Stay away from my wife. Stay away from Blackthorne Hall when she visits there. Or she will be the one to suffer.''

The duke turned and started up the stairs. ''Reggie!'' he shouted. ''Are you up there? Come down! I want to see you! Are you well? Are you all right?''

''Papa, is that you?'' Reggie yelled back.

Blackthorne halted on the stairs at the sound of her voice. ''Come down, please! Now!''

''I'm coming, Papa,'' Reggie shouted. ''Wait for me. I'm coming!''

''She will pay for your mistake,'' Clay repeated.

He saw the struggle on the duke's face. The need to stay and see his daughter. The fear of what would happen to her if he did. ''I only want to see that she is well,'' the duke said. ''To make certain that no harm has come to her at your hands.''

''No harm has come to her . . . yet. Whatever harm she suffers from this moment forward will be on your head.'' Clay took a step back, folded his arms, and looked up the staircase, waiting for Reggie to make her appearance.

The duke looked from Clay to Pegg and then back up the stairs. He crossed swiftly down the stairs and confronted Clay. "Do you swear on your honor as a gentleman that no harm has come to her?"

Clay sneered. "My word of honor? As a gentleman? Would you believe me if I gave it to you?"

The duke looked physically ill. He glanced up the stairs again and then met Clay's dark stare. "I will accept your word that she is well."

"I swear it," Clay said. "If you wish to keep her safe, you will leave now."

Blackthorne had already opened the front door and was halfway through it when a word stopped him.

"Papa!"

Both men looked up to see Reggie at the top of the stairs. She was barefooted, wrapped in a sheet that she clutched around her with both hands, her bare shoulders shining with beads of water, her blue eyes glistening with tears. "Oh, Papa!"

Clay turned to meet Blackthorne's distraught gray gaze and murmured, "The choice is yours."

The duke swore an oath and stepped through the door, slamming it behind him.

Chapter 13

REGGIE GRABBED HANDFULS OF THE TRAIL-
ing sheet she had draped around herself when she climbed out of the tub
and ran down the winding wooden staircase as fast as
she could.

"Help me!" she begged as she struggled to pry open
the massive front door. She bit back a moan as her
wounded hands protested the effort.

"He's gone," Carlisle said, keeping his arms folded
across his chest, to avoid the temptation to touch.

Reggie shot him a look of disgust and returned to her
struggle with the door. By the time she managed to open
it, her father's horse was too far down the road for her
even to call out to him. She whirled and confronted Carlisle. "What did you say to him? Why did you send him
away?"

"Your father left of his own accord," Carlisle replied.

"I cannot believe he would go without speaking with

me," Reggie said heatedly. "You must have said something!"

"The choice to stay or to go was entirely his."

"Pegg? Is that true?" Reggie turned to challenge the one-legged Scotsman, only to discover he had withdrawn. The tiled entryway to the castle, the hall, and every room that opened from it seemed abandoned. "Pegg?"

The sound echoed back to her from the cavernous ceiling.

Reggie turned back to Carlisle. And discovered an avid look on his face that both frightened and excited her.

Reggie suddenly realized she was wearing nothing more than a cotton sheet tucked around her breasts, rucked up in front to reveal not only her bare feet, but her limbs all the way to her knees. She shivered as a draft from a broken window slithered across her damp shoulders. The feral look in Carlisle's dark eyes made her throat feel tight. She tried to swallow, but her mouth was dry.

"Clay . . ." He could not expect her to lie with him now. Not after he had so ruthlessly sent her father away. Especially when she had just warned him he would never get his heir on her unless he made peace with her father.

He reached out and tucked a finger into the front of the sheet between her breasts and drew her toward him. She stared at him defiantly, daring him to touch her. When she felt the sheet coming free, she grabbed at it with both hands to keep herself decently covered. "Don't do this," she warned. "I will never forgive—"

His mouth closed over hers, stopping speech, stopping breath. Her knees collapsed, but before she could fall, his arm circled her waist to hold her tight against him.

Reggie knew she had to fight him now, or she would lose the battle forever. She bit his tongue, and he reeled back, staring at her in surprise.

"You bit me!"

"I said no and I meant it."

He lifted her into his arms and started up the stairs.

She grabbed his hair and yanked hard. "Stop this, Clay!"

"Ow! That hurts!"

"Put me down!" she shouted, pummeling his head and shoulders as he carted her up the stairs. "Let me go!"

He threw her down hard on the bed. When she looked up Reggie was appalled at the hunger she saw in his fierce gaze. All her resistance had done was increase his passion.

She scooted across the bed and off the other side. "Get out! I don't want you here."

Unfortunately, he had grabbed the sheet, and she found herself on the other side of the bed stark naked. She ran for the dressing screen, but he caught her before she had gone more than a few steps and threw her back onto the bed. This time he used the weight of his body to hold her captive.

"I don't want you," she said, determined to resist him. Her breath caught in her lungs as Carlisle lowered his head and kissed her breast. Before she could recover from that assault on her senses, his mouth closed over her nipple, and he began to suckle her.

Reggie grabbed handfuls of his hair, intending to shove him away, but she moaned deep in her throat, and her body arched toward him as his fingers intruded between her thighs and forced their way inside her. "I—will—not—do—this," she grated out.

And yet her body responded to his skilled touch. He seemed to know where to kiss her, where to fondle her to create the greatest sensation. She writhed beneath him, feeling so much—too much—and surrendering at last to the desperate need for relief from the tension building inside her.

"Clay," she moaned. "I cannot bear it."

His mouth found hers, and the thrust of his tongue mimicked his fingers below. She heard a guttural sound in his throat as her body arched instinctively—against her reason, against her will—toward his.

He freed himself from his clothing, and a moment later he was inside her, filling her deeply, fully.

This time she was the one who mimicked the sex act with her tongue, urging him to completion. Their tongues dueled as their bodies danced together, the pace frenzied, the pleasure enormous, building until it seemed they could reach no higher. And yet he took her further, faster, in a wild and reckless race toward something . . . someplace . . . wonderful.

Reggie cried out in fear. There was nothing she could do to stop what was happening, what she was feeling. Her body seemed caught in a never-ending spiral of desire. She heard Carlisle cry out as well, and her eyes opened in time to see his head thrown back, his jaw clenched tight as though in pain. She stepped over the cliff with him and fell deep into a well of unbearable, unbelievable pleasure.

Reggie felt her husband's weight settle onto her. His face nuzzled against her throat, his breathing as tortured as her own. He should have been too heavy, but the feather mattresses cushioned them both, and he provided a warm cover as her sweaty flesh cooled in the evening air.

The tears came without warning, and Reggie turned her face away and blinked hard to keep them from falling. She did not understand herself. How could she have made love to Carlisle? Although *making love* hardly seemed to describe what had just happened. She should have fought harder. She had not only surrendered to her husband's attentions, she had *enjoyed* them!

Reggie knew she had to find a way to make Carlisle understand this could never happen again. Not until he had forgiven her father. Not until good relations between the two men had been restored.

"Clay?" When he did not answer, she nudged his shoulder. "Clay?"

The rogue was asleep.

Reggie half-shoved, half-slid her way out from under him. She was surprised to discover, when she tried to stand, that her knees were still wobbly. She crossed to the copper tub of bathwater, frowning when she saw the soap scum on the surface. Reggie shivered when she dipped a toe in and felt how cold and slimy the water was, but she would have jumped into a murky, icy pond, if necessary, to free herself from the musky smell of lovemaking that clung to her.

She stood and sluiced herself with the cold, soapy water using a sponge, noticing how tender her breasts were where Carlisle's day-old beard had rubbed and how tender she was between her thighs. Reggie wasn't sure when she realized she was being watched. Her gaze skipped to the bed. She hissed in a breath when she met Carlisle's dark, intent gaze.

Her first instinct was to cover herself, but he had already seen all there was to see. Instead, she turned her back to him, ignoring him as though he were not there, and continued her ablutions. Reggie was so determined not to pay Carlisle any attention that she was startled when she felt his hand touch her back.

She jerked upright, but managed at the last instant not to turn around. She kept her back to him and glanced over her shoulder. "What are you doing?"

She held her breath as his fingertips traced a line on her back, and then another, and another.

"I never noticed these scars before," he said. "Did he beat you?"

She stared at him in confusion. "What?"

His jaw was taut, his dark eyes dangerous. "I recognize the mark of a lash, my dear," he said in a harsh voice. "Someone beat you. Was it your father?"

She shook her head. "No. A governess. Miss Tolemeister."

Carlisle lifted a brow. "And your father allowed it?"

"Of course not! He was the best of fathers."

"Obviously not," Carlisle countered.

Reggie felt his fingertips once again trace the three marks where Miss Tolemeister had wielded her rod so efficiently. "Papa is not responsible for those welts. He left me and my sister with my uncle Marcus while he traveled to Scotland. He was gone for a year. We later learned that he had been shipwrecked and had amnesia from a blow to his head.

"It was not long after Papa left that Uncle Marcus was wounded grievously at Waterloo. He did not want anyone to see him scarred so horribly, so my sister and I had a series of governesses during the year Papa was gone, six or seven in all. And one of them . . ."

She felt his lips against her back, kissing her, as his hands captured her waist. Goose bumps rose on her flesh.

"You're cold," he said, abruptly releasing her. He turned to look for a towel and found one near the fire, which he wrapped around her from behind and tucked around her breasts. Then he lifted her out of the tub and turned her to face him.

As he kissed her throat beneath her ear, she continued breathlessly, "I am trying to explain—"

"Your lips are swollen," he said, kissing them gently. "Does that hurt?"

"No," she murmured.

He walked her toward the looking glass, staying behind her, and reached for the jar of salve that Pegg had left on the dressing table. He opened it, dipped in his fingers, and began to smooth the figwort concoction onto her blisters.

She hissed at the sting as the salve touched her skin.

He bit her ear, distracting her from the pain, and she moaned with pleasure. He continued kissing her the entire time he ministered to her hands. Reggie closed her eyes and concentrated on the feel of his lips, instead of the sting in her hands, until she heard the lid being replaced on the jar.

When she opened her eyes, she saw herself reflected in the looking glass. Her eyes were heavy-lidded, her body languid in Carlisle's embrace.

He was seducing her again! As Reggie jerked herself free, she nearly fell over backward into the tub. She grabbed hold of Carlisle's arms to keep her balance, wincing as her blisters brushed against his flesh. Once she was steady, she stepped away from the tub and turned to face him, wrapping the towel more securely around her, forcing herself to keep her eyes on his face and not the rest of his very aroused body.

"I was explaining why my father was not responsible for the scars on my back," she said. "I think it is a story that bears telling. It proves he is a good man, not at all the kind of person who would unjustly accuse another."

Night had fallen, and besides a single candle lit beside the bed, the only light came from the flickering fire. She could not help admiring the breadth of Clay's shoulders and the muscles in his arms. She could make out each of his ribs and found her gaze moving to his flat stomach and to the dark line of hair that led downward from there.

She forced her gaze back to his face and blurted, "Pegg will be waiting supper for us." Then she escaped behind the Chinese dressing screen, where she had left one of the several dresses Pegg had hung in the wardrobe while she had been working in the rose garden. The garments were of the sort a woman of her station might wear, but smelled slightly of camphor and were years out of style. She had chosen a long-sleeved copper silk dress.

"Where did these clothes come from?" she asked.

"I asked Pegg to bring down a trunk from the attic," he said. "They belonged to my wife."

Reggie froze, staring down at the dress which, aside from being a trifle too long, fit her perfectly. How could Carlisle bear to see her in his wife's clothes? Then she realized it was the surest way of reminding him of who she was, and why he had married her.

Reggie felt sick. Their courtship, during which she had believed she was so cleverly testing Carlisle for flaws, had merely been a game to him, with the winner long since decided. She had just collected another bit of proof that Carlisle had married her for only one reason. And it was the wrong one.

When Reggie came out from behind the screen, Carlisle was already dressed in trousers and boots and was pulling on a shirt. She crossed to the wing chair near the fire and sat down, ignoring him. She stared into the fire, wondering how she could ever hope to unscramble the mess she had made of her life.

Carlisle startled her by speaking directly over her shoulder. "You were telling me what you did to get those stripes."

She continued staring into the fire. "Miss Tolemeister objected to a prank I had played and wanted me to admit

I was a bad child. I refused. She applied the rod to convince me of the error of my ways. It infuriated her that she could not make me cry."

His hands caressed her shoulders. "And yet I managed to provoke a tear the first time I met you."

"I . . . you . . ."

"Go on, my dear," he said.

"There is not much more to tell. At long last, the most wonderful and kind lady, Miss Eliza Sheringham, became our governess and then my aunt, when she married my uncle Marcus. That was the end of any beatings by stern governesses for misbehavior. While my father was in Scotland, he met his future wife, Lady Katherine MacKinnon."

"And me," Carlisle interjected.

Reggie rose and turned to face him. "I know you have suffered greatly as a result of being transported," she said. "But can you not leave the past where it belongs? Can we not go on from here?"

She was close enough to feel the tension in his body, to see the way the muscles in his jaw jerked as he ground his teeth. For a moment she thought he would refuse to speak. At last he said, "Your father humiliated me. He had me treated like a common felon!"

Reggie was horrified by the venom in Carlisle's voice and took a step back. "He must have had some evidence—"

"None besides his word! And that of Cedric Ambleside."

She reached out a careful hand, as she would to appease a snarling dog. "I think it is time you found this villain, Mr. Ambleside," Reggie said, crossing to Clay. "It seems he is more responsible for what happened to you than my father. I'll help you. We'll make him tell the truth, and—"

"That is not enough. Ambleside must die."

"You cannot kill the man," Reggie said. "That would make you a murderer!"

"That is justice, not murder."

"What kind of monster have I married?"

"The Sea Dragon, my dear," Carlisle said, bowing to her. "Terror of the Seven Seas, savage plunderer, vicious pirate, convicted criminal . . . courtesy of your very own papa."

Reggie flushed. "Anyone can make a mistake."

"Not all of them have such deadly consequences."

Reggie lifted her eyes to meet Carlisle's fierce, unrelenting gaze. "Can you not find it in your heart to forgive him? For my sake?"

"No."

She swallowed over the sudden knot in her throat. "Very well. If you will not relent, I must resort to drastic measures."

"Meaning?" Carlisle asked.

She took a step back. "I will not willingly lie with you again, my lord. Not until you have forgiven my father."

Carlisle's eyes narrowed. "Don't threaten me, my dear."

" 'Tis no threat." Reggie balled her hands into fists to keep Carlisle from seeing that they were shaking. "You can, of course, take me by force. You may even manage to seduce me." He had already proved he could. "But I will hate you for it."

"You are my wife. You must obey me."

"I am yours to command, my lord. Except in bed."

"Bloody hell, woman. You're my wife!"

"When you're ready to treat me as a beloved help-mate, when you're willing to make my family—all of my family—your own, then we may address the subject again. Until then, I will not couple with you again."

Clay stared at his wife, knowing that if a string of severe London governesses had failed to break her spirit, he was unlikely to succeed. "Are you coming down to supper," he asked.

"I'm not hungry."

He looked at Reggie's wan features and realized she was exhausted. The stubborn chit was probably starving as well, but he was in no mood to cajole her. A night without supper would do her no lasting harm. And having her at the supper table was sure to interfere with his own digestion. He might have found the chit's defiance exhilarating, if it were not equally exasperating.

"Good night, wife," he said, as he left the bedroom. "I trust you will sleep well. Alone."

"I will!" she retorted.

He opened his mouth to reply, but decided it was entirely acceptable to give her the final word, so long as the final action was his. He grabbed the candle from the bedside table to light his way downstairs and yanked the door closed behind him.

Which was when he realized he had just denied himself a place in the only bed in the house.

Clay searched the rest of the upstairs bedrooms to see whether there might be some other place to lay his head. But the wooden bedframes possessed no mattresses, nor were there chairs in any of the rooms that he might draw together for a makeshift bed.

He stomped down the stairs, furious with Reggie for denying him. Even more furious with himself for not taking what was his due.

"Threw ye out, did she, lad?"

Pegg stood at the bottom of the stairs, a lantern in one hand, a covered tray in the other, and a disgustingly smug grin on his face.

"Stubble it, Pegg. I am in no mood for your wit."

Pegg headed up the stairs.

"Where are you going?" Clay demanded.

"I have a wee bit of a supper here for yer wife. There's a plate for ye in the library, if the rats ha'na gotten to it. Maybe ye can make up a bed in there."

Clay didn't question how Pegg knew his wife wasn't coming down to supper, or that he wasn't sleeping upstairs. He simply turned and stalked down the hall toward the one room he knew had a chair and a fire and food.

The library smelled even mustier than Clay remembered. Many of the leather bookbindings were moldy. His father's elegant mahogany secretaire had survived by virtue of being in a corner away from the windows that framed the French doors leading out into the rose garden. An armed wing chair appeared to be in good

enough condition to provide comfort. Clay picked it up
and moved it in front of the fire, then found a wooden
stool that had been used to reach books on the upper
shelves, and hauled it over to provide a footrest.

He found the plate of food on the secretaire and discovered a meat pasty and some cheese beneath the cloth
cover. He looked for something to drink and saw that
Pegg had provided a bottle of port and a chipped crystal
goblet. He carried everything over to the chair in front of
the fire, where it was warmer, and sat down to eat with
his food in his lap, the goblet and bottle of port on the
floor beside him.

He practically swallowed the meat pasty whole and
had devoured the cheese as well before Pegg returned.
He was still hungry, but loath to ask Pegg to wait on
him—since the older man looked as tired as Reggie—
and reluctant to leave the warmth of the fire to wait on
himself.

"Have you eaten?" he asked Pegg.

"I have."

"Would you like some port?" he asked, offering the
bottle.

Pegg shook his head.

"Then pull up a bed," Clay said.

Pegg shoved a small sofa over next to Clay's wing
chair, then took several books from one of the shelves
and put them under the corner of the sofa where a leg
was missing, until he had it leveled out. He stretched out
with his head cushioned at one end of the sofa and his
legs below the knee hanging off the other end.

Shortly, both men were settled down before the fire.

But even that did not provide enough warmth to counter the cold sea wind that whistled noisily through the broken windowpanes.

"It's damned cold in here," Clay grumbled.

"We've endured worse," Pegg said.

"Not when there's a blanket to be had." Clay jumped up and crossed to the windows, where he tore down a pair of moth-eaten drapes. He gave half to Pegg and snuggled down under the rest of the heavy velvet himself.

Clay stared into the fire for a long time without speaking. At last he said, "I hadn't counted on liking her."

"Mmm," Pegg said.

"She's refusing me, you know. Threatened to fight me if I tried to have her. Expects me to make peace with Blackthorne. To forgive him. Little chance of that!"

"Mmm," Pegg said.

"I have no doubt she will try to see her father, even though I have forbidden it."

"Mmm," Pegg said.

"If she does, I will be forced to punish her."

Pegg said nothing.

"She's been beaten before. Did you know that?"

Pegg said nothing.

"I don't think she will break, Pegg. I am not even sure she will bend. What am I going to do with her?"

Clay glanced at Pegg and saw that his eyes were closed. A soft, ragged snore confirmed that he was asleep. Clay reached out to adjust the moth-eaten velvet over Pegg's remaining foot.

He had not really expected Pegg to provide him with a

solution to his dilemma. He was almost glad his friend was not awake to witness his confusion. In all these years Clay had never wavered in his determination to ruin Blackthorne's life. And yet now, when his goal was in sight, a rebellious young woman was threatening to turn his carefully laid plans upside down.

"I cannot forgive him," Clay murmured. "I will have my vengeance."

And if she is lost to you because of it?

Then she is lost.

You will be alone again. Forever. Is that what you want?

Clay knew what it felt like to be hollow inside, to be completely disconnected from everyone and everything one had ever held dear. He had come back to Scotland, to this house where it had all begun, in order to keep the memories of everything that had happened fresh in his mind. While he had been suffering, the duke had continued with his life, raising his children, loving his wife.

He was entitled to retribution.

Clay put a hand to his chest, feeling the ache there. The pain of all he had lost was a shadow that haunted him always, though he had buried it deep in order to survive. He thought of the woman he had loved. The child who had been lost to him. He remembered the plans he had made after his brother's death to restore Castle Carlisle. Anything had seemed possible.

Reggie had made him want it all again. Made him begin to dream again.

But twelve years later, the innocent fool who had believed in the goodness of his fellow man was gone. What remained was a ruthless devil who demanded his due. And no angel, however tempting, was going to sway him from his course.

Chapter 14

AFTER A NIGHT SPENT IN A WING CHAIR with a moth-eaten drape for warmth, his legs stretched out on a footstool that barely served to keep him safe from marauding rats, Clay had woken the next morning in a foul mood.

Sometime during the night he had decided it would be better to have Reggie's family come to visit her, rather than going to Blackthorne Hall. That was the only way to be sure she did not see her father. He was certain she would object, but in his present temper, he would have welcomed a fight with his wife.

In the end, the weather proved a friend to both of them. It had begun to rain during the night, a gentle Highland mist. By morning the mist had become a torrent of wetness that left the sky blackened and turned the roads into mudholes that made any sojourn, either on horseback on in a carriage, impossible. For three days the rain poured as an icy north wind lashed at the castle.

It should have been simple for Clay to avoid his wife.

Any sane woman would have remained tucked up warm and cozy in her bed. Reggie was a whirlwind of energy. She insisted on clearing everything from the upstairs rooms and scrubbing down the floors. She asked him which pieces of furniture he wanted to save and which should be relegated to the attic or given away. She tore down every drapery in the house, making it obvious that the windows must be next in line for repair.

Apparently, word had passed through the neighborhood that the Earl of Carlisle had returned, and those seeking to become footmen and underfootmen and maids-of-all-work arrived on foot despite the deluge. Carlisle relegated the hiring to his wife, until he realized that she had employed four footmen when two could have done the job, three maids-of-all-work when one would have sufficed, and even a tweeny, when they needed none at all.

When he asked for an explanation, she replied, "It is only a temporary measure, my lord, while we repair the house. The more helping hands, the more quickly the labor proceeds."

It had sounded perfectly logical, though he suspected it might be difficult for her to decide which servants to let go when the time came. And then she gave herself away.

"Betty's mother is sick with consumption, and I have promised her enough work to pay the doctor. George's wife is expecting their tenth child, but I have told him not to worry about being able to feed them all. Mercy is in the family way—oh, that is a secret—and until she can persuade her John to make an honest woman of her she must have a place, don't you agree? Simms is a little hard of hearing, but he looks the part of a butler, and I am sure he will manage. Terrence's face and hands were badly scarred by a fire, but he feels sure he can deal with—"

"Did you turn anyone away?" he interrupted.

She fiddled with her apron string—when was the last time anyone had seen a Countess of Carlisle in an apron, he wondered?—before she lifted her chin and said, "'Tis common knowledge you possess a fortune. If the little we pay our servants is too great a burden, I will gladly make up the difference from my own funds—as soon as your friend Mr. Kenworthy works out the amount of my quarterly allowance."

Clay was torn between laughing out loud and shaking her silly. "Just make sure you leave room enough in the house for us to walk the halls," he said.

She smiled at him and said, "Thank you, Clay."

He had stood there long after she was gone, wondering how she had managed to talk him into anything so foolish as an excess of servants—and make him feel good about it in the bargain.

Worn Turkish rugs showed up on the wooden floors upstairs. A pianoforte appeared in the corner of the drawing room, though a single keystroke revealed it was in sad want of tuning. An ormolu clock suddenly graced the mantel in the library, attractive but useless, since it did not keep the correct time. And a beautiful but chipped Sèvres vase now sat on a new-found half-table across from the door as one entered the castle.

Even though he spent most of his time in the library,

working on the estate books at his father's secretaire, Clay could not help but note the improvement. "You have found a few things to brighten up the drabness," he said at the supper table that evening.

"I have," she said.

She did not offer him any explanation of where she had found her prizes, and he would not give her the satisfaction of admitting his curiosity by asking.

On the second day of rain, a sleigh bed appeared in the bedroom that connected to the one in which Reggie slept. Clay wondered if the appearance of the bed was some sort of signal that Reggie had rescinded her pledge to keep him at arm's length. But when he checked that evening, the door between the two rooms was locked.

Clay arrived at breakfast on the third day of rain to discover an enormous epergne in the center of the dining room table filled with spiky purple blooms from the only flower growing near the castle—the thorny Scottish thistle. He stopped and stared. Cherubs holding trumpets were etched into the polished silver. It was the same epergne his mother had always filled with roses. He had believed it had been sold to pay his debts before he was transported, along with everything else of significant value.

"Where did you find that?" he asked, his voice husky with emotion.

"Wrapped in rags and hidden in a corner of the attic," Reggie replied. "Is it the one you remember?"

Unable to speak, Carlisle nodded.

"I am glad you have at least one valued memory restored," Reggie said.

"This makes me wonder what else might be up there," Carlisle murmured.

"It is a veritable treasure trove, my lord."

Carlisle lifted a disbelieving brow.

"I don't mean there is anything of true value. At least, none that I have found so far except the epergne. But there are a great many furnishings and trunks and portraits. Since the attic is entirely enclosed, with only a tiny opening at either end for ventilation, everything has been marvelously preserved. There is one particular trunk I think you might want to explore."

The last thing Clay wanted was to be in an enclosed space with his wife, who was looking more desirable every day he was denied her bed. He suspected, from the way she kept her distance, that she felt the same tension in his presence that he felt in hers. "Is it really necessary for me to be there with you?"

"I would appreciate having your opinion," she said.

Their eyes met, and she quickly looked away. Yes. She felt it, too. "Very well," he said. "I—"

He was interrupted by the nearly deaf butler, Simms, who entered the dining room, came to rigid attention, and shouted, "She's hanging, milady. In the library."

Clay leapt to his feet. "Who's hanging?"

"Banging? Yes, milord. A great deal of it, trying to get her up there," Simms shouted.

"Bloody hell! I said, who's *hanging*—" Clay cut himself off. By the time he got a word of sense from the senile old man, whoever was hanging in the library would be dead. He raced from the dining room and sprinted down the hall to the library, his coattails flying, leaving stunned and slack-jawed servants in his wake.

"Clay! Wait!" Reggie cried as she ran after him.

Clay slammed open the library door and stood stunned at what he found. A grotesque-faced man—the servant who had been scarred by fire—was balanced on a ladder near the fireplace. But there was no noose around his neck. Nor was there anyone else in the room in imminent peril.

"What the devil are you doing up there?" Clay demanded, his heart still hammering in his chest.

"Hanging the lady's portrait," the man replied in a painfully raspy voice. The burned man leaned away, and for the first time, Clay saw the gold-framed painting beyond the ladder.

"I found it in the attic," Reggie said as she stepped into the room beside him. "One of the maids said it was your mother. I thought you might like to have it hung in here. I'm sorry if Simms—"

"I had forgotten how beautiful she was," he said, staring at the painting.

The woman in the portrait had large, dark eyes and black hair that she had obviously passed on to her son. It was equally clear that Clay could only have inherited his sharp nose and square chin from his father.

The scarred man tipped the portrait one more time, until it was precisely square with the ceiling, then made his way awkwardly down the ladder.

"Thank you, Terrence," Reggie said. "You can come back later to remove the ladder."

"Very well, milady," Terrence said in his raspy voice.

Clay struggled not to wince when the disfigured servant turned to make his bow. He knew from his experiences with fire as a pirate that Terrence was lucky to have survived such severe burns, but he did not envy the man a lifetime of horrified looks and hidden revulsion.

Once the servant was gone, Reggie said, "I found a portrait of you and your brother as well. Is there someplace you would like me to hang it?"

"Hang it anywhere you like," he said. He could not afford to care. This was not a home. It was a hovel.

He glanced around the library and realized the description no longer fit. The leather books had all been wiped with a clove-scented oil to kill the mildew. The fireplace was cleaned of soot, and a new leg had been fashioned for the sofa. The mahogany secretaire had been polished to a glossy shine, and a selection of his father's pipes stood in a wooden stand on one corner, while an inkwell and quill pen occupied the other.

He could almost imagine himself sitting there, quill in hand, the French doors open wide, the smell of his pipe smoke at war with the delicious scent of roses wafting inside.

Something was missing from the picture, and his imagination conjured the sound of children laughing. On the lawn beyond the rose garden he could almost see Reggie cavorting with twin, black-headed boys.

"Shall we return to the dining room and finish our breakfasts?" Reggie asked.

Clay was shocked out of his reverie. To accept the

fantasy was to deny the pain of the past. He would never live in this house. And any child he and Reggie had together would not know his mother.

"I'm not hungry," he said brusquely.

"Shall we go up to the attic, then?"

"You go," Clay said. "I will meet you later." He was no longer so anxious to unearth the memories of the past. They were far more poignant, more powerful, than he had ever imagined. "I have some estate business that must be handled first."

She hesitated, started to say something, then stopped herself, before she finally turned and left him alone.

Clay crossed to close the library door behind her, but paused when he encountered the burned man waiting just outside the door.

"May I collect the ladder, milord?" he rasped.

Clay realized it would only take a moment and stepped back to allow the scarred servant to enter. The ladder was tall enough to be awkward for one man to handle alone, and Clay reached out to help angle it from a vertical to a horizontal position.

"Thank you, milord," Terrence said. "Your mother would be proud to see the improvements you are making to the castle."

Clay started. "You knew my mother?" Clay believed he would have remembered a servant as scarred as this one was.

"It was a long time ago, and my circumstances were not what they are now."

Clay wondered what disaster had befallen the man. He started to ask, but realized it was none of his business. "Can you manage?" he asked as Terrence headed for the door, ladder in hand.

"Yes, thank you, milord," the servant said as he carried the ladder out the door and headed down the hall.

Clay sat at his desk and tried to work, but his gaze kept returning to the portrait of his mother over the fireplace. He almost believed he could smell the lavender water she had used. He could hear her burbling laughter as his father teased her about the youthful bows she insisted on wearing in her hair.

What else from his past life was left in the attic? he wondered. A sudden, urgent curiosity propelled Clay from the room and up the stairs to the attic. The cramped space was frigidly cold, and the rain drummed loudly on the slate roof, drowning out the rest of the world.

He was surprised to find Reggie alone, bent over an open trunk, her hair bound in a scarf like the most menial servant, her long-sleeved gray wool dress covered with an apron that gave evidence of the amount of dirt she had encountered that morning.

"We have an army of servants," he said. "Where are they?"

She jerked upright, her hand to her heart. "You frightened me, my lord."

He weaved his way over to her through a maze of boxes, trunks, and furniture. "You haven't answered my question."

"I imagine they are having their luncheon."

He raised a brow. "And you are not hungry?"

She smiled. "I was enjoying myself too much to quit."

"What has you so intrigued that you're willing to give up Cook's blackberry tarts?"

She closed the trunk lid and stepped in front of it. "Nothing that would interest you."

"Let me see."

Reluctantly, she stepped aside.

He lifted the lid and barely suppressed a gasp. The trunk was filled with baby clothes, with rattles and teething rings and toys. He shot her a questioning look. To beget children, they would have to couple. Was she ready to ask him to come back to her bed? He was willing, his eyes said, whenever she was.

He could feel her need as palpably as his own, but he felt certain that if he reached for her now, she would keep her promise to resist him. So instead, he bent down and picked up an embroidered, lace-trimmed satin gown so tiny across the shoulders that it was barely wider than his hand. "Are babies really this small?" he asked.

"My niece was," she replied. "Though Lily has grown so big in three years, it is hard to remember she was ever so tiny." She took the gown from him and held it by the shoulders. "I believe this was your christening gown."

"*I* wore that?" Clay asked incredulously.

Reggie laughed as she held the gown up close to his chest, measuring the difference in the child and the man. "You have grown a little since then, my lord."

Their eyes caught again. And held again.

"I want a child, Clay," she said at last. "But you can see it would be wrong to bring any child into a household where its parents were at war."

"My war is not with you." He tugged the christening gown from her hand and dropped it back into the open trunk. Then his arm circled her waist, and he drew her close and lowered his mouth to cover hers.

He had not expected to feel so much. He had not expected to need so much. He had not expected her hands to clasp so ardently around his neck or her body to cleave so closely to his own. His arms tightened around her, holding her as though he would never let her go.

He tasted the flesh beneath her ear, then bit her earlobe. She made a coarse sound deep in her throat that caused his body to draw up tight in anticipation. He wanted to feel the shape of her and slid his hands from her waist up along her ribs to cup her soft breasts, which filled his palms to overflowing.

He felt her stiffen, felt the beginning of resistance, and whispered, "Let me love you, Reggie."

She took a gasping breath as his thumbs found her nipples beneath the wool. Her hands grasped his wrists, but she did not push him away. Her blue eyes looked dazed as she searched his face for further explanation of the words he had uttered.

He did not give her time to think. His mouth found hers, and he kissed her deeply, hungrily, thoroughly. There was not a part of her mouth he did not taste with his tongue. He nibbled at her lips until they were swollen and then sought other pleasures, sucking hard on the flesh at her throat in response to the raw, feral sounds she made to urge him on.

Her dress had a high, square neck that left only the base of her throat exposed to his kisses. It was not enough. He tore his hands from her breasts in order to unbutton the dress enough to pull it down off her shoulders, leaving her wearing a simple cotton chemise.

He paused to stare at what he had. Her breasts were full and high, and the dark rose nipples had visibly peaked beneath the fabric. He lowered his head and took her nipple into his mouth, sucking on it through the cotton.

He felt her fingernails digging into his shoulders, felt his body clench and swell and harden at the sound of her moans as she clutched at his hair and kissed any part of him she could reach. At last she tugged his head away and sought out his mouth with her own. His tongue thrust deep, and he pressed his hips against hers, mimicking the action of his mouth.

Something cold and hard hit the bridge of his nose.

He jerked backward and reached up to see what it was. His fingers came away wet.

"Clay . . . What . . . ?" Reggie murmured breathlessly.

A drop of icy rainwater plopped on her cheek. It might as well have been a bucket of cold water. Her eyes shot open in alarm, and she took a startled step backward.

She stared at him as though he were a perfect stranger, and he had no doubt he had the look of someone dark and dangerous. Her eyes followed the direction of his, until she focused on the wet stain where he had suckled her, which revealed her rosy nipple through the white cotton.

He watched the myriad emotions—need, shame, then

need again, before shame won out, and she grabbed frantically at her dress and pulled it up over her shoulders, in a vain attempt to recover some shred of composure. She scrabbled awkwardly to redo the buttons, but she was too distressed to make much headway.

He did not ask permission to help her. She would not have given it. He merely grasped her shoulders, turned her around, and finished buttoning the dress.

When he dropped his hands, she turned slowly to face him, her color high, her eyes wary. "You should not expect a repeat of this lapse," she said, her chin angled so high he thought it might strain her neck. "I was caught off guard by—"

A plop of rainwater landed on her cheek, cutting her off.

Clay looked up. Another drop hit him right in the eye. He swore as the drop became a deluge. Squinting at Reggie, he asked, "Have you got a bucket?"

"What?"

"A bucket? Do you have one?"

She seemed to welcome the chance to put some distance between them. "I saw one here somewhere." She hurried from trunk to trunk lifting lids and slamming them with a bang, before she pulled out what looked like a child's tin sand pail, painted with a picture of a blue and yellow sailboat.

"That's it?" he asked when she handed it to him.

"You're welcome to look for yourself, if you think you can do better," she retorted.

Clay decided he was better off accepting what she'd brought him. He gauged where the drips were landing and set the pail on the wooden floor. Each drop made a tinny sound as it hit the metal pail, but he could see the floor was still getting wet. He leaned over to adjust the pail slightly. When he stood again, he realized Reggie had stepped back completely beyond his reach.

"Am I so fearsome?" he asked with a smile he hoped would both allay her suspicion and cloak his disappointment.

A breath shuddered out of her, and he knew she had not yet recovered from their recent encounter any more than he had. His blood still thrummed. His heart still hammered. He still wanted her more fiercely than it was decent for a husband to want his own wife.

But despite her arousal, he could see in her eyes that she no longer welcomed his advances. If he pursued her further, he would have to force her. And this time she would fight, despite the fact she was obviously still as choked with desire as he was. If he chose to take her now, he might regret it forever.

"What happened was a mistake in judgment," she said, inserting reason where emotion was too dangerous to indulge. And then reason fell away, and she pleaded, "I need more time, Clay. We need more time."

"For what?" he said.

"To find our way."

"I chose my direction a long time ago," he said. His course was set, and there was no turning aside. Not for anyone. Most especially not for her. "I won't change my mind, Reggie. And I won't back down."

Her eyes looked sad as she replied, "Neither will I."

Chapter 15

BECKY STOOD AT THE OPEN DOOR TO THE library at Blackthorne Hall, quiet as a mouse, and peered inside. Her father sat hunched over his desk, studying the document before him. His head rested on his palm, while he pensively brushed the feather of a quill pen against his pursed lips.

She could remember a time when Papa would have sat ramrod straight in his chair, when he would have greeted her with cold eyes and a stern voice, when something as human as a hug would have been unthinkable. Thankfully, those days were long past. Papa had come to Scotland and found her stepmother Kitt, and Kitt had taught him how to love.

"Papa?"

He sat up and looked at her with surprise. "Becky! What are you doing here?"

Before she could answer, he had crossed the entire distance of the room and grabbed her up in a tight hug. "I've missed you," he said in a gruff voice.

She clung to his neck, feeling the sting in her nose, feeling the tears pool in her eyes until they blurred, and she could no longer see the wall of books behind him. When he tried to step back, she held on, until she felt his arms once more tighten around her.

"What's wrong?" he murmured in her ear. "How can I help?"

"Oh, Papa," she wailed. "Oh, Papa, everything is wrong. And no one can help!"

A moment later she found herself sitting in her father's lap like a child, her hands still grasping his neck, her face hidden against his throat. He had retreated to the sofa near the fireplace and sat holding her, saying nothing, waiting for her to speak.

Becky was grateful for the warmth of both the fire and her father's greeting in light of the chill inside and out that had plagued her the whole trip north. She could hear the steady beat of her father's heart, or thought she could. "I have tried to be as strong as Reggie, Papa, truly I have," she said. "But I am not."

"No one expects you to be like Reggie," her father said. "You have your own strengths, Becky."

Becky lifted her tear-streaked face from his shoulder and said, "Name one, Papa."

"There is not a gentler soul in all of England and Scotland combined," her father replied. "You have the patience of Job, and the cleverness of Machiavelli, without any of his cruel intent."

"What good is all of that, when I am a coward?" Becky asked.

Her father tenderly brushed a stray curl from her forehead. "You don't lack courage, my girl. It took courage to come here and confess you are in trouble. Will you tell me what is wrong?"

Becky laughed through her tears. "I love you, Papa. No one but you could make my hasty retreat from London, like some hound with its tail between its legs, sound like a courageous act."

"You still have not told me what calamity has sent you haring off to Scotland."

She could feel the tension in his legs beneath her thighs, in his shoulders beneath her hands. More difficult to bear were the questions she saw in his worried gray eyes. Her throat constricted, making it difficult to swallow, making it impossible to speak. Stifling a sob, she laid her head back on his shoulder, clasped her hands around his neck, and begged, silently, for a little more time. Soon enough she would have to tell him the awful truth.

Though she was ultimately grateful to be free of an oppressive marriage, Penrith's rejection had left her feeling savaged, like some poor beast torn to pieces by hungry winter wolves. And because she was essentially a peaceful person, she had no experience dealing with the suddenly unbottled rage that threatened to erupt and spill over onto everyone around her.

But her father had never been a patient man. "Are you ill?" he asked, when she did not speak.

She shook her head.

"Is something wrong with Lily?"

"No," she croaked.

"Has some disaster befallen Penrith?"

"No. But . . ."

"There are problems with your marriage," he deduced.

"Oh, yes. It is . . . There are . . . Penrith has . . ." She felt his palm on the back of her head, pressing her cheek against his shoulder, while his other hand made soothing circles on her back.

"Marriage is never easy," he began. "When two people marry they have differing ideas on many subjects."

Becky had desperately needed the nonjudgmental comfort her father had offered. But she realized as he began to speak about the importance of compromise in marriage, that in allowing herself to be comforted as a child, she had given him the impression that she had come to him seeking a parent's wise counsel.

In fact, Becky had made up her mind during the trip north what she was going to do with her life. And advice on how to appease her husband was useless, when her marriage was, even as her father spoke, being annulled.

She let go of him and sat up. "Please let me up, Papa."

He released her and helped her to stand, then rose and crossed to the mantel before turning to face her. Waiting.

Becky took a deep breath and said, "Penrith has left me." She put up a palm to hold her father in place, but that did not keep his hands from balling into fists, nor his lips from flattening into a knifelike line. "He has left the country, Papa. But before he did, he signed all the legal documents necessary to annul our marriage."

"We can have that stopped," he said in a deadly voice.

"No!" And then more calmly, "No, Papa. William was not everything a husband should be. I am glad to be free."

Emotions skidded across his face like a fallen kite bumping along the ground, struggling to catch the wind and soar effortless once more in the sky. She saw sorrow and pain and fury and frustration, before he regained his poise.

"You will stay with us," he said.

It was couched as an order, and once again Becky had to remind him—and herself—that she was no longer a child. "I would like to stay with you until the annulment is final," she said. "Meanwhile, I plan to look for a manor house nearby where Lily and I can live."

"There is no need—"

She met his gaze unflinchingly and said, "My mind is made up, Papa."

He smiled, though she could see the effort it took. "Did I mention you can be as tenacious as a bulldog when your heart is set on something?"

She felt the tension ease out of her shoulders. She had expected more resistance from him than she had gotten. Then she realized he was not the greater obstacle. She would still need to convince Kitt that she and Lily would be happier living in a home of their own. She knew Reggie would approve.

"Have you spoken with Reggie, Papa?" she asked.

"Not yet," he said, his eyes bleak. "But now that you are here, perhaps a visit can be arranged."

"Were you very angry when you found out she had married Carlisle in such haste?"

"My only concern is for Reggie's happiness," he said quietly. "And yours."

Becky made herself smile. "Then you do not need to worry about me, Papa. For I am determined to be happy from now on."

"I thought you were still upstairs, ridding yourself of all that dust from your journey."

Becky pivoted to find her stepmother in the doorway.

"Look who I found," Kitt said with a smile, as she linked her arm with Michael O'Malley's and stepped into the room. "Mick just returned from London himself."

Becky was not ready to see Mick. Not ready to speak to him about what had happened to make of her once more an unattached female. But her gaze was caught by the blanket-wrapped bundle in Mick's arms, and she was drawn helplessly, inexorably across the room to his side.

Without a word being spoken between them, Mick turned the bundle toward her and peeled the blanket away to reveal the tiny, perfect features of her baby sister.

"Oh. She is so beautiful," Becky said.

"We think so," her father said.

The baby started to fuss, but rather than hand Meg to her mother, as another man might have done, Mick rocked the tiny child in his arms and made cooing sounds and even sang a few verses of an Irish lullaby in a beautiful tenor voice.

Becky was suddenly stuck with the realization—as

though it were another physical blow—that she had never once seen William hold Lily in his arms as Mick was holding Meg. It was as though she were seeing in that instant all that had been wrong in her marriage by observing a moment of how life could have—should have—been.

"Excuse me, please," she said, brushing past Mick and heading for the door. "I am feeling a bit hagged after my journey. I will see you all at supper."

She caught a glimpse of the frown on Kitt's face at her abrupt departure and knew she had not seen the last of her stepmother. But at least she could postpone the moment when she must confront Mick.

Becky was afraid of what Mick might ask of her when he discovered she was free. She did not want to hurt him, but she could not marry him. What if he did not want her except as a wife? What would she do then? Becky felt a sharp ache in her chest, a sense of such total and utter devastation at the thought of losing his friendship that she almost cried out with the pain of it. Oh, God, she had not realized how deep her feelings for him ran.

But marriage was impossible. Impossible.

"Are you sure Becky is all right?" she heard her stepmother ask.

"Penrith has had the marriage annulled and fled the country," her father replied.

Becky glanced over her shoulder, unable to resist looking back to see Mick's response to her father's announcement. Their gazes locked, and she could feel everything he was feeling, as though they were connected by some invisible thread.

Pain. Sorrow. Concern. Distress.
Those she had expected.
Need. Hunger. And . . .
She felt her heart begin to thunder. Oh, God. It was there.
Unreserved. Unabashed. Unrepentant. Love.
Becky whirled abruptly and fled up the stairs.

Mick wondered if he should have let Becky see what he was feeling. He knew he had frightened her. That was why she had run away. But the time for pretending was over. He loved her. He wanted her. And he intended to pursue her until she either rejected him in words that could not be misunderstood or agreed to become his wife.

Mick watched as Kitt crossed the room and walked right into Blackthorne's embrace. He knew the momentous problems the duke and his wife had overcome to find happiness together, so he knew that love could survive great tribulations. But Mick might have gone too far to be forgiven.

It had been done with the best intentions, but he had rearranged Becky's life without her knowledge or consent. The agreement Penrith had signed, which gave him a large sum Mick had borrowed in expectation of his inheritance, had required Penrith not to divulge Mick's part in convincing him to give up his wife. Mick wanted to choose the right time and place to tell Becky what he had done.

The balance of Mick's fortune would go to Penrith

when Mick finally inherited it from his grandfather. He knew most people would think him crazy for the decision he had made. But he would choose a lifetime with Becky over a fortune every time.

Mick had not demanded that Penrith leave the country, but he was not sorry the man had gone. He wondered how Becky would react when she finally learned who was really responsible for the end of her marriage. He was worried that if he told her how he had traded his fortune for her freedom—and assuming she felt grateful rather than enraged by his efforts on her behalf—she might agree to marry him out of a sense of obligation. He did not want that. Mick wanted her to come to him out of love. He wanted the duke's daughter to agree to marry a whore's bastard son.

It might not be fair of him to want Becky to give up everything for love, but it was the only way he could be sure she was marrying him for the right reasons. He wanted her to commit herself to Mick O'Malley, her father's steward, before she discovered he was really Michael Delaford, Earl of Stalbridge.

The title, of course, was deceptive, since he had signed away most of the wealth that went along with it. But he would still inherit several entailed properties, and he had kept the trust fund of five thousand a year from his mother's estate. If Becky married him, she would have to sacrifice many of the luxuries she now took for granted. But Mick hoped to make up to her in love whatever else she might lose in the bargain.

However necessary it was to continue deceiving Becky, Mick had decided it was equally necessary to tell her father the truth about his changed circumstances before he began to court her. It was the only honorable thing to do, considering everything he owed the duke.

And the sooner it was done, the better.

"I have some business to conduct with the duke," Mick said to Kitt. "And I think Meg needs your attention."

"Oh, dear," Kitt said. "Did she get you very wet?"

Mick held the baby away from his waistcoat, which was, in fact, a little damp. "It will dry," he said with a smile, as Kitt took the child from him.

"Will you be very long?" Kitt asked. "Should I hold supper?"

"This won't take long," Mick said. Although, if Blackthorne opposed the match, there would likely be one less at the table.

As Kitt left, Mick closed the door behind her.

The duke had already crossed back to his desk and picked up his pen.

Mick stood by the door, his heart in his throat. *My palms are as damp as Meg's bottom,* he thought wryly, as he wiped them on his trousers.

The duke glanced up from his ledger and said, "I wasn't sure we ought to plant wheat again this year, but it looks like you were right, as usual."

Mick stood frozen in place as Blackthorne continued his discourse on wheat, comparing the promise of this year's yield with figures in the ledger, as though that were the matter Mick had come to discuss.

Mick had never been shy in the duke's presence. In fact, he was one of the few persons who had been given the privilege of addressing Blackthorne by his Christian name. The honor had come as a result of his having done the duke a kind turn. It was the sort of story one told to children at bedtime, and Mick hoped someday to be able to tell it to his own.

A long time ago, he would begin, the Duke of Blackthorne was shipwrecked on the Scottish coast. His head was injured on the rocks and when he reached the shore he could not remember who he was. He wandered into the town of Mishnish, his face battered black and blue, and sought food and drink at the Ramshead Inn, where Mick was a serving boy.

The Scottish innkeeper refused to help the Englishman without being paid first. He had already turned the duke away without succor when Mick, a gangly boy wearing too-short trousers and too-large shoes, took pity on him and offered the stranger a mug of ale and an oatcake.

The landlord repaid Mick's generosity with a blow and the loss of his job. The stranger, who called himself Alex Wheaton and claimed to be one of the Quality, offered Mick work as his valet. Mick had accepted, even though he believed the stranger was dicked in the nob.

In the end, Alex Wheaton had turned out to be Alastair Wharton, sixth Duke of Blackthorne. Once the duke was himself again, he had insisted Mick continue calling him Alex. The duke had repaid Mick's kindness three-fold. By sending him to Oxford to be educated, by giving Mick's sister and brothers employment at Blackthorne Abbey, the duke's estate in Kent, and by employing Mick as steward at Blackthorne Hall, the duke's largest estate in Scotland.

Mick and Alex had become good friends over the years, and despite the duke's elevated station, he had always treated Mick as an equal. Even so, Mick wasn't sure what the duke was going to say when Mick told him he intended to marry his daughter.

"Is something troubling you, Mick?" the duke asked, noticing at last that he did not have Mick's attention.

"There is something I need to discuss with you," Mick said, forcing himself to approach the imposing Sheraton desk where the duke sat.

"If you need time to spend with Becky, take it," the duke said. "You've always been a good friend to her, and she could use one right now."

"Uh. I will, but—"

Blackthorne leaned back in his chair and brushed the feathered quill back and forth across his lips. "I still cannot believe Penrith abandoned her. If I had him here . . ." He sat forward and said, "Maybe you can think of some way to cheer her up. Take her riding, or for a picnic along the coast."

"I plan to spend as much time with her as I can," Mick said. "Courting her."

The feather stopped moving. The quill dropped to the desk. "Would you like to elaborate on that statement?"

Mick knew Alex Wharton well. So he knew the duke was agitated. And trying hard not to show it.

Mick could prove he was no longer a bastard. But he was still a whore's son. What if Blackthorne would not permit the match? Mick forced himself to speak before fear silenced him.

"My circumstances have changed, Alex. In the most unexpected way." The knot in Mick's throat made speaking painful. "I was recently contacted by a solicitor in London. It seems I am legitimate, after all. My mother was married to Thomas Delaford when she bore him a son named Michael. My late father was the eldest son of Harold Delaford, Marquess of Tenby."

Blackthorne hissed in a breath.

Mick made an elegant bow, as though greeting the duke for the first time. "Michael Delaford, Earl of Stalbridge, at your service, Your Grace." He felt constrained to add, "Though I am no longer a bastard, Alex, I am still a whore's son."

"What happened? Why did your mother—?" The duke interrupted himself and said, "Sit down, Mick. Make yourself comfortable while I hear the whole of this incredible tale of yours."

"It is a long story that reflects badly on my grandfather," Mick began as he settled into one of the leather chairs in front of the earl's desk. He told Alex how his grandfather had searched for years before finally locating him.

"I'm glad for you, Mick," Alex said. "Very glad. I suppose you're telling me this so I can find myself another steward."

Mick shook his head abruptly, then rose from his chair. He stood anxiously, like any other young English nobleman before the father of his chosen bride, and said, "I came to get permission to court Becky."

"I see," Blackthorne said. He eyed Mick speculatively. "How long have you loved her?"

Mick hesitated, then said, "Since the first moment I laid eyes on her."

Mick was watching Alex's face, so he saw the slight flicker of concern in his eyes, the tightening of his mouth. "Does Becky know how you feel?"

"I believe she does."

"Does she feel the same way?"

Mick's lips curved in a rueful smile. "I wish I knew. I am hoping to convince her we belong together."

The duke stood and crossed around his desk. For a moment Mick wasn't sure whether Alex intended to hit him or hug him. In the end, the duke extended his hand. "Good luck, Mick. You're going to need it."

"Then you don't oppose the match?" Mick said.

The duke laid an arm on Mick's shoulders, as though he were already his son-in-law. "I know she likes you as a friend. I'm equally certain you'll take good care of her. And now, of course, you can. Delaford has a fortune, and as his heir—"

"I won't inherit his fortune," Mick interrupted.

The duke's arm slid off Mick's shoulder, and he took a cautious step back. "Why not?"

"Carlisle managed to ruin Penrith financially. When the opportunity arose, I offered Penrith my inheritance in exchange for Becky's freedom."

The duke's features tightened. "Are you telling me that *you* encouraged Penrith to annul his marriage to my daughter? That *you* are the source of Becky's current misery?"

Mick swallowed hard. "He beat her. I could not bear it."

The duke was clearly incredulous. "*Beat* her? She said nothing—"

"How could she?" Mick replied heatedly. "He was her husband. He would never have let her take Lily if she left him, and she would never have left her daughter behind. She could not tell you, for fear you would challenge him."

"I would have sent him to hell, where he belongs!"

Mick laid a hand on the duke's arm. "He is gone from England. And Becky is free."

"That wife-beating brute should be punished," the duke ranted as he paced the breadth of the carpet. "I will find him wherever he has gone and make him suffer, as my daughter has been made to suffer."

"Then you become another Carlisle," Mick said. "Is that what you want?"

The duke paused near his desk, then slumped into the chair behind it. He shoved his fingers through his hair, leaving it on end. "At least you could have left him in penury," the duke muttered.

He suddenly looked up, focusing his gaze on Mick's face. "If you have signed over Tenby's fortune to Penrith, with what funds did you propose to set up housekeeping with my daughter?"

"I will inherit several entailed properties, a farm in particular, where I thought I might put my knowledge and experience to good use," Mick said. "And I still have a trust fund my mother left me—five thousand a year—to provide for necessities."

"You propose to make a farmer's wife of a duke's daughter?" Blackthorne asked in a quiet voice.

"She will want for nothing so long as I draw breath," Mick said. "And she will be greatly loved."

"She cannot—" The duke cut himself off. "She will not—" He cut himself off again and finally said, "What makes you think she will have you under those circumstances."

Mick smiled. "Oh, I don't intend to offer her even that much hope of a comfortable life."

The duke sat forward. "What?"

"I do not intend that Becky should know of my connection to the marquess at all."

"But why not, man?" Alex asked. "You cannot expect her to agree to marry a whore's penniless bastard son!"

"Oh, but I do."

The duke's brow furrowed.

"Don't you see, Alex? I cannot tell her the truth. If I explained what I've done, she might accept me out of some feeling of obligation. I want to know she's marrying me because she loves me and wants to make a life with me."

"Becky has never been the strong one," the duke cautioned. "She may never find the resolve to take such a risk. Especially since she knows I would never condone such a match."

Mick stood, braced his shoulders, and lifted his chin. "I believe Becky has more spirit than you think. But I suppose we will simply have to wait and see."

"Why not at least tell her I will allow the marriage?" the duke offered.

Mick shook his head. "She will expect—and rightly so—that your approval means an appropriate dowry to ease our life together. I don't want her to make that assumption. I want her to understand that she will be giving up everything if she chooses to marry me."

"Is that fair to her?" the duke asked. "If you love her, why are you forcing her to make such a choice?"

Mick met Alex's hard look with bleak eyes. "If she truly loves me, nothing else should—or will—matter."

"You belong in Bedlam," the duke muttered.

Mick shrugged. "Perhaps. But I want to know if she can learn to love the man she sees before her," he said, letting Alex see his hope that she might, and his fear that she might not. "Not my title. Not my fortune. *Me.*"

"If that was your intention all along, why did you tell me the truth?" the duke asked.

"Because I owe you too much to court your daughter without your permission. Do I have it?"

The duke hissed out a breath of air. He stood and walked the few steps that put him face-to-face with Mick, then held out his hand and said the words that Mick had been waiting to hear.

"If Becky will have you, she's yours, with my blessing."

Chapter 16

REGGIE WAS SO BUSY WITH WORK INSIDE the castle over the next two days, while she waited for the muddy roads to dry enough to make travel to Blackthorne Hall possible, that she never had a chance to start the work outside. However, she had a great deal of help, since she managed to hire two more maids, a groom, a falconer (she decided Carlisle would want gerfalcons once he realized he had a man to train them), a huntsman (whom she immediately sent out to find game), and a wizened gatekeeper named Cameron MacTavish.

Of course there was no gate for MacTavish to keep, since the outer stone walls that had once surrounded Castle Carlisle had long since crumbled. But Reggie had heard MacTavish tell such a glorious tale of jousting knights and their fair ladies at the kitchen table—where he had been offered a cup of tea, hot-from-the-oven butter biscuits, and a place to warm his bones—that she had begged him to stay and tell more stories.

"I canna stay without wor*rr*king for my hir*rr*e," the Scotsman said in his thick burr.

"What can you do?" Reggie asked.

"In days of old, when Scottish lair*rr*ds lived in these castles, I was a *gille-coise*," the old man said.

"What is that?" Reggie asked, not recognizing the Scottish word.

"A bodyguar*rr*d to the clan chief."

"I don't believe I could convince Lord Carlisle to accept a personal bodyguard," Reggie said hesitantly. Then she had come up with what she thought was a positively inspired alternative. "But you could guard the gate to his castle."

"The gate?" he said. "Ther*rr*e's no gate her*rr*e."

"Well, no," she conceded. "Castle Carlisle does not actually have a gate. But you could keep watch and make sure that all who live and work here are safe."

So Cam MacTavish had become *gille-coise*—though his title was gatekeeper—of Castle Carlisle.

Reggie was ever mindful of the fact she must make do with what was available for repairs, but she was equally determined that the castle should become a comfortable place to live. So she took unbroken windows from the third-floor nursery and used them to replace the broken panes in the second-story bedrooms. She made sure the rotten treads on the stairs were replaced with solid wood from the floor of the attic. And she cleaned. And cleaned. And cleaned.

She emptied every cupboard in the kitchen and scoured everything she found. She washed all the floors and walls and windows. She dusted every corner of the ceiling. She scrubbed the fireplaces free of soot. She stripped the draperies from all the windows, because they were uniformly faded, moth-eaten, and moldy. In any case, they were nothing but decaying decoration, since the dense growth of ivy allowed little sunlight inside.

Reggie wanted desperately to cut away the ivy from the windows and let in more light, but it made no sense to do so until she could replace the rest of the cracked windowpanes and find a way to restore the missing draperies. She would gladly have used her own money, but upon her marriage, all her funds had legally passed into Carlisle's control, and she had been unable to cajole him into releasing any to her.

"You will suffer nothing by it," she had argued, standing across from him, as he sat behind his desk in the library. "Since the money was never yours in the first place."

"It is mine now," he pointed out, yielding nothing.

"Do you plan to keep me destitute?" she demanded.

"Do you plan to keep me out of your bedroom?"

She had taken a step back, shocked at the turn the conversation had taken. "Are you suggesting you would *pay* for the privilege of sleeping with me?"

"That was not my intent, but now that you mention it—"

She had already whirled and started for the door when she heard his amused laughter. She stopped in her tracks and marched right back to him. "I do not find it in the least amusing that you would make a whore of me. All I asked for was enough of *my own money* to make a comfortable home for us. Only a dastard would—"

"Enough!" he roared, coming out of his chair, his palms slapping the desk in front of him with enough force to send papers flying. "I never asked you to make this a home. And you are the one who mentioned bartering yourself for draperies and furniture, not I! We are husband and wife, yet you lock your door against me at night. Bloody hell, woman, make up your mind. You want a wife's allowance. Are you willing to be a wife?"

Reggie had retreated without a word. Her bedroom door had remained locked, and she had made do with what she had. She had worked each day until there was no more light to see the dirt, pushing herself and every servant in the house to their limits.

By late afternoon of her sixth day at Castle Carlisle, Reggie was satisfied that she had done everything she could, with the few resources she had been given, to make it a comfortable place to live. However, so far as she had been able to determine, Carlisle would have been just as happy if she had left the castle teeming with cobwebs and vermin.

Reggie decided to give the servants the rest of the afternoon off as a reward for their unceasing labor and to give herself the afternoon off as well. Even God had rested after six days of labor. All day as she worked, she had been eyeing the distant pond that was half-hidden by white-trunked birch and rowan and elderberry trees, imagining how wonderful it would feel to immerse herself and wash away all the sweat and grime she had accumulated after a day spent dusting and scrubbing.

She waited until the sun was headed downward, depending on the dusk to hide her from prying eyes, before she grabbed a towel, a bar of scented soap, and some clean clothes and picked her way down the hill across the untended lawn to the pond. The surface of the water was smooth, and the sun reflected a perfect mirror image of the spoor-ridden ferns and graceful cat-o'-nine-tails that grew along the bank.

Reggie looked around to make certain she was alone, but the shadows were already growing among the trees, and it was difficult to see to the farthest reaches of the pond. It would have been wiser to survey the area completely, but she was in a hurry because, once the sun set, it would take with it what little warmth there was. Besides, she reasoned, if anyone had been in the pond, the currently unbroken surface would have been rippled by his presence.

Reggie said, *"Brrrr,"* as she dipped a toe into the pond, then laughed aloud with delight as she strode into the cold water. She was quickly immersed up to her waist and used the washcloth and soap she had brought along to clean herself briskly and thoroughly, humming one of the more ribald sea chanteys she had learned on her recent voyage to Scotland.

She washed her hair last, laying the washcloth over her shoulder while she worked. When she was done rinsing her hair, she squeezed out the cloth, wrapped the cake of soap up in it, and threw both soap and cloth onto the bank.

Once both her hands were free, Reggie dove underwater and swam for the sheer love of it, heading for the mound of large flat stones located in the center of the pond. When at last she came up for air, she realized she was not alone.

Carlisle was sitting atop the stones, his arm resting on one upraised knee, which coincidentally hid certain parts of his body. He was stark naked. His hair was still damp and slicked back from his face, and although his skin was mostly dry, here and there a pearl of water clung to him.

"Where did you come from?" she demanded angrily, treading water, unwilling to swim any closer, since she was equally naked. The ravenous look in his dark eyes left no doubt what he would like to do with her. To her. "How did you get there?" she snapped.

"I swam here," he replied with a wolfish smile.

Reggie realized that the large flat stone was shaped like a step. Carlisle must have been hidden from view on the lower level. "Why didn't you make your presence known sooner?"

He lifted a brow. "You must know the answer to that."

"How would you like it if I—" That line of reasoning would not work. He obviously did not care if she saw him bare-bottomed, since he was sitting naked before her.

Reggie had been keeping her eyes cast downward, trying *not* to see him, and suddenly realized that the only way he could know what it felt like to be scrutinized was to do the deed herself. She lifted her gaze and did a slow, thorough survey of his body, starting with his face—

meeting his eyes to let him know what she intended—and then moving downward.

His hand dangled off his knee, and she noticed how large it was, how long and narrow his fingers. She was spared a full view of his masculine endowments, but there was enough of a shadow for her to realize he was aroused.

So was she, by the time she had finished. Which was the last thing Reggie wanted to be, when she had no intention of satisfying either him or herself. So far Carlisle had not made a move toward her, but Reggie did not think it would take more than an eyelash flickered in invitation for him to join her in the water.

The lesson she had hoped to give him had miscarried miserably. She sought some other way she might punish him for his flagrant behavior and realized reprisal was within her grasp.

"Where are your clothes?" she asked, backpeddaling in the water, slowly but steadily putting more distance between them, hoping he would not notice.

He pointed toward shore, a short distance from where she had left her own. "There. On the bank."

While his gaze had been distracted, she had put even more distance between them. Then, before he could discern what she intended, Reggie turned and swam as fast as she could toward the bank. She expected Carlisle to come after her, but it took him an extra few seconds to realize her intent, unwind his body, and dive off the rock.

In that time, she reached the bank, pulled her dress

over her head, yanked on her half boots, and ran as fast as she could toward where he had left his clothing.

She discarded his trousers, shirt, and smalls, but grabbed up his shoes and stockings.

"Reggie, I do not find this amusing!" he shouted as he ran toward her along the slippery mud bank.

"Have a nice walk home through your manicured lawn, my lord," she said with a laugh as she raced for the castle.

"It is full of thistles!" he shouted. "And prickly weeds I cannot even name. And sharp stones!"

"I will make sure Pegg has some figwort waiting to salve your wounds," she called back.

She was grinning from ear to ear, running as she had not run since she was a child. In those long ago days, she had pretended to be a wild horse, leaping from green hillocks and galloping down grassy vales, Becky chasing after her with a noose made of knotted scarves, trying in vain to capture her. Reggie had forgotten what it felt like to be so free. She had forgotten the feel of the wind in her hair, the aching stitch in her side, the burning in her thighs as she pushed herself harder and faster.

A figure stepped out of the darkness, and she started in fear and dropped everything in her hands. She paused, ready to dart away again, lungs heaving, side aching, legs burning.

"My lady, are ye in dangerrr? What's wrrrong?"

Reggie managed a ragged, relieved laugh. "I'm fine, MacTavish. I'm only playing a trick on my husband." She huffed out a breath, then reached down to retrieve her clothes, managing to hold up one of Carlisle's Hessians. "He's walking back from the pond barefooted," she explained.

The wizened old man laughed. " 'Tis a good joke, my lady. Is he likely to be ver*rry* angr*rry* with ye?"

Reggie sensed the old man was ready to protect her, to be her *gille-coise,* if she had need of him. "He will do me no harm, MacTavish. Although, I believe I will play least in sight when he returns," she said with a grin.

"I'll take those boots for ye," he said. "And give them a shine before I r*rr*eturn them," he said with a gleam in his eye. "That way, if yer*rr* husband comes askin' if ye have them, ye can honestly say no."

Reggie laughed. "Thank you, MacTavish."

She was inside before she realized she had been talking to MacTavish with her dress still unbuttoned! Reggie blushed when it was too late for anyone to notice, then finished dressing quickly and quietly by the fire in the empty kitchen, before she fulfilled her promise by seeking out Pegg.

She found him sitting in the wing chair in the library, a warm plaid wool blanket across his lap, a glass of brandy at his side, a book in his lap, looking very much like the lord of the manor. Except he wore a black eyepatch and a golden earring and only one foot stuck out from beneath the blanket.

"Carlisle will be needing some of your famous salve this evening," she said as she stepped into the room.

He looked up from what he was reading and asked, "Why is that?"

"I believe he misplaced his boots and had to walk back from the pond barefooted," she said with a grin.

"Ye can be a trial, lass," Pegg said, returning her grin.

"What are you reading?" she asked, curious because she had not expected someone who had made his living as a card sharp to be an educated man.

"'Tis a pamphlet Clay asked me to look over."

"Oh? What is it?" She crossed to Pegg, leaned over his shoulder, and read aloud, "*How to Make Your Farm Produce a More Substantial Yield*. Carlisle asked you to read this?" she said, her brow furrowing.

"I think, given the chance, the lad would rather farm than sail the seas," Pegg said.

"But he has the chance," Reggie said. "Castle Carlisle is surrounded by land he could farm."

"Did ye not know, lass? His brother sold all the land to yer father. None of it is Clay's. It all belongs to the duke."

Reggie suddenly felt chilled. She walked around the chair and stood directly before the fire, searching for warmth. "No wonder he hates my father." She had a sudden thought and turned excitedly back to Pegg. "Carlisle could buy it back!" she said. "He's rich now, and I know my father would be willing to part with the land if I asked."

"I don't want any favors from your father," Carlisle said from the doorway.

Reggie wished she had gone straight to her room. She glanced down and saw Carlisle was still barefoot. Blood wept from a dozen tiny cuts she could see on his ankles and toes. She did not wish to imagine the condition of the soles of his feet. She swallowed hard and met his eyes. She had not intended to hurt him seriously. "Are you badly injured, my lord?"

He sighed and limped his way across the Turkish carpet. "There is no damage a good soaking and some figwort won't cure," he conceded.

"I'll leave ye to tend to yer husband, lass," Pegg said as he rose and stumped out of the room.

"But, Pegg—" It was plain she would get no mercy from him. "Will you sit, my lord," she said, gesturing to the chair Pegg had vacated. "I will send one of the maids for some hot water."

Then she realized she had given all the maids the rest of the day off. "Oh, dear. There is no maid to bring water. I will have to do it myself. Will you wait here for me, my lord?"

He raised a brow and said wryly, "I am not inclined to do a great deal more walking this evening."

Reggie hurried away to boil some water and happily discovered that someone had put a large pot of water over the fire in the kitchen to heat for tea. She decided that Carlisle's feet needed the hot water more, and she carried the teapot, and a pan large enough to hold both of Carlisle's feet, back to the library with her.

She set the pan down without speaking and poured in the steaming water. She dipped her fingers in to check the temperature. "Hot, but not too hot." She sat back on her heels and watched as Carlisle eased one foot into the pan of water, making a hissing sound like steam, as though his foot were a hot poker being dipped into cold water.

Reggie lifted the other foot and hissed in his stead as

she eased the wounded limb into the water. Once both feet were ensconced, she looked up and said, "I'm sorry, Clay. I didn't think such a silly joke would have such cruel consequences."

"There is a way you can make amends," he said.

She met his gaze and saw the need he made no effort to hide. She rose and took a step back. "I think not, my lord."

Reggie turned and walked away, leaving Carlisle alone to nurse the wounds in his flesh—and in his unforgiving heart.

Simms entered the dining room at breakfast the next morning and announced in a loud voice, "Company has come to take you riding on a pig, milady. Or it might be rowing in a bog. I could not quite make it out."

Reggie glanced at Carlisle, who was rolling his eyes at the deaf butler's mutilation of whatever message he had been asked to bring. "Never mind, Simms. I will shortly know for sure," Reggie said. "Please excuse me, my lord, while I see who has arrived."

"As long as you return and tell me what was said. I must admit my curiosity is aroused."

Reggie hurried to the drawing room and stopped in the doorway, moved beyond words by the sight that greeted her. "Becky! Mick! What a wonderful surprise!"

"We grew weary of waiting for you to come to us, so we decided to come to you," Mick said with a grin.

"We're here to have a picnic and go boating on the pond."

Riding on a pig and rowing in a bog. Reggie laughed with delight. "But what are you doing here, Becky? Where is Penrith?"

"Penrith has left the country," Becky said.

While Reggie was still trying to absorb that astonishing piece of news, her sister added, "Actually, he has left me. My marriage has been annulled."

"What?" Reggie cried. "What about Lily?"

"Lily is with me."

"Thank God!" Reggie said, gripping Becky in a hug that threatened to crack both their ribs. She let go enough to search Becky's face. "How are you faring? How did this happen? I have so many questions!"

"I will answer them all," Becky promised, freeing herself from Reggie's grasp. "But the day is so beautiful. And Mick has planned a wonderful picnic."

"Of course," Reggie said. "I will tell the servants to put together—"

"We have everything we need except you," Mick said. "Kitt, your brother Gareth, and your sister Meg are all waiting in the landau."

"And Papa?" Reggie asked excitedly. "Did he come?"

"I'm sorry, Reggie," Becky said, laying a hand briefly on her sister's forearm, communicating more in that small touch than in a thousand words. "He had estate business that could not wait."

Reggie was certain Carlisle's threat was the true culprit. She was sorry her father had allowed the warning to keep him away, but she was not going to ruin what should prove to be a congenial afternoon's visit with everyone else by worrying about it now. If she had to, she would sneak out in the middle of the night and visit her father.

"Let me go get Carlisle," she said. "We were just finishing our breakfast."

"Must he come?" Mick asked.

Reggie stopped and turned back to Mick, annoyed that he should want to exclude her husband, even if she understood his reasons. "I want him to meet Kitt."

"He already knows Kitt," Mick said.

"What?"

"Carlisle courted Kitt before your father married her," Mick said.

"What?" Reggie was aghast. *"Carlisle* and *Kitt*? He must have been a puppy at the time, years younger than she was!"

"Actually, only a year younger," Mick said.

"You are not making me feel better," Reggie informed him. "Why did you not say something sooner?" She rounded on her twin. "Did you know about this, Becky?"

Becky shook her head. "I am as astounded as you are."

"It was a long time ago, and nothing ever came of it," Mick said. "I am sorry now I mentioned it."

"Was Carlisle in love with her?" Reggie asked, her heart beating frantically, frightened of what Mick's answer might be, but needing to know it.

"Of course not," Mick said. "It was to be a marriage

of convenience for both of them. Neither was ever enamored of the other.''

"How can you be sure?'' What if Carlisle still loved Kitt? Reggie wondered. What if it was not his dead wife he grieved for, but the living woman he had lost to Reggie's father?

"If you don't believe me, ask Kitt this afternoon,'' Mick said.

Easier said than done. Now Reggie was not at all sure she wanted Carlisle to come along on the picnic. Her stepmother was still a very beautiful woman. And Reggie could not imagine how she might casually ask Kitt if she had ever been in love with the man who was now Reggie's husband!

"Wait a minute,'' Reggie said, even more bizarre thoughts racing through her head. "Do you think Papa might have accused Carlisle of all those crimes to get him out of the way, so he could have Kitt for himself?''

"That would be horrible, if it was true,'' Becky said, reaching out to take both of Reggie's hands in hers. "I cannot believe it of Papa.''

"It isn't true,'' Mick said flatly. "Kitt had already married your father before he accused Carlisle of anything.''

"Thank goodness for that,'' Reggie murmured.

"We can discuss this all morning, or we can go on a picnic. Which is it to be?'' Mick asked.

"Let me get Carlisle and tell Terrence to have the groom prepare the gig for us,'' Reggie said, dropping her sister's hands and turning for the drawing room door. "We will join you shortly.''

Reggie looked at Carlisle with entirely new eyes when she reentered the dining room. She had never much considered the difference in their ages, since it was commonplace for a man to be from fifteen to twenty years older than the young miss he married. Now she realized Carlisle had done a world of living—and loving—in the twelve years that separated their ages.

She had never felt jealous before, Reggie realized, because she had never cared enough about any particular man to want him for herself. She had known for a long time that she enjoyed Carlisle's company. She had known she craved his body. But her feelings went much deeper than that.

I am impossibly, completely, and totally in love with him.

The thought was startling—and dismaying—when she considered what it might mean if Carlisle refused to give up his quest for vengeance against her father. What if she was forced to choose between them? Would it come to that?

While loving a man was new to her, Reggie was only beginning to realize that her husband had loved before, courted before, married before, even been a father before. She could believe in happily ever after because she had never lost a first love . . . a spouse . . . a beloved child.

Reggie tried to imagine how she would feel if Carlisle were suddenly gone from her life.

It hurt to breathe. Dear God. Did she care that much? Despite everything? What if their marriage floundered, and he left her? Or she was forced to leave him? How did one go on? How did one live with the awful grief of such a loss?

"Well, my dear, will we be riding pigs this morning? Or rowing in a bog?" Carlisle asked.

"You will be glad to hear the promised 'ride on a pig' is a picnic, and 'rowing in a bog' is rowing in a boat."

Carlisle raised a brow. "Who has invited us to share such entertainments?"

"My family."

Carlisle cocked his head and eyed her intently. "Your entire family?"

"Everyone except my father," she said. "He had estate business that could not wait."

"I see," Carlisle said. "Where are they now?"

"Waiting for us to join them. I asked Terrence to have the groom prepare the gig for us. Mick says he has taken care of everything else. All we need bring is ourselves. Will you come?"

"I would not miss it," Carlisle replied.

Reggie grabbed a woolen shawl in case a chill moved in from the sea and a parasol in case the sun got too warm.

When Reggie and Carlisle joined the rest of the party in front of the castle, she realized Mick had not exaggerated. Not one, but two wagons waited behind the landau transporting her stepmother and siblings. One was piled high with tables and chairs and numerous baskets, which she supposed held cutlery and glasses and linen and mounds of food. The other held two small rowboats.

While Reggie had been to a great many picnics on the outskirts of London where such elaborate preparations had been made, this was the first time she could remember it being done for a country picnic. Then she realized Mick knew the sad state of disrepair in which Castle Carlisle had been only a week past. Apparently uncertain whether she would have tables or chairs or even foodstuffs, he had left nothing to chance.

When Reggie saw how much baggage Mick had brought, she insisted that Terrence and George join the party, to be of whatever assistance they could to Kitt's servants, and they climbed on the second wagon.

"Come and be introduced to my stepmother," Reggie said, taking Carlisle's hand and leading him to the landau.

"Lady Blackthorne and I have already met," Carlisle replied. "But I am looking forward to seeing her again."

Reggie noticed that Carlisle did not mention he had previously *courted* her stepmother, but she was not willing to risk an argument that might cause their picnic to be postponed or interrupted entirely.

"You are looking wonderful, Kitt," Reggie said, as she stood beside the landau. She reached up to take her stepmother's hand and gripped it tightly. "And Meg is beautiful," she said, eyeing the baby sleeping in the crook of Kitt's arm. "I am so very happy for you."

She met Kitt's eyes, knowing they would never speak of the three babies who had not lived to be born, but wanting her stepmother to know that she understood why Kitt must cherish Meg all the more.

She stepped back alongside Carlisle and said, "May I present my husband, Clay Bannister, Earl of Carlisle."

"You are looking well, my lord," Kitt said, as she and Carlisle exchanged nods.

"And you, Your Grace," Carlisle replied formally.

Reggie was watching for any signs of romantic interest, but all she saw was a guarded look from Kitt that was even less cordial than the formal greetings they had exchanged.

And then Carlisle said, "You are still very beautiful."

"And very much married," her stepmother replied. "My husband was sorry he could not be here."

Reggie held her breath. She could not believe Kitt had mentioned Papa under the circumstances.

Whatever cordiality Carlisle might have felt toward her stepmother was extinguished like a burning candle whipped by a chilly wind. His features hardened, and his eyes turned a cold, obsidian black that Reggie thought must reflect the darkness in his soul.

"Come," Reggie said. "Let us join my family—"

"It is not a family I have any desire to join," Carlisle said.

"I am sorry to hear that," Kitt replied in even tones that denied the flare of temper Reggie saw in her stepmother's eyes.

"Damned scoundrel," Reggie heard Mick mutter under his breath.

"Please," Becky whispered, begging him to control his anger.

Reggie could feel the situation spiraling out of control. Any moment, polite courtesies would become hurled epithets and any chance of a rapprochement with her father would need to include her stepmother as well.

"When are we going to eat?" eleven-year-old Gareth blurted.

That mundane question broke the tension and focused every eye on her brother.

"We have only another mile or so to travel," Kitt reassured him.

"But how long before we get there?" the boy asked plaintively. "I'm starving!"

Reggie reached out to ruffle Gareth's black curls and said, "And I can see why. You are growing like a weed!"

Gareth grinned. "Papa says I will probably grow up to be as tall as he is."

"I can easily believe it," Reggie said. Though in fact, Gareth was rather small for his age. Seeing the look on Carlisle's face, she quickly changed the subject away from her father. "How do you like having a baby sister?"

Gareth wrinkled his nose like a schoolboy facing a bowl of cold gruel. "All she does is cry and eat and sleep."

Reggie laughed. "Soon enough she will be tagging along behind you begging to do everything you do." She turned back to her stepmother, and said, "I want very much to hold Meg, but I think it might be better to wait until she wakes up. And if we don't get on the road soon, it seems Gareth will die of hunger."

Reggie slipped her arm through Carlisle's and urged him toward the gig in which they were traveling, partly to make sure he did not argue further and partly to make certain that he did not turn around and walk back inside.

She could feel the tension in his arm and see a muscle working in his jaw.

"Please, my lord," she whispered. "Do not spoil the day."

"Perhaps you would rather go without me." he suggested.

She gripped his arm tightly. "I love my family, and I love—" She cut herself off abruptly. She had been about to say *I love you*. She did not dare put that much power in his hands. She had spoken the words on her wedding day, but she had not repeated them since. And would not, until she was certain her feelings were returned. "—the sea," she said instead. "But neither would be as much fun, if you are not there."

"Very well, my dear. You win. We will picnic by the sea."

She had not realized a contest was in progress, but she did not stop to relish her triumph. She hurried toward the gig and climbed in without waiting for his help.

Mick mounted his horse and signaled the coachman to start the landau. Reggie and Carlisle followed in the gig, and the two overloaded wagons brought up the rear. As they were pulling away, Cam MacTavish hopped onto the last wagon.

Reggie opened her mouth to call out that he needn't come, but she was certain George and Terrence would appreciate the help unloading the boats, and if the picnic got dull, MacTavish could liven it up with one of his stories.

"Where are we going?" Reggie asked Mick, once they were on the road.

"Down to the sea," Mick said. "Where you and Becky and I used to go. Do you remember?"

"Of course I remember." Not more than a mile farther down the road, the cliff declined gradually until it became a grassy verge nearly at sea level. After picnicking on the grass, a gentle climb down would lead them to an inlet where they could boat in a small bay where the water was nearly smooth, because the waves broke against a rocky reef that nearly enclosed it.

"I can hardly wait," Reggie said. "Will you come boating with me, my lord?" she asked Carlisle.

"I am at your service, my dear," he said.

Reggie raised a brow. "Do you mean you are willing to do whatever I wish for the rest of the afternoon?"

"I am," he replied.

"Then I want you to be nice to Mick and to Becky and to my brother, Gareth. And most especially, I want you to be on your best, most courteous behavior with my stepmother. Will you promise to do that?"

Carlisle wore a grimace exactly like the one she had just seen on Gareth's face, but he said, "Very well. I promise."

Reggie rewarded him with a smile, then scooted closer along the torn leather seat of the gig and twined her arm with his. "Oh, this is going to be a wonderful day. I just know it!"

She ignored the ticklish worm of foreboding, inching its way down her spine.

Chapter 17

AFTER WHAT COULD ONLY BE DEEMED A shaky start, Reggie did her best to keep herself between Carlisle and her family, thus ensuring a pleasant time at the picnic for everybody.

While Kitt's servants set up the tables with Mick's help, and Carlisle supervised the unloading of the boats by her three men and helped carry the boats down to the shore, Reggie managed to find out what few details Becky knew about Penrith's defection. When Reggie had heard it all, she could not help but think her sister was better off without him.

"Now tell me about you and Carlisle," Becky said. "Whyever did you agree to marry him on such short notice?"

"He did not give me much choice," Reggie said.

"Are you saying you were forced?" Becky asked, aghast.

Reggie told Becky the details of her kidnapping, her marriage, and the ruins she had found when she arrived at Castle Carlisle. "I cannot say I am mistreated," Reggie finished, "but I cannot honestly say I have my husband's love. Though I am still hoping for happily ever after."

Becky shook her head. "It does not exist."

"It must," Reggie said.

"Only in fairy tales," Becky said as she glanced longingly at Mick.

Lily had not come along on the picnic, since she had a bit of a stomachache, so Reggie did her best to play matchmaker and threw Becky often into Mick's path. Mick seemed more than happy to be caught there. He helped fill Becky's plate and sat beside her while she nibbled at it. Neither seemed hungry, though their eyes devoured each other.

Reggie sat beside Carlisle on a blanket and let him feed her choice morsels of his chicken, pretending for her family that all was right with her world. His eyes focused intently on her mouth, and her body squeezed up like a drawstring as she tasted his fingertips with her lips, even sucking the tip of one briefly inside her mouth.

She glanced around surreptitiously to see if anyone had noticed her indiscretion, but Becky and Mick were entranced with each other, Kitt's eyes were centered on Meg, and the servants were all busy. And then she met her brother's gaze.

His lips curved in a crooked grin. And he winked.

Flustered, Reggie crossed her eyes and stuck out her tongue at him.

Carlisle snickered.

Reggie blushed.

Gareth turned away and concentrated on the chicken leg he was gnawing to the bone.

The instant Meg was awake, Reggie was there to hold her newborn sister. "I am surprised Papa would allow you to make such a journey with her, after what happened when you—" Reggie cut herself off, suddenly remembering that Mick believed Carlisle to be responsible for the carriage accident that had injured her stepmother. "I was only thinking that newborns are so fragile," Reggie said.

Kitt opened the blanket more completely so that Reggie could see the baby's ten perfect fingers and ten perfect toes. "Your papa wanted you to meet your sister," she said simply.

Reggie felt the tears sting her eyes and blinked quickly to banish them. She missed her father terribly. How sad that he could not share her joy at seeing this new addition to the family for the first time. Reggie turned to Carlisle, feeling resentful, but saw the stark look in his eyes and said, "Would you like to hold her?"

She felt the stillness, as everyone around her froze. Mick frowned at her, and she glared back. Kitt's brow furrowed, but she made no word of protest. Becky sucked in a breath . . . and held it.

Reggie could hear the flies buzzing the scraps of ham. The distant surf pounding against the shore. The snuffle Meg made as one of the dandelions Gareth had picked landed momentarily on her cheek before being carried away by the cool sea breeze.

"I want to hold her now," Gareth said. He didn't wait for Reggie to agree. He simply leaned down, plucked the tiny child out of Reggie's hands, and threw her up over his shoulder.

"Careful!" four adults said at once. Only Carlisle did not speak.

Gareth gave them all a pitiful look of schoolboy disdain. "She's a baby, not a piece of china," he said. "She won't break."

To Reggie's amazement, Meg laid her head down on Gareth's shoulder, stuck her thumb into her mouth, and stared at the rest of them in complete contentment.

"You are a marvel, Gareth," Reggie said with a relieved smile.

"I know," Gareth said, grinning back.

Mick snorted.

Becky laughed.

And the tension was broken. In an effort to find some harmless subject to discuss, Reggie said, "You will never guess what Carlisle gave Pegg to read the other evening."

"What?" Becky asked.

"A pamphlet on improving the yield on crops!" Reggie said as she shot Carlisle a teasing look.

"You used to be quite interested in farming," Kitt said.

When Reggie raised an inquiring brow, Kitt explained, "The earl once told me that he hoped someday to put into practice a great many new ideas about farming he had learned from books."

"That was a long time ago," Carlisle said curtly.

"Are you planning to farm the land around the castle?" Mick asked.

"As you must know, the land around the castle is not mine to farm," Carlisle said. "My brother sold it to Blackthorne."

"Blackthorne deeded it back to you twelve years ago when he realized how badly he had misjudged you," Mick said, meeting Carlisle's embittered words with a steady look. "I suppose you would have no way of knowing that, since it was done so long ago, and you haven't been in communication with the duke."

Reggie saw the flash of astonishment in Carlisle's eyes before they turned dark and unreadable again.

"I don't want anything from him," he said.

Mick shrugged. "It is already done. The land is yours to do with as you wish. Farm it. Leave it fallow. The choice is yours."

Reggie watched as Carlisle opened his mouth to retort, then shut it again before saying the words she could imagine were on the tip of his tongue: *He can have it back.* It was plain to see that he was moved by her father's gesture. Or maybe the better word was *disturbed* by it.

Before the situation had a chance to deteriorate further, Gareth blurted, "When are we going boating?"

Reggie smiled, thinking how Gareth's interruptions had helped them avoid more than one nasty confrontation that afternoon. She might have gone on believing Gareth's interruptions were merely luck, if she had not happened to meet his gaze—his shrewd, entirely perceptive gaze—at that moment.

He knows exactly what he is doing, she realized suddenly. She wondered how her brother had learned to be such an effective peacemaker. She did not think her parents fought often, which only left boarding school. It must be a hellish place, for him to have acquired such a talent so young.

Taking advantage of his timely interference, Reggie said, "Why not go boating now? Mick, you and Becky and Gareth can go in one skiff, and Carlisle and Kitt and I will—"

"I prefer to stay here with Meg," Kitt said.

Gareth had handed the sleepy child to his nurse, and there were two additional servants to guard Meg's safety. It was possible her father had asked her stepmother not to leave the child with anyone else. But Reggie believed Kitt was merely giving an excuse to avoid being in the same boat with Carlisle.

Reggie could have confronted her stepmother, but what was the use? Carlisle was the one with the problem. Until she could convince him to make peace with her father, she would have to bear the loss of her family's company.

"Fine," Reggie said. "Carlisle and I will go alone in the second boat."

The small wooden rowboats had been set just far enough away from the water that the tide could not catch them and carry them out to sea. The two men each pushed a skiff into the water, while Gareth stood holding a rope attached to each. Then each man returned and picked up one of the twins and carried her out and set her in his boat. Finally, Gareth climbed in, followed by each man, and Mick and Carlisle began to row away from shore.

To no one's surprise, they rowed in opposite directions. Reggie might have protested, except she wanted to talk to her husband, and a little distance was necessary to keep her voice from carrying to the occupants of the other boat.

"It must be good news to learn that the land surrounding Castle Carlisle is yours again," she said.

"Should I be grateful that your father sought to sop his conscience by returning land he bought from my brother at a pittance of its worth?" Carlisle said.

"My father is not to blame for mistakes your brother made," Reggie returned heatedly. "Will you farm the land, or not?"

"I will not."

"Then I shall."

"What?"

"I see no reason why the land should go to waste," Reggie said. "And it will put a great many people to work."

He stared at her as though she belonged in Bedlam.

"Of course, if you are inclined to offer any suggestions concerning how I should go about getting started, I would certainly—"

Carlisle threw back his head and laughed. "You are a constant delight, my dear. I make no doubt you would be successful . . . if you had the slightest idea what you were doing."

"Does that mean you will help?" Reggie asked hopefully.

"I will—"

"HELP! REGGIE, HELP!"

The boat waggled in the water as Reggie lurched to her feet to see why Mick was yelling. "Their boat is sinking!" she shrieked at Carlisle. "Becky can't swim!"

"Sit down," he ordered, "before you fall out and I have to stop and rescue you!"

Reggie plopped onto the wooden seat and clasped her hands desperately on either side of the skiff. "Hurry, my lord. Please hurry! Gareth is not a strong swimmer!"

Reggie leaned forward and back with each stroke of the oars, as though that would help Carlisle row faster. "There is no way Mick can save Becky and Gareth both. He will need help," she said, feeling a desperate sense of doom.

"Don't do anything foolish," Carlisle warned.

"I must do something!" she snapped back.

"Drowning yourself won't help your sister," Carlisle said. "If you jump in wearing that dress, it will drag you under like a stone. We'll be there in a minute or two—"

"That may be too late!" Reggie cried, feeling all the more helpless because she was so close—and yet so impossibly far away.

She did not understand what she saw happen next. Mick picked Becky up, kicking and screaming, and threw her into the sea, then forced Gareth over the side. While the two of them flailed in the water, he jumped onto one edge of the skiff, flipping it upside down!

Then he was in the water himself, grabbing Becky and Gareth each by the scruffs of their necks—like two drowning pups—and hauling them over to cling to the upturned boat.

Within another minute, Reggie and Carlisle were beside them.

"Becky, Gareth, are you both all right?" Reggie asked, leaning over the side to reach out to them. She managed to grasp Gareth's shirt and heave him over to her.

Carlisle reached over her shoulder, caught the boy under his arms and hauled him in. A second later, Mick handed Becky over to him, and he lifted her into the boat. Reggie took her shivering sister into her arms and held her tight, as Gareth huddled beside them.

"I can manage by myself if you will balance the boat," Mick said through chattering teeth.

A moment later he had levered himself into the skiff, which was now dangerously overloaded. Carlisle picked up the oars and began rowing back toward shore.

"What happened?" Reggie asked. "Why did the boat start to sink?"

"Someone put a hole in the bottom, that is why," Mick said furiously, glaring at Carlisle. "The gash was concealed under the seat and apparently plugged with something that came loose once it was wet enough."

"Maybe the hole was there when you left Blackthorne Hall," Reggie said.

"I checked the boats myself before we left. There was no damage to either of them. Someone sabotaged that boat today and trusted it would not be discovered until it was too late."

"When would someone have had the opportunity to do such a thing?" Reggie asked.

"Carlisle helped unload the boats. He helped carry

them down to the shore. He stayed there alone until we called him to come and eat."

Mick's accusation stunned Reggie. It was horrible to imagine Carlisle wanting to hurt Mick or Becky or Gareth. She simply could *not* imagine it. If Mick would only think, he would realize that Carlisle had stayed on the beach merely to avoid further confrontation with her family.

"Carlisle is innocent," she said. "Think, Mick. How could he know which boat you would choose?"

"He chose first," Mick snapped back.

"What if you had chosen first? You might have."

"Then the two of you would have gotten wet," Mick said. "Instead of nearly drowning Becky and Gareth."

Reggie could see the futility of trying to convince Mick that Carlisle was not to blame. She looked at Carlisle's face, to see how he was reacting to Mick's accusation. It might as well have been made of stone.

But if Carlisle had not sabotaged the boat, then who had? None of Kitt's servants had gone down to the shore. That left only the three men Reggie had brought along, Terrence, George, and MacTavish, as suspects. Her gaze immediately sought out MacTavish.

Of the three, he was the one she had not asked to come along. She remembered how he had appeared from nowhere the previous evening when she had been returning from the pond, frightening her out of her wits. Why had he been there? And why had he come today?

Reggie realized she knew very little about the *gillecoise* turned gatekeeper. He kept to himself and did not socialize with the other servants. He lurked—yes, that was the word that fit—around the castle. And despite his age and his small stature, he was wiry and, she was certain, quite strong. And he must be clever to have managed to sabotage the boat without being caught.

There was only one enemy who could want to hurt both Carlisle and her own family—Cedric Ambleside. Reggie wondered if Mr. Ambleside might have hired MacTavish to do what harm he could.

The party on shore had seen the disaster and were waiting with warm blankets. "What happened?" Kitt asked, as she pulled Gareth to her and held him close.

"Another 'accident,' " Mick said, glancing sideways at Carlisle.

Carlisle did not bother defending himself, but Reggie knew as well as he did that where Mick was concerned, it would have been wasted breath.

Reggie saw the shadow of concern that flickered in her stepmother's eyes before Kitt said, "We had better get started home."

"You can get into some warm clothes at the castle," Reggie said, knowing they would not want to drive home in cold, wet, sea-salty clothes.

"We can be home in the time it would take us to stop and change," Kitt countered.

Reggie stared at her stepmother, then met Mick's eyes, and Becky's. It was clear that all of them suspected Carlisle.

He is innocent! she wanted to shout.

As a last resort, she turned to Gareth. Surely a child as canny as he had proved to be would recognize the truth. But Gareth would not meet her eyes. He lowered his gaze to the toe of his wet shoe, which was burrowed into the seagrass.

Reggie did not say another word. There was nothing more she could say.

Kitt left the servants to repack the wagons and immediately headed back in the landau. Reggie and Carlisle followed in the gig.

"Why do you bother to defend me?" Carlisle said at last. "They will never believe you."

He was staring straight ahead, so there was no way to catch his eye. But she slipped her arm through his and said, "Because I believe you are innocent."

He eyed her askance and said, "Despite all evidence to the contrary?"

Reggie considered telling Carlisle her suspicions about MacTavish, but he was likely to simply terminate the old man on the spot. And if MacTavish was not guilty of anything, the poor man would be put out into the cold again through no fault of his own. Reggie decided to wait and to watch on her own.

"When the real culprit is discovered," she said, "I will make sure they all apologize to you."

He pulled his arm closer to his body, giving her arm a gentle squeeze, which was all the response she got. It was enough. It was a start. Maybe if someone believed in him, he would begin to believe in the good in himself again.

Becky woke up gasping for air. She had been dreaming that her mouth and nose were filled with saltwater, that her dress was tangled in her legs, and that she was suffocating in the murky depths. She sat up and took a slow, deep breath.

I'm alive. I'm safe.

But her escapes from a watery death—both the real one, and the one she had conjured in her dream—had left her too agitated to sleep. She got up, jammed her feet into cold slippers, yanked on a dark green wool dressing gown, and stalked over to the window to stare out at the moonlit darkness.

She had been horrified when Mick suggested that the only way he could save both her and Gareth was to flip the skiff so they would have something to hang onto until Reggie could reach them with the other boat. Becky was embarrassed to remember how terrified she had been, refusing to go over the side, until Mick had been forced to pick her up and throw her in. She had swallowed a mouthful of seawater as she flailed ineffectually toward the surface. Suddenly, Mick's strong arms had been there to haul her up for a gasp of life-giving air.

I might have died today without ever loving Mick . . . or telling Mick I love him.

It had been her intention when she first came to Blackthorne hall to visit Mick's manor house and tell him she wanted to be his lover. But the rains had come, and she had used the weather as an excuse to delay her sojourn. When the rain finally stopped, she had told herself it was indecent to leap into Mick's bed when she had so recently been another man's wife.

Excuses. I have always had a great many excuses for why my life is not as I want it to be. It is time to stop being chicken-hearted. It is time to reach out for what I want. And I want to make love with Mick.

That was as far as she would let her fantasy take her. Love, marriage, any kind of future together, all seemed quite impossible. Becky laughed softly. She did not even know if she could persuade Mick to make love to her. She only knew she had to try.

She managed to go back to bed, but not to sleep. In the hours before the sun rose, she tried to imagine how she might induce Mick to take her to bed. Unfortunately, this was her first attempt at seducing a man, and she lacked any useful experience. In the end, she decided she would arrive in her best looks and leave the rest up to Mick.

Becky took special care with her toilette, making sure a few curls were freed from the knot at her crown so that Mick might imagine pulling out the rest of the pins and letting it all fall down.

She chose a peach-colored, sprigged muslin dress with puffed sleeves and a V neck that revealed a mere hint of the feminine assets that had never been enough to satisfy her husband, but which she had caught Mick admiring. She put on her best straw hat, tying the blue plaid ribbon a little askew, hoping Mick would want to adjust it, providing an easy way for him to reach out to her.

Finally, she wore white gloves, which she planned to get dirty along the way, giving her an excuse to remove them, and opted for a parasol, rather than a fan. No sense getting needless freckles before she saw him.

Becky made sure Lily had breakfast and sent her off

with her nurse to play before she went looking for Kitt to explain her absence from the house, so that no one would get worried and come looking for her.

She found Kitt in the library with her father and announced, "I'm going for a walk to see how many different wildflowers I can find."

"What a wonderful idea! Perhaps I'll go with you," Kitt replied.

Ordinarily, that would have been the end of that. Becky would have conceded defeat and come home with a faceful of freckles and a handful of wildflowers. With a willfulness that was frightening, it was so new, she said, "Actually, I would prefer to be by myself."

"Oh," Kitt said. "Well. Of course."

Her father gave her a probing look that usually had the effect of launching her into a confession of whatever sin she was contemplating.

Becky resisted the urge to blurt out the truth. "Do not worry if I am not back for luncheon. I have asked Cook to prepare a basket to take along with me."

Her father arched an inquiring brow, and she hurried from the room before she could succumb to the desire to confess everything.

It did not occur to Becky until she had walked half the distance to Albury Manor, where Mick was living, to wonder whether he would be there when she arrived. Becky thought she remembered Mick telling her yesterday on the ride back from the picnic that he would not see her the following morning, because he had bookkeeping that must be done at home. But what if he had since changed his mind?

Looking for a reason to turn around and go home? The sky would make a better one. It is filling with dark clouds. And that frilly parasol you brought along will not do you much good against a hard rain.

In the end, Becky's careful toilette proved a waste of time, since it began to pour while she was yet half a mile from Albury Manor. She was wearing a pretty cape, which quickly became soaked, and her straw bonnet began to sag under the weight of the rainwater. With every step she took, her slippers slung mud halfway up her back, and her hem was soon dirtied as well.

By the time she reached the back door of Albury Manor, Becky did not much care whether Mick was there or not. She doubted seriously whether the bedraggled female arriving on his doorstep would prove an irresistibly tempting feminine morsel. She was so frustrated, she could have cried, except that would only have added reddened eyes and a dripping nose to the list of her deficiencies.

The medieval stone manor house was much smaller than she had thought it would be, rectangular in shape, with a steeply peaked shingled roof. There were two narrow windows in front and two in back, which she thought must correspond to what could not be more than four rooms on the single floor that comprised the whole of it.

If she were ever to defy convention and marry Mick, this house—or one very like it, if her father dismissed Mick in outrage, and they had to move away—might be where she lived out the rest of her life. There was not even a separate room for Lily, let alone space for the army of servants who now cared for her needs. It was daunting to contemplate such an existence.

But she had not been able to resist contemplating it. As she had learned only yesterday, life could end with frightening suddenness. It seemed foolish to deny herself the chance for happiness with Mick simply because people would talk. What she feared—what she doubted—was her own ability to learn how to do all the tasks that servants now performed for her.

She had decided to start with seducing Mick, and see how things progressed. There would be time enough later to decide whether she would make a good wife for him.

Becky knocked on the door, and when it was not answered immediately, she realized Mick probably was not at home after all. She had no idea whether he had any servants—there certainly was no room for them to live on the premises—but when she tried the doorknob, it opened without a sound, and she let herself in.

The house felt empty. The floor was made of uneven stone, so there were not even any creaking boards to give away her presence. She started to call out, but then felt silly. If anyone had been at home, they would have answered the door.

Becky found herself in a kitchen containing a cooking stove and a counter with a water pump attached. Everything was put away in its place, hanging on the wall or in a cupboard.

The room looked far larger on the inside than it had from the outside. Perhaps that was because there was so little in it. She set down her basket and wet parasol on the small round table where she suspected Mick ate his meals. The door to the kitchen led to a hall, and she headed for it, intent on finding a fire to warm herself and dry her clothes.

Directly across from the kitchen she discovered a bedroom, the bed neatly made, the room uncluttered, quite spare in its furnishings. She spied one of Mick's favorite waistcoats hanging from the bedstead and deduced it was his bedroom.

Shivering with cold, Becky hurried forward down the hall toward an open door on the left. A quick glance revealed a sofa and chairs, but otherwise the sitting room was empty. The fire had burned down to ashes without the grate being cleared and a new fire being laid. Becky had never shoveled ashes in her life, much less carried wood and laid a fire.

There were obviously no servants to do the work. If she lived here with Mick, either he must do it, or she must. Becky shivered again. Perhaps there was a fire in the other room or at least some wood near the other fireplace, so she would not have to go back outside hunting for it.

As she left the sitting room, Becky noticed for the first time that the door on the opposite side of the hall was closed. Was Mick inside? Was the closed door the reason he had not heard her knock.

It was tempting to let herself out as quietly as she had let herself in. Seeing where Mick lived—how he lived—forced her to acknowledge how difficult it would be for them to have any future together. Even if she could learn to do without, was it fair to subject Lily to such a fate?

To be honest, Becky was not sure she could adapt to a life where so much would be expected of her. What if she could not learn? She could not bear to become an additional burden on Mick.

All roads led back to the one great weakness in her character. It would take courage to give up the familiar. Courage to learn a new way of life. Courage to face the tabbies. And Becky had always been notoriously faint of heart.

She was standing in the hallway, still uncertain which way to turn, when the door opened, and Mick stood before her.

"Becky! Good grief, girl. What happened to you? What are you doing here? You're soaking wet. Come in here by the fire and get warm. Here, let me get that bonnet off of you. Bear with me, the knot is stuck tight."

Well, Becky thought, *the bonnet has done its job. The rest is up to me.*

She smiled.

"I'm glad to see you have not lost your sense of humor," he said. "There, that does it." He held the sodden bonnet out in front of him. "Perhaps if I set it on the mantel it will regain some of its shape as it dries." He came right back to her and started to work untying her cape. "This has to go as well. It's sopping wet."

She wondered if it had occurred to him that he was undressing her. She decided not to point it out to him, but concentrated instead on taking off her gloves.

"Here, sit down in this chair by the fire and let me get those half boots off. You'll catch your death."

She curled her fingers around his hand as he led her

over to a ladder-back chair that he pulled away from his desk and angled toward the fire. He pressed her into the chair with a hand on her shoulder, then knelt and took off her muddy half boots one at a time. He wiped the mud from his hands onto his trousers, which she could see were already soiled from whatever physical labor he must have done that morning.

"Your stockings are damp," he said, reaching up under her skirt all the way to her knees and pulling first one down and then the other. "Better let them dry out, too."

After he had pulled off the second stocking, but before he could rise and move away, Becky reached out and laid a hand on his head, running her fingers through his hair.

Mick froze.

She let her hand drop back into her lap. And waited to see what he would do.

Without looking at her, and without leaving his knee, he carefully untangled her white stockings and laid them across a wrought-iron bar that held tools for the fireplace.

In case Mick thought she had touched him accidentally, Becky reached out again. This time she brushed the backs of her fingers across his cheek, then traced his lower lip with her thumb. She saw the pulse beating hard and fast in his throat. His eyelids were lowered, hiding his eyes from her.

Mick reminded her of a wild buck she had come across in the forest that was curious enough to stand and see what she would do, but ready to bolt at the slightest hint of danger.

"What are you doing, Becky?" he asked in a low, husky voice.

She put her hand beneath his chin and tipped his face up, forcing him to look at her. Forcing herself to look him in the eye. She tried to smile, but could not get her mouth to cooperate. "I had a hope you might undress me completely in the interest of getting me warm. That would have been a great help in accomplishing what I came here to do."

"What was that?" he asked.

She managed a crooked smile. "Seduce you."

She waited for him to smile back, but his eyes had never looked more sober. His face had never looked more serious.

"I have never wanted anything in my life as much as I want you," he said. "But—"

She put one hand on his shoulder to keep him from rising, the other across his lips to cut off his speech. "Please don't say it would not be honorable to lie with me. Please don't say you owe my father too much to take advantage of me. And don't tell me I will regret this later. The only thing I will regret is leaving here as un- touched as I was when I came through your kitchen door."

"Becky . . ." His eyes looked tortured. His shoul- der had turned to iron beneath her hand.

"Love me, Mick," she pleaded. "Show me how it feels to be loved."

As he rose, her hand fell away, but her gaze remained locked with his. A second later he had lifted her into his arms. She linked her arms around his neck and laid her head on his shoulder as he carried her out of his study and down the hall to his bedroom.

It was cold, because there was no fire, but he pulled down the covers on the bed and set her on the edge of it.

"Let's get you out of this dress and under the covers where you can get warm," he said quietly.

She turned her back so he could unbutton her dress, and lifted her bottom so he could peel it off of her without her setting her bare feet on the rough stone floor. She scooted under the covers before he could remove her chemise and pantalets, as modesty finally reared its head, and pulled the sheet and quilt up to her neck.

She stared at him with wide, frightened eyes, wondering what would happen next. Afraid, because she had no experience pleasing a man—she had never pleased Penrith—and she wanted very much to please Mick.

"Let me light a fire in here," he said.

She wanted to shout, *"Can't that wait?"* But she realized he was right. They would both be warm so long as they were making love, but afterward, when he was damp with sweat, as Penrith had often been, Mick was likely to get chilled.

She sat forward and watched what he did, thinking that she would need to pay attention to everything from now on, just to see if she could learn. In the end, it did not take very long to lay a fire. Just long enough for her nerves to begin to jump.

Mick must have seen the fear that had risen like an ensnaring snake to choke her, because he came to her without removing any of his clothes and sat down beside her and slowly began taking the pins from her hair.

Joan Johnston

"What has you grinning like the cat that got the cream?" he asked.

"When I tried to think of ways I might seduce you, I imagined you taking the pins from my hair."

"What happened next?" he said, removing the last pin.

"I have no idea," she answered with a nervous laugh.

"How about a kiss?"

Fortunately, he did not require a response, because her heart leaped into her throat, preventing speech entirely. His hands caught in her hair and angled her face up to his. The kiss was tender—for about two seconds—and then it was hungry, ravenous, voracious.

Becky had always believed there must be something wrong with her, because she had never felt any great desire to be kissed by her husband. Had never very much liked the way he touched her. Never wanted to have him inside her, because it was at best uncomfortable and at worst hurtful.

Everything was so different with Mick. She could not touch him enough, could not get close enough to him, could not get enough of his kisses. She could hardly bear to let him go long enough to strip off his clothes or the rest of her own. For the first time, she asked for what she wanted.

"I want you inside me. Now."

Becky gave a sob of joy when Mick thrust deep inside her.

He paused, his weight braced on his straining arms, his features taut, his eyes burning with need. "Have I hurt you?" he asked. "Shall I stop?"

306

"Penrith said a man cannot stop."

He brushed a curl away from her forehead. "I can always stop, though sometimes it may be difficult. Shall I stop?" he asked again.

Mick started to withdraw, but Becky wrapped her arms around him and held him where he was. "No," she said. "It feels good, Mick. It never did before. Never!"

She heard his agonized moan and reached up to stop it with her mouth. She had never kissed a man; she had always been the one who was kissed. She let her tongue slip into Mick's mouth, enraptured by the taste of him, mimicking the movement of their bodies below.

When at last they lay sated together, *both* their bodies slicked with sweat, Mick's arms wrapped tightly around her, and their bodies spooned together as though they were one, Becky said the only words she knew to thank him for what he had done.

"I love you, Mick."

She heard him catch his breath, felt the muscles tense in his arms and thighs, before he replied, "I love you, too, Becky. Will you marry me?"

Chapter 18

REGGIE HAD NEVER REALIZED HOW MANY customs must be observed from springtime until harvest when one wanted to begin farming. She had come home from the picnic ready to put a plough to the land the very next day, but George had told her, "It canna be done, milady."

"Why not?" she asked.

"Ye canna begin ploughing until the moon be on the wane. Then there is the blessing by his lordship, and—"

"What blessing?"

Reggie had listened for another half hour to everything George had to say before she sought out Carlisle in his library.

"Caught you!" she said, when she saw what he was reading.

His ears pinkened. It was the pamphlet on improving yield. "It was sitting here on my desk when I came in."

"I am glad you are studying, because it seems there is a great deal we both need to learn about farming," she

308

said. "In fact, I came here to see if you are aware of all the folk customs that must be observed if we are to have a good crop."

He raised an arrogant brow. "If I farm at all, I intend to use modern methods."

"That makes a great deal of sense," she agreed. "But what would be the harm in following the old customs? As George described them to me, they seem relatively simple and absolutely harmless."

His brows arrowed down. "Give me an example of these simple, harmless customs."

"Well, you will have to bless the plough."

Carlisle snickered. "You're joking."

"I am entirely serious. You must drink a glass of whiskey, then fill the glass again and pour it over the bridle of the plough, and say, 'God speed this plough.' Of course, there can be no further work the day of the blessing, and usually there is a dance to celebrate."

"Celebrate what?" he asked.

"Why, the blessing, of course."

"It is a moot point, because I have not made up my mind to farm."

"Oh, you will not have to do anything," Reggie said. "I will manage it all. Except the blessing. You will have to be there for that."

"Reggie, I—"

"Please, my lord," she said, crossing to where he sat at his desk. "Think of all the hungry mouths this work will feed. And consider how much richer you will be when the crops are harvested."

"I am rich enough," he said.

"The land is yours," she said, refusing to take no for an answer. "You might as well use it."

"Giving me back the land does not make up for everything else he did," Carlisle said, leaning forward across his desk.

"No one said it did," Reggie replied. "But I believe my father must have felt very bad about what he did to return so much valuable land without asking for anything in return."

"He got his pound of flesh from my back," Carlisle snarled.

"For Christ's sake, lad. No one says ye have to give up yer blasted revenge. Just farm the damned land!"

Reggie started and whirled to find Pegg sitting in the wing chair before the fire. "I didn't see you there," she said, laying a hand against her pounding heart.

He rose from the chair and stumped across the room to join them. "In all the years we spent at sea, ye never opened yer mouth but out came dreams of comin' home and farmin' the land. Why pretend now ye dinna care?"

"Blackthorne killed those dreams!" Carlisle shot back as he rose from his chair to confront Pegg.

"Aye, some dreams are dead," Pegg agreed. He glanced at Reggie, then met and held Carlisle's brooding gaze. "But others may still come true. Grab what ye can, lad, and forget what's lost."

Pegg stumped out of the library, leaving Reggie alone with her husband. It always came back to the same sad refrain, she thought. Carlisle could not live in the present, and could not see any future, because he was still mired in the misery of the past.

"Will you farm, my lord?" she asked.

"Bloody hell," he said.

"Will you bless the plough?" she demanded.

"Yes, damn it, I will bless the bloody plough! Are you happy now?"

Reggie smiled. Brilliantly. "Oh, yes, my lord. Quite happy."

Simms entered the library and announced, "I have escorted someone claiming to be a sinner to the drawing room. If I may be allowed to say so, the iniquitous female bears a startling resemblance to your ladyship."

"It must be my sister," Reggie said to Carlisle. "Something must have happened to bring her back here so soon."

"Do you want me to come with you?" he asked.

Reggie was both surprised and grateful for Carlisle's offer of support. "If I need you, I will send one of the underfootmen to find you." She was at the door when she turned back and said, "Thank you, Clay."

Reggie would have run all the way to the drawing room if she had not been so aware of all the eyes focused on her. Apparently the word had spread that she was a twin. The same superstitious Scots who demanded the observance of certain rituals to guarantee a good crop were ogling her as though she were a freak of nature. She felt like yelling "Boo!" and watching them scatter but managed to control the impulse.

She arrived in the drawing room to find Becky wrapped in a shawl and standing close to the fireplace.

"Has something happened to Father or Kitt? Are Gareth and Meg and Lily all right?" Reggie asked.

"Everyone is fine," Becky hurried to reassure her.

That was when Reggie stopped to take a good look at her sister. Becky's face glowed with joy, but her eyes were red-rimmed and shadowed by dark half-moons. "What on earth has befallen you?"

"I am in love," Becky said with a smile and a shrug.

"With Mick, of course," Reggie said, returning the smile with a grin. She crossed the room and hugged her sister hard. "I'm so happy for you. I'm presuming Mick has confessed to loving you as well."

"Yes," Becky said. "And he has proposed marriage."

Reggie's hands dropped, and she took a step back from her sister. "And you said . . ."

Becky paced away toward the fireplace and held out her hands to the flames. "I have told him I need time to think before I answer him." She pivoted to face Reggie. "I have done nothing but think all night, and I don't see how I can marry him."

Now Reggie understood the contradictory reddened eyes and dark half-moons that accompanied the glow of joy on her sister's face. "You want to marry Mick, but you don't think the marriage will work out because Mick is not the least plump in the pocket, has no title, and Society will not approve," Reggie said, speaking what she guessed were her sister's conclusions.

Becky nodded miserably.

"Do you really care what anyone else thinks?"

"I am concerned what Papa may say."

"Papa likes Mick."

"As a son-in-law?" Becky said dubiously. "I am the

daughter of a *duke*. Mick has no father at all. It is not done.''

''What is the worst Papa can do if you marry Mick without his approval?'' Reggie asked.

''Let Mick go without a reference,'' Becky said promptly. ''I could not bear it if Mick was to suffer as a consequence of loving me.''

''I am sure Mick has weighed the danger and must be willing to accept any consequences, if he has asked for your hand. Has Mick said he will speak to Papa?''

''I have told Mick I will do it . . . if I agree to marry him.''

''You had better let me do it,'' Reggie said. ''You are likely to—''

''I said I will do it,'' Becky said, her chin lifting. ''And I shall. If I decide to marry Mick.''

''Well, well,'' Reggie said with a grin. ''My sister has acquired a backbone. It seems love agrees with you.''

''I do love him, more than I ever believed possible,'' Becky said. ''But there are so many ways I am afraid I will not measure up to what he will expect of me.''

''Do you think Mick would ask you to do anything he did not think you capable of doing?'' Reggie asked.

''I suppose not.''

''Then you have your answer,'' Reggie said, spreading her hands wide, as though the problem were solved.

''You are forgetting Lily,'' Becky said. ''She is Penrith's daughter, and a duke's granddaughter. Is it fair—''

''What Lily needs most is love, and she will have more of it from Mick than she ever got from Penrith. If you are worried whether Lily will be able to make a good match, watch and see if Papa does not give her a large enough dowry to ensure that she takes when she makes her bow to Society.''

"And our other children?''

Reggie smiled and took Becky's hands in her own. "Will be blessed to have the two best parents in the world and an aunt who will sponsor them in London whenever they wish to go.''

A tear slid onto Becky's cheek. "You make it sound so simple.''

"It is. Love is too wonderful to waste. Be happy, Becky. And make Mick happy.''

"I will,'' she said, laughing through her tears.

"When are you going to tell him?'' Reggie asked.

"Papa is planning a dance for the St. John's Eve celebration next week. I suppose I will tell Mick then, so he can make the announcement of our engagement during the festivities. That way there will be no turning back.

"Papa has invited everyone—Uncle Marcus and Aunt Lizzie, the Duke of Braddock and his duchess, the Earl of Denbigh and his countess, the earl's friend Percival Porter—''

"Denbigh is Trent now,'' Reggie corrected, "since Denbigh's grandfather cocked up his toes.''

"Oh, I had forgotten. Which makes Charlotte a duchess, not a countess. And of course, the entire neighborhood has been invited, since all of them are farmers who will be celebrating St. John's Eve along with Papa.''

"We have not been invited,'' Reggie said, her eyes bleak.

"But you have. I helped Kitt pen the invitations, and I know she sent one to Carlisle. Perhaps he has not shared it with you yet."

"I suspect he does not intend to share it with me at all," Reggie said. "He is determined I shall not see Papa, and that Papa shall not see me."

"Why not come without him?" Becky suggested.

"I may just do that. I don't want to miss the announcement of your engagement to Mick. Since Carlisle has not shared the invitation with me, he will think I know nothing about it, so I should be able to sneak away to attend."

"It is too bad you cannot come together," Becky said.

It was as close to a criticism of Reggie's marriage as Becky was likely to make. Reggie wanted to defend Carlisle, but the truth was, though she loved him, she thought he was wrong. Her eyes twinkled with mischief. "Perhaps I will leave enough clues for him to figure out where I am—after I am safely gone."

"You are incorrigible," Becky said with a laugh.

"I know. And impossible and hopeless. But I am determined to make a silk purse from the sow's ear I have married."

Becky giggled. "Oh, do not let Carlisle hear you describe him in such terms."

"Of course not," Reggie said with a grin. "To his face he is always 'my lord.' "

•   •   •

Becky could not keep the smile off her face. She had never been so happy as she was in the days preceding the St. John's Eve celebration. She had made up her mind to marry Mick, and she was determined to live her life as happily as she could from now on. She was a little uncertain what her father's grand company—a houseful of dukes and lords, and even a marquess she had never met before—would think when Mick announced their engagement that evening, but she was determined not to quail before them.

Becky had not attended the supper preceding the St. John's Eve dance, because Mick had declined his invitation, and she knew she was too excited to make idle conversation with company when she had not yet told him her decision. Mick was a guest at Blackthorne Hall, because he needed to be on hand to supervise the preparations for the outdoor St. John's Eve festivities to be held later in the evening, which included a bonfire. He had a room upstairs where he stayed whenever his business with her father kept him overnight.

Becky sought him there.

She was wearing a gown of sapphire blue silk that matched her eyes, with a low-cut square neck, short, capped sleeves, and a flounced hem. She knocked on the door and waited with bated breath for Mick to answer it.

"Oh!" she said when he opened the door. "You look so . . . elegant."

He was dressed in exquisitely tailored evening clothes, including a light blue coat in a shade that complemented her gown, a silver waistcoat, gray trousers, white stockings, and black patent leather shoes. He could easily have passed for one of the noblemen dining downstairs. But he was not and never would be. Once she married him, her life would change forever.

Mick peered into the hall and said, "What are you doing up here, Becky? Someone may see you. Do you want to ruin your reputation?"

She grinned. "Since I have decided to marry you, I don't give a fig what anyone thinks."

Becky had not meant to blurt it out like that. When she saw the look of utter joy on Mick's face, she was glad she had. He grabbed her by the hand, dragged her inside his room, and closed the door behind her. A moment later she was in his arms being soundly kissed.

It was a long time before they came up for air, and they were both grinning with delight when they finally looked at each other.

"I promise you will never be sorry," Mick said, covering her face with kisses. "I will devote myself to making you happy. I will try to be a good father to Lily and our other children you do want more, don't you, Becky? We never spoke of children."

"I do," Becky said. "I want as many more as we can manage on your salary. I do not intend to let Papa discharge you if he disapproves of our decision to marry, even if I have to go to Kitt and ask for her help to make him keep you on."

"About that . . ." Mick said. He caught her face between his hands. He was smiling, but there was concern in his blue eyes. "There is something I have not told you."

"Whatever it is, I do not want to know," Becky said,

suddenly certain it was not good news. "Please, Mick. Say we can be married. I don't care how hard our lives will be. I am willing to endure any hardship, if only we can be together."

"Oh, my darling. Heart of my heart. You have filled my cup to overflowing. It will *not* be hard. There is something I must tell you that—"

A knock on the door interrupted him.

"Your presence is requested downstairs in the dining room, Mr. O'Malley," an underfootman said.

Becky exchanged an uneasy look with Mick. "I thought you had refused Papa's supper invitation."

"I did," Mick said. "One of the guests has commanded my presence, someone I . . . never expected to see at Blackthorne Hall."

"Who?" Becky asked.

Mick sighed. "I suppose you will have to know sooner or later. Will you come with me?"

Mick offered his arm and Becky took it, but she could tell from the grim look on his face, that she was not going to like whatever was coming.

There was an even number at the supper table, even though Reggie had not made it after all. Another gentleman took up the extra setting needed to partner Trent's bachelor friend Percival Porter, Viscount Burton.

"Tenby was telling us about your good fortune, Mick," Uncle Marcus said. "Quite a coincidence, finding you after all these years. We all wanted to toast your good fortune."

All the gentlemen stood, while the ladies raised their glasses.

"Please do not—"

Mick's protest was drowned out by the Marquess of Tenby's toast. "To my long-lost grandson, Michael Delaford, Earl of Stalbridge. Welcome back to the fold."

"Here, here," the gentlemen said as they emptied their wine goblets.

Becky had heard what the marquess said, but she was still not certain she understood what it meant. She turned to Mick and asked, "Are you Michael Delaford?"

"Yes, but Becky—"

"How long have you known?" she demanded, aware that she was making a spectacle of herself, but unable to stop.

"Since I was last in London."

She felt her heart begin to ricochet. Felt her ears begin to roar. "And yet you let me believe that if I married you we would live as paupers?"

"We won't be rich," Mick replied. "I traded my inheritance to Penrith for your freedom."

The blood leached from Becky's face. "How could you?"

"You are still rich, my boy," Tenby volunteered. "I forced my solicitor to reveal what you intended to do and bought off Penrith myself. Sent him out of the country for good, so he would never cause another worry to you or your lady. Your inheritance is intact."

It was Mick's turn to blanch. "Becky, I had no idea—"

"Do not speak to me," she said. "I don't know if I can ever forgive you for what you've done. Or trust you.

Or love you. And I most certainly will not marry you!''
Becky turned and fled from the room.

"What was that all about?" Blackthorne asked Mick.

"It appears your daughter has just refused my pro-
posal." Mick met his grandfather's penitent eyes and
said, "I didn't ask for your help, and I don't want it.
Stay out of my life. You've done enough damage!"

Mick pivoted on his heel and left the suddenly silent
dining room, desperate to find Becky and make his apologies. But he did not hold out much hope that she would
forgive him anytime soon. "Damn, damn, damn!"

"Why do I think that is *not* a toast to your coming
nuptials."

"Reggie!" Mick cried. "Thank God you have come.
You must talk to Becky."

"Why? What is wrong?" she asked, stopping inside
the door to hand her cape to the butler.

"A stupid misunderstanding."

"I presume you are the one who has been stupid."

"Do not play games with me," Mick snapped. "My
whole life is at stake—and both Becky's and my happiness."

Reggie eyed the butler and said to Mick, "Perhaps we
should go somewhere private to continue this conversation."

"The drawing room should be empty," Mick said,
leading her in that direction. Once they got inside, Reggie settled onto the sofa, while Mick paced before her.

"The last time I spoke with Becky, she had made up
her mind to marry you and live a life of sacrifice. What
has happened since then?" Reggie asked.

"I have become an earl as rich as Croesus," Mick retorted.

Reggie was startled onto her feet. "What? You cannot be serious."

"When I was last in London I met with a solicitor who informed me I am Michael Delaford, the long-lost grandson of the Marquess of Tenby. Because of his shabby treatment of my mother, I wanted nothing from my grandfather, so I pledged my inheritance to Penrith in exchange for Becky's freedom."

Reggie gasped and sank onto the sofa.

"A moment ago, Becky found out everything."

"And refused to marry you," Reggie said.

"Yes."

"Why didn't you say something to her sooner?" Reggie asked.

"It seems foolish now, but I wanted her to give up everything for love."

"And she did, and then found out you had made a fool of her. I cannot blame her for being angry," Reggie said rising again to confront him. "I am furious with you! How could you go to Penrith without asking Becky first? I thought her marriage wretched, but it should have been her choice whether to remain in it."

"I cannot be sorry for ridding her of Penrith," Mick retorted. "I cannot even be sorry for testing her as I did. It is a sweet thing to know one is loved for oneself, not for any title or fortune. Surely Becky can forgive me."

"How can she trust you after this?" Reggie asked. "After you manipulated and deceived her so cruelly?"

"I love her, Reggie. Tell me what to do. Tell me what to say."

Mick looked so miserable that Reggie took pity on him. "I saw Becky walking in the garden when my carriage arrived. If you want her back, I suggest you beg her pardon and promise never to mislead her again. It cannot hurt if you point out that you will be wealthy enough to support her comfortably, and that when your grandfather sticks his spoon in the wall, she will become a marchioness and take precedence over me when we go in to supper."

Mick grinned. "You are incorrigible, Reggie."

"I know. Hurry, Mick. You have a lifetime of love to arrange."

Mick kissed her on the cheek. "You have been a good sister, Reggie, to both me and Becky. Is there anything I can do to help you in return?"

Reggie shook her head. "Go. I am bound to see Papa at last. Then I will deal with that beast I have married."

"You will deal with me now," Carlisle said.

Reggie turned and saw the devil had come to life. Carlisle was dressed entirely in black, with a cape that covered even his white linen.

Mick put himself between Reggie and her husband and said, "You will have to go through me to get to her."

"Please go, Mick," Reggie said, adroitly stepping around him. "I need to speak with my husband alone."

"I don't trust him not to hurt you," Mick said.

Reggie saw the flash of affront in Carlisle's eyes. He had never physically harmed her, though he had not made her life as easy as it could have been. "You have business of your own that must be tended," Reggie reminded Mick. "My husband will do me no harm."

Reggie worked to keep her demeanor calm, knowing Mick would make his judgment whether to leave or to stay based on her behavior. "Go," she urged. "Becky is waiting."

A moment later Mick was gone, and Reggie was alone with her husband.

"What are you doing here, Reggie?" Carlisle asked.

"I was invited," she replied flippantly. "Though you neglected to advise me of the fact," she said in harsher tones.

"I have forbidden you to see your father. You must know he is here tonight."

"Yes. And a great many other friends with whom I hope to visit," Reggie agreed. "Now that you are here, I will be able to dance. I have missed dancing with you, my lord."

"I did not come to dance."

"Neither did I," Reggie admitted. "I came with the sole purpose of seeing my father. You cannot keep us apart forever, my lord."

"Come home with me, Reggie," he said, holding out his hand to her.

"And if I refuse?"

"I will carry you out of here kicking and screaming, if that is your choice."

She believed he would do it. It was dreadful to get so close, and yet not speak with her father. If Mick had not delayed her, the deed would have been done, and she would not have been left with the choice that Carlisle now gave her. If she did not go quietly, her husband intended to forcibly remove her from her father's house. If she resisted, he would doubtless make a scene and create a scandal and perhaps even provoke her father into a duel.

It would not be hard to do. Both men were proud and stubborn and opinionated.

"Very well, my lord," she said. "I will postpone my visit to Papa until another time."

She was not giving up. She was only giving in for the moment. At least she had gotten her husband to cross the threshold of Blackthorne Hall. That was a feat she would have believed impossible, except he was standing in her father's drawing room. It was a small step, but enough small steps might eventually get Carlisle where she wanted him to go.

Her husband escorted her directly back to the door, where the butler returned her cape. Carlisle draped it over her shoulders and said, "I have brought my carriage to take you home."

"I have transportation of my own," she replied.

"I have sent Terrence home with your carriage. You will need to ride with me."

Reggie bit back the unladylike word that was trying desperately to get out and allowed Carlisle to escort her to his waiting carriage. Before she stepped inside, the elderly coachman, a retired army sergeant whose name she remembered was Dick Hobson, but who only answered to Sergeant, handed her something wrapped in linen.

"Terrence left this for you, my lady," Hobson said. "It is a piece of cake from the St. John's Eve celebration. He was sorry he could not stay to give it to you himself, but he thought you might like to have it."

"Thank you, Sergeant," Reggie said. Terrence had surely divined, when Carlisle ordered him home, that she would not be allowed to stay and enjoy the festivities. The thoughtful gesture moved her almost to tears. She opened the small napkin and stared at the moist, fruit-laden cake.

Her stomach suddenly rolled, and she knew she would never be able to eat it. She handed it back to Sergeant Hobson. "You enjoy it, Sergeant. I have no appetite now, and it will be better eaten fresh."

"Thank you, milady," Hobson said. He picked up the square of crumbling cake from the linen and shoved the whole of it into his mouth. "Delicious," he said, grinning wide enough to reveal mushed-up cake between his teeth.

Reggie was afraid she might cast up her accounts and hurried to step inside the carriage door, which Carlisle held open for her.

"Are you unwell?" he asked as he sprang into the carriage and sat down beside her.

"I am sick at heart," she retorted, though her stomach was none too steady.

"We will be home soon," Carlisle said.

"Home?" she replied sharply. "I have tried to make it that. But so little light seeps in beyond the ivy choking the windows, that it remains a dark and gloomy place. Won't you at least allow me to purchase windowpanes, my lord? I cannot bear the darkness," she cried. "I cannot bear it anymore!"

He lifted her onto his lap and held her close enough to hear his heartbeat, while she quivered with tears she refused to shed. It was Carlisle's darkness she could not bear. His black soul that so desperately needed light. But she had found no way so far to free either of them—the house or the man—from the crippling wounds of the past.

The carriage slowed and then stopped, but when Reggie looked out, she did not see any welcoming lights. "Where are we?" she asked. "Why did Hobson stop?"

"I will find out," Carlisle said, setting her back down on the seat next to him and then exiting the carriage.

Reggie waited only a moment before she was out of the carriage behind him. She stepped to the front of the carriage and saw that Hobson was slumped sideways on the coachman's seat. Carlisle was up on the seat beside him, his hand pressed against the pulse beneath Hobson's ear.

"What is wrong with him?" Reggie asked, alarmed.

"He's dead," Carlisle replied. "His heart must have failed. I will have to drive us the rest of the way. Get back inside."

As Carlisle moved the coachman aside, the two lanterns on either side of the seat revealed his face. Reggie gasped. From the look on Hobson's face, he had died an agonizing death. Suddenly, the napkin that had held Terrence's offering slipped off the seat and onto the ground in front of her.

Until that instant, Reggie had not imagined foul play

was involved in the coachman's death. But something about the look on Hobson's face, together with the sudden reappearance of the napkin, made her wonder if the cake might have been poisoned.

If it was, then you were meant to die.

Reggie shivered. And felt nauseated again. But this time she was forced to turn aside, as her body betrayed her, and she lost what little food her stomach contained. She was aware of Carlisle standing beside her a moment later, handing her his handkerchief to wipe her mouth.

"I am sorry," she said. "When I saw his face . . ."

"Come, let me help you back inside the carriage."

She opened her mouth to tell him about her suspicion that poison might have killed Hobson, but shut it again. There was no way to prove the issue one way or the other. And she was probably letting her imagination run away with her, suspecting plots where none existed.

But Terrence had been on the beach with the boat that had been sabotaged. And now he had given Hobson the cake to deliver into her hands. Perhaps Terrence was the one in Mr. Ambleside's employ, not MacTavish. She would have to question the scarred man about the cake and watch for any signs of guilt. Reggie had learned enough from her father's experience to know she did not want to unjustly accuse anyone. Better to wait and be certain before she said anything to Carlisle.

Tomorrow she would confront Terrence with what she knew.

Chapter 19

As soon as Reggie was safely in the house, Clay had sought out Pegg and asked him to come out to the stableyard and look at Sergeant Hobson. "I didn't want to frighten Reggie, so I told her Hobson's heart had failed. He is old enough for that to be the case. But I think the man's been poisoned."

Pegg pried open Hobson's mouth and looked at his tongue, then peeled back his eyelids—which Clay had closed so the man would not stare at him the entire way home—and peered into the sergeant's eyes to study his tortured features.

"Looks like poison, right enough," Pegg said. "But why would anyone want to poison one of yer servants?"

"The poison was intended for Reggie," Clay said. "It was in a piece of cake Terrence left for her with Hobson. She wasn't feeling well and told Hobson he could have it. Hobson ate it and died."

"Ye think Terrence knew the cake was poisoned?" Pegg asked.

"I intend to find out," Clay said. But when he and Pegg went looking for the scarred man, he had disappeared.

"Terrence said this afternoon that his mother was ill, and he was spending the night with her in Mishnish," Cook said, when she learned of Clay's search for the missing servant. "I expect he will be back at work tomorrow morning."

Clay exchanged a look with Pegg. It was coincidental that the man was gone, and perhaps, if Reggie had died, he would not have come back. But the next morning he returned at dawn.

When he was told that Hobson had been poisoned, Terrence expressed horror and regret, but no guilt. In fact, the scarred man exhibited none of the nervousness and anxiety that Clay would have expected, if he were actually guilty of Hobson's murder.

In the end, Hobson's murder remained a mystery. But Clay was convinced his inquiries about Cedric Ambleside had made the man anxious enough to want to be rid of him. Murdering Clay's wife was one way of doing it, since Clay would likely be accused of the crime. Hobson's death, combined with the sinking rowboat and the slashed carriage traces, left Clay in no doubt that Ambleside was intent on seeing him back in chains. The attacks on Blackthorne's family were especially effective in pointing a finger at Clay, because his animosity toward the duke, and the reason for it, were so well known.

Clay redoubled his efforts to find the man, knowing

that he must be close. He did not give up his search for Ambleside during the rest of the spring and summer, but he found little evidence that Cedric Ambleside had ever existed. Clay gave the balance of his attention to farming the rich land Blackthorne had returned to him.

In the three months since St. John's Eve, Clay had overseen each step of the ploughing and planting. He had seeped the seed in water, following the precise instructions in his pamphlet. But he had also allowed his workmen to observe the traditional custom of placing the soaked seed in a basket on top of an egg and an iron nail, which supposedly ensured germination.

He had listened to prayers for the land's fertility and allowed the sowers to walk sunwise and drop their seed from a triangular cloth. But he had also made sure the rows were spread generously with manure first, as his pamphlet advised.

His corn had grown fast and tall and was already tasseling. His wheat was so heavy-laden that the stems bent and shimmered like green waves in the wind. His mangel-wurzels threatened to burst, they were so large. In short, his fields promised a yield greater than any other in the neighborhood.

Clay should have been the happiest man alive. He had achieved the dream that had kept him alive during the five cruel years he had spent on Captain Taylor's frigate. It was only now, when success was in his grasp, that Clay realized his dream meant nothing to him, compared to the thing he did *not* have: his wife's love.

Ever since Clay had gone to fetch Reggie from her father's home on St. John's Eve, she had kept her distance. It was no longer a matter of the bedroom door being locked against him. She had removed herself entirely from his company. If he came into a room, she left. If he joined her on horseback, she ended her ride. They ate at different times or in separate places. She never argued with him. She hardly spoke to him at all.

And yet his house ran with a smoothness he had never imagined. His servants—there were too many of them to count—functioned with great efficiency. Reggie had even been there at each step of the ploughing and planting, in the background observing and helping in any way that would not bring her into his sphere.

Clay wanted his wife back in his life. Especially since he had discovered she was in expectation of a happy event.

He would never have known Reggie was pregnant if he had not caught her bent over the stone wall behind the garden one morning a week past, casting up her accounts.

He had wiped her face with his handkerchief, and then demanded, "Did you get too much sun? You should wear a bonnet when you work in the garden. Although why you would need to dig in the dirt when we have two gardeners—"

"I am expecting a child," she had blurted.

Clay felt his stomach pitch. "Are you certain?"

"As certain as a woman can be," she said, wavering unsteadily on her feet. "I have not yet seen a doctor—"

"Sit down," he said, "before you fall down."

He had lifted her bodily and sat her on the repaired stone wall that separated the garden from the lawn beyond it. "Take a deep breath," he instructed. She looked wan and pale and even a little thin. "You must take care of yourself better," he said brushing the back of his hand gently across her cheek. She flinched, and he withdrew his hand. "Is my touch so repugnant to you?"

She met his gaze and said, "Quite the opposite, my lord. But I will not be seduced. You know the price of my acquiescence."

"So now your favors are for sale?"

Two angry spots of red appeared on her pale cheeks. "I want my child to know his grandfather. Will you make peace with my father?"

"I have no intention of—"

She jumped down from the stone wall so abruptly, she nearly fell. He caught her, and she jerked herself away. "Keep your distance, my lord."

He had watched her stalk away, her chin up, her arms akimbo, and wanted her desperately. But not on her terms.

He had finally come up with a peace offering he thought she might accept. He had ordered new windowpanes for all the broken windows.

Of course, Clay had not told her yet what he had done. He planned to have the broken windows replaced some afternoon when Reggie was out of the house visiting the Scottish Home for Orphans she had found in Mishnish and surprise her when she got back. He hoped it would work to melt the ice that surrounded her heart.

Forgive her father, and she will burn in your embrace.

Clay had tried. He simply could not.

He watched every day for the wagonload of windows.

Maybe when the castle was full of light once more, Reggie could find her way to him.

In the three months since St. John's Eve, Reggie had not discovered which of her servants, if any, was in Cedric Ambleside's employ. Terrence had pleaded innocence. MacTavish played least in sight. Meanwhile, Carlisle had not forgiven her father, Becky had not forgiven Mick, and she found herself unable to convince either one to relent.

Reggie spent her days so agitated in heart and mind that her appetite suffered even more than it would have under the circumstances. She often felt too sick from her pregnancy to eat, and when she did, she could not keep anything down. She was tired of waiting for her father and Carlisle to make amends on their own. So she had sent a note to her father asking him to meet her this afternoon at a spot halfway between Blackthorne Hall and Castle Carlisle. The glen had a hazelnut tree for shade and a fallen log where they could sit and talk.

She was going to make sure Carlisle met her at the same place a half hour later. Once the two men were face-to-face, with her to keep peace, of course, Reggie was certain they could be brought to some understanding.

As she entered the barn to saddle a mount for herself—she had found Freddy a better job as an apprentice blacksmith in Mishnish—a man suddenly stepped out of the shadows.

Reggie stumbled backward, tripped over a pitchfork

someone had left on the ground, and would have fallen onto the sharp tines, if two strong hands had not caught her first.

"MacTavish!" she exclaimed, when she saw who had rescued her. "What are you doing here? You scared me half to death."

"Ye asked me to meet ye her*rr*e," he reminded her.

She shot him a chagrined smile. "So I did. I would like you to find his lordship and tell him to meet me at the glen halfway between here and Blackthorne Hall in half an hour."

MacTavish frowned. "Ye'*rr*e *rr*idin' there by your*rr*-self, milady?"

"Don't worry, MacTavish. I won't be on my own for very long. I've arranged for someone else to be there when I arrive."

MacTavish's beetled white brows rose to his absent hairline. "What t*rr*ouble are ye b*rr*ewin', lass?"

"Please do as I ask, MacTavish," Reggie snapped. She was nervous enough about the coming encounter without adding MacTavish's qualms to her own.

Because he insisted, Reggie allowed MacTavish to saddle a mount for her and then to help her into the sidesaddle. She would have preferred to ride astride, but she had no intention of giving either man the opportunity to turn his wrath on her for something as paltry as how she mounted a horse, when there were much more important issues to be debated.

Reggie could see her father's gray stallion, almost the size of a medieval warhorse, grazing in the shade of the hazelnut tree as she approached the glen. Unfortunately, she could also hear pounding hoofbeats behind her.

Reggie groaned. At the farthest hill, just heading into a concealing copse of trees, she saw Carlisle's black stallion, Balthazar. She should have known better than to trust MacTavish!

She kneed her mount, hoping to reach her father before she was overtaken by her husband. She had just reined her horse to a stop in the glen and was leaning forward so her father could lift her down, when a bullet zinged past her. If she had not leaned over, it would have struck her in the head.

Her father yanked her down and threw himself protectively on top of her. "Are you all right?" he asked. "Were you hit?"

He had landed on her with his full weight, which was enough to drive the breath from her lungs, leaving her unable to tell him she was fine. When she did not reply, he raised himself up enough to do a survey of her gold riding habit with its black military frogs, searching for a spot of blood red.

"I am fine, Papa," she managed at last.

"I will kill him," her father said.

He leapt up from the ground and headed for Carlisle, who had just arrived in the glen, vaulted down from his horse, and was running toward where she lay on the ground, apparently oblivious to her father's lethal intent.

Reggie knew she had to do something immediately, or disaster would result. "Papa!" she cried. "No!"

Her cry alerted Carlisle to her father's attack and put

him on guard, but the two men stood bristling a foot away from each other.

"I want to see my wife."

"You've done enough harm today."

Reggie clambered to her feet and slid into the narrow space between them, a flat palm against each man's chest to ensure they did not move a step closer. "Stop it, both of you!" she ordered.

She angled her chin up toward her father and said, "You can see Carlisle has no weapon. Someone else must have taken that shot at me. Ask yourself who could want to harm both you and my husband? Who has a motive to want you separated from those you love most and to want Carlisle blamed for it? What common enemy do you both have, Papa? Think!"

Her father frowned. "It cannot be Cedric Ambleside."

Reggie turned to her husband. "And you must long since have realized, my lord, since we both know you are innocent, that some evil force must be at work, the same force that set you and my father at odds twelve years ago."

"Cedric Ambleside," Carlisle supplied.

"Can the two of you not find some common ground on which to fight your common enemy?" Reggie asked. "For my sake?"

"Ambleside is a ghost," her father said. "I have found no trace of him."

"Nor have I," Carlisle said.

"But who else could it be?" Reggie asked.

She saw her father glance sideways at Carlisle. "No, Papa. It is not my husband."

"How do you know?" her father demanded. "He was out of sight in the trees when the shot was fired. Perhaps he set aside his weapon before he rode into the glen."

"You never believed the truth twelve years ago, when it was right before your eyes," Carlisle snarled back. "Why should I expect you to see it now?"

"Clay, please!"

"Come with me, Reggie," he said. "I have heard enough. I am through here."

"No, Clay. I—"

"Either come with me now, or I am done with you," he said.

"I cannot choose between the two of you," she said. "Please stay and make peace with my father."

"He does not want peace!" Carlisle snapped.

"Papa, tell him you are willing to forgive and forget—"

"I have done nothing for which I must be forgiven," Carlisle interrupted angrily. He turned to Blackthorne. "And I will never forget the harm you have done me and mine."

"Then why did you marry my daughter?" the duke demanded.

"To destroy the thing you loved most," Carlisle raged back.

Reggie felt as though she had been stabbed in the heart. "Clay, please—"

"Your father can have you," Carlisle said, shoving her toward the duke. "I will come for my child when it is born.'' He strode to his horse, mounted, and rode away without another word.

Reggie felt the sting in her nose and blinked hard to clear her blurring vision.

She felt her father's hand on her shoulder. ''Go after him, child. I would rather you stay with him than have your child torn from your arms. That is a wound no parent should have to bear.''

Reggie hugged her father as much to comfort him as to comfort herself. ''If he cannot forgive you, he does not truly love me,'' she said. ''But there is something I must do before I leave him.''

''What is that?'' her father asked.

''Let in some light,'' she said. ''To chase away the shadows.''

Her father had ridden halfway home with her before they encountered MacTavish, who escorted her the rest of the way. Reggie was starving by the time she arrived back at the castle. She did not search for Carlisle. She did not wish to see him. She stuffed down one of Cook's cherry tarts on her way through the kitchen, where she collected George and Terrence.

''We will need that ladder you used to hang the Countess of Carlisle's picture in the library, Terrence,'' she said. ''Would you get it please, and bring it outside.''

''Yes, milady,'' Terrence said.

''What do you think would be best to use to cut that ivy away from the windows?'' she asked George as she headed out the kitchen door with him.

''A pair of garden shears, milady.''

"Do we have such a thing?"

George scratched his head. "I saw a small shed near the barn. Perhaps I might find something there."

"Will you please go look now?"

Within an hour of Carlisle's ultimatum to Reggie, Terrence was holding the ladder braced against the outside of the castle near the ivy that covered Carlisle's bedroom window, while George clung to the third rung from the top, pruning away the thick ivy in a neat square.

Reggie was standing nearby, watching the sun sparkle off a speck of newly revealed windowpane, when a boy of nine or ten appeared at her side.

He glanced up, shading his eyes with his hand. "Is that my papa?"

"Who is your papa?" Reggie asked.

"George Dunswell, milady."

"Then that is your papa," Reggie confirmed.

"Ma says he's to come right away," the boy said. "She's havin' the baby, but it isna comin' right, and she needs the doctor."

"Terrence, would you please call George down and tell him it is his wife's time, and she needs him to go for the doctor?"

Reggie wondered if she should go with the boy and see if she could help Mrs. Dunswell. She knew nothing about childbirth, but she could at least entertain the other children and keep them out of the way.

Moments later, George was on the ground. He was so excited he handed Reggie the shears and said, "Dinna fash yerself, milady. Sadie says it isna comin' right every time, and every time, out pops another bairn, as easy as ye please.''

Reggie was flustered by his frank talk, but relieved that Mrs. Dunswell was apparently in no real danger. ''Would you like me to come—''

She had no trouble reading George's face, though he had more difficulty explaining in words, stopping and starting and stuttering, that a great lady in the house would only make his wife anxious, and besides, her sister was staying with them and could manage the children.

''Very well, George. I will remain here,'' she said at last, to cut him off.

When George and his son were gone, she was disappointed to realize it would not be possible after all to clear the windows of ivy this afternoon. But she could not spend another day at Castle Carlisle.

She opened and closed the shears once. That was not so hard. She looked up at the window, judging the distance. She had climbed trees taller than that. And she and Becky had not once, but twice, tied sheets together and descended from a window at least that high.

''Will you hold the ladder for me, Terrence,'' she said.

''You are not going up there, are you, milady?'' Terrence said.

''Why not?'' Reggie said. ''Everyone else is busy with another chore, and I cannot bear to leave the house in gloom another day. I want Lord Carlisle to see the sun rise tomorrow morning.''

''Why not let me—''

"I would be little help if the ladder began to tip under you, Terrence. While you will be here to catch me if I fall."

Terrence gave her a dubious look. "Perhaps Lord Carlisle—"

Reggie gave Terrence her most charming smile. If he went to Carlisle, she would never be allowed to finish what George had started. "Lord Carlisle will be grateful to see the work is done." Or maybe not. But by then it would be too late. She started up the ladder, afraid that if she waited, Terrence might betray her as MacTavish had and search out Carlisle after all.

It was not until Reggie had reached the third rung from the top, where she had seen George stand, that she realized the difference between standing on the solid branch of an oak and standing on the narrow rung of a rickety ladder. It was necessary to use both hands to manipulate the shears, and every time she leaned over, the ladder swayed beneath her weight.

"Hold tight, Terrence," she called down to him.

"I will, milady," Terrence promised.

It was harder work than Reggie had thought it would be. The awkward way she was forced to bend made her shoulders ache. And her hands began to blister under George's too-large leather gloves. A large horsefly kept buzzing around her head. She had swiped at it often enough to know it was not going to leave her alone, so she was trying to ignore it.

Reggie had almost the entire window cleared and was working on the farthest corner, stretching her whole body across the window to reach the last of the ivy, when the horsefly settled on her nose.

And bit her.

She yelped and jerked upright. At the same time, the ladder seemed to rock beneath her feet. She struggled to retain her perch but was overbalanced by the heavy shears, which not only pulled her body forward, but also occupied both hands, making it impossible for her to grab on to the ladder. She finally dropped the shears and reached for the ladder, but it was too late.

Reggie's arms flailed in vain, as she felt herself plummeting toward the ground.

Chapter 20

REGGIE'S TERROR WAS SO GREAT, IT stopped her breath in her chest, so she could not even scream. She fell silently, arms and legs scrabbling for purchase in the insubstantial air. Until today, she had never imagined what it might be like to die, that prospect had seemed so far in the future. In the few seconds Reggie had left, she thought of Clay, wishing she did not have to leave him so wounded. And of Becky, who was the other half of her. And of Papa—

She got no further than picturing him in her mind before she struck something solid. If Reggie had thought at all of the pain she would have to endure when she landed, it had been to have a brief hope that she would die instantly. It was immediately apparent that her wish was not to be granted. On the other hand, her landing was much less violent than she had anticipated.

She had forgotten entirely about the unkempt boxwood hedge that surrounded the castle. Because the hedge was so high, she had not plunged the entire way to the ground. The soft leaves and new growth gave way, breaking her fall, but she quickly encountered more substantial limbs that gouged her back and buttocks. Those same boxwood limbs crackled and popped and finally broke away under her weight. And she found herself once again diving through the air.

The second drop was much shorter, and Reggie managed at the last second to stick out her right hand to keep her head from hitting the ground first. Her hand eventually collapsed under the weight of her body, and her right shoulder bore the brunt of her tumbling fall. What little air was left in her lungs was crushed out by the force of her landing.

She lay dazed, breathless, feeling the sting of the salty sea air on dozens of cuts and pricks made in her flesh by hardy Scottish thistles, but very grateful to be alive.

"Reggie?"

Reggie recognized Carlisle's voice, but it took too much effort to open her eyes. There was no air in her lungs to speak, and breathing, she realized when she tried it, hurt. In fact, moving at all was out of the question.

"You little fool," she heard him mutter, though he sounded more tender than irate. Of course, the hope that he would not be angry with her did not last long.

"Damned stubborn, willful woman!" he swore. And then, "Bloody, bloody hell!"

By then she had taken a few careful, shallow breaths, so there was enough air in her lungs to cry out in agony when he tried to lift her.

"I'm sorry, love," he murmured in her ear, as he gently slid his hands under her, curled her body against his own, and stood up. "Those cuts need to be tended, and lord knows whether you have any broken bones."

She bit back a moan as he shifted her in his arms and started walking. Her right wrist and shoulder hurt worst, but her back and buttocks ached, and it seemed that every place her skin came in contact with his, he rubbed against a tear in her flesh.

"Terrence says you hit the hedge first, or you would not be alive to hurt so much," he said. "Wake up, Reggie," he ordered in a voice that demanded obedience. And then, more urgently but more quietly, "Open your eyes, Reggie, please."

Her eyelashes flickered open, but the sun was too bright, and she closed them again. "Clay," she murmured.

"Yes, love," he said.

"My shoulder hurts."

"I suspect it does. What were you doing up on a ladder, Reggie? Don't waste the breath to answer. I can see for myself my bedroom window is clear of ivy. But we have servants to do that sort of work."

"The baby," she murmured.

"You should have thought of the baby sooner. I cannot believe you were climbing a ladder in your condition! Are you mad, woman?"

She was trying to tell him that George's wife was having a baby, and that was why she had gone up the ladder herself. But she was so cold and so very tired, and it took entirely too much effort to explain. And he was right. She should have been more careful. But it had been so important to let in the light. More important than anything. . . .

He started walking faster, jostling her, making everything hurt more.

She gave a sharp cry when he stumbled once and jarred her shoulder.

"Sorry," he bit out. "I will try to be more careful. Terrence has been sent to find a doctor. With God's help, he will be back before you suffer much more."

Tears seeped from beneath her eyelids, but she endured the excruciating pain without further complaint.

"Don't give up now, Reggie. Keep fighting, love. We have a great many years ahead of us together."

That was the last thing Reggie heard before she sank into a blackness that summoned her with soft whispers that promised surcease from the pain.

Clay paced anxiously outside Reggie's bedroom door. Dr. Wren had been inside for nearly half an hour without offering a word of information on Reggie's condition. Clay knew she was alive, but she had lost consciousness soon after he laid her down, and she had not regained it before the doctor arrived several hours later. He was frightened.

What if she never woke up? What if he never had a chance to say he was sorry? What if she never had a chance to see Castle Carlisle with all its windows open to the sunlight?

Suddenly, Reggie screamed.

Clay's heart skipped a beat. Dear God! What had happened now? He burst into the room, saw the doctor bent over her, and shouted, "What are you doing to her!"

"I have just reset her dislocated shoulder," the doctor said calmly. "Now, if you will please wait outside, your lordship, I can finish my work."

Clay stood staring, unable to move. Reggie's right shoulder was horribly bruised, and her right wrist was swollen nearly double its size. He was appalled at the enormous number of cuts and smaller bruises he could see on her face and arms despite the sheet that was drawn up to protect her modesty. Her face was wan, her eyes closed.

But if she had screamed, she was obviously no longer unconscious. Surely that was a good sign. "Will she be all right?" he asked.

"I will know more when I have completed my examination," the doctor said. He turned to the plump, white-haired—and white-faced—housekeeper and said, "Mrs. Stephens, will you please take his lordship downstairs and get him some brandy."

"I can see myself out, Mrs. Stephens," Clay said, backing out of the room. "You stay and assist the doctor."

He headed downstairs to the drawing room and found Pegg there before him. The big man was sitting in the single wing chair that occupied the room, leaving Clay with a choice between the stool at the pianoforte or the Grecian sofa, with its flaking gilded arms. The rotted red velvet that had once covered the sofa had been replaced with a piece of bottle-green brocade drapery salvaged from an upstairs bedroom window.

Clay could not bear to look at the sofa. It reminded him too much of Reggie. He marched to the rolling cart in the corner, poured himself a glass of brandy—both the chipped crystal goblets and the slightly cracked decanter having been scavenged by Reggie from the attic—and swallowed it in one reckless gulp.

The heady fumes made his eyes water, but did nothing to ease his fear. He was tempted to pour himself another but realized it would take the whole bottle to drown his dread. He set the glass down and began to pace again.

"Sit down, lad. Ye're makin' me nervous," Pegg said.

"If she dies—"

" 'Twill serve ye right if she dies," Pegg interrupted, lurching out of the chair to confront Clay. "Ye never valued the lass, and look what's happened. Are ye ready now to give up this foolishness?"

"Are you suggesting I forgive her father because she fell off a ladder doing something I never asked, never intended, never even wanted her to do?"

"If ye love the lass, why not?" Pegg retorted.

Clay ignored the first half of Pegg's statement to focus on the question he had asked. "Do you really think Blackthorne has suffered enough? He endured a slight financial setback when he tried to sell his wheat crop this year, but he has made arrangements to keep that from happening again.

"I have bankrupted his son-in-law, but Blackthorne

merely welcomed his daughter home with open arms. And I have taken his other daughter to wife, forcing her to live apart from her father for—is it three months now or four that we have been in Scotland?'' Clay asked sarcastically.

''Where have I done Blackthorne any harm that can equal the harm he has done me. Where are we even? Whatever my personal feelings for his daughter, the duke must not be allowed to escape unpunished. I made a vow to God, to my wife and son, and to myself, that if I lived to return to England, I would do my best to repay the duke by making as thorough a ruin of his life as he made of mine. I have not yet begun to repay that debt!''

Clay marched out of the room without allowing Pegg to speak. There was nothing his friend could say to him that would change his mind.

But his feet took him back up the stairs, where he paced outside Reggie's door as nervously and anxiously as any new bridegroom threatened with the loss of a beloved wife.

''Milorrrd? I must speak with ye.''

Clay turned to find Cam MacTavish standing before him. The gatekeeper had no business in the house and none at all upstairs where the family lived. ''What are you doing here, MacTavish?'' Clay asked irritably. ''If you have come to ask about my wife's condition, I have nothing to report.''

''I havena come for that. I've come to tell ye 'twas no accident yer*rr* wife fell. 'Twas done on pur*rr*pose by the scar*rr*red man holding the ladder*rr*. He meant for her*rr* to fall. He meant to kill her*rr* if he could.''

349

Clay's breath was caught in his chest. He had already interrogated Terrence about how the accident had happened. The man had not acted like a murderer. He had been in tears.

"She was swatting at a horsefly, my lord," Terrence had said, his voice breaking, "and lost her balance."

"What was she doing up there in the first place?" he had asked.

"When George was called away, Lady Carlisle insisted on climbing the ladder herself to finish what he had started. She said I could hold the ladder for her, but she would not be able to hold it for me."

He remembered thanking Terrence for coming to find him so quickly and Terrence apologizing for how long it had taken to locate the doctor.

If what MacTavish said was true, it was entirely possible Terrence had delayed finding the doctor on purpose.

"How do you know Terrence is guilty?" Clay asked. Having been a victim of false accusations himself, he was not ready to accept MacTavish's word without some further evidence.

"I was the*rr*e, milo*rr*d, watchin' ove*rr herrr* like I was ordered to do and saw the whole thing. Ye*rr* wife *did* lose he*rr* balance, but she wouldna have fallen if that blackgua*rr*d hadna tipped the ladde*rr*."

"Who ordered you to watch over my wife?" Clay asked in a silky voice.

"I was sent by the Lai*rr*d of Clan MacKinnon."

It took Clay a moment to decipher the meaning of MacTavish's words. The Laird of Clan MacKinnon, by virtue of his marriage to Katherine MacKinnon, was Reggie's father, the Duke of Blackthorne.

"The duke sent you to watch over her?" Clay confirmed, feeling a flush of anger spread upward from his throat.

"Aye, milorrrd. He couldna be surrre ye didna wish the lass ill. I suspected Terrrrence when the skiff sank, but I didna see him do it. I'm only sorrrry I didna say somethin' before the lass was hurrrt."

"Do you know where Terrence is now?" Clay asked.

"Aye. That's why I came huntin' ye, milorrrd. He's in the barrrn, saddling a horrrse."

"Find Pegg," Clay ordered as he headed for the stairs. "And bring him with you to the barn."

Clay did not know why he had not seen the similarities sooner.

Terrence was Cedric Ambleside.

The scarred man was the same height as Cedric Ambleside. Had the same hazel eyes, though one rarely looked past the scars on his face to see them. What was left of his hair had gone completely gray, and where he had been soft before from sitting behind a desk, now he was muscular and wiry. But once Clay was willing to accept the possibility, it seemed obvious: *Terrence was Cedric Ambleside.*

When Clay arrived in the barn, his certainty faded. The scarred man did not look like a murderer. He looked like a humble servant. Which was probably why he had remained undetected for so long, Clay realized, once the burns had disfigured him enough to disguise his true identity.

"Good afternoon, Mr. Ambleside."

The scarred man froze. And Clay realized he had his man.

"How did you get burned?" Clay asked.

Mr. Ambleside continued saddling the horse, buckling the cinch and laying the stirrup back down over it. "I was hiding in the attic of a tavern, and it burned down."

"When?" Clay asked.

"A week after I escaped from your drawing room," Mr. Ambleside said. "So you see, I have been quite disguised for the past twelve years."

"And continuing to cause mayhem wherever you go," Clay accused.

Mr. Ambleside ceded him the matter with a tip of his head. "However, I believe I have accomplished what I set out to do here. Blackthorne will never stop hounding you now, and while his attention is focused on you, it is diverted from me. It is time to take my leave."

Clay shook his head. "Not this time."

Mr. Ambleside pulled a pistol from the bag that was tied to the saddle and pointed it at Clay. "My argument was never with you," he said. "You were only a means to harm my half brother, the Duke of Blackthorne."

"You and Blackthorne are brothers?" Clay asked incredulously.

"I am the bastard son who was kept hidden and never acknowledged," Mr. Ambleside said. "I should have had half of everything Blackthorne owns in Scotland. That is the law here. The bastard inherits equally with the legitimate son. But my father made certain my existence was never acknowledged. And my brother has done nothing to remedy the situation.''

''He made you his steward,'' Clay said. ''He put you in charge of his estates in Scotland. You had control of everything. You lived comfortably and well.''

''I deserved more,'' Mr. Ambleside said.

''So you tried to murder your half brother and steal away his land,'' Clay said. ''And involved me in your plot.''

Mr. Ambleside shrugged. ''You were young and gullible. A convenient tool. My plan would have worked, if those fools had killed Blackthorne before they threw him off his ship and into the sea.''

''Your murdering days are over,'' Clay said.

''I am the only one holding a pistol,'' Mr. Ambleside pointed out.

''Look again,'' Clay said.

Mr. Ambleside's eyes darted from side to side. Pegg stood at one door to the barn with a pistol. MacTavish stood at the other with a shotgun. Mr. Ambleside aimed his pistol at Clay's heart and said, ''Tell them to leave, or I will shoot you where you stand.''

Clay realized Ambleside had nothing to lose. He was a dead man whether he tried to leave and got shot, or gave up his gun and got hung. That made him dangerous.

MacTavish signaled Clay that he planned to fire the shotgun into the air. In that instant, Clay leapt forward, tackling Ambleside, fighting him for his pistol. The two men rolled on the ground, as Clay tried to keep the gun aimed away from his face.

Ambleside's finger was locked in the trigger, and Clay knew he was waiting for the chance to pull it. They were rolling around so much, there was no way Pegg or MacTavish could shoot without taking the chance of hitting Clay.

"I might have forgiven you for what you did to me," Clay said through gritted teeth, as he turned the gun from his chest toward Ambleside's heart. "But never for what you did to my wife."

The pistol fired.

Clay saw the shock in Ambleside's eyes and realized the older man had accidentally pulled the trigger. The ball had hit him in the heart, and the light died quickly from his eyes. He was dead within moments.

Clay raised himself from the villain's body and stood on shaky legs staring down at Cedric Ambleside. He was such a small man to have caused so much harm.

Pegg kicked Ambleside's ribs, as though to assure himself the man would not rise up again. MacTavish spit on him.

"Good rrriddance," the Scotsman said.

Clay realized suddenly that it was still light outside. It felt like he had been gone from the house for hours. In reality, the confrontation with Ambleside—for which he had waited twelve years of his life—had taken only a few minutes. "Will you two take care of him?" he said. "I need to find out how my wife is faring."

Clay waited barely long enough to see Pegg's nod before he was gone. He ran most of the way to the house and bounded up the first few stairs before he stopped, paralyzed by fear.

Please let her be all right, he prayed.

When had God ever answered his prayers?

Clay forced himself to walk the rest of the way up the stairs and down the hall to Reggie's bedroom door. It was still closed.

When at least another half hour had passed, Mrs. Stephens opened the door and stepped outside, closing it behind her. "The doctor would like to speak with you now, milord. I will be bringing a tray to her ladyship. Will you be wanting to eat supper downstairs this evening?"

"I will dine with my wife in her room," Clay replied. "Please have something sent up for both of us."

"Very well, milord," Mrs. Stephens said.

Clay was not sure what to expect when he entered Reggie's bedroom. But he was astonished to see her sitting up, wide awake, several pillows stacked behind her. Her hair was neatly combed and had been caught up in a knot of curls at her crown. She was wearing a simple white cotton nightdress, and her arm was angled in front of her, resting in a cloth sling.

What he found most difficult to credit was the smile on her face.

"Dr. Wren has been telling me that I need only stay in bed for a couple of days, my lord," she said brightly.

He took the few steps that brought him to her side and said, "You are certainly looking . . . better." *Better* was definitely the right choice of word. To say, "You are looking *well,*" would not have been correct. She was no longer as pale as milk, but her right cheek had been scraped raw by the fall, and there were several small cuts on her forehead, nose, and chin.

He was sorry Ambleside was dead. He wished the villain were alive, so he could kill him again.

"It turns out Terrence was Mr. Ambleside," he told her.

"How did you discover it was him?" Reggie asked.

"MacTavish saw him tip the ladder out from under you. When I confronted him, he admitted the truth."

She smiled wanly. "See. It helps to hire a gatekeeper to keep an eye on things."

"Your gatekeeper was sent here by the Laird of Clan MacKinnon with orders to keep an eye on you."

Reggie started to laugh, but gasped instead and grabbed her ribs with her good hand. "Please don't make me laugh. But it is a wonderful joke."

He could see she was in a great deal of pain, though it was equally plain she was going to some effort to make it seem like less than it was. But the tightness of her mouth and the careful way she held her body gave her away.

"May I speak with you privately for a moment, my lord?" Dr. Wren said.

"Excuse us, please, Reggie. I will return as soon as I have seen the doctor on his way."

"Promise me you won't allow him to sentence me to stay in bed any longer than he already has," Reggie said.

From the sudden flush on the doctor's cheeks, Clay realized that that was precisely what Dr. Wren must have intended. Clay shot Reggie a grin and said, "No matter what the doctor says, you will stay in that bed until I am convinced you are well enough to leave it.''

''But, you cannot—''

That was as much as Clay heard of her protest before he and the doctor were outside in the hall with the bedroom door closed behind them.

''Now, doctor. What is it you did not wish to say in front of my wife.''

''Lady Carlisle is in very good condition, considering the height from which she fell, my lord. But I am concerned that there may be some damage inside. Several of the bruises, especially those low on her back, are quite severe. You will need to watch through the night and make certain they do not become any larger.''

''And if they do?''

The doctor looked grave. ''It will mean she is still bleeding inside and needs the assistance of a surgeon. Unfortunately, the local surgeon has gone to visit his mother in Glasgow. Even if you sent someone for him this very moment, he could not return in time to save your wife.''

Clay felt his throat tighten. ''Are you saying my wife may die?''

''If the bleeding continues unchecked, it is a possibility.''

''Is there nothing anyone can do?''

''I am very sorry, my lord,'' the doctor said. ''I have done all I can.''

''When will I know for sure if she is bleeding inside?'' Clay asked.

"If she survives the night, you may take it as a sign that she will ultimately recover," the doctor replied.

"My wife is with child," Clay said.

"There was no bleeding to indicate she is in danger of losing the child. If your wife lives, I see nothing to suggest the child will not be born healthy and whole."

"What can I do? What should I do?"

"Keep her calm and warm," the doctor said. He hesitated, met Carlisle's dark gaze and added, "But if there is anything you would like to say to her, I would say it now."

Chapter 21

CLAY LOVED HIS WIFE. AND HATED HER father. Should he contact Blackthorne and let him know his daughter might die? If he did nothing, he would have his revenge. Blackthorne would lose his child without ever having the chance to bid her farewell, just as Clay had lost his wife and son.

But when he thought of denying Reggie the solace of her father in what might be the last hours of her life, Clay felt a stab of pain that was as real as a knife piercing flesh.

"Can you get the door for me, milord?" Mrs. Stephens asked. The housekeeper had returned with two maids, each carrying a tray piled high with what Clay could see were Reggie's favorite foods. Mrs. Stephens carried a third tray that contained a teapot, two chipped china cups, and unmatched saucers.

Clay followed the three of them into Reggie's bedroom. Mrs. Stephens supervised the arrangement of a tray on short legs that fit over Reggie's lap, then asked, "Where would you like me to put your tray, milord?"

"On the foot of the bed, Mrs. Stephens," Clay replied.

One of the maids collected the chair that sat at Reggie's dressing table and carried it over to set it next to his tray, then both maids curtseyed and left the room.

"Shall I pour, milord?" Mrs. Stephens asked, standing beside the tea tray she had placed on the dressing table.

"No thank you, Mrs. Stephens. I can manage."

A moment later they were alone in Reggie's room.

Clay watched as Reggie looked at each delicacy that had been provided and rejected them one by one. He had been worried before, but Reggie with no appetite was reason for concern. "Is nothing to your taste?"

"You must know they are all my favorite dishes," she said with a sigh. "I am simply more tired than hungry, my lord."

"You must eat something for the baby's sake."

She shook her head. "I don't think I can. Did the doctor say the baby is all right?"

"He said the baby will be fine."

"I am so glad," she said with a smile. "So very glad. I want so much to have your child, for us to be a family."

And then her joy dimmed, and he knew she was remembering everything that had led up to her accident. As he was remembering himself. He had told her that he would come and take the child from her when it was born. And then he had abandoned her, as he had promised himself he would.

"Why did you come back here today, after I left you at the glen?" he asked.

"I had not finished the task I had set for myself," she said. "The windows . . ."

He glanced at her bedroom window, which allowed no starlight, no moonlight—and tomorrow would allow no sunlight—to stream into the room.

He did not know how to tell her that he loved her. He did not know how to tell her that nothing mattered if she was not a part of his life. His throat felt tight, and his nose stung with the threat of tears.

"I have ordered new windowpanes," he said.

It was a plea for absolution. And a promise for the future.

She reached out and clasped his hand. "Thank you, Clay. That is the nicest gift you have ever given me."

There was an even greater gift he could give.

"I thought I might invite your father to come visit you here at Castle Carlisle," he said.

"Oh, Clay," she said, her eyes gleaming with unshed tears. "When?"

"Tonight."

Her brow furrowed in confusion. "Are you saying you want everything between the two of you settled now? Tonight?"

"Yes," Clay said.

"Then by all means, summon my father," Reggie said. "The sooner things are mended between you, the better."

"Will you eat something while we wait for him?" he asked.

Reggie wrinkled her nose at him. "Must I?"

"I think for your sake—and the baby's—you must." Clay broke off a piece of cherry tart and held it to her lips. "It is sweet," he promised. "Eat."

She sucked the cherry from between the flaky crust, then licked the pastry and leftover sauce from his fingers. She shot him an impish look that told him she knew however aroused she might make him, there was nothing he could do, when she was all over cuts and bruises from her fall.

Clay left her long enough to explain the situation to MacTavish, making it clear that if Blackthorne wished to be certain he would see his daughter alive, he must come at once.

He spent the next two hours, while he waited for the duke to arrive, entertaining Reggie. He managed to coax her to eat a few spoonfuls of leek soup, some stewed haddock, and nearly half a bowl of Mother's Eve pudding, before Mrs. Stephens and the two maids came to take the trays away.

Reggie was obviously sleepy, but Clay had seen too many sailors, who had fallen from high in the masts and hit their heads, go to sleep and never wake up again. He wanted her to stay awake at least long enough to bid her father good-bye. Even if she did not realize that was what she was doing.

"Stay awake, Reggie," he said, adjusting the pillows behind her. "It cannot be long now until your father arrives."

"Please, Clay. I must sleep."

"You have not kissed me good night," he said, in a desperate attempt to distract her.

She closed her eyes and pursed her lips.

He stared at her and laughed.

She opened her eyes, saw his smirk, and said, "Take it now or lose it forever."

She had no idea how prophetic her words might be. Clay braced his arms on either side of her, then leaned down and kissed her softly on the mouth. She was infinitely sweet. The Mother's Eve pudding, no doubt. He kissed her again and tasted cherries. And again, and tasted sweetness and goodness and all the things she meant to him.

Clay felt Reggie's hand in his hair, felt her lips soften as she responded to him. He did not dare to touch her anywhere. There was nowhere she was not scratched or bruised. But he could kiss her lips. So he did.

Gentle kisses. Nibbling kisses. Long, deep, sensuous kisses. Delicate kisses. Passionate kisses.

"Clay," she murmured. "I ache."

"I am sorry, love," he said, willing to abandon even this small pleasure, if he was hurting her.

But she circled his neck with her arms and pulled him back to her, whispering, "I yearn. I need. I desire."

And then she kissed him. Soft, subtle kisses on either side of his mouth. She sucked his lower lip into her mouth and nibbled it with her teeth. She thrust her tongue deep into his mouth.

"Reggie," he said in a raw voice. "I ache."

"Good," she whispered in his ear. "I want you al-

ways to remember what waits for you here in this bed
. . . as soon as I am well.''

That was how her father found them.

Clay stood abruptly and took a step back from the
bed. "I assume MacTavish told you what happened.''

Blackthorne surveyed his daughter and made a *tsk*ing
sound as he sat down beside her on the edge of the bed.
"Climbing on a ladder, my girl. That is easily as repre-
hensible as sliding down knotted sheets.''

"This is not as bad as it looks,'' Reggie said.

"I am glad to hear that, because it looks awful,'' her
father replied with a crooked smile.

"Papa, Clay invited you here tonight to make peace.
Will you not greet him? Will you not shake his hand?''

Blackthorne stood and turned to Clay and held out his
hand. "I hope you will accept my apology, Carlisle. I
was wrong about you.''

Clay heard all the things Blackthorne did not say
aloud. That he knew Clay could have kept him away and
wreaked a terrible vengeance, but had not. That he was
sorry for his mistake, sorry for the harm he had caused.
That he wanted to make amends.

Clay reached out and felt Blackthorne's strong right
hand grasp his own. He wanted to say something, but his
throat was clogged with feeling. He looked up and saw
there were tears in the duke's eyes.

Clay pulled his hand free and said, "I will give you
and Reggie some time alone to talk.'' If he did not escape, he feared he would lose control and give away the
game.

Blackthorne turned to Reggie and said, "I have

brought Kitt and Becky and Mick with me. Do you feel well enough to see them?''

"Of course," she said with a smile for her father. "Bring them in."

Reggie shot a quick look at Clay before he left the room, and for the first time, he saw alarm in her eyes. She was clever enough to realize that if her entire family had come to visit, she might be in worse shape than she had been told. But he had no intention of staying to confirm her suspicions.

"I will be back soon," Clay promised her.

As he crossed the threshold and saw the worry in Mick's eyes, the panic in Kitt's, and the terror in Becky's, his own fear increased a hundredfold.

"It is not certain she will die," he managed to say. Then he was stumbling his way down the stairs to the drawing room and a bolstering drink of brandy.

Reggie could feel the fear that entered the room with her family. It was a tangible thing. She could almost smell it. There was only one reason she could think of why they should be so frightened. The aches and pains she felt must be much more serious than either the doctor or Clay had told her.

Her heart began to hammer. She tasted copper in her throat. Their fear was contagious, she realized. But if her family was determined to pretend this was an ordinary social call, she was willing to indulge in this one last fiction.

"Have you heard the good tidings?" she said brightly. "Carlisle and I are expecting a child."

She saw her news had created horror, rather than joy, and realized she must have even less time to live than she had imagined.

"That is wonderful news," Becky choked out.

"Meg will have someone to play with," Kitt said with a watery smile.

Her father said nothing, simply turned away.

A sudden lump grew in Reggie's throat. *Oh, Clay. I do not want to leave you. Not now.*

At least she had been able to help Clay make peace with her father. She glanced up in time to see Mick reach out to touch Becky's shoulder and witness her rejection of his offer of comfort. Neither had spoken a word directly to the other since they had entered the room.

Perhaps her accident could provide the necessary impetus for another reconciliation.

"Why haven't you forgiven Mick?" Reggie asked her sister.

Becky looked flustered. "This is not the time—"

"This is a perfect time to discuss forgiveness," Reggie said, daring any of them to contradict her. "If Clay can forgive Papa, surely you can forgive Mick."

"How can I ever trust him again?" Becky asked.

"Perhaps you never will trust him in the same way again," Reggie replied. "But when you love someone, you give them a second chance."

"And sometimes a third chance and a fourth," Kitt interjected, exchanging a glance with Reggie's father.

"Apologize to Becky, Mick," Reggie ordered. "And mean it."

Reggie watched as Mick took Becky's hand in his, then tipped her chin up, so she was looking at him.

"I'm sorry for hurting you, Becky. Please give me another chance to make you happy."

Reggie nodded. "Very prettily done. Your turn, Becky."

Becky's chin had taken on an uncharacteristically mulish tilt. "How do I know he will not hurt me again?"

"You don't," Reggie said flatly. "The truth is, he probably will. And you will hurt him," she said from her vast store of marital experience. "But if you both try very hard, the good times will surely outweigh the bad."

Reggie forgot she was hurt and tried to move her wounded arm, then cried out as she felt the pain in her dislocated shoulder and sprained wrist.

Her father was immediately at her side. "Are you all right? Shall I call back the doctor?"

Reggie made a face and then groaned, because she had broken open one of the cuts near her mouth. That made her father even more anxious, and she hurried to say, "Please, Papa, don't worry so. I'm fine, really."

The distressed look in Becky's eyes gave her pause, but she was determined to finish what she had started. "Well, Becky? Do you have anything to say?"

Her sister turned to Mick and said, "If you still want me, I accept your offer of marriage."

Reggie watched as Mick twined his fingers with Becky's and replied, "I love you, Becky. I always have, and I always will."

"Now that we have that settled," Reggie said, "when is the wedding?"

Her sister's eyes goggled. "We cannot set a date now."

"Why not?" Reggie asked.

"Because . . ."

Of course no one was inclined to mention that it was indecent to be talking about weddings when she might be dying, so Reggie said, "How about right after the harvest? Everyone will be in the mood for a celebration then."

She watched her parents exchange looks, saw Mick and Becky shift uncomfortably. "It will be perfect. You will have time enough to become friends again before the wedding, now that you are speaking to each other again."

Becky managed a smile. "You are incorrigible."

"I know," Reggie said with a lopsided smile. "And impossible and hopeless. And right now, very tired. As much as I am enjoying your company, I need sleep," she said, settling back against the pillows.

Becky impulsively hugged her, jostling her injured shoulder, but Reggie bit back her cry of pain, put her good arm around her twin, and pressed her cheek hard against Becky's. "I love you," she whispered fiercely. "Be a good wife to Mick."

Mick ruffled her hair and said, "Sleep tight. Don't let the bedbugs bite." And then he met her gaze and added, "Don't worry about Becky. I will keep her safe."

Kitt kissed Reggie's cheek. "Rest. Take good care of that baby."

Her father pressed a tender kiss against her forehead and said, "Good night, Reggie. I will see you in the morning."

Reggie felt the tears welling in her eyes and turned away so her father would not see them. She was no watering pot, even if she was dying, even if, for her, there might be no morning.

Reggie imagined the farewells her family must be saying to Clay. It was most likely a very stilted meeting, considering how recently all had been forgiven. But she knew her father and stepmother would not leave Clay to mourn alone once she was gone. And Becky would urge Mick to help Carlisle with the farm. And Pegg would be there to keep his spirits up.

Reggie lay staring at the ceiling for a very long time, waiting for sleep or death—whichever came first—to overtake her. The odd thing was, now that she had given in to the fatigue that had plagued her since the accident, she was suddenly wide awake. She wondered where Clay was. And why he had not returned.

Reggie decided to go hunting for her husband.

She was infinitely careful getting out of bed and adjusted the sling so her dislocated shoulder and sprained wrist would not get jolted as she eased her way down the stairs. She was able to slide her feet into slippers, but maneuvering into a robe was beyond her capabilities.

She found her quarry in the drawing room.

"What are you doing out of bed?" Carlisle rose abruptly from his chair as he spoke, crossed to her, and slid a supportive arm around her waist. "Are you all right?"

She gave him a rueful grin. "After all my complaining that I needed to sleep, I found I could not."

Clay eased back down into the wing chair, settling Reggie in his lap. She leaned her head against his shoulder and let her legs hang over the arm of the chair. They sat for a long time without speaking, silently loving one another.

At last she said, "Am I dying, Clay?"

She heard the sharp intake of air before he said, "What makes you ask a silly thing like that?"

"The fact that my entire family came to visit me, including my father—who was never welcome in our home before tonight—suggests I must be hurt more seriously than I was led to believe. Will you tell me what is wrong with me?"

"You may still be bleeding inside," he said quietly.

"Can nothing be done?"

"The local surgeon is in Glasgow. Dr. Wren seemed to think that if you are bleeding, the surgeon cannot possibly get back in time to save you."

"And if I am not?"

"Then you will live to be an old woman, presuming you stay off ladders," Clay said. "In any case, the doctor says we will know for sure by the morning, one way or the other."

"Is there no way to know sooner?"

"I suppose I can check the bruises on your back from time to time during the night and see if they are growing larger," Clay said.

"Will you do it now?"

"Reggie, I—"

"Please, Clay."

He nodded his acquiescence.

Reggie reached up and untied her gown but let Clay lower it from her shoulders. She could not move freely enough to turn around and see the damage. "How does it look?"

"Horrible," he muttered.

She felt his fingertips graze her back, making her shiver, and stifled a groan as her dislocated shoulder protested the movement.

"I wish I had seen these bruises earlier this afternoon," he said. "So I would know whether they have grown."

"Perhaps you will be able to judge better when you check again in an hour or two," Reggie said.

"Right now, I think the best place for you is bed."

She felt him kiss Miss Tolemeister's welts before he replaced her nightgown and retied it at her throat.

"May I stay with you tonight?" she asked.

"Wouldn't you be more comfortable in your own bed?"

"I would rather spend tonight with you."

"All right," he agreed at last.

But she was suddenly tired again, and she did not think she could get up the stairs by herself. "Will you carry me?"

"I am bound to hurt you."

"Please, Clay."

He picked her up as gently as he could, but there was no way it could be done without causing some pain. When they got upstairs, he laid her down on his bed long

371

enough to go around and pull down the covers on the opposite side, then carried her around, set her down, and tucked her feet under the quilt.

"Where are you going?" Reggie asked, when he started to leave the room.

"I'm only closing the door." When Carlisle returned, he lay next to her on top of the covers, fully dressed.

"Could you hold me in your arms?"

She saw the struggle on his face, and knew he was worried he might accidentally hold her too tight and hurt her. Finally, he said. "All right. Come here."

They both edged toward the center of the bed, and Carlisle eased his arm around her and pulled her close.

She tugged on his chin, angling his face down so that she could kiss his lips. "Good night, Clay. I love you."

"Good night, Reggie."

She waited a heartbeat before he said, "I love you, too."

Reggie closed her eyes and let sleep claim her. She had never been so happy. Or so unbearably sad.

Reggie thought she could see a light. A very bright light. So bright she needed to squint to keep it out.

"Wake up, sleepyhead."

Reggie opened her eyes to find bright sunlight streaming through the window. "I'm still alive," she marveled.

"That seems to be the case," Clay agreed with a grin. "How do you feel?"

"My shoulder aches, my wrist hurts—actually, I ache all over. Otherwise, I feel fine." Reggie smiled back at him. "In fact, I feel wonderful."

She was lying in her husband's embrace. Carlisle's

hair was flattened on one side and standing straight up on the other. His face was shadowed with a dark beard, his eyes were shadowed with purple half moons, but those were the only shadows in the room.

Bright sunlight filled the space from corner to corner, spilling over the two of them and bringing with it hope and joy . . . and the promise of love.

Epilogue

C~LAY~ COULD HEAR THE SOUND OF CHIL-
dren's laughter. He looked up from behind the mahogany secretaire where he
was reviewing the latest profits from the harvest and saw
his wife sitting on a stone bench amidst a profusion of
pink roses, their two-year-old daughter, Nicole, giggling
on her lap. Their five-year-old twin sons, Daniel and
Donald, raced in a circle around the bench, being chased
by a small terrier that yapped at their heels.

Clay smiled, closed the books before him, and rose to
join them. A knock on the library door interrupted his
escape.

"The marquess and his wife have arrived to play tag
and drink beer," Simms announced.

Clay no longer needed Reggie to translate for the deaf
butler that *Mick and Becky had arrived to talk for a
while and were glad to be here.*

"Thank you, Simms," Clay said with a grin. "Send
them out to join us in the garden, please."

Clay walked out the French doors and down the steps into the rose garden. He met Reggie's eyes and felt his heart begin to race. Even after all these years, he only had to look at her to want her. When the boys saw him, they came running, and he reached down to pick up each one as they leaped into his arms and grasped him around the neck.

He pretended to stagger as though they were too heavy, and they gripped him with their legs and clung desperately to his neck.

"Careful, Papa!" Donald cried. "You're falling!"

"He's only joking," Daniel told his brother. "Papa's as strong as an ox."

Clay pawed his feet like an ox and made grunting, oxlike sounds just to hear his sons giggle.

"It's Julia and Jeanine!" Donald said, struggling to be set down. A moment later his sons were greeting Mick and Becky's five-year-old daughters.

Lily crossed to the bench, sat down beside Reggie, and said, "Can I hold Nicole?"

Reggie relinquished their daughter and crossed to join Clay as he moved to greet their company. Mick and Becky were walking toward them along the gravel path, arm in arm.

"Well, are you ready to play tag and drink beer?" Clay asked, just avoiding the two sets of twins as they raced past.

Mick laughed. "You should fire that butler."

"Not a chance," Clay replied. "I've finally learned how to translate what he's saying."

"Well, why not play tag and drink beer?" Reggie asked. "It sounds like a lot of fun to me."

"My wife has a point," Clay said.

"We'll have to go with *the talk* and *being glad to be here*," Mick said, "since Becky is in a delicate condition."

Reggie took the few steps to reach Becky and hugged her sister. "Oh, my goodness," she said with a laugh. "How wonderful!"

"Well, to be honest, my dear, you have no business playing tag or drinking beer, either," Clay said.

Becky's eyes went wide. "Oh, my goodness. You, too?"

Reggie laughed. "Me, too!"

The sisters put their arms around each other's waists and began to walk along the gravel path sharing stories of their trials with the early stages of pregnancy.

"Well, we certainly are *de trop*," Mick said as he watched their wives walk away without looking back. "I think I'll go play tag with the children."

"I'll get us some beer," Clay volunteered with a grin.

As he looked out across his mother's rose garden, Clay realized how blessed he was. Reggie had chased all the shadows away. Every day he loved her more. And he had never been so aware as he was now, with another child on the way, that everything he had ever wanted, everything he had ever needed to be happy, was his because of her.

Good friends. A loving wife. And, of course, the laughter of children.

Dear Readers,

This novel concludes the Captive Hearts series, which includes *Captive, After the Kiss, The Bodyguard,* and *The Bridegroom.* Next, I'm taking the Blackthornes to modern-day Texas in a new series which chronicles the adventures of their descendants in America. Hope you'll come along for the ride!

I love to hear your suggestions and comments. You can reach me online at www.booktalk.com/jjohnston. Or send a self-addressed, stamped envelope to P. O. Box 8531, Pembroke Pines, FL 33084, if you would like a written reply.

Happy Reading,

Joan Johnston